Matt Gemmell is a former consultant software engineer, and the author of *CHANGER* and *Raw Materials*. He lives in Edinburgh, Scotland with his wife Lauren and their labradoodle named Whisky, and can be found on the web at mattgemmell.com.

For an exclusive bonus chapter of this book, plus previews of new novels and more, sign up for his readers' newsletter: mattgemmell.com/news-toll

KESTREL BOOK TWO

TOLL

Matt Gemmell

TOLL is book two in the KESTREL series, following *CHANGER*.

Each book stands alone, and you can read them in any order — though you may enjoy some additional (but non-essential) references if you've already read the earlier stories.

TOLL

toll

noun

1. A price paid for a privilege or service.
2. An amount or extent of loss or destruction.
3. The sound of a bell being struck.

PROLOGUE

The breeze coming in over the bow was bitingly cold, and the small ship was constantly buffeted by dark waves on all sides.

She was named *Hjørdis*, and she had been a shrimp trawler during her working life, but that time was now in the distant past. Her hull was scarred and patched, but still seaworthy, and hadn't seen fresh paint in many years. She was an outrigger, with her superstructure forward, but the booms were long gone from the base of her mast. A solitary capstan still poked up from her aft working deck, rusted solid and hazardous, and the sounder in her wheelhouse was smashed beyond repair. Her current occupants had no use for such equipment anyway.

The 48-foot vessel was a patch of grey against the deep blue of the Norwegian Sea, under a cloudy late-afternoon sky. Its destination was already in sight, breaking the featureless horizon ahead like something from another world.

Mark Cross lifted the binoculars to his eyes for at least the third time in as many minutes.

Sverdfisk Gamma, he thought.

The oil platform was an alien-looking thing, profoundly unnatural to the eye, towering many storeys above the waves. It was a fifth-generation semi-submersible drilling rig, and it looked like the scaffolding for some absent gigantic machine, floating on the ocean's surface. It was run by the Norwegian petrochemical giant, CHX INFERIS Group, and officially it was now decommissioned.

Liars.

Cross was one of four people on the *Hjørdis*, each of them a member of a radical environmentalist group that was the bane of the Scandinavian and North Sea energy industry. They called themselves the Green Defence Front, and their voyage was more accurately described as a mission.

The rumours had been reaching them intermittently for weeks now, from contacts in shipping companies, chartered helicopter operators, and various other less reputable sources. *Sverdfisk Gamma* wasn't as inactive as was generally believed. There had been reports of inbound night-time helicopter flights, and supply vessels without properly-filed route plans. Sea-level lights were seen by a fishing vessel, from far off.

There had been a much-publicised though allegedly

minor spill from the platform three and a half years earlier, after an apparent accident that damaged the drilling apparatus, and the rig had begun its long de-commissioning process immediately afterwards. The company said that repairs weren't economically feasible, given the minimal projected remaining yield from the oil field below. The rig was fully down-manned eight months ago.

But now you're up to something again on the quiet, you polluting bastards, Cross thought.

His assumption was simple: despite what the oil company had told the public, the spill hadn't been fully contained at all, and they were continuing remedial work in secret, hoping to avoid further enormous fines from the EU and even more negative publicity. Cross had no direct evidence of it yet, but that was one part of what this mission was about. There were video cameras set up on the trawler's bridge that had been recording continuously since the platform was sighted, and once they'd made an initial close pass by the legs and a few circuits around it, at increasing distances, they would return to port to inspect and upload whatever footage they managed to get. With any luck, they'd catch something that the world media would be very interested to see.

The second aspect of the mission was more enjoyable, and the main reason that Cross volunteered for this particular voyage: to annoy the hell out of the oil company, and make sure they knew they were being watched.

We're onto you, he thought, lowering his binoculars and drawing his heavy coat closer around his neck against the bitter wind. They were barely twenty minutes out, and overhead the sky had begun to darken.

The *Sverdfisk Gamma* platform now filled the air above the small ship. They were only sixty feet or so off one of the primary support legs — too close, ordinarily, but Cross had insisted on getting as near as possible, to get the best vantage point. Ugo, the surly middle-aged Italian piloting the vessel, was muttering to himself in irritation.

Cross stood out on the rear deck, some way back from the wheelhouse, craning his neck to look up at the vast installation. He could see the slate-grey clouds through various walkways, gratings, and gaps in the superstructure, and there were two bright orange lifeboats, covered with red tarpaulins, slung against the nearest side of the platform and attached to pairs of small cranes. The windows of the accommodation block were only tiny black rectangles, far overhead.

The rig seemed to be deserted.

The third crew-member of the *Hjørdis*, a wide-eyed, nervous young Romanian who Cross knew only as Nic, had already tried using a megaphone to hail any possible occupants of the platform, but he had quickly given up. The sound of the wind and the waves had made the exercise seem faintly ridiculous, and if Cross was being honest, it was unsettling to be here. Their own ship was dwarfed by the enormous construction that loomed above them, and there was clearly no-one and nothing else nearby, unless you counted the ocean's residents below.

Cross glanced over his shoulder at the fourth and final of his rag-tag and sombre companions, and grimaced. She wore the same frown she always did, and for the hundredth time, Cross wondered if she actually had any other facial expression. She'd told them her name was Sarah, but it had the air of an alias, indifferently chosen, and she hadn't been forthcoming with any other details. There were many people who viewed some of their group's actions as terrorism, and in that context it paid to be circumspect with your true identity.

Sarah — or whoever she was — cradled a black .45 calibre pistol in her right hand, restlessly turning it over and then back again by rotating her wrist, as if she was weighing it. Her forefinger lay along the side of the barrel, away from the trigger, and her shoulders were tense. Antagonistic exchanges with private security personnel were common during trips like these, and it was wise to be prepared. Cross had never been involved in an actual exchange of fire, and he didn't like weapons of any kind, but if it meant the difference between being boarded and detained or being allowed to leave, he could see the sense in at least showing that they weren't defenceless.

All the same, the woman troubled him. She was

twitchy, which was neither uncommon nor unjustified in their organisation, but it didn't seem like a desirable quality for someone holding a firearm.

He was about to order Ugo to take them back out and begin a slow circuit of the platform, when there was a sudden sound from above. A metallic clunk, like a latch releasing, then a moment of silence, and then the whirr of a heavy-gauge motor. Looking up, his eyes immediately registered movement of the rightmost of the two covered lifeboats.

They're lowering it down, he thought, turning immediately to wave to the Italian in the wheelhouse, but he already knew his command was unnecessary: the deck shuddered for a moment under his feet as the engines went into reverse, and a moment later the *Hjørdis* began to move slowly backwards, putting distance between herself and the platform above.

The lifeboat continued its unhurried descent, and Cross sensed the presence of Sarah beside him. There was a barely-audible click, and he looked quickly around at her in alarm, but she only gave him a brief derisive glance. Her finger now lay across the trigger-guard, and Cross realised that the small noise had been her disengaging the pistol's safety.

"Just… wait," he said, hoping that there was some authority in his tone. "It's only a boat. They always fuck with us. They'll pull it back up in a minute." Sarah made no acknowledgment at all, and Cross took a quick breath and returned his attention to the lifeboat.

The tarpaulin was still attached, but only at the two furthest-away tie-down points, the nearest side of it already flapping wildly in the breeze. As the boat approached the water's surface and its topside came fully into view, they could see that something had been installed on it, still partly hidden by the red tarpaulin. A heavy umbilical cable snaked upwards, clearly being spooled out from above as the launch gantry was lowered.

Abruptly, the lifeboat's downward motion ceased, with a clunk that made Cross visibly flinch. Its hull was still almost six feet above the waves, and he knew that under normal circumstances, the retaining latches would now be hydraulically disengaged, and the boat would drop smoothly into the water.

It hung there, motionless.

"We should go," Nic's voice said from nearby, unease causing his Eastern European accent to thicken. "I don't like this."

Cross felt his pulse kick up a notch, and he nodded. Discretion was the better part of valour, after all, and they had the video evidence of continued occupation of the rig.

"Alright," he began, "tell Ugo to turn us around, and —"

The sound seemed to come from every direction at once. A gentle and almost sonorous hum, rhythmic and pulsing every two or three seconds. Its pitch was low, and it didn't seem to be loud, but it nevertheless effortlessly drowned out the slap of the waves and the howl of the wind. It had the odd quality of being superimposed over the scene around them, and Cross felt the hairs on the back of his neck stand up.

Something's wrong here, he thought. In his peripheral vision he saw Sarah raise her pistol instinctively, though she had no target. Then the tarpaulin was caught by a gust of wind, snapped twice against its remaining moorings, and finally tore away, flitting out over the waves like a strange airborne manta ray, before finally dropping into the water.

The machine mounted on the lifeboat's deck was black, and secured by its own support gantry. It looked to be about two metres in height, cylindrical in general outline, and rounded at both the top and the bottom. The thick umbilical cable was anchored at its topmost point, and there were what could have been vents of some kind running in a belt about three-quarters of the way down its surface, where it widened. It was clearly the source of the deep, pulsating hum — and then, as Cross watched, it seemed to burst open.

He realised his error a moment later, for the machine was still fully intact — but it was nevertheless now leaking something from everywhere on its surface. It was... *light*, a rich golden-orange colour, but it moved like liquid. It curled and ran, billowing laterally through the air, blooming outwards from the device with shocking speed.

Jesus, Cross thought, staggering back several steps as

the first real feeling of panic gripped at his throat. He felt the ship's engines jolt into higher gear, propellers chopping at the water in an effort to pull away faster, but the eerie and uncanny waves of roiling light from the black machine were moving much faster, and would reach the bow of the trawler any moment.

Sarah darted forward, raised the pistol, and took three shots directly at the machine on the lifeboat's deck. Cross heard the flat report of the gunshots, muted by the omnipresent hum, but nothing else happened. Whatever was emanating from the device continued to billow and flex towards them like liquid fire, and then at last it reached the bow of the ship. The light played harmlessly over the metal, only a couple of metres from where Sarah stood holding the pistol in a death grip, unsure of what to do.

"For god's sake, get *back!*" Cross shouted, but the strange light seemed to surge, and in an instant it engulfed her. The only sound Cross heard was the dull clang of the pistol falling to the deck, and he blinked in disbelief.

Sarah was no longer there.

Over the side? his mind asked, frantically, but there was no way she'd gone overboard. There was a guard rail all around, and he'd have seen and heard it happen. The woman was just… gone.

The light oozed through the air, twisting and expanding, running with gold and the colour of flame, like ink through clear water. It washed across the deck towards the remaining three of them, flowing over surfaces, leaving the ship untouched and unharmed.

Cross heard a splash from over his left shoulder, and somehow he knew that the young Romanian had dived into the sea, surely to his death. He also knew that the action was futile; the light was now an undulating wall of luminescence, twelve feet high and growing, and it spanned at least forty feet on either side of the trawler. Ahead and just above, he could still barely see the black machine that was producing it, and the hum filled his skull.

The light licked across the deck, only a few feet away now, and he screamed.

Less than a minute later, the *Hjørdis* was deserted.

PART 1

Chapter 1

Captain Jessica Greenwood ran.

Narrow streets, with cobblestones and cracked pavements, glowed in the evening light. She hadn't passed a car or even one of the ubiquitous mopeds for several minutes. The lane looked like it might be a dead end, but she spurred herself onwards, all too aware that time was ticking away.

She could hear bells from somewhere behind her, but that wasn't unusual — there were many churches here, all painted pale yellow and trimmed with white. The scent in the air was of the day's fading heat, with just a hint of lemon from the groves that dotted the region.

Faster, she silently commanded herself.

She rounded a final corner and the vastness of the Mediterranean sky opened out in front of her, beyond a low wall that lay just up ahead. She could hear the sea now, and she pushed her burning leg muscles even harder, feeling the coastal breeze cooling the sheen of sweat on her face.

The soles of her shoes thudded rhythmically against the ground as she raced towards the short stone barrier, and the hundred-foot drop to the ocean that she knew lay on the other side of it.

Greenwood was aware that only scant seconds were left, and as she came within the last few metres before the precipice, she felt the expected vibration of the device strapped to her wrist.

She skidded to a halt, both palms dropping onto the waist-high wall, and took several deep breaths, feeling her pulse thundering in her chest. After a few moments, she straightened, then she lifted her left arm and read the two words blinking on the display.

PERSONAL BEST

"Damned right," she panted, clenching her fist in victory.

The terrace looked out over the Gulf of Naples, and the Tyrrhenian Sea was ablaze with a spectacular sunset, painting the waves and sky in orange and gold. She had run this same route on each of the four previous evenings, and today was the first time the humidity had appreciably dropped. She was in the *comune* of Sant'Agnello, just a twenty-minute walk from the popular tourist town of Sorrento, with its limoncello makers and world-renowned *prosciutto crudo*.

Greenwood put her hands on her hips and enjoyed the smell of the salt air as perspiration ran freely down her neck and back. Her heart was pounding from the exertion of the run, and she felt completely at peace. She smiled.

Now this is what I call a holiday, she thought.

Greenwood was the commanding officer of the elite European Special Tactical Force, Group One — code-named *KESTREL*. A small and highly secret unit attached to the European Defence Agency in Brussels, and operating uniquely under the direct authority of the European Security Council, their remit included surveillance, infiltration, extraction, and combat missions throughout the EU and beyond.

Her close-knit team were her family, but everyone needed a break from time to time. She was a workaholic, driven by an unshakeable sense of duty and responsibility, and she found it difficult to ever fully relax. Greenwood had learned to look forward to her mandatory personal leave each year, and she invariably used the time to visit someplace new and not too busy. She occupied herself with good food, several books, and of course a daily run. As a soldier, vigorous exercise was as natural and essential as breathing.

It had been a difficult year, culminating in the *Destiny* mission at the very end of winter. Despite the heat of the day, she felt a chill run down her spine.

The event in Germany.

It was only a few months ago, but already it had taken on the quality of a half-forgotten nightmare. Much of Western Europe was just moments from being destroyed, and the means by which Greenwood's team managed to narrowly avert disaster was still barely believable — yet she had witnessed all of it with her own eyes.

And we gained our fifth member, she thought, a small frown creasing her forehead for a moment.

She was pulled from her reverie by an insistent vibration pattern from her wristwatch. She lifted her arm to view the display again, and then she raised one eyebrow. It was as if her train of thought had summoned the man. The screen showed an incoming call, alongside a single word: ALDRIDGE.

She glanced out at the ocean once more, pretending that she was deciding whether or not to answer, but barely five seconds passed before she tapped the green icon on her watch to accept the call. She heard a chime in her wireless earphones when the connection was made.

"Why are you calling me, Aldridge?" she asked without preamble, and there was a brief pause before he replied.

"Why are you out of breath, Captain?"

Greenwood rolled her eyes. "I hardly think that's any of your business," she said.

"Catch you at a bad time?"

She could hear the smirk in his voice, and could readily picture what it looked like. "I'm on holiday. Of course it's a bad time. Any time when I'm not supposed to be at work is a bad time."

"Enjoying yourself, then?" he asked, and now the amusement was gone from his tone. There was a note of curiosity, and she knew he was fishing for information.

"Until very recently, yes," she replied, and she heard him huff out a small laugh. Then a thought occurred to her, and her eyes narrowed. "How did you even get this number?"

There was another pause before Aldridge spoke. *"It's in the staff contact directory. Under 'Greenwood'."*

She rolled her eyes. "No it bloody well isn't," she replied, and she heard him clear his throat.

"Well, it was in the emergency contact list," he said at last.

"Now we're getting somewhere. So what exactly is the emergency, Aldridge?"

"I'm bored," he said, then he quickly continued before she could interject. *"And I thought it was sensible to check up on you. You disappear off on holiday and don't tell anyone where you are, or who you're with. It's not safe."* His Scottish accent somehow made the words sound both prudent and petulant.

Greenwood laughed. "Not safe?" She knew that he was grinning too.

"Alright, maybe that was a poor choice of words. But I think I deserve credit for the sentiment."

Dr. Neil Aldridge was a physicist, formerly specialising in theoretical subatomic particle interactions, and the newest member of KESTREL. He crossed paths with Greenwood's team in his native Edinburgh earlier in the year, while being pursued through alleys and back-streets by a pair of trained mercenaries. He had been abruptly pulled from the safe world of academia and thrust into a race to save not only his own life, but those of millions of others. The *Destiny* mission was a success, though victory came at great personal cost for Aldridge, and the intervening months had found him pursuing his new life with the ceaseless dedication of a man who didn't want to have enough time to dwell on his memories.

The nature of KESTREL's work made Aldridge's skills very valuable, especially with secrecy to be considered, but when they found him, he was anything but a soldier. Accordingly, he'd been undergoing a strict training regime: physical conditioning, tactical thinking, use of firearms, high-speed driving, military protocol, and more. He was a very different man than he'd been half a year before.

"I seem to recall explicitly telling you not to bother me until I got back," Greenwood said, closing her eyes again to let the evening sunlight wash over her. She was looking forward to a long shower, and then a leisurely evening meal somewhere within walking distance of the apartment she'd rented for the week on the *Viale Del Pini*.

"I don't remember that. Maybe I wasn't paying attention."

She didn't give him the satisfaction of a response, instead choosing to remain quiet, knowing full well he'd fill the silence himself. Sure enough, Aldridge spoke again after just a few seconds.

"So you never did answer me, Captain. Why were you out of breath?"

"I was running, Aldridge, until you interrupted me. It's something you should be doing every morning, as I recall from your physical conditioning schedule."

"Favourite part of my day," he replied. *"And were you running... alone? That doesn't sound like much fun."*

"That's none of your business either," she said. "And how *is* the training going? I'll be evaluating you at the end of the month."

"I've got the appointment circled in my diary," he replied. *"But I'm glad you brought that up. Dowling is a monster. A sadist. I have a tab open in my browser about reporting people to the European Court of Human Rights."*

Greenwood laughed at that one. Sergeant Lawrence Dowling, or rather Larry to almost everyone, was just about the nicest man you could meet — provided he wasn't your opposite number in a conflict situation — but he made for a formidable sight. He was KESTREL's weapons and explosives specialist, and he was built like a tank. He stood 6'4" tall, with tattoos on his biceps, and close-cropped, sandy-blonde hair. As Greenwood's second in command, he was very much her brother-in-arms.

The big man's soft Welsh accent belied his stature and lethality, but when left to his own devices he was a gentle and good-natured giant, and optimistic to a fault. All the same, when he had a mission to complete, he was all business — and Greenwood knew that Dowling was greatly enjoying his latest task of turning Aldridge the scientist into Aldridge the soldier. Dowling would demand nothing but the best from their new team member, as Aldridge had no doubt discovered.

"Since we're a covert military force, I doubt the Court would ever hear your case," Greenwood replied. "And you really ought to raise any legitimate concerns with your commanding officer first."

"Is it too late to say that's actually my reason for calling?" Aldridge asked, after a brief pause. *"I think a formal complaint is already overdue."*

Greenwood shook her head, ignoring his remark. She'd had an update from Dowling only a week ago, and knew that Aldridge was taking to the programme very well indeed. He would readily be cleared for full operational field duty at his next assessment.

"Since you haven't said anything that's actually important, much less an emergency, I'm going to go now," she said. "I'll talk to you when I get back."

"And when will that be, exactly? Just so I know when to tidy up the lab. Hide the video games; that kind of thing."

"A week on Monday," she replied. She expected him to make some remark about the duration of her holiday, but he remained silent. Just when she was about to ask if he was still on the line, she heard the rustle of paper.

"Huh," Aldridge said, clearly to himself. *"Weird."*

Greenwood looked out over the bay again. The sea breeze had changed from refreshing to slightly chilly since she'd stopped moving, and she knew that she should end the call and get back to her evening. She also knew, however, that curiosity would always get the better of her.

"What's weird, Aldridge?" she asked. "And give me the brief version."

"Hmm? It's… huh. Now that's strange."

He was suddenly distracted, and she could hear that the levity was gone from his voice. The rustle of paper continued in the background, and now she also heard the rapid clicking of a computer keyboard.

"Aldridge," she prompted, and the sound of typing paused abruptly.

"Sorry," he replied. "It's just this thing. I thought it was the results of those tests on my DNA after the Destiny mission, but it's actually the stuff that came across my desk a few weeks ago, from Spindelbauer at the… actually, I don't even remember what agency he was with. I met him at a conference during my first month with you. He thought I was in materials research, and I didn't correct him. We talked about lab equipment."

"Please get to the point," Greenwood replied, resting her hands against the low wall of the terrace and beginning some stretching exercises. The sun seemed lower towards the horizon, but it might just have been the sudden chill.

"I got a package forwarded from the Defence Agency, and there was a dossier and a box of medical stuff. Dental fillings, surgical implants; that kind of thing. Spindelbauer passed it

to me because he didn't have access to the right equipment for a detailed analysis. I read the file then sent the other items to the bio lab. The results just came back, and they're weird."

Greenwood sighed. "Weird how, and where were they from, and why is this my problem?"

"It's not your problem," Aldridge replied, *"and I was going to send it all back, but if I'm reading this correctly then there's no organic material at all on any of these. Which is odd, since they were apparently the only trace left of a four-man trawler crew in the Norwegian Sea."*

She frowned, trying to put the pieces together, but there was too little to go on. "What was a trawler crew doing with medical supplies?"

"What medical supplies?" Aldridge asked, and Greenwood started to jog on the spot to ward off the ocean breeze.

"What you said. Implants, fillings."

"Oh, they weren't supplies. That's the thing. I've got health records on three of the four crew members. This stuff came from inside them."

There was a long moment of silence.

"Inside them," Greenwood said. "As in… their own fillings."

"And pins from a shoulder reconstruction. And a small metal plate from the young guy's right hip, which came from a pretty amazing mountain biking accident a few years ago."

"How—" Greenwood began, feeling a headache developing, then she shook her head and began again. "So what's your explanation for how a trawler crew vanished, except for their hip plates and shoulder pins and dental fillings, but none of it has any organic residue after removal?"

"I don't have one," Aldridge said, cheerfully. *"But I can tell you that they weren't a trawler crew either; not the way you're thinking. They were environmental activists, and they were on their way to a decommissioned oil platform."*

Greenwood didn't reply, her mind now filled with questions. She had started to feel the vague annoyance that always rose up when she was confronted with a mystery. She was about to respond, but Aldridge was already talking again.

"The leader of the group had a sister, and she works in the petrochemical industry. She's the one who put the dossier together. She wants answers about his disappearance, and she's not getting them from the oil company. She says she'd be happy to take the proper authorities to inspect the trawler vessel."

Greenwood bit her lower lip. They had no current assignment, hence her holiday, but she'd been looking for an opportunity to take Aldridge out in the field again, to assess him. It was required before she could grant full duty clearance.

"It might all be a mistake, of course."

"It might be," she replied.

"And I wouldn't want to interrupt your holiday."

"You already interrupted it, Aldridge." Again she could vividly imagine the smirk on his face.

"All the same, though, you've got more than a week left. I

can just make some enquiries myself; maybe go and talk to the sister. See if there's anything to it. You should get back to your run."

There was another long pause, then Greenwood sighed in exasperation, but the man already knew her too well. She wasn't just a workaholic; she also couldn't bear to leave a question unanswered.

"It's hardly within our remit, but *if* I think it's worth the trip, we'll make it a field observation exercise for you. And I'll be observing very closely," she said, and she was almost certain he pumped his fist in the air in victory. "Have a briefing ready for midday tomorrow."

"Already working on it, Captain," Aldridge replied, and then the line went dead.

Greenwood took a final look out at the ocean. It was a darker shade of blue-orange now, and the sun boiled on the horizon. She tapped her wristwatch's screen several times to reactivate the fitness program, then she turned and ran back in the direction of her hotel.

Chapter 2

It was barely 11:30 AM when Greenwood switched off the engine of one of the nondescript and interchangeable black fleet SUVs her team used. The parking area was a small, concrete-enclosed structure with space for thirty vehicles. Just outside, she could see the familiar view of the Royal Library of Belgium.

The library was an interlocking series of cuboids of light-yellow stone, studded with windows including dramatic floor-to-ceiling panes above the main entrance, and bordering the *Boulevard de l'Empereur* on one side and the *Jardin du Mont des Arts* on the other. It stood on the site of its predecessor institution, in a neighbourhood of Brussels which was dotted with museums. The tourist buses trundled ceaselessly by on the road outside, but their sound was largely muffed within the modern, airy building itself. Its collection extended to more than six million volumes, 700,000 engravings and drawings, 150,000 maps and plans, and over a hundred and fifty kilometres of bookshelves.

I really should visit the main library sometime, Greenwood thought for perhaps the hundredth time since her relocation to the city several years earlier. Her destination, just across an open-air footpath bordered by abstract decorative columns, was a plain exterior door bearing a numeric keypad and a sign indicating in six languages that only authorised personnel were permitted to enter. It stood well away from any of the primary entrances and exits, and was deliberately forgettable.

She reached the door, glanced around, and entered an eight-digit code. There was no sound, but when she pushed the door, it swung inwards. Greenwood stepped inside, allowing it to close behind her. Lights came on automatically when the door's lock had reengaged, revealing a short corridor with an elevator at the end. Above the silver doors, there was a wall-mounted sign with *LIBRARY FREIGHT* printed in English, French, and Dutch.

She walked to the elevator and pressed the call button, and after only a moment the doors slid open. The interior was clean and spartan, and the control panel bore only four buttons: those for floors zero, one, and two, and an emergency intercom. Greenwood pressed the intercom with her right thumb, her eyes focused on the cheap-looking red LCD display that currently showed only the digit zero.

The thumbprint and retinal scans were instantaneous

and unnoticeable. She knew that she had been under constant surveillance since she drove into the parking area, and that armed guards and various automated defences were all primed to repel any intruders — though the first line of defence was simply to connect the emergency intercom to a bored-sounding elderly custodian, who would politely explain that the freight elevator was out of order, and that the main library entrance was back out the door and to the right. Any wayward interloper who'd managed to obtain the current week's eight-digit exterior door PIN would of course be detained before ever leaving the upper corridor.

The doors slid shut, the red zero in the small display vanished, and Greenwood felt the elevator begin its descent.

The Royal Library of Belgium was conveniently located within Brussels, only a twenty-five minute drive from the airport and less than ten minutes from the headquarters of the European Defence Agency. Unbeknownst to its many staff and visitors, the Library also formed the cover — both figuratively and literally — for KESTREL's own headquarters, located in a four-storey subterranean complex accessible from several locations over a three-block radius.

It took just under seven seconds to reach the topmost level of what Larry Dowling had always called *the bunker*. The elevator slowed smoothly to a halt, and the doors remained closed as hidden cameras in all eight corners of the small space scrutinised its occupant. Clearing her throat, Greenwood spoke aloud in the small space.

"Jessica Greenwood," she said.

After only a further fraction of a second, at the confirmation of her voiceprint, the doors opened to reveal two alert guards armed with semi-automatic weapons, in a staggered firing formation within another short hallway. Neither of them smiled, but the nearest nodded respectfully.

"Captain," he said. Greenwood knew that his name was Lafferre, and she nodded in return.

"Gentlemen."

She stepped forward and then stopped between strips of dark glass panels which lined the walls on either side and the ceiling above. A soft chime sounded, and the guards lowered their weapons.

"Welcome back, Captain," Lafferre said, in heavily French-accented English, and Greenwood gave him a polite smile, also nodding at the other guard as she walked past them to the end of the corridor. She was faced with the familiar blast-door, which slid open just as she approached it. With entrance security successfully traversed, she stepped into the base proper.

The space she walked into was surprisingly large, given the confines of the corridors leading up to this point. Greenwood was on a metal balcony which ran around the upper perimeter of an area approximately twenty-five metres squared, and three storeys high. Two criss-crossing walkways stretched across the open void, and there was a further balcony level below, with the ground floor visible beyond. The upper two levels were connected by stairways at their midpoints along one wall. She stood on level one, with levels two and three beneath. The fourth level was kept under even higher security, and only a single elevator led to it, from a secure room at the rear of her own office on the third level.

Various rooms opened off the atrium, which was harshly illuminated with fluorescent strip-lighting overhead and along each wall. Colour-coded signs indicated the directions of each section of the base. Greenwood turned left and headed along the suspended walkway, passing a blue-bordered sign which read SCIENCES.

She could already hear the music long before she reached the physics lab on level two. Aldridge had recently developed the habit of playing his own phone's music collection through the lab suite's speaker system, and while Greenwood herself — one floor further down, and on the opposite side of the atrium — could never hear it, she'd overheard a couple of chemistry technicians in the cafeteria grumbling about the *noise pollution* a few weeks earlier.

So I had a word with him about it, and he clearly didn't listen, she thought.

Aldridge's playlist of choice was an eclectic mix of everything from rock to classical, pop, and soundtracks

— so it was guaranteed to annoy everyone equally.

When she reached the lab, she pressed her thumb to the small plate next to the door, and an adjacent panel illuminated green. She pushed the door and it swung open, and the music's volume abruptly increased.

Aldridge glanced around as soon as she entered, even though Greenwood had no idea how he could hear the door over the racket. He grinned, then picked up his phone from a workbench and tapped the screen. The music was silenced immediately.

"Welcome back," he said, and Greenwood folded her arms.

"What did I tell you about the music?"

"It helps me focus," he replied, and then when she continued to glare at him, he raised one hand in a placating gesture. "But I'll turn it down in future."

"I'd appreciate that," she said, "and I don't want to have to talk to you about this again."

Aldridge nodded, a contrite expression warring with his continuing grin, then he sat down on a lab stool and looked at her expectantly.

"What?" Greenwood asked, but he just shrugged.

"Just hoping I didn't inconvenience you too much, pulling you away from your holiday a bit early. And anyone you were travelling with, of course."

Still fishing, she thought, brushing off her mild annoyance on account of feeling well-rested, despite her unexpectedly early return to work. The break had done her good, however brief it was.

"No inconvenience," she said. "I can pick up where I left off once we sort this out. Whatever this is."

Now it was Aldridge's turn to fold his arms, and he nodded thoughtfully. "Well, the briefing's ready, and on the system. Do you want to go down now?"

"No time like the present," Greenwood said.

Aldridge stood up, removed his lab coat, and draped it over a stool before crossing the room to join her. She assessed the man as he moved, seeing with satisfaction that his training had clearly progressed even since the last time she spoke to him. He had an energy about him that had been absent when they first met in Edinburgh, under circumstances that had become stranger by the hour. His physique had changed, too; he was slimmer in the waist but with some bulk to his chest and arms, and his latest scores in armed and unarmed combat reflected his single-minded and almost obsessive approach to meeting the required standards.

She had learned that things — including people — fell into two main categories for Aldridge: worthwhile, and unimportant. He would go to any lengths for something he believed was worthy of his time and devotion; everything else would fall by the wayside and be forgotten. He was many things — flippant, borderline disobedient at times, occasionally childish, a brilliant scientist, and more — but there was no question about his dedication to becoming a full member of her team. The others had quietly remarked upon it on more than one occasion, and Sergeant Dowling's only additional comment about the training process was that Aldridge never failed to make either a sarcastic comment or a gratuitous complaint about every exercise.

She had reminded herself again and again that Aldridge had been a life-long civilian until a few months ago, and that he'd already demonstrated his bravery and sense of responsibility several times during the events of that period. He just had some rough edges, and they'd be smoothed off in due course.

"Something on your mind, Captain?" Aldridge said, as Greenwood had hesitated for a moment at the doorway.

"Just deciding how much extra interval training I'll tell Larry to give you tomorrow, for the music."

He grimaced as he stepped past her to grasp the handle and pull the door open, allowing her to precede him. "You're grumpy when you get back to the office. You should relax more. I have a playlist you'd like."

Greenwood strode away ahead of him, not even acknowledging his remark.

It's good to be back, she thought.

Chapter 3

When they reached the conference room, the other members of the team were already there. Larry Dowling leaned against the wall near the large display screen mounted at the front of the room, his powerful arms folded across his chest, head back, and his eyes trained on the ceiling. His expression was serene, as it usually was, and he glanced over and smiled at Greenwood when she entered.

"Welcome back, chief," he said. His warm Welsh accent was a greeting in itself.

"Thanks, Larry," she replied. "I see we're all here."

Seated around the large wooden conference table were KESTREL's remaining two members. Lieutenant Gerrit Goossens — their electronics specialist, driver and pilot, and occasional field medic — was a tall, rangy Dutchman with a shaved head. His dark skin contrasted with the vivid yellow t-shirt he wore, and he nodded respectfully when Greenwood looked over at him. He was a quiet man; soft-spoken and contemplative, with a deferential manner. After a stint in the Dutch armed forces, he'd become a communications expert for private industry, and he was recruited by KESTREL following an encounter a few years before. He'd proven to be a flexible and able soldier, and a skilled tactician — as well as a thrill-seeker during his leisure time. It made for quite a contrast from the rural upbringing he'd infrequently mentioned.

Goose, as he was universally known, had sustained an injury during the *Destiny* mission: a gunshot wound to his left thigh. He'd been in a physiotherapy programme, and then restorative training alongside Aldridge. According to the latest progress reports Greenwood had received, he'd made a full recovery.

KESTREL's final member sat at the far end of the table, observing the others. Corporal Alicia Ramos's slight build and large, dark eyes gave her a fragile look that could easily mislead a casual observer. Her olive skin and shockingly short, raven-black hair drew the attention of plenty of men, which Greenwood knew was a subject of continuing amusement to Ramos's wife.

She was the group's surveillance and infiltration specialist, as well as a markswoman and sniper of unmatched skill. While Goose was simply quiet by nature, Ramos was positively inscrutable, and shared very little of herself with her colleagues. She was a keen watcher of people, and always carried an air of dark humour about her. She was never without her silver pendant on a fine, short chain around her neck, but only she knew its significance. Greenwood had heard that Ramos had a very religious family back home in Spain who she didn't get on with, but much of the rest of her personal life was a mystery. Ramos was utterly calm and dependable in a crisis, and displayed an efficiency that bordered on coldness at times. She was a valuable ally, and not someone you'd want to be on the wrong side of.

They were an interesting blend of personalities, backgrounds, and talents, but they worked effectively together and were unfailingly loyal. They were all still learning where and how Aldridge fit into the group, as was Aldridge himself, but Greenwood was confident that he would continue to be an asset to her team.

"Let's get started, then," Greenwood said, taking a seat at the head of the table, and Aldridge walked over to a small podium which held a lectern with a touchscreen display. He tapped a couple of controls, and the large screen on the wall brightened, the room lights dimming automatically. Dowling took a seat next to Greenwood, and Aldridge cleared his throat.

"Alright, here's what I have," he said, tapping another panel on the lectern's display. A magnified image appeared on the large screen, showing a series of small, metallic items of several different shapes and sizes.

"A week ago, I received these objects along with a dossier via an acquaintance from an EU scientific conference. They're dental fillings, shoulder pins from reconstructive surgery, and a hip plate. They're all that's left of the four people whose bodies they were inside, including the brother of the woman who put the dossier together. She wants answers about his disappearance and presumed death."

Dowling cracked his knuckles, drawing a brief glance from Greenwood. "It's never just a lost puppy in this job," he said, which earned a rare look from Ramos at the far end of the table. "So somebody what, cremated the poor buggers?"

"Nope," Aldridge said, "but I'll get to that." Dowling gestured at him to continue.

"The owners of these items," Aldridge said, "were the crew of a small trawler vessel, but they weren't out on a fishing trip. They were environmental protestors, making their way towards a decommissioned oil platform in the Norwegian Sea, about three months ago."

"I've been wondering about that since you called me; why would protesters visit a *decommissioned* platform?" Greenwood asked, and Aldridge nodded at her.

"Why indeed?" he replied. "Well, the word on the street was that the rig was actually still functional — or rather, still doing *something*. The protest group had seen reports of supply activity, transport in and out, lights moving about, and that kind of thing. It's the same rig that had a spill almost four years ago; you might recall it being in the news for a while."

"The one that hurt CHX INFERIS's stock value? I remember reading about that," Goose said, and

Aldridge nodded.

"That's the one. And they began the shutdown process soon afterwards, because it was no longer economically viable — or so they said. When our merry little group of environmentalists set sail, it had been sitting empty for five months."

Ramos frowned. "They started to shut it down almost four years ago, but it was only empty for five months when this happened?"

Aldridge shrugged. "I wondered about that too. I checked, and apparently it takes a long time to decommission an oil platform. They have to remove any oil and gas, shut it all down, make it safe, remove equipment, clean it, and all sorts of stuff. Takes years — in this case, just over three, and that's a pretty fast job."

Ramos tilted her head to one side. "Alright," she replied, her Spanish accent making the word sound exotic. "So couldn't the activity have been the last part of the shutdown?"

Aldridge shook his head. "Not according to the company. It was fully down-manned — which is what they call taking everybody off it — just over eight months ago."

No-one replied, and Aldridge knew they were all waiting for him to fill in the blanks.

"The *really* interesting thing is that there's no original organic residue on any of these items. They were found rattling around on the boat, so there's some miscellaneous crud, but nothing like what you'd expect for objects that had until recently been implanted within human bodies."

"What condition was the trawler in?" Goose asked, and Aldridge looked towards him.

"Same condition it was in when they bought it, so I'm told. Seen better days, but undamaged. Certainly no sign of anything like a fire, or an explosion."

"That's a bit odd, then, right enough," Dowling said, leaning forward in his chair. "If they died on the boat, there's no sign of how. If they died somewhere else, how did that stuff get back onboard?"

"Could someone have been sending a message to the environmental protest group? A threat, maybe?" Greenwood asked, but Aldridge shook his head.

"The vessel was apparently stripped of any identification and quietly towed to a salvage yard on the Norwegian coast, then sold for virtually nothing. It was only because of the sister's tenacity that she even found it in the first place. Hell of a strange way to send a message."

He tapped a control on the lectern, and another image came up on the large screen: the hull of a grey-black ship, perhaps fifty feet long, perched on struts in what looked like a vast workshop or storage area. There was a noticeably defaced area where the vessel's name would usually be.

Greenwood raised an eyebrow. "It's in a dry dock now?"

Aldridge nodded. "The sister has some resources. And it's her *brother's* death we're talking about; she wants answers. It's the salvage yard's own premises. She's renting the space."

"Bit of a mystery, chief," Dowling said, turning slightly in his chair towards Greenwood. "Not really our thing, though."

Greenwood's gaze remained fixed on the large screen. "No, ordinarily not. But Aldridge here needs an observed field excursion, and I've got to admit that I'm curious. I think we can put a couple of days into it. It won't need all of us."

Dowling nodded, then he made eye contact with Aldridge and winked before turning back to Greenwood. "Thought you might say that."

"What about jurisdiction?" Goose asked. "Norway isn't part of the EU."

Greenwood gave a small shake of her head. "It won't be a problem. They're the second biggest energy trade partner for the European Union, and part of the Single Market, EEA, and Schengen. We have agreements on all manner of things, and the EU imports over sixty billion Euros of goods from Norway every year. A tenth of that is seafood, and they're our largest supplier. Anything that poses a threat to shipping or fishing, in particular, would be a subject of bilateral concern."

"You just happened to know that stuff, off the top of your head?" Aldridge asked from the podium, with a note of amusement in his voice.

"It's my job to know that stuff," Greenwood replied. "Areas of legislative or diplomatic leverage are always tactically relevant."

"I bet you looked it up on your phone before you came in here," Aldridge said, *sotto voce*.

"Tell us more about the sister," Greenwood said, and Aldridge picked up a small tablet computer sitting on one side of the lectern and interacted with it for a few moments.

"Her name is Dr. Lily Cross. She runs her own consultancy to the energy industry," he replied. "A dozen or so employees. She used to work for one of the bigger firms as a process engineer, based in various places. The Hague, Paris, Aberdeen, Baar, Abu Dhabi; the list goes on."

Greenwood folded her arms. "Quite a traveller. And you know all this how, exactly?"

Aldridge placed one palm against his chest, pantomiming indignation. "I didn't misuse any resources, Captain. It's in her professional biography, on the website for her business."

"And one of the protestors was her brother," Dowling mused. "Must have been a bloody awkward Christmas dinner if she was working for big oil and he was saving the whales."

Aldridge tilted his head to one side in acknowledgement. "Mark Cross was her elder brother, by four years. I think it's safe to say they were estranged, and yes, probably because of her work. She said in the cover letter that they hadn't spoken in some time. I get the feeling he was the one who hadn't been in touch."

"Why do you have the dossier in the first place?" Ramos asked. "You said it arrived via an acquaintance."

Greenwood turned in her chair to address the question. "Aldridge met a colleague at an EU conference. They got talking about their lab equipment." She rolled her eyes, and Ramos might have grinned ever so slightly. "It was this other man who actually received the package, but he didn't have access to what was needed to perform a detailed analysis. He remembered Aldridge's boasting about his lab here, and decided to send it along, via the Defence Agency."

"Pretty much," Aldridge added, drawing a glance from Greenwood. "Cross doesn't know we have it, and of course she doesn't know who we are. And for the record, I *wasn't* boasting. I just... have a lot of great equipment."

Dowling shook his head and re-folded his arms, but Greenwood ignored the remark entirely. After a moment, Goose spoke up.

"I assume she already tried raising her concerns with the company and with the Norwegian government?"

"Says she was given the run-around," Aldridge replied. "Which makes sense. No-one wants a scandal. It's a huge company, and politically powerful too. And Cross is Swiss; neither Norwegian nor an EU citizen."

Goose nodded thoughtfully. "What's your colleague's connection with Ms. Cross?"

Aldridge lifted one hand, palm upwards, in the universal gesture for *I don't know.* "I assume she knows him the same way I do; she's a regular attendee at energy symposiums and research conferences too. More of an academic than you'd usually expect for someone who runs their own business. It pays to stay in touch with people in related fields."

Goose nodded. "It seems so."

"Anything else?" Greenwood asked, and Aldridge glanced at his tablet computer again.

"Well, she's… blonde. Pretty," he added, with the characteristic gleam in his eyes that showed he was being deliberately irritating. Greenwood glanced wearily at Dowling, who only gave an exaggerated shrug in response, then she stood up.

"Alright. I'll talk to the Director," she said. "I'll let you all know what we decide. Be ready for a deployment at short notice. Dismissed." With that, she began walking towards the door of the conference room. From the lectern, Aldridge looked from Greenwood to Dowling and back again.

"Oh, and she likes Italian food, and long walks in the Scottish countryside," he added. "Wait, no; that last part is actually me."

Greenwood didn't so much as glance in his direction, and after another moment, she had left the room.

"You shouldn't test her patience, mate," Dowling said, but his tone and the smile on his face bore no real warning. Aldridge grinned back at the big man.

"I don't know what you're talking about," he replied.

* * *

Less than half an hour passed before the door to Aldridge's lab once again swung open, and Greenwood walked in. She noted with satisfaction that the music was playing at a much lower volume than earlier.

"That was quick," Aldridge said, swivelling his lab stool around to face her. Greenwood just approached the lab bench adjacent to where he sat, picked up his phone, and pressed the Home button to see the title of the instrumental track that was currently playing.

"*Local Hero*?" she asked, and Aldridge nodded.

"You haven't seen the film?"

Greenwood shook her head, and when he opened his mouth to speak again, she held up a hand. "Spare me the synopsis and review. Suffice to say that it's a classic, and I really ought to see it, and you're shocked that I haven't been brought up properly."

Aldridge folded his arms and leaned back, amusement dancing in his eyes, and there was a moment of silence before Greenwood continued.

"Wuyts approved your little outing, so you can contact Dr. Cross to schedule a meeting. Tomorrow morning would be preferable. We need to arrange transport, so the sooner you call her, the better."

Aldridge wasn't surprised that the excursion had been given a green light by the Director of EUFOR's Special Tactical Forces; Greenwood's judgement was trusted implicitly. Janne Wuyts had oversight of KESTREL and several other groups besides, and was nominally accountable to the European Defence

Agency, where she kept a permanent office. In practice, she had significant latitude to conduct operations in the best interest of the European Union and its citizens.

Wuyts made for an intimidating figure in the handful of encounters Aldridge had with her since arriving in Brussels. She was slender, elegant, always immaculately dressed, and her fine white hair never had a strand out of place. Her hazel eyes were perpetually steely, and many of the world's foremost power brokers dreaded being the focus of her intellect and attention. She had previously been the Minister of Defence for Belgium, and was independently wealthy, and fiercely protective of her people. Her political and private-industry connections made her a powerful ally, or a formidable opponent.

"I'll get right on it," Aldridge said, picking up his phone and silencing the music. He brought up Lily Cross's contact information, and was about to place the call when Greenwood spoke again.

"The Director gave us some leeway, but this isn't a school trip," she said. "We've got two days. She doesn't think it warrants any kind of official investigation; it's strictly a field exercise for you."

Aldridge nodded, giving her his best disarming smile. "Understood, Captain."

Greenwood raised one eyebrow slightly, then half-turned away from the bench before meeting his gaze again. "This is your show, so coordinate with Logistics for transport and equipment. You, me, and Ramos.

Larry's going to stay and sign off on Goose's return to active status. Send me a message when it's done."

Aldridge snapped off a crisp salute, then tapped his phone's screen and raised the device to his ear while Greenwood turned and walked over to the door. There was a magnetic noticeboard mounted along the adjacent wall, and she saw a laser-printed sheet of A4 paper attached to it with a bright purple magnet. The paper was slightly askew, and bore the words *Thank you for visiting the Mikkel Anfruns Memorial Laboratory*.

She rubbed the bridge of her nose briefly, but she said nothing, and a moment later she opened the door and stepped out into the corridor.

Chapter 4

Tsutomu Miwa stared at the blank wall without really seeing it.

It was cool and quiet in the chamber he'd chosen for his office, and the furnishings were functionally minimal to the point of asceticism. A large metal desk sat in the rear half of the space, with a cable-routing channel running away from it along the floor, which disappeared into a small hole that had been drilled into the wall decades earlier. The desk bore a sleek, lightweight laptop, a small potted plant, a single button recessed into the surface, and nothing else. The ergonomic leather office chair was sculpted and precisely adjusted to suit Miwa alone. The left wall had a doorway to a private bathroom, and also a large video screen, which was currently switched off. The right wall had no embellishments whatsoever, and it was in this direction that his gaze was focused.

He knew that he was high above the valley, but still underground, and surrounded on all sides by rough, blue-grey stone. Many of the installation's rooms and hallways had been excavated recently, but some were older than Miwa himself, bored into the rock by slave labour, when a different country owned these mountains.

Balance in all things, he thought.

It had been his grandfather's favourite phrase. The old man used it in various contexts, sometimes to teach and sometimes to amuse, but for Miwa it had become the cornerstone of his personal philosophy of utilitarianism. His overriding sense of the greater good was the principle that guided his life — and his business empire.

He was a tall and slender man, with the dark eyes and hair of his Japanese ancestry. Always immaculately dressed in light colours, and in a starkly contemporary and minimalist style that only heightened the mystery of his age; he could have been twenty-eight, and he could equally have been forty.

Miwa carried himself with grace and poise, but those who worked for him also knew his other side: the directness, ferocious conviction, and the disquieting force of his intellect and will. He was a fiercely driven man, pursuing his own personal quest throughout the entirety of his adult life so far, and he demanded absolute loyalty from his employees and partners — who were many.

He was the founder and CEO of Miwa Environmental

Consulting Ltd, a multinational eco-strategy and energy solutions business focusing on sustainable fuel sources, environmental technology, hybrid power, carbon reclamation, and considerably more. Miwa's career had begun in the nuclear industry, via his uncle's engineering firm which specialised in reactor safety, and he held a Master's degree in mechanical engineering from the University of Tokyo. The rest had been a matter of timing.

As the world awakened to the growing evidence of climate change and environmental damage, his company was there. As the political reality of an increasingly media-fuelled popular desire for cleaner industry embedded itself in mainstream culture, his company was there. Providing guaranteed carbon offsetting, and reducing fuel consumption. Advising and coordinating on clean-up operations in the aftermath of oil spills and toxic chemical releases. Exerting pressure on governments to improve their energy profile, expand recycling programmes, and enact pollution laws. And whenever there was a disaster with environmental consequences, from south-east Asia to western Europe and further afield, his company was there too.

By the time of the Tōhoku earthquake in Fukushima, Japan, on 11th March 2011, Miwa's vast staff included a multidisciplinary team of engineers, analysts, strategists, lobbyists and more, spread over multiple locations across several continents. Miwa himself was worth several billion Euros, and his company was the *de facto* emergency management and planning consultancy for an ever-lengthening list of nations. The tsunami which followed the earthquake, and the resulting generator and coolant pump failure that led to meltdowns of three of the six reactors at the Fukushima Daiichi nuclear power plant the next day, was a personal turning point for Miwa himself.

I warned them, he thought, still staring at the blank wall without seeing it. *More than once. The generators were too near the ground.*

The power plant's seawall was three metres too short to deflect the largest wave of the tsunami, which reached thirteen metres in height, and the primary emergency diesel generators were housed in low-lying rooms beyond. The ingress of water flooded them, and then, as predicted, the situation became a horrifying sort of race: the secondary emergency coolant-pump generators were battery powered, but couldn't sustain the pumps for the several days of continuous operation needed to sufficiently cool the fuel rods after the post-earthquake *SCRAM* shutdown procedure. The workers toiled tirelessly to restore power in time, but they were ultimately unable to. The batteries drained, the secondary pumps failed, and the rods inevitably began to overheat.

And so we had our second 7.

The International Nuclear and Radiological Event Scale, or INES, was created in 1990 by the International Atomic Energy Agency to grade the severity of nuclear accidents. It was designed as a logarithmic progression, whereby each increasing value represents an accident ten times more severe than the previous level. Its levels run from zero up to a maximum of seven. The Fukushima incident was only the second ever incident to attain the maximum severity on the INES scale. The first was Chernobyl.

But they still haven't learned, Miwa thought.

Fukushima was also a personal tragedy. Tōhoku region was both his birthplace and where he spent his childhood, though none of his employees or associates knew anything of his background. It was profoundly difficult to see an example of some of his worst fears for the world striking so close to his home. It only strengthened his resolve.

Miwa walked a fine line, all through his career: an enigmatic figure personally, but also a reluctant darling of the world media. He built his company himself, and was now one of the pre-eminent last great hopes of environmentalism. He regularly reminded the great and the good about the signs and portents all around. His company's persistent lobbying was largely responsible for China's decision to cancel the building of new coal-fired power plants. But he knew that ultimately these were token gestures.

Pollution grows worse and worse across Asia; permafrost melts in the Arctic; insect and bird populations dwindle; winters are ever more unpredictable, and summers more scorching; icebergs calve off from ice shelves and plunge into the sea. Reefs are destroyed. Forests are cut down. Species become extinct.

He stood up, and took three measured steps towards the blank rock face.

Miwa knew that he had already captured the zeitgeist of eco-urgency, as a businessman, as a hands-on lobbyist, and as a scientist by training. He ran his company and also actively participated in projects, right there on the front lines if the project was high-profile or interesting enough, often making use of his considerable skills as a scuba- and free-diver, yachtsman, and submersibles enthusiast. He had significant resources at his disposal. He issued press statements often, but he was usually only seen in person at elite gatherings and conferences. Especially lately. Because he also knew that time was running out.

He glanced off towards the single door that led from this room into the nerve centre of the facility. His subordinates knew that when the door was closed, he wasn't to be disturbed. His focus was entirely on his mission — his life's work.

Having predicted, warned of, and then watched the effects of human encroachment into the natural world, and of civilisation's relentless hunger and consumption without due regard to consequences, his greatest frustration was that his own culture's sense of harmony and modesty was not more widely shared by the rest of the planet's population.

But so be it, he thought, just as he had done countless

times before. *Humanity is doomed to poor decisions.*

His unshakeable sense of moral rectitude came from the realisation that those who could not make choices in their own best interests ought to have those choices made *for* them. Miwa wrestled with his own discomfort about the great project he'd undertaken during these last several years, but he never wavered in his determination to see it to completion. It was his *ikigai* — his reason for being. And it seemed that the planet surely agreed with him.

The gift from the past.

Even now, years later, his skin still prickled with gooseflesh at the thought of it. The testing installation was just two levels below the room he now stood in, returned there after decades of absence, and the experimentation and refinement were in their closing stages. Very soon now, it would be ready — and then things would change forever.

He glanced at his wristwatch, an elegant Swiss timepiece which was worth more than most people's homes. Its bracelet glinted dully in the artificial light. He nodded.

Miwa was no stranger to the concept of difficult decisions. The foregoing of one thing in favour of another. The greater good, above all. He understood, as few others did, that sometimes progress meant making sacrifices.

Even if others must make the sacrifice on my behalf.

* * *

After a brief pause, Miwa walked to the door of his office, turned the utilitarian metal handle, and opened it. The area outside was a muted hive of activity, with a sunken floor area holding dozens of metal-framed desks, each bearing a series of laptop computers. Workers wearing headsets were so engrossed in their tasks that most didn't even notice that their employer had joined them. It was how Miwa preferred things to be.

He walked directly past the control area and out into a wide corridor, carved through solid rock. Turning left, it took him only twenty paces to reach the narrow steel doors of an elevator, which in turn took him down two further storeys into the heart of the mountain.

It was cooler here, and quieter, especially given the large blast doors that sealed away the vast chamber which sat fifty metres beyond the elevator's lobby area. There was an access portal set into the rightmost blast door, with a small black panel embedded in the surface adjacent to it. Miwa pressed his thumb against the panel for a moment, and the portal unlocked with a muffled click.

No matter how many times he saw it, he was still awed by the machine.

It sat in its testing harness, overhanging the pool — it didn't seem to be susceptible to thermal stress itself, but without manual intervention to cool its exterior surface after use, it would continue to dangerously heat the surrounding air indefinitely — and even though they now knew so much more about it than when they'd discovered it almost four years earlier, many of the specifics of its function remained frustratingly shrouded in mystery.

But we can control it, he thought, and that was more than enough. *Better than its creators ever could. Because they lacked modern technology.*

Towards one side of the sixty-metre-wide cavern, there was a free-standing reinforced metal control booth, with thick cable trunking exiting from its rear corner into a channel cut through the rock floor. The mechanised gantry above the pool was operated from within the booth, as was the device itself.

The machine's black exterior glinted in the shifting light from the pool below. It was precisely two metres in height, a squat cylinder which flared towards the bottom, rounded at each end. Mounting brackets of the same material as its casing were affixed to a ring running around the upper section, and a single, thick umbilical cable ran directly from the top. The emission array vents around the lower third were obscured with steam at the moment, a byproduct of its warm-up cycle and the humid environment of the test chamber. Those amongst Miwa's staff who wore spectacles had to periodically wipe the lenses clear, as the ambient temperature and water vapour levels fluctuated constantly.

Miwa knew that there were three ventral access panels encircling the angled lower portions of the machine, whose securing bolts had been replaced by a more sophisticated locking mechanism by his own engineers. It was one of only two external modifications they'd made; the other was the removal of the etched symbol plate which had been attached to the machine's upper surface when they discovered it.

Some things are best consigned to the past, he thought. That was what the machine was all about, after all — and his plans for it.

He was pulled from his thoughts by the rumble of rubber wheels against the rock floor. A smaller shuttered door had been opened on the far side of the chamber, and an electric cart drove through, pulling several interlinked trailers, not unlike airport luggage transport vehicles, but the cargo wasn't suitcases. Each trailer unit was a wheeled cage, and visible through the mesh were a pig, a large breed of dog, a variety of smaller mammals, and in the final unit, a man with a shaven head and a dramatic tattoo of a dragon curling up his neck. All were unconscious, and the man wore the gown of a hospital patient.

Miwa's brow furrowed. He felt considerable unease at this part of the work, especially given its unsettling echo of what occurred in this place decades before, but it was necessary. Science was both the problem and the solution, and as the foundation of his education and his worldwide business, he would follow the principles of controlled experimentation rigorously — no matter how much personal distaste he felt.

The pool below the machine's harness was only twenty by twenty metres, but it was three full metres deep. It was situated near to the centre of the chamber, and the control booth was as far from it as was practicable. Whilst the booth's walls were metal, and safe from the effects of the machine's operation, there was no known way to protect the scientists inside if the shutdown cycle wasn't triggered in time after each test cycle. As a result, everyone's mind remained firmly focused on their work.

It had been hypothesised — both by Miwa's own scientists, and by the project's progenitors in the previous century — that removal of the liquid cartridge at the machine's core would effectively render the device inert, even if power were still present. Exactly two attempts had been made to do so, seventy years apart. In each case, everyone in the immediate vicinity had died instantly, without ever managing to dismantle the central mechanism.

And so we treat you with respect, because we cannot seem to destroy you even if we wanted to, Miwa thought, looking once again at the machine itself. *In exchange for that respect, you will perform a great service for this planet and its foolish inhabitants.*

The trailer units had been decoupled, and were now arranged in a loose circle around the edges of the cooling pool. The technicians had withdrawn, and Miwa saw that he was the only person left standing out in the open. He glanced towards the control booth's two-inch-thick perspex viewing port — a useless precaution, they had long ago realised — and saw the current team leader watching him patiently. Miwa nodded in his direction, then turned and walked unhurriedly back towards the access door that led to the elevator lobby.

The door closed behind him and the lock engaged with the same muted click. As Miwa began to walk back down the corridor, his footsteps echoing sharply around the hard surfaces of the subterranean space, he felt the hum of the machine's startup cycle begin to vibrate through his bones.

When the doors of the elevator opened once more upon the complex's primary hub level, Miwa found his trusted lieutenant, a small, elderly man named Tien, waiting for him a short but respectable distance away. Miwa stepped out of the elevator and approached the other man, coming to a halt without speaking. Tien gave the barest bow from the waist.

"There may be a matter of concern," he said. His voice was dry and quiet, as ever, lending a note of calm to the words he had spoken. "Dr. Cross received a phone call on the intercepted line. She's to meet a small delegation from Brussels regarding her brother's disappearance."

Miwa raised an eyebrow. "A delegation?"

"They were circumspect. A man; another scientist. She asked the name of his agency, but he declined to elaborate. The call's origin could not be traced. We have the place and time of their meeting tomorrow morning."

Miwa considered this information for a moment.

Cross had been pursuing the mystery of her brother's fate for the last several months. *Understandably. The loss of a beloved relative is a tragedy.* Up until now, though, as far as his operatives could determine, she had met with little success in obtaining any more actionable information — but she hadn't been under close surveillance either. If external parties were now interested, there could be an element of risk to the vital work they were conducting here. He refocused his gaze on Tien, who spoke immediately.

"You wish to learn of the nature and participants of this meeting," Tien said. It wasn't a question, but Miwa gave the barest nod.

Tien made another rudimentary bow, and then hurried away.

Miwa watched for a moment as the other man departed, then he resumed his course back towards his office. There was much to do, but he would also monitor this developing situation diligently.

It was always wise to be prepared.

Chapter 5

The sky was overcast in Bergen, the bustling *city of seven mountains*, and the second largest settlement in Norway.

KESTREL's jet landed at Flesland just before 08:00 local time, the flight north from Brussels taking only a little under two hours. Aldridge, Greenwood, and Ramos were on board, plus a duty pilot, even though Ramos was also qualified to fly the aircraft if necessary.

A rental SUV was waiting for them. The European Defence Agency had operational resources in both Bergen and Oslo, but Greenwood had decided to use civilian transport. Meeting a consultant engineer with a lost brother was unlikely to require much in the way of tactical hardware. Nonetheless, all three team members wore a concealed SIG P226 Elite Dark pistol, chambered for 9mm ammunition, in a shoulder holster beneath their jackets. Aldridge also carried an equipment case with a variety of portable scientific instruments.

Lily Cross had asked Aldridge to meet her at a quayside warehouse adjacent to a small marine salvage yard, less than two kilometres from the historical Bryggen district lining the east side of the Vågen harbour. In the morning traffic, the drive from the airport took almost forty minutes, with Ramos at the wheel. The temperature had risen a couple of degrees by the time they arrived at their destination, but it was more than offset by the breeze coming in from the fjord. Ramos parked the SUV in the concrete lot that bordered the warehouse. The building had two sets of corrugated metal shutters, and one set had been drawn up, allowing entrance to the structure. Aldridge glanced at Greenwood, who simply gestured for him to lead the way.

The interior of the vast wooden building was gloomy, and smelled strongly of diesel. The single dominant feature was one they all recognised from the briefing photos: the trawler, mounted on struts in the rear half of the warehouse, near the seaward wall. A floatation channel led away from it towards enormous slatted wooden doors which presumably opened onto a harbour area, but the channel had been drained and now held only scattered puddles of oily-looking seawater. The place was deserted.

"We're a little early," Aldridge said, checking his wristwatch. "She should be along soon."

Greenwood took a few steps towards the trawler, its grey bulk looming silently above them. There was a movable staircase gantry positioned halfway along the port side, giving access to the deck. She considered telling Aldridge to begin his survey, but before she could speak, they all heard the sound of footsteps coming from the parking lot outside. A moment later, Lily Cross appeared in the doorway.

The woman's gaze flicked between Aldridge, Greenwood, and Ramos. She was barely 5'3", with tied-back blonde hair, and grey-blue eyes. She was dressed casually, but there was tension in the set of her shoulders. Her expression was one of determination and confidence, but there was also the barest hint of weariness around the edges. Aldridge took a step towards her, and then stopped.

"Dr. Aldridge?" Cross asked, and he nodded, giving her a small smile. Her accent was perfectly neutral. Aldridge knew that she was Swiss, with an English father, but she'd grown up in various cities throughout Europe.

"It's a pleasure to meet you, Dr. Cross," Aldridge said warmly, closing the remaining distance between them to shake her hand. "Thank you for seeing us at such short notice."

Cross nodded, giving a momentary smile that barely touched her eyes, then she glanced towards the other two women again.

"These are my colleagues, Jessica Greenwood and Alicia Ramos," Aldridge said, indicating each woman in turn. They both nodded at Cross, who returned the gesture, then she cleared her throat.

"Which EU organisation did you say you were with, Dr. Aldridge?" she asked, and he gave a bashful smile.

"I'm fairly sure I didn't," he replied. Cross held his gaze for a long moment, and Greenwood stepped forward.

"We're attached to an agency with jurisdiction over commercial shipping matters," Greenwood said. "We've been assigned to follow up on the dossier you submitted to make sure there's no question of illegal or dangerous activity in an oil-producing area."

"By which you mean piracy," Cross said, already sounding mildly frustrated, and Greenwood tilted her head to one side.

"Amongst other things," she replied. Ramos and Aldridge exchanged a look, which Cross didn't see. They all knew that Greenwood had made the story up, but the more complex truth would only invite difficult questions as to the true nature of their group, and their purpose here.

"This isn't the eastern coast of Somalia, Miss Greenwood," Cross said. "The responsible party is somewhat larger and better-organised than that."

"By which you mean CHX INFERIS," Greenwood replied, and now it was Cross's turn to give a half-nod.

"And last time I checked, Somali hijackers don't remove dental fillings and surgical implants," Cross said. Greenwood's lips were pressed into a thin line, and Aldridge knew it meant that she was conceding the point.

"Why don't you show us what you've found?" Greenwood said, and after a moment, Cross nodded again.

Aldridge knew this was his cue to take charge of the meeting, and so he smiled broadly and gestured towards the trawler. "After you," he said, and Cross led the way across the floor of the warehouse towards the forlorn-looking ship.

"If you don't mind me asking, are you a medical doctor?" Cross asked, and Aldridge blinked at her for a moment before realising that the question was logical, given the unusual remains that had been found on board.

"Ah, no," he replied. "My background is in physics, actually."

Cross's brow creased in momentary confusion, and she threw a brief glance towards the other two women who were following at a distance of several metres. "And your colleagues? Are they scientists too? Because that's what we need here."

"They're both experts in their respective fields," he said, giving her another smile which probably looked as strained as it felt. "And I assure you, Dr. Cross, we're here to help. This is a fact-finding meeting, and I intend to do everything I can to get you answers about what happened to your brother and those other people. But to do that, I need you to show me exactly where you found those objects, and tell me once again how you managed to locate this vessel."

Cross sighed, but she looked less suspicious than she had a moment before. Aldridge knew that they hadn't given her much reason to trust them, and he also knew that the biggest reason for her compliance so far was simple desperation. The dossier had detailed how she'd been investigating her brother's disappearance (*and almost certain death*, he thought) for several months already, and it was only via her dogged persistence that she'd heard about the unnamed and stripped-clean ship being quietly sold for a nominal fee to this modest salvage business. There was also a large dose of luck involved, and he knew that she was aware of it too.

Hell of a situation to be in, he thought, feeling profound sympathy for the woman. Field exercise or not, he was going to get to the bottom of this somehow.

Cross and Aldridge climbed the stairs of the deck-access gantry first, followed by Greenwood. Ramos remained on the ground, on the pretence of inspecting the hull, but Aldridge knew that it was actually both prudence and protocol. Ramos would keep an eye on their surroundings, because on the fairly lengthy list of things she didn't care for, surprises were near the top.

Cross guided Aldridge and Greenwood to several different points on the deck's surface in turn, and one just inside the doorway of the wheelhouse, pointing out where each object had been found. She seemed to know each of them off by heart, and Aldridge had a vivid mental image of her making this macabre tour on her own, over and over again during the past several weeks.

"I don't think the distribution means anything, of course," Cross said, and Aldridge nodded without making eye contact.

"The ship was brought here after... whatever it was that happened," he said. "Either towed or under her own power. Everything would probably move around en route." Nevertheless, he sat his equipment case down on the deck plates, pressed his thumb to a small panel to open the twin metal catches, and took out a small, hand-held device. He passed it over each area, paying close attention to the display screen.

"You're looking for a radiation signature," Cross said, and it was a statement rather than a question. "There isn't one. And I don't know of any kind of radiation event that could... do that... to people, and leave the ship itself completely intact and unmarked."

"Nor do I," he replied, then he frowned.

Greenwood, who had been standing silently a short distance away, moved closer. "What are you thinking, Aldridge?"

Instead of replying, he returned the device to its foam-padded compartment within the case, then took out a different tool, which looked very much like the sort of scope you'd find attached to the top of a rifle. He re-fastened the catches and stood up, looking at Cross.

"Did you check the general area under magnification?" he asked, and she shrugged one shoulder.

"As much as I could, and at a limited factor. I don't have a mobile lab at my disposal here."

"Mm," Aldridge said, already walking towards the bow of the ship and the location where two of the dental fillings had been found. When he reached the low guard rail, he got down on his knees and leaned forward, bracing one palm against the deck to support his weight, and aimed the cylindrical device directly at the metal plating. He pressed a pair of small controls inset into the barrel, and Cross could hear the barely-audible whine of a miniature motor.

"Huh," Aldridge said after a moment, slowly turning around on his knees as he peered through the device towards several different points on the deck's surface.

"What is it?" Cross asked, but Aldridge didn't immediately reply.

After a further moment, he opened his mouth and then closed it again. Two more seconds passed before he spoke. "It's just that… huh."

"He does that," Greenwood said, and Cross glanced briefly at her. "Aldridge, what have you found?"

"Something's odd about the decking. All of it, as far as I can see," he said. "It's been cleaned, very recently, and incredibly thoroughly."

"Define 'thoroughly' for me," Greenwood said. "You mean to prevent forensic analysis?"

Aldridge shook his head. "I can't imagine why anyone would go to this kind of trouble. Aside from whatever's been picked up during its journey to this yard, and from Dr. Cross walking back and forth across the deck for the last few weeks, there's *nothing* here. It's been stripped back to the metal. I'm using five-hundred-times magnification, and even the ridges and pits in the metal are completely clean. It's like someone immersed the whole deck in a strong solvent, power-washed it, and reattached it to the ship. But—"

He tailed off, getting up from his knees to move to the nearest section of railing, at the base of which was a metallic runner that partially covered a line of bolts fastening the top-plate of the deck to the superstructure beneath. He knelt down once more, this time bending fully forward to lay the side of his head against the deck, and he aimed the magnifying scope at one of the bolts. Then he frowned again.

"But?" Greenwood asked, and this time it was Cross who spoke before Aldridge could respond.

"But there's no sign that the decking was ever detached, is there?"

"None whatsoever," Aldridge said, continuing to inspect the bolts at various angles. "Some scuffing on the interior side, but the outsides are remarkably well preserved. No boots to kick them for the last thirty years, or however old this thing is, since they face outwards from the deck. No tool marks either. The last time these plates were separate from the ship was on the day they were installed."

Aldridge shook his head. "And still weirdly clean, right to the back. How would you even get in there, assuming you didn't dismantle the whole thing?"

"Good question," Greenwood said, but her tone was distracted, and she was glancing along the entire stretch of railings, back past the wheelhouse and towards the stern. After a few moments of silence, Aldridge looked up from the scope to see what she was doing.

"What are you thinking?" he asked.

"I'm wondering how thoroughly Dr. Cross checked along that channel that covers the bolt heads," Greenwood replied, looking towards Cross, who only shook her head.

"As I said, my resources are limited. You think I missed something? It's certainly possible."

"Alright," Greenwood said. "Then let's have a look. Aldridge, do you have anything that could help speed this up?"

Aldridge thought for a moment, then looked again at the line of railings. "It's a straight line along most of the deck. I have a rangefinder, with a 500-nanometer laser. Should be pretty visible in here, given the dust and other particulates hanging around. It'd at least rule out anything larger than a centimetre or so, wedged behind any of the posts."

Greenwood nodded, already opening the equipment case with her own thumbprint and taking out the relevant device. It was black metal, cuboid in general shape, and had prominent yellow-and-black warning stripes along both of the largest sides. She crossed to the port-side railing, placed the rangefinder on the decking at the outermost point, and slid a small switch along the top of its casing.

A vivid green dot of light appeared against the terminal point of the railing's mounting, off to one side of the ship's bow. A faint beam of green light was visible running along the base of the entire stretch of railing, interrupted by the support posts from their perspective, but clearly unimpeded. Dust was visible in the beam, dancing languidly in an unseen air current.

"Nothing there," Aldridge said. "At least, nothing big enough to interrupt the beam. But there's got to be five millimetres of clearance below the emitter. Most of the fillings that were recovered would fit underneath it."

"I'm aware of that," Greenwood said. "Let's try the starboard side." She deactivated the rangefinder and picked it up, carrying it across to the opposite side of the deck before setting it up in a similar position. Again, she activated it by sliding the switch forward. Three pairs of eyes flicked towards the forward terminus of the starboard railing.

There was no green dot.

It was Cross who hurried over to the railing, shielding her eyes from the rectangle of bright light that marked the open door of the warehouse. She traced the faint green beam with her finger. It came to an abrupt stop behind the fourth support post from the rangefinder.

"Don't touch anything," Greenwood said, appearing at her side. "Aldridge, you're up."

"I know," Aldridge replied, retrieving tweezers from

the equipment case, and a transparent plastic envelope. He joined the two women, who stepped back to give him room, then he crouched down and gingerly fed the tweezers behind the post, with their grips held closed. There was a metallic scraping sound, and then a small object rolled out into view.

"Is that…?" Cross said, watching as Aldridge snagged the brass-coloured cylinder with the tweezers and deposited it in the envelope.

"Yes, it is," he replied. "Bullet casing, .45 calibre." He handed the envelope to Greenwood.

"Do you know if your brother was in the habit of carrying a firearm, Dr. Cross? Or any of his crew?"

Cross's face had noticeably paled. She hesitated before she spoke, then she shook her head. "I don't… I can't imagine him having one. And his group gets into enough trouble with naval authorities and the drilling companies as it is. It would be madness to carry weapons."

"A lot of protest groups play fast and loose with the law," Greenwood said, drawing a sharp look from the other woman, and she raised one hand in a placating gesture. "Just an observation, not an accusation."

Aldridge had retrieved the magnification scope and was inspecting the bullet casing through the envelope. "It's the same as the other stuff. No surface contaminants of any kind. I don't even see any powder or gas residue, but it was definitely fired."

That's impossible, Greenwood thought, but she didn't

say the words aloud.

Aldridge thought for a moment, then lowered the scope and stood up, turning to face Greenwood and Cross. "We'll never get a fingerprint from this. There's just nothing there. But I can tell you one thing."

Greenwood raised an eyebrow in a silent question, and Aldridge looked again at the envelope in his hand. He felt the fine hairs prickling on the back of his neck.

"Whoever thought they'd need a handgun for this expedition of theirs… I think they were right. And it still didn't do them any good."

"That's speculation," Greenwood said, her gaze pointedly flicking from Aldridge to Cross and back again, and Aldridge shrugged.

"I know," he replied. "But there's something wrong here, and we both know it."

"I think he's right," Cross said, and after another moment, Greenwood nodded and looked towards the wheelhouse.

"Well, if they didn't usually carry firearms — as far as you know — then what *did* they bring along? What's probably been removed? They'd want to document whatever they found, if the oil platform did turn out to still be secretly in use. They'd have had cameras, surely."

Cross nodded. "Several. Mark spoke about it once. They always hid multiple cameras, in the hope that if the ship was boarded they might not all be found. The wheelhouse is the logical place, but I've checked it a dozen times."

"Let's check again," Greenwood said, and Cross gestured towards the small structure.

"Go right ahead."

Aldridge picked up the equipment case and followed them to the doorway. The interior consisted of a bridge area at the front, with exits to the deck on either side, then a partition leading towards a larger rear space with a fold-down bunk along one side, a long but shallow work surface opposite, and what looked like the rusted mounting points for a folding table of some kind at the back. There was no machinery to speak of, but plenty of less-faded areas of the interior walls where some sort of equipment or furniture had once been.

Greenwood glanced at the rearward space, but only for a moment. There was nowhere that a camera could be hidden, and there wouldn't be a clear view through the bridge area's windows from this far back. If there was anything to be found, it would be nearer the front.

"I've checked at least five times," Cross said. "There's nothing left in here. Whoever cleaned it out did a thorough job."

"They did," Greenwood agreed, "but there's a chance that they missed something. I doubt they meant to leave behind the objects you found either."

Cross conceded the point, and simply stepped back out of the way, arms folded. Aldridge had placed the case on a desk area to the starboard side, and removed another device. It had a compact, roughly cube-shaped plastic casing, with a black lens taking up most of one end. There was a small LCD display set into the top, and a handful of recessed controls alongside. It looked similar to an SLR camera's hot-shoe flash, but there was no coupling point on the underside — instead, there was a radiation warning label.

He pressed two of the controls, then began slowly and methodically passing the device's lens over every surface in the bridge area, including the undersides of work surfaces, behind structural supports, and even overhead. He noticed Cross watching him, and he briefly raised an eyebrow before continuing with his task.

"And what's that supposed to be?" she asked. Greenwood opened her mouth to respond, but Aldridge had already spoken.

"It's just a battery detector. It can find lithium- or nickel-based battery cells even if they're behind up to an inch of structural material. Well, depending on the specific material, its density, and the environmental conditions, of course."

Cross gave Greenwood an incredulous look, but the other woman's face was perfectly neutral.

"A *battery detector*," Cross said, and Aldridge nodded without looking around.

"I'm fairly sure there's no such thing, Dr. Aldridge," Cross said, now with a clearly audible note of suspicion in her voice. "And I don't appreciate being misled."

"Next you'll be telling me Santa Claus isn't real either," Aldridge replied with a slight grin, and then Greenwood stepped forward.

"Dr. Cross, I can assure you that no-one is misleading you. But we're not at liberty to discuss this subject further."

Cross looked from Greenwood to Aldridge and back again, her lips pressed together in a narrow line. "Just who exactly *are* you people?" she asked.

"We're here to help," Greenwood said. "Now, why don't you tell me again about your brother's—"

She was interrupted by a single, crystalline beep from the device Aldridge was holding. He'd been moving the device across the very frontmost strip of the bridge's ceiling, which came down slightly lower than the large windows, as if the internal structure of the ceiling had sagged during the ship's decades in use. It was covered in a spotted, yellowed linoleum, tucked and pinned into retaining plastic rails which ran around its edges.

"Lithium-ion cells, weak trace here," Aldridge said. "There's definitely a portable power source. Very low draw. My money is on electronics, which is just what we're after."

Greenwood stepped past Cross to join Aldridge in front of the windows which looked out onto the dimly-lit dry dock, and she raised her arm to poke at the ceiling's surface. It gave slightly under the pressure of her finger, and she reached into her jacket to retrieve a pocket knife multi-tool, deploying the box-cutter. It took only a few seconds to prise the plastic railing from its pins, and the sheet of linoleum obligingly flopped downwards at the front, releasing a small black object. Greenwood caught it easily with her free hand.

"Bingo," she said.

It was an ultraportable video camera, barely larger than a pack of cigarettes, with a fold-out screen on the side to review captured footage. The drooping front edge of the ceiling meant that the camera would have had a narrow view straight out of the bridge windows, even though it was concealed in the roof structure, but would still have been invisible from the outside. Greenwood flipped the screen open, but it remained darkened even when she pressed the power button. Aldridge retrieved a portable nine-volt DC power unit from his case, and plugged it into the device before pressing the power button again. This time, the screen illuminated immediately, showing a simple menu system. The battery icon in the top-right showed no charge.

"Did it record anything?" Cross asked, having joined them at the windows, making the fairly spacious bridge feel crowded and claustrophobic.

"I think so," Greenwood said as she used the controls on the camera's body to rapidly seek forwards through the video from the beginning. There was digital noise flickering all over the screen; jagged blocks and bars of colour, but nothing recognisable.

"Looks like data corruption," Aldridge said, and both women could hear the frustration in his voice. "It's like it wasn't encoded properly. Or it's not being decoded in the right way."

"What could cause that?" Cross asked, and Aldridge shook his head.

"Any number of things. Equipment failure or damage. Badly formatted or corrupted storage media. Electromagnetic interference."

There was a flash of coherent colour on the screen, and the barest hint of a human figure. Greenwood immediately moved her thumb to the rewind control to move backwards in the video file, until the footage was a jumble of smeared colours again. Then, she pressed the Play button.

Aldridge flinched at the hissing sound that came from the camera, not expecting it to be equipped with a speaker. The sound was tinny and clipped, but gave the impression of the omnipresent hum of some kind of machinery. The images were much more troubling.

The video quality wasn't great, particularly on the small and low-resolution screen, but it was exquisitely well-lit. They could see the bow of the *Hjørdis*, and a woman standing there, holding a pistol in a classic two-handed grip. She was aiming at something off-camera and at a slightly elevated angle, and dimly visible beyond was one of the mammoth support pylons of an oil rig. It was what lay between the rig and the trawler that sent a chill chasing up Aldridge's spine.

There was a wall of eerie, golden-orange luminescence, billowing over the water towards the ship. It moved like liquid, flowing through the air, and after another second the woman discharged three shots in quick succession. There was no indication of whether she'd hit her target, but her posture slackened in what very much looked like defeat. A moment later, the light surged forwards, licking over the bow of the ship, and engulfed her, then briefly ebbed before continuing to spread over the deck towards the camera's position. During the second or so that the tip of the bow had been revealed again, it was clear that the woman was no longer there.

There was no scream. No splash. No suggestion of a human form tumbling over the safety railings and falling towards the waves below. She was simply gone.

This time it was Cross who flinched when the footage abruptly degraded again into a meaningless jumble of visual artefacts, and the constant hissing sound was replaced with silence.

Greenwood flipped the camera's screen closed, disconnected the power supply, and slipped the device into her pocket, turning to give Aldridge a look that he understood immediately.

The mission parameters have changed.

Cross looked stunned, but when Greenwood pocketed the camera, the other woman's expression became one of anger. She was clearly about to protest, but then all three of them heard the sound of footsteps on the access stairway. A moment later, Ramos appeared in the doorway of the wheelhouse. She glanced briefly around, then focused her attention on Greenwood.

"I think I left my phone in the car. I'm going to go and get it."

Greenwood nodded, and casually unfastened her tan leather jacket, leaving it hanging open at the front. Ramos turned and went back down the stairway to the floor of the warehouse, putting her hands in her pockets as she walked towards the entrance.

Without a word, Aldridge quickly packed up the equipment case. He'd recognised Ramos's words as a prearranged code phrase. Its meaning was simple.

We're not alone.

Chapter 6

The dark red Volvo S90 was parked directly across the road from the warehouse, in a small side street that led to a connecting alleyway bordered with wooden sheds. The car faced away from the warehouse but within sight of it, and its two occupants sat low in the front seats, never turning around. The engine ticked as it cooled in the pronounced breeze.

The car was rented, and a small camera was mounted below the rear central headrest, its footage displayed on a tablet computer in the lap of the man who sat in the front passenger seat. His name was Venter, and he was a man of few words. His companion and driver was called Reddy, and both were private security contractors hand-picked by Miwa when he'd visited Cape Town several years earlier. They had been members of his organisation ever since. According to their employee records, they were Site Survey and Liaison Managers, which was a euphemism for their real speciality: covert surveillance, and when necessary, direct intervention.

"Anything?" Reddy asked, and the other man shook his head.

"The black-haired woman went further inside," Venter said. "They must still be looking at the boat."

Reddy shifted position in the contoured leather seat, and reached inside his thick jacket to adjust the position of the snub-nosed pistol that sat in a holster against his rib cage. Their orders were to avoid engagement, but they never deployed without concealed weapons, which were always waiting for them when they arrived in whichever country Miwa sent them to. He was a powerful man, and had connections that made such arrangements straightforward. Reddy hated this sort of work: watching and waiting. He would have preferred to take his chances by approaching the building, come what may. His job involved a great deal of alert inactivity, and on the infrequent occasions when conflict was called for, he found it both a relief and a pleasure.

Venter glanced up from the tablet and out of the windscreen, but the rest of the side street was still deserted. It hadn't been long since the Cross woman arrived at the warehouse, only a minute or two after the others. Venter's briefing said that this would be the first time in several days that she'd visited the site, though she'd spent plenty of time here during the last few weeks.

But her companions are the more pressing matter, he

thought.

Miwa was obviously concerned about these people from Brussels, and understandably so. It was vital that no scrutiny was placed on the oil platform. The disappearance of a group of misfit environmental protestors — several with criminal records — on the open ocean was normally unlikely to prompt more than a cursory investigation. Dr. Cross, however, had proven persistent, and far more resourceful than anyone had expected.

No doubt driven by grief and guilt, against all expectations she'd managed to locate the stripped trawler, and take ownership of it. Miwa's organisation had only found out about this development very recently, and there had been no time to once again make the vessel disappear. Things had evidently moved very quickly during the past several weeks, and now the situation was in danger of spiralling out of control. Miwa hadn't foreseen the possibility that Cross would successfully involve the European authorities, but that was now his working assumption about the identity of the two women and one man who'd arrived in Bergen this morning.

Via a private jet, no less.

Enquiries regarding the aircraft's registration number yielded an ominous lack of information, and Venter had received an additional briefing via satellite phone less than twenty minutes ago: *Operational discretion granted.*

The video feed on the tablet computer still showed no

movement. The small camera had an impressive optical zoom capability, and could also be remotely panned within a ninety-degree horizontal range, and rotated vertically within forty-five degrees, via the tablet's on-screen controls. Even so, the only openings on the street-facing side of the warehouse were a high, boarded window, and the two metal shutters, of which one was closed. Through the open shutter, they had seen the black-haired woman moving within the warehouse more than once, appearing to casually examine the building's interior perimeter. But Venter had seen no sign of Cross or the other woman and man since they all entered. He was growing impatient — to say nothing of his companion. Venter had worked with Reddy for more than five years, and while he was a strong asset, he also had a certain thrill-seeking quality that needed to be moderated.

"Alright," Venter said, drawing a glance from the other man. "Tag their vehicle."

Reddy zipped up his black goose-down thermal jacket, and slipped out of the car without a word. Stuffing his hands into his pockets, he started walking back down the side street. After a moment, he appeared in the video feed on the tablet computer, moving purposefully towards the junction with the main road.

"Stay on this side of the road until you have an opening," Venter said in Reddy's earpiece, and the other man snorted under his breath.

"Not my first time, *boet*," Reddy replied, his Afrikaner

accent thickening in proportion to his newfound cheer-fulness.

Venter shifted slightly in his seat. Attaching an electronic locating and eavesdropping device was a risky move when they had no means to observe the interior of the building and track the positions of those within, and he knew that the Cross woman was both observant and highly motivated about determining her brother's fate. Nevertheless, the priority was to obtain more information about the identities of the three others who were meeting with her, and their intentions.

Reddy reached the junction and turned the corner, moving parallel to the warehouse. He slowed, pretending to check his phone, and then glanced disinterestedly towards the structure across the street. There was no-one visible through the open shutter.

"Proceeding," he said quietly, as if talking to someone standing right next to him, and then he dashed across the road, his rubber-soled boots making remarkably little sound against the tarmac. He stepped over the low wall which bordered the parking area, withdrew a small magnetic device from his jacket pocket and concealed it within his fist, then carefully approached the rented SUV. There was silence in his earpiece, and he knew that Venter was watching the dark void leading into the warehouse via the camera's zoom function.

There was no sign of the black-haired woman, though, and Reddy reached the back of the vehicle without trouble. He crouched near the axle at one side, extended his arm underneath, and smoothly placed the device high up within the right rear wheel arch. Then he immediately turned and crouch-ran back to the perimeter of the parking area, straightened to step over the low wall again, and casually walked off down the road, in the opposite direction from the side street.

Once he was fifty metres past the warehouse, he spoke two words under his breath.

"It's done," he said.

"Aldridge, you and Cross should check the rear cabin again, just in case," Greenwood said, taking a position at the open door of the wheelhouse with one hand on the handle. Ramos was visible at the open metal shutter where they'd entered the warehouse, standing inside the doorway and off to one side. Greenwood had just seen a concealed hand-gesture from her, indicating the presence of an unknown person outside.

"What's going on?" Cross asked, again with suspicion in her voice. "The rear area is completely empty. You know that."

"Let's go anyway," Aldridge replied, gesturing towards the spartan area beyond the bulkhead. Cross hesitated, and Aldridge shifted his stance slightly.

"Have you noticed anyone hanging around? Perhaps keeping this building, or you, under surveillance?" he asked. Cross looked from him to Greenwood and back again, but the other woman's gaze was fixed on her colleague at the entrance.

"No, I haven't. Is that what's happening? There's someone else here?"

Aldridge was about to reply, but Greenwood spoke first. "Yes," she said. "Now please do as Aldridge suggests. Both of you wait here."

She stepped out of the wheelhouse without a backwards glance, closing the door behind her. Aldridge looked briefly at Cross, then pointed to the rear starboard corner of the enclosed space.

"If you could wait there for just a few minutes, Dr. Cross," he said. "You're safe with me, I promise. We're just making sure everything is alright."

Aldridge saw her face go slightly pale, but after a moment she stepped over towards the corner he'd indicated. He nodded gratefully, and then half-turned so he could keep an eye on both her and the wheelhouse's door facing the access stairway.

It didn't escape Cross's notice that he'd also left his jacket unfastened.

Ramos stood silently just within the warehouse, off to one side of the open shutter, listening to the receding footsteps.

From years-long habit, she always carried a compact monocular scope with her wherever she went. As a sniper, she was used to being able to see distant areas up close, and as the group's surveillance expert, constant watchfulness had become so ingrained that it now felt like it was in her genes.

She spotted the car in the side street before she drove into the warehouse's parking area earlier, and had been keeping an eye on it while Greenwood and Aldridge were up on the trawler's deck with Dr. Cross. An area of shadow at the edge of the shutter afforded a suitable vantage point, and on her first pass she'd picked up both men. On her second pass, she saw the rear-facing camera, even though it would have been virtually unnoticeable to anyone who walked right past the parked car.

Ramos's training told her to treat every situation as having the potential for escalation and conflict, and to never consider a location to be completely secure. She didn't like the combination of Dr. Cross's brother and his associates disappearing, and now the trawler — or Cross herself — apparently being under surveillance. She didn't like it at all.

Donde hay humo, hay calor, she thought, as she reached inside her coat and unsnapped the tough loop of leather that kept her weapon in its holster. *There's no smoke without fire.*

She knew that the man outside had approached their vehicle, and then retreated again. His likely goal was to plant a bug, but there were darker possibilities too. Ramos herself would need less than a minute to rig a vehicle to explode when the ignition was triggered, but that wasn't the kind of work that KESTREL did. Her last glimpse of the unknown intruder had been when he reached the main road and was about to cross towards the warehouse, and her trained eye had noticed the characteristic small bulge of a handgun on the left outer edge of his chest beneath his ski jacket.

Ramos craned her neck upwards to follow the line of the shutter, and saw that it was pinned open via a lever at the opposite side. Her assessment was that the man wouldn't return, but she wanted options in case he did. She would need to move across the open space to close the shutter.

In the next instant, she heard the sound of an approaching engine, and she knew that the other man in the Volvo had driven off after his colleague. As the vehicle passed and then receded, Ramos refastened the retaining loop over her pistol, and zipped up her coat once more. It was time to see what exactly had been done to the SUV. First, though, she turned and made a hand-gesture towards Greenwood, who was at the foot of the access stairway alongside the trawler, poised to move at a moment's notice.

Greenwood acknowledged the gesture and then jogged over to where Ramos stood. "Well?" she said, and Ramos nodded in the direction of the parking area outside.

"Two men, in a rented vehicle", she replied. "They were parked in the street opposite, keeping the warehouse under surveillance. One of them just paid a visit to our car. He was armed."

Greenwood's expression tightened, and she briefly glanced back towards the trawler before meeting the other woman's eyes again.

"Perimeter and vehicle check," Greenwood said. "Be careful, Alicia."

Ramos just nodded again, then stepped out into the daylight and slowly approached the rear of the parked SUV, at a distance of several metres. Her gaze swept over the road for several seconds, but there was no longer anyone else around. The side street was likewise deserted, so she turned her attention to their transport.

She took almost a full minute to circle the vehicle, visually checking its bodywork, handles and locks, and chassis, then she reached into her pocket and took out the one other device she always kept on hand besides the scope: an RF signal detector. She'd used it while surveilling the interior perimeter of the warehouse, and had found nothing. Now, though, she knew exactly where to look — inside the rear right wheel arch, the part of the vehicle that offered the best balance of opportunity for concealment, proximity to the approach point from the road, and an obscured view from within the warehouse itself. She pulled her phone from her jeans pocket for just long enough to enable its flight-safe mode, which would prevent interference.

Ramos knew that a bomb was very unlikely. Her team was unknown to whoever had planted the device, and intel was always more valuable than casualties. An exploding rental vehicle would also draw enormous attention and a thorough investigation. She was virtually certain it would be a bug, but caution was always indicated. She crouched down beside the wheel arch, craned her neck to look inside at the highest point of its interior surface, and sure enough, she found the device immediately.

The signal detector made no sound, but displayed an animated histogram on its display showing the characteristics of the homing transmission. The familiar bug was modern and efficient, of most use within metropolitan areas, relying on an embedded universal cellular radio with GPS antenna to provide tracking data anywhere in the world over the existing mobile telecoms infrastructure. It would be useless in most rural areas, unlike the older and more bulky devices that broadcast a powerful signal designed to be intercepted locally, but within the city it could run for days — and be tracked at the user's convenience.

It was a flattened cuboid about seven by seven by two centimetres, in a rugged housing, with no display or indicator lights of any kind. Ramos knew that the antennae were looped around the outward-facing edge, and that the rear panel was magnetic. It contained a trip switch that would instantly send a repeated warning signal to its owner if the device was pulled away from the surface it was attached to. She also knew that it contained a sensitive dual-microphone directional assembly, mounted towards the metallic attachment point, which used sound conduction to eavesdrop on any conversations taking place nearby. It was remarkable how much could be picked up even through the chassis of a moving vehicle, with modern equipment.

She returned the detector to her pocket, stood up, and made her way back inside the warehouse to where Greenwood stood waiting.

"Cellular tracker with acoustic bug," Ramos said. "Someone is interested in us."

Greenwood's eyes narrowed. "Still in place?"

"Of course," Ramos replied. "The model has a removal failsafe. What do you want to do?"

Greenwood thought for a moment, but there was really only one course of action. "We'll let the situation play out for now. I'll talk to Dr. Cross. Get us ready to move, Alicia."

Ramos nodded, and went out into the grey daylight once again.

Aldridge waited behind the wheelhouse's closed door, opposite the hinged side, his attention focused on the sounds from outside. He could feel the SIG Elite in its holster against his body, and he was conscious of his own pulse, but it was steady and moderate. He felt focused, and in control. The edge of adrenaline was there, but he was still able to think clearly, and he felt prepared — no matter what the situation outside might be. His training had worked wonders.

His shoulders tensed slightly as he heard the clang of boots hitting the lowest step of the access stairway, but their pace was unhurried, and he knew the gait well. A few moments later, he wasn't in the least bit surprised to hear the familiar sequence of four knocks on the door.

"Coming in," Greenwood's voice said from outside.

"Be my guest," Aldridge replied, taking two paces back and watching as the door opened and Greenwood stepped inside, looking unbothered to find him looming near her. She closed the door again, and only then did Aldridge allow himself to stand at ease.

"They've gone," Greenwood said, looking from Aldridge to Cross. "You can relax now, Doctor."

"Ramos?" Aldridge asked, and Greenwood nodded.

"I think she's a little disappointed, to be honest. Two men, watching the building. They just bugged our car."

"The plot thickens," Aldridge replied. "I'd be keeping watch too, if I knew what happened to the people on this ship. I probably wouldn't want anyone nosing around asking questions."

Greenwood inclined her head in agreement, and turned her attention to Cross. "Are you alright, Doctor? You're safe," she said, and Cross looked at her as if she was insane.

"Of course I'm not alright!" she replied, with a surprising level of anger given how shaken she looked. "Who was out there? Why were they watching the building? And the woman in the recording... she just vanished. What is going on, and *who are you people*?"

Instead of answering immediately, Greenwood went over to one side of the small compartment, folded her arms, and leaned her shoulder against the cold wall, apparently deep in thought. After a few moments, she looked at Cross once again, and saw that the other woman looked marginally less upset.

"As I said to Dr. Aldridge, there were two men, and they had this location under surveillance," Greenwood said. "They've attached a tracker and listening device to our vehicle. I don't know any more than that. The recording we found is as much of a mystery to me as it is to you."

"I'm pretty sure that *Doctor* Aldridge here has a concealed firearm," Cross said, glancing at Aldridge's face and then his chest in quick succession, "and I assume that you and your other colleague out there—"

"Alicia Ramos," Greenwood supplied patiently.

"—have them too."

Again, Greenwood just nodded. *You don't miss much, do you?*

She saw that Cross was about to make some kind of demand, and she suddenly felt some of the stress of the early flight, strange discovery, and unexpected encounter all catching up with her. She raised a hand, and Cross remained silent for the moment.

"I understand how you feel," Greenwood said. "I do. And there'll be time to answer your questions, if we can. But right now I need to ask *you* something: since this all began, have you had any sense that you were being watched? Unfamiliar faces you've noticed more than once. Anyone paying too much attention. Things looking like they've been moved, either here or wherever you're staying. Anything like that?"

Cross's cheeks had almost returned to their normal colour, but now they paled again. "No," she replied in a small voice, after several moments of silence. "You think they've been here for a while. Not just because you're here."

"Aldridge and Ramos could both tell you that I don't believe in coincidences, Dr. Cross," Greenwood said. "Your brother and the other people on this ship disappeared, under what now appear to be very suspicious and unusual circumstances. The trawler was stripped and cleaned, then anonymously sold for scrap a long way from its last known location. Then you sent a dossier to a contact in the European government, and we arrived to find men in position, keeping an eye on the building."

Greenwood stood up straight now, no longer leaning against the wall. Her expression was compassionate, but her voice was as firm and clear as ever.

"Whoever they are, I think they're connected to what happened to your brother," she said. "They've bugged our vehicle, and they're also armed. I don't know who they are, but I can tell you that those men don't have *any idea* who they're dealing with."

"Nor do I," Cross said, with a hint of defiance creeping back into her voice. "And if you'll just let me leave now, I think it's definitely time I talked to the police." She paused for a moment before continuing. "I don't have to mention that you were here."

Greenwood raised one eyebrow wearily.

"I appreciate the thought, but your conversation with the police will have to wait. As for who we are, that's one of the things we can talk about later," Greenwood replied, lifting her hand again to preempt the question she saw forming on Cross's lips. She spoke before the other woman could say anything.

"Gather your things, Doctor. You're coming with us."

Chapter 7

Venter kept the car at the speed limit as he merged onto Riksveg 555, the national road winding westwards through Laksevåg and eventually connecting south towards Flesland and the airport. He habitually checked the rear-view mirror every fifteen seconds as the Volvo cruised smoothly across the Puddefjord Bridge. The waters of the Damsgårdssundet were a dull, gunmetal blue under the increasingly cloudy sky.

"Shouldn't be long," Reddy said from the passenger seat, already using the tablet computer to remotely connect to the tracking device. The operation had gone like clockwork, and now they simply had to wait for Dr. Cross's companions to conclude their meeting, or inspection, or whatever it was, and return to their vehicle.

"Any bets?" Reddy asked, drawing a quick glance from Venter. "About who they are, I mean," Reddy continued, but he knew he wouldn't receive much more than a grunt in response. His colleague was a trained soldier just like him, but much more cautious, and not given to speculation or impulsiveness. Reddy often found his partner's carefulness annoying, but it had also saved their lives on more than one occasion. Besides, he was mostly just needling him.

"The one with the short hair," he said, "I think she was military. Just the way she moved. You know how it is."

Venter did indeed know how it was, and he'd had the same disquieting instinct, which he hadn't been planning on voicing yet. He frowned. No-one was expecting a delegation from the EU government to be anything except scientists, investigators, or the omnipresent administrators and bureaucrats. The presence of security personnel of any kind could mean that Cross knew more than they'd assumed. It also meant that her new acquaintances were much less likely to go to the police, and instead would potentially pursue matters at a higher level — if they'd found anything to arouse their suspicions.

He shifted in his seat, feeling his appetite for lunch fading, to be replaced with a growing sense of impatience. They would proceed to somewhere in the vicinity of the airport, and wait to monitor whatever the tracker picked up when Dr. Cross's visitors made their own return journey. Later in the day, they would retrieve the tracking device from the vehicle, then get rid of their own car, which would never again be in the service of the rental agency.

"Let's keep the speculation to ourselves for now," Venter said. "We'll see what we can learn, then we'll report in. He won't be happy until we've got something concrete."

"Is he ever?" Reddy replied, his gaze fixed on the tablet device. Venter didn't respond.

As they cleared the bridge and felt the slight bump as they rejoined the tarmac, he checked his mirrors again and then pressed the accelerator down just a little further.

Cross had taken a taxi to the warehouse, as always, and was returning to the airport immediately, which was the ideal scenario from Greenwood's point of view: they could offer her a ride to their mutual destination, talk during the drive, and feed misinformation to those who were listening in.

All four of them were in the SUV now, and Ramos was being careful to keep her speed down, to minimise the amount of road noise the tracker would pick up. Greenwood had already briefed Cross on what to expect.

Aldridge and Cross sat in the rear, with Greenwood in the front passenger seat. They had only been driving for a few minutes, and would soon be leaving the harbour district.

"We appreciate you seeing us today, Dr. Cross," Greenwood said. "I know this has been a difficult time for you."

"And apparently also a waste of both my time and yours," Cross replied. Aldridge's lips quirked into a grin, impressed at how convincing the remark had sounded.

"As I said," Greenwood replied, "we're sympathetic to your situation. But without anything more substantial to go on, I don't see any justification for involving further investigative resources, or engaging the Norwegian naval authority. But rest assured that I'll be forwarding a recommendation to recheck all unidentified hospital admissions in port cities during the period in question, in case your brother and his crew did make it back from their expedition."

"How kind of you," Cross replied. Her tone was convincingly withering.

Greenwood cleared her throat before continuing. "At the moment, I see no indication of a continuing threat to commercial activity in the area of the oil platform, and I'm satisfied that the vessel was obtained via the usual marine salvage procedures. I've also been assured by the Norwegian Ministry of Petroleum and Energy that the platform was fully down-manned some time ago, and remains in a decommissioned state."

"And how exactly do you explain the disappearance of four people?"

Greenwood's voice became kindly, and in a flash of awareness, Aldridge knew that she really had been in the position of having to give difficult news to bereaved relatives more than once. His brow creased into a frown for a moment as he continued listening to the conversation.

"The ocean can be treacherous at the best of times, and it's fair to say that your brother's crew made a very dangerous voyage without sufficient experience or safety equipment," Greenwood said. "I'm sorry, but I believe they probably underestimated how challenging the conditions would be. Tragically, it's still all too common for people to be lost at sea."

There was silence for at least half a minute, and Aldridge sighed. "It's a terrible situation, Dr. Cross, and we're all deeply sorry for your loss. I agree with my colleague's judgement. If we do hear anything more, though, we'll naturally be in touch immediately."

"You'll forgive me if I don't find that thought particularly comforting, or of much help," Cross said, folding her arms across her chest and turning to look out the window.

The rest of the journey back to the rental agency at the airport passed almost entirely in silence, and when they arrived, Cross immediately bid her travelling companions a perfunctory farewell as soon as Ramos parked the SUV in an available bay. She got out and stormed off in the direction of the terminal building, and was soon lost to view. Ramos locked the vehicle, and the remaining three walked to the agency office beyond the parking lot in silence, concluding the rental at a leisurely pace before continuing towards the terminal themselves, at least fifteen minutes behind Cross.

They went inside, ignoring the check-in and baggage drop areas, and proceeded straight to an exit at the far side. A black sedan with tinted windows was waiting for them; their direct transport to the private hangar out on the airfield. The very brief journey was also made in silence, and when they finally entered the hangar's waiting area, Aldridge smiled. Seated at the small coffee area in the farthest corner, facing away from the entrance, was Cross.

Greenwood had made a call from the warehouse, arranging for Cross to be taken from the terminal building to the hangar, to get her out of sight of any possible surveillance in the public part of the airport. Evidently, she had arrived without incident. There was a cup of black coffee in front of her, but it looked like it was untouched. Her mobile phone sat beside it.

"Very convincing," Aldridge said, taking a seat beside Cross as Greenwood and Ramos also sat down. Cross nodded at him.

"So what now?" she asked. "Do you think they followed us?"

It was Ramos who replied. "They'll be somewhere in the area, but airports are dangerous for direct surveillance. Too many cameras, and police. It'll be risky enough to retrieve the device from the vehicle. They'll probably do it after it gets dark."

Cross thought about that for a moment, then looked down at the black liquid in her cup. After a few seconds,

Ramos spoke again.

"Do you come to the warehouse regularly, Doctor? Was today a normal day for you to be there?"

Cross shook her head. "I was there almost every day after I had the trawler brought in, for a while. But lately it's been less often, and only when I could manage. I had to fly in, just like you."

"And yet there were men in position, with equipment, when we all arrived," Ramos said. The implication was clear.

"Oh, god," Cross replied. She was only now putting the pieces together. "They weren't just watching me *here*? They knew my travel plans?"

"Probably simpler than that," Greenwood said, her eyes flicking down to the phone sitting beside the coffee cup. "I assume that's the number you included in your dossier, which Aldridge used to contact you."

Cross's face paled again, and she looked at the device as if it were suddenly primed to explode at any moment. "I put it in flight mode as soon as I got into the terminal, as you asked. Now I understand why."

"Well, they can't see us in here — and you're going to visit the toilet and drop your phone into the bin before we leave. We'll also be boarding within this building, not out on the tarmac. We're leaving as soon as the tower gives us clearance, so you should go and ditch the phone now."

Cross understood what the other woman was saying. "Where are you taking me?" she asked, and Aldridge glanced at Greenwood. Ramos was listening, but she ceaselessly scanned the general area, ever wary of any potential eavesdroppers.

"Brussels," Greenwood replied after a moment. "We need to consult with some of my other colleagues."

"I'm not going with you to—" Cross began, but Aldridge cut her off by raising his hand slightly to get her attention.

"Doctor, I understand that a lot has happened this morning, and that you're frightened, but I promise you: we only have your best interests in mind," he said. Cross was looking at him now. The expression on his face was sympathetic, and he knew without having to look that Greenwood was listening carefully.

"You also have to understand that you may be in danger, and we can protect you. What we saw in the recording changes things for us. The truth is, we visited you today as a courtesy, but it's my judgement now that your brother's disappearance bears active investigation."

Cross looked at Aldridge for another moment, then glanced towards the other two women. Greenwood and Ramos said nothing, but Greenwood nodded.

"And if I'd rather take my chances with the local police?" Cross asked. This time it was Greenwood who replied.

"I'm afraid you're temporarily not at liberty to do so," she said, "but I promise that I'll give you more of an explanation when I can. You're safe with us, and we represent the proper authorities, at a higher level. I'm asking you to trust us for the time being. I know it's asking a lot."

Cross looked at Aldridge once again, and he just gave her a smile that he hoped was reassuring.

"Alright," she sighed. "Since I don't seem to have much choice. And… I'm glad you were there."

"I'm glad of that too," Greenwood said. There was a long pause before Cross spoke.

"What did you say your name was, again?"

"Jessica Greenwood."

"But not *Doctor*," Cross said.

"Actually," Greenwood replied, "it's Captain."

Chapter 8

It was a little after 1 PM in Brussels when the heavily customised people-carrier finally rolled to a halt, after descending several ramps in what felt to Cross like a multi-storey underground parking structure.

They'd been picked up within another private hangar at Bruxelles-National airport just moments after their jet landed, and the driver — a stocky, powerful-looking man in nondescript clothing, with close-cropped dark hair — hadn't said a word during the twenty-five minute journey. Greenwood and Aldridge sat in the middle row of seats, with Ramos and Cross behind. The vehicle had windows which had looked tinted from the outside, but curiously, they were completely opaque from within, too, and there was a partition between the passenger area and the driver's compartment, affording no visibility outside at all. It was like being in the back of a van, albeit a comfortable one.

Cross had heard the usual traffic and city noise for most of the trip, but several minutes ago the sounds had all dropped away, and she felt the vehicle slowing and beginning to traverse a downwards incline. There had been several long, smooth turns, with brief stretches of level ground, but the overall tendency was to move further and further downwards. Just as she began to wonder where they could possibly be, she felt the brakes being gently applied again, and the vehicle came to a halt. There was a muted clunk from both sides, and she realised that the doors had just been unlocked, presumably by the driver. Less than a second later, the sliding door on the right was opened from the outside.

A man in a military uniform stood there, holstered sidearm on his hip. When he saw Greenwood, he immediately saluted. It was Aldridge who returned the salute, though, and Greenwood momentarily fixed him with a look which had him immediately lowering his arm again. They both got out of the vehicle, and Ramos gestured to Cross that she should exit now too.

The flight had been a quiet one, on an aircraft that had clearly begun its life as a luxury private jet, but had been retrofitted into something very different. There were banks of flat panel monitors and computer equipment, working spaces, and lockers too. The seating still seemed to be the customary leather recliners, but everything else was functional and utilitarian. There were no identifying marks on the fuselage except the tail number, nor anything in the interior to shed any light on its owners' identities. There was also no paper what-soever, besides the drinks napkins in a dispenser on the conspicuously non-alcoholic minibar. Finally, there was a floor-to-ceiling metallic cabinet of some kind, with an inset small glass panel and no handles. Cross wasn't sure what to make of it, but she knew it only made her feel more on edge.

Having arrived at their destination — which Green-wood had refused to disclose the location or nature of in advance — Cross now stepped out of the people carrier to stand beside Aldridge and Ramos. Aldridge gave her a small smile again.

"Home sweet home," he said. "We'll get you some-thing to eat, if you'd like."

"Thank you," Cross replied, and Greenwood turned to face the other three after exchanging a brief word with the soldier who stood nearby.

"We appreciate your cooperation, Doctor," she said, then she nodded towards the soldier. "This gentleman will take you to have some lunch, then bring you to meet us again later. Aldridge, take the video camera to Tech. I want to know if the intact footage has been tam-pered with, and whether we can restore any of the dam-aged sections. Alicia, bring the others up to speed. We'll meet in the conference room once I have our orders."

"Going to talk to Her Majesty?" Aldridge asked, drawing a startled glance from Cross, until she realised he wasn't speaking literally.

"That's how the chain of command works," Greenwood replied, already turning away. "You should read up on it."

Miwa sat behind his desk, listening calmly to the report from Tien about the surveillance operation in Bergen.

On the surface, the news seemed positive: the mysterious delegation from some part of the web of EU governmental agencies had found nothing worthy of further investigation, and had now left the country. It would be even more difficult for Cross to attract additional interest from the authorities now that resources had already been expended fruitlessly.

And yet Miwa still felt uneasy. His agents in the field hadn't been able to pin down any details of the delegation's identity, and it was unusual for investigators of shipping-related incidents to have access to a private aircraft. Granted, this matter related to Norway's petrochemical industry, and the safety of commercial vessels in an oil-producing region, but even so. Something felt wrong.

"Do we have any further information on Dr. Cross's travel plans after she left Norway?" he asked, and Tien shook his head.

"She has made no further calls, but depending on her destination it may be some time before she lands."

Miwa nodded. On balance, the situation had not changed. Preparations were almost complete, and the facility in which he now sat was completely unknown to anyone outside his organisation, including those who had previously been involved with their work on the oil platform. The platform itself was now genuinely decommissioned, and there was nothing to be found there.

Unless they looked below, he thought. But even then, any discovery would only bring questions without answers, because he had taken all the answers away with him — and his people had been as thorough as ever. The object beneath, while certainly shocking, couldn't be linked to him, and nor could it throw any light on his larger plan.

There was also virtually no time left for anyone to interfere.

"Very well," he said. "Inform me if anything changes. In the meantime, we proceed."

Tien bowed and silently withdrew from the chamber, closing the door behind him.

Miwa steepled his hands together for a moment, his gaze focused on the cold metal surface of the desk. His instincts told him that he might be facing an unforeseen element of risk, and he'd learned to trust that inner voice.

It may be wise to put a contingency plan into operation, he thought, and in the silence of the room within the mountain, he clenched his fist.

Chapter 9

The next hour passed agonisingly slowly for Cross. She ate lunch in silence, amidst the bustle of some kind of canteen that was peopled with a strange mix of uniformed soldiers, scientists, and nondescript other people. They were in tight-knit groups, all mutually respectful, but there was an unexpected lack of conversation. Cross, with her conspicuous military minder sitting diagonally opposite her at their otherwise-empty table, suspected that she might be the reason for the general lack of chatter.

Once she'd eaten, she was taken to a room not unlike a waiting area in an upmarket office building; there were magazines and newspapers in a dozen languages, all the latest editions, and refreshments for the taking. The windows of the small room were also oddly opaque from within, making the otherwise comfortable space seem like a luxurious holding cell. Her minder, whose name was Di Giorgio according to the tag on the flap of his uniform's left breast pocket, remained in the room with her, never eating or drinking, and saying very little. She tried to read a newspaper, but the surreal quality of the day she'd had gave the mundane news an air of unreality.

Eventually, the room's door opened to reveal Aldridge, and he smiled at her.

"There you are, Doctor," he said. "Did you manage to get some lunch?"

She nodded. "Yes, thank you."

"Good, good," Aldridge replied, still holding the door open. "Well, I'm sorry to have kept you waiting. If you'll come with me, I've got someone I'd like you to meet."

Cross stood up, and glanced towards the soldier standing impassively nearby. Aldridge followed her gaze, and nodded at the other man.

"I think I can keep an eye on her from here," Aldridge said genially. "You're dismissed."

"Sir," the other man replied, then he left the room immediately and walked off down the corridor. Aldridge smiled at Cross again and made a small gesture, inviting her to precede him, and he allowed the door to close behind them as they left.

During the next few minutes, Cross was ushered through a maze of corridors and up a stairway, and she briefly saw a large open area too, with walkways criss-crossing overhead. The entire installation seemed to be underground, and there were uniformed guards patrolling each area. Everywhere she looked there were people engaged in muted, purposeful activity, and again she wondered what she'd stumbled into.

"I remember the first time I saw the place too," Aldridge said, as he pointed towards the right fork of an approaching junction, just past a set of metal double doors with radiation warning symbols emblazoned upon them. "Admittedly, they brought me in the front door instead."

"What is this place?" Cross asked, and Aldridge only grinned enigmatically.

"I'll let our fearless leader answer that one, if she so desires, otherwise I'll be in trouble."

"By which you mean Miss... or actually *Captain* Greenwood?"

"Definitely the latter," Aldridge replied. "But I'm pretty sure the former exists somewhere in there too."

Cross quirked an eyebrow at the remark, but she was coming to realise that Aldridge was often indirect in his responses. She changed tack, and asked something that she'd been wondering about since they left the waiting area.

"The soldier back there; he called you *sir*, and followed your orders," she said, "but frankly you don't strike me as the military type. Did you mean it when you said your background is in physics?"

"Very much so," Aldridge replied. "I have a Ph.D in theoretical subatomic particle physics, and I've conducted research in that field for most of my adult life. I have a lab here that rivals anything at the universities I've worked at."

"So how does a scientist have soldiers under his command?" she asked, and Aldridge glanced briefly around at her as they walked.

"Suffice it to say that my position here carries a rank, and that we're a rather unique group," he said. "To get clearance to tell you more than that, you wouldn't *believe* the number of forms I'd have to fill out. Ah, here we are now."

Aldridge slowed as they drew level with a large sliding door. There was a blue-bordered sign on the adjacent wall reading SCIENCES, and additional boldface lettering below, spelling out a single word: BIOLOGY. Aldridge pressed his thumb to a small panel mounted at waist height on the door frame, and the door itself gave the barest hissing sound as it slid open automatically.

Cross's eyebrows shot up as she surveyed the room within. Her consultancy work for the energy industry involved a great deal of travel, and she had seen industrial sites and offices, boardrooms and drilling platforms — but rarely had she encountered a laboratory as well equipped as this. It was a far cry from any academic facility, and instead reminded her of documentaries she'd seen about the private labs run by multinational pharmaceutical corporations.

The room was big enough for an impromptu indoor soccer match, if not for the rows and rows of equipment and the multitude of personnel. There were a hundred sounds coming from a bewildering array of apparent experimental stations, fume cupboards, temperature-controlled storage facilities, several mass spectrometers, dozens of computer terminals, and a bank of articulated robotic machines which were relentlessly active at a series of conveyor stations bordering the far side of the huge space.

The work surfaces were at a variety of different levels, and as Cross watched, several of them smoothly altered in height as one or another of the staff approached them.

"It's not *real* science, of course," Aldridge said, and he smirked at the incredulous look she gave him. "Nothing wrong with a bit of physical-versus-life-sciences rivalry."

Cross was saved from having to formulate a response by the whisper of movement nearby, accompanied by a barely-audible electrical humming sound. For the briefest moment, she thought it was another automated device, but then a man came into view, seated in a motorised chair of sleek aluminium. He looked middle eastern, with black hair and a neatly trimmed beard, tanned skin, and a powerfully-built chest. He bore a gentle smile. The chair had a small joystick set into the end of the left armrest, and a series of other controls on the opposite side, and it moved almost noiselessly across the floor towards them.

"Dr. Lily Cross," Aldridge said, "I'd like you to meet my arch-enemy: our very own Q."

The man in the wheelchair grinned broadly, showing an impressive array of white teeth, then raised his right hand and placed it over his chest. When he spoke, his deep voice filled the air around him. "It is a pleasure to meet you, Doctor. Pay no attention to this disreputable man."

His tone was cheerful as he nodded in the direction of Aldridge, and Cross found herself liking him immediately. "The pleasure is mine, I'm sure," she replied. She turned her head to look at Aldridge again. "Q?"

"Dr. Qadir al-Ahmed, at your service," the other man interjected before Aldridge could reply. He pronounced his given name as *kadeer*, and his head bobbed in the slightest hint of a bow as he introduced himself.

"Qadir analysed the foreign objects you found on the trawler," Aldridge said. "His report flagged the lack of any expected biological residue."

"Then I have you to thank for your… organisation's timely involvement," Cross said, smiling at Ahmed. The man made a dismissive gesture, as if to say he was simply doing his job, and then his expression became sorrowful.

"I'm saddened to hear of your brother's disappearance," he said, and Cross nodded.

"I appreciate that, and your help. I'm very impressed by this facility. Were you previously working in academia like Dr. Aldridge?"

"I obtained my degree in Baghdad as a young man, but my doctorate came later, after a period in the military," Ahmed replied.

"He worked in bomb disposal," Aldridge said. Cross was unable to prevent her gaze from flicking downwards to where the other man's trouser legs sat flat against the chair's seat, clearly without limbs inside them. Her cheeks flushed slightly. Ahmed smiled.

"Don't be uncomfortable, Doctor," he said kindly. "I disposed of one final anti-personnel mine in an unconventional manner, then decided to resume my studies of the life sciences."

"I see," she said, unsure of how else to respond, shifting her position awkwardly.

"Now he runs this temple of impure science," Aldridge said, gesturing exaggeratedly towards the gleaming equipment all around them before checking his wristwatch. "And with that, we should probably be heading towards the conference room. The Captain will be calling for us soon."

Cross nodded, then turned her attention back to al-Ahmed. "Thank you again." The man nodded, once again bowing his head slightly.

Aldridge grinned at Ahmed, giving him a cursory salute before leading Cross back to the door of the lab. As they went, he loudly said "By the way, Q holds the pull-ups record in the gym. Six years running. One of the few things he doesn't cheat at, unlike our Mario Kart tournament."

They both heard the other man's voice booming out behind them in amusement. "What possible advantage could I have?"

Aldridge allowed Cross to exit the room first and then he stepped out after her, turning to look back towards his friend as he rested his thumb on the panel to close the door. He tilted his head in the vague direction of Ahmed's wheelchair.

"Joystick proficiency," he said.

The other man's laughter followed them down the corridor.

Cross looked up when a muted chime came from over their heads, and she saw speakers set into the ceiling at regular intervals. A moment later, she heard a female voice she didn't recognise.

"Group One to conference, on the double. Group One to conference."

"Nearly there," Aldridge said, confirming that the announcement was meant for them. Cross felt a twinge of unease as she wondered who else she might find when they reached their destination, but she also finally felt a sense of momentum and encouragement.

The recording they'd found gave a very strong indication that Mark was indeed gone, and in truth she'd already accepted the fact of it during the past several months. The time would come for grief, but for now her focus was to bring those responsible to justice, and it seemed like the strange group of people she'd become involved with might just be able to help her do that.

"You said that you initially came to see me as a courtesy," she said. "What did you mean by that?"

Aldridge looked around at her briefly, seemingly untroubled by the question, and they both came to a halt. "I was wondering when you'd ask about that. Just as I said, really; your dossier arrived on my desk almost by accident. Missing relatives aren't exactly our bread and butter around here, as you can imagine."

Cross was silent for several moments as she considered his answer, and then she met his eyes again. "Then I'm especially grateful that you decided to investigate regardless. Thank you."

She reached out and placed her hand on his forearm for just a moment, and saw the brief flash of surprise in his eyes. He cleared his throat.

"Uh, of course," he said. "You're most welcome. Shall we go in?"

Her brow creased for an instant before she realised that they'd stopped beside an open doorway which led into a brightly-lit room dominated by a large wooden table surrounded by chairs. There was also a compact podium with a lectern, and a display screen mounted on the wall.

Within, she saw Greenwood standing with a man and woman she didn't recognise, and Ramos was sitting at the table alongside another man. Greenwood was looking in their direction. They went in.

"Dr. Cross," Greenwood said, and Cross smiled at the other woman.

"Captain."

"Please take a seat wherever you'd like," Greenwood continued. "I understand that you'll have questions, but please keep them for the end of the briefing, if possible."

Cross nodded, then she approached the large table, choosing the nearest vacant chair. As she sat down, she noticed an unfamiliar insignia mounted on the wall, or perhaps a sculpture of some kind. It was made of a silver-coloured metal, was circular in general outline, and looked to be almost two metres in diameter. It was fashioned in the shape of a ring, containing the silhouette of a bird in flight. Around it lay the twelve stars of the European Union flag. She considered asking Aldridge about it, but Greenwood spoke before she had the chance.

"Let's begin," Greenwood said, taking a seat at the head of the table, and both Aldridge and the man who had been talking with Greenwood also sat down. The other woman went to the lectern.

"You all know Olsen from Tech," Greenwood said, indicating the young woman standing at the lectern behind her. Greenwood briefly met Cross's eyes, in acknowledgement that Cross of course didn't know any of the staff here, but her tone indicated that time was of the essence. Cross assumed that any necessary introductions would come later. Greenwood swivelled her chair around to face the podium. "Please go ahead, Inge."

The room lights smoothly dimmed, and the large display screen on the wall behind the podium brightened, showing the video footage recovered from the hidden camera they'd found on the bridge of the *Hjørdis*. The sound was muted, and the video was playing at one-quarter speed.

"Thank you, Captain," the young woman said. "We've analysed the recording and the hardware, and the data storage card was partially corrupt — that's the reason for the damaged footage."

"Caused by?"

The question came from the bald, dark-skinned man sitting towards the rear of the room, two seats along from Ramos. Cross glanced at him, then returned her attention to Olsen. There was something unusual about how the young woman looked in a fixed direction, never lowering her eyes to the control panel set into the lectern's surface. She also wore a small earpiece in her right ear.

"There's no indication of tampering or damage. Most likely, the card was just beyond its useful life. The technology allows a finite amount of data to be written before sections of the storage become unusable."

"And the footage we did manage to recover?" Aldridge asked, and Olsen's head turned slightly in his direction, but her eyes never moved.

"It's genuine," she said. "According to every analysis, there was no manipulation — digital or optical. What you saw is what happened."

"Thank you, Inge," Greenwood said quietly. "That'll be all."

Olsen nodded, tapped a control on the lectern to dim

the main screen and increase the room's lighting, then she reached behind the lectern and retrieved an object that Cross hadn't noticed before: a long white stick, with a small plastic ball at the end.

She's blind, Cross realised. *The earpiece is for audio descriptions of the computer interface she was using.* Assistive technologies for people with visual impairments had become much more widespread with the advent of mobile phones and tablet devices, and Cross had witnessed such systems in use before. Even so, she found it remarkable that it was only upon seeing the woman's cane that her lack of sight had become apparent.

Olsen left the room, and Greenwood turned around again in her chair to face the table. Five pairs of eyes looked back at her. She focused on Cross.

"Considering that you've already seen the recording, Doctor, and also due to your personal connection, I'm going to reveal a number of things to you," she said. "You're an intelligent woman, and I assume you understand implicitly that everything said here, as well as this morning's events in Bergen, the existence of this facility, and the identities of anyone you've encountered here, are all matters of the utmost secrecy."

She paused for emphasis. "Any disclosure would result in severe penalties including immediate imprisonment, fully sanctioned by the European Union as well as your own Swiss government. I do hope that's clear."

Cross's expression, to her credit, remained unperturbed. "Perfectly," she said, and Greenwood nodded.

"You heard the results of the analysis; what we saw in the recording actually took place. The phenomenon was within the visual spectrum, and doesn't represent anything that our people can readily identify. We're concerned."

"The director thinks it's a weapon, chief?"

It was the other man that Cross hadn't met yet who spoke. He was enormous, with a chest like the trunk of a tree and arms to match. He had cropped, sand-coloured hair, and his posture was absolutely relaxed. Cross couldn't quite place his accent, but she knew it was one of the more colourful and pleasant-sounding ones from the United Kingdom.

"She's not sure what to think, Larry," Greenwood replied, "but she's worried, and so am I." She turned her attention to Aldridge. "I assume you'd have spoken up by now, but just in case..." she tailed off, and Aldridge leaned forward, shaking his head.

"Nope," he said. "It's not familiar to me, either, and I spent most of the last hour trying to find something similar, without any luck. The mechanics of it are wrong, no matter how I try to categorise it."

"Meaning what?" Ramos asked, and now Aldridge leaned back in his chair, putting his hands behind his head. He shrugged.

"Meaning that it's not radiation, because that doesn't occur in the visible spectrum under those conditions. But it's not a gel or a foam either, because it moves contrary to the ocean current and wind direction, and its speed of movement contradicts the viscosity or structural integrity it would need in order to show those characteristics. It's also not a liquid, because it travelled in a vertically-oriented plane, moving across and above the ocean's surface, and spreading outwards through the air. But then it's equally not a gas, or a combustion phenomenon, again due to the environmental conditions and wind direction, to say nothing of the nature of the luminescence."

He took a deep breath, and let it out as a frustrated sigh. "I have no bloody idea what it was, but I think that it's responsible for four deaths, and it's definitely not a naturally-occurring event."

"The director agrees," Greenwood said. "Identifying the source and nature of the... disturbance in that recording is now our priority, effective immediately. This is an active mission."

The large man cracked his knuckles, and Cross flinched at the sudden sound. He smiled at her apologetically across the table.

"We've seen the trawler," Aldridge said, his gaze focused on Greenwood, "and we've seen what was left behind of the people on board — so you know there's only one other place to look for answers."

Greenwood nodded. "We deploy tomorrow at first light. Wear layers, and your thermals. It'll be cold."

"Are you...?" Cross began, drawing the attention of the others. "You're going to *Sverdfisk Gamma*? But it's private property, and the company will never allow it.

Besides, it's unmanned!"

"A skeleton crew will be in place within six hours," Greenwood said. "They'll receive us in the morning. And you're right that CHX INFERIS isn't happy about our visit. They claim that the rig was completely idle and deserted on the day in question, and for a long time before, so there's nothing to see. We're going anyway."

"How can you do that?" Cross asked, looking not just at Greenwood but around the table too.

"Our resources are substantial," Greenwood replied. "Perhaps now would be the time for some introductions, since you'll be remaining in our care until we've determined that you're not in direct danger."

Cross opened her mouth to object, but she seemed to realise either the futility of any argument, or the wisdom of laying low until the situation was clearer. She took a breath, and then clasped her hands on the wooden surface in front of her.

"You've already met Dr. Neil Aldridge, Corporal Alicia Ramos, and myself," Greenwood said. "This," she said, motioning to the large man who sat with his arms folded as if they were discussing nothing more consequential than the weather, "is Sergeant Dowling."

"A pleasure," Dowling said, with a smile that seemed entirely genuine. Cross nodded at him, recalling that Greenwood had called him Larry a few minutes earlier.

"Last but not least, Lieutenant Goossens," Greenwood continued, tilting her head in the direction of the bald man at the back. "But we call him Goose."

"Doctor," he said.

Cross was silent for a moment as she looked around the table once more, then she fixed her gaze on Greenwood again. "And collectively, you're Group One, according to the announcement I heard in the corridor. But what exactly does that mean? This isn't the headquarters of any shipping-related agency, or anything remotely related to one."

"Oh, I like this bit," Aldridge said gleefully. "It seems like just a few months ago that I was hearing the speech myself. And honestly, I think the Captain likes doing it."

"It *was* a few months ago," Greenwood replied. "It just feels like years." She made the remark without breaking eye contact with Cross, and immediately continued without waiting for Aldridge to make another quip.

"This installation facilitates the mission of the five people in this room, Dr. Cross. We're a covert investigation, surveillance, infiltration and combat force operating under the direct authority of the European Security Council. Our discretionary remit spans the whole of the EU — and beyond, if necessary."

Cross looked around the table once more, and each pair of eyes told the same story. She knew that Greenwood was telling her the truth.

"You're part of the European Defence Agency," she said.

"We're notionally accountable to the Agency, yes, but officially speaking, we don't exist. Nor does this base.

We're the sharp end of the stick."

"And why does the EU need all of this?" Cross asked. Her question sounded defiant, but her voice had lost much of its confidence.

"Because of what you saw on the recording, and plenty more besides. We live in a world with a growing number of unknown, unquantifiable, novel, and profound threats to the security of nations and populations alike. The people you see here make sure everyone else can sleep a little more soundly — mostly by never having to know what we do."

Even a day earlier, Cross would have scoffed at the justification, but things had changed. Something much larger than she'd anticipated was going on, and it was certainly out of the ordinary. Her attention was drawn by a shift in Greenwood's posture as the woman sat back in her chair.

"To answer your earlier question, we're in the headquarters of the European Special Tactical Force, Group One — and you're looking at it. Beyond these walls, you'll never meet anyone who will know or acknowledge that name."

"Because it's such a bloody awful one, and a mouthful," Aldridge interjected with a frown, causing Greenwood's eyes to narrow. "They should permanently replace it with the codename, if you ask me."

Cross's curiosity was once again piqued. "Codename?" she asked. Aldridge returned his hands to the table surface and opened his mouth to respond, clearly eager to do so, but Greenwood beat him to it.

"*KESTREL.*"

Cross's eyes flicked up to the oversized metal insignia on the wall. A bird in flight, the universal symbol of freedom — within a shield, and spanning the whole of the European Union.

"Now tell me you didn't enjoy that," Aldridge said as he pointed at Greenwood, who simply shrugged.

"Maybe a little," she replied.

Chapter 10

"We may have a problem."

The face of Leif Magnusson filled the video screen on the stone wall. He was the CEO of CHX INFERIS, the company which owned the *Sverdfisk Gamma* platform and many others besides, and he was a powerful man. Today, though, his expression was one of discomfort, and even concern.

Miwa didn't react, because he had been expecting such a call for the past several hours. His instinctive sense that something was wrong hadn't left him, and when Tien informed him that Magnusson was requesting an urgent video conference, he knew that he'd been right. He simply waited for the other man to continue, and after a moment, Magnusson spoke again.

"I've received diplomatic notice that an EU delegation will visit the platform for a mandatory inspection. Crew are being diverted to await their arrival. I had no choice."

Miwa simply nodded. "When?"

"Tomorrow morning," he said, and now Miwa's expression did flicker for a moment. *A demanded visit, virtually immediately, with no regard to inconvenience or cost* — it was highly unusual. Surely Cross herself would not be taken out to the rig, but presumably the other three people from the warehouse in Bergen would make an appearance once again.

"How many?"

"I was not told," Magnusson replied, a note of defiance in his voice. *"A single helicopter."*

Miwa nodded again. "Yours?"

Magnusson frowned briefly, not understanding the question, and then he shook his head. *"Their own transport. They will refuel on the platform, of course."*

"Of course," Miwa replied, lowering his gaze to the floor, deep in thought. "And you are not aware of this delegation's precise identity, I take it?"

"The instruction came from the Directorate-General of the European Commission," Magnusson said, but they both knew it wasn't really an answer to Miwa's question.

"Naturally," Miwa replied.

The European Commission of the EU had ten political priorities, and energy security, affordability, and sustainability was understandably high amongst them. Its directorate on energy, or *DG ENER*, had wide-ranging responsibilities regarding power generation, fuel import and export, decarbonisation, migration to renewables, and much more. The directorate's attitude was cautious and defensive, and with good reason. It was at least a plausible source for this surprise inspection — but just barely.

The actual forces at work remain in shadow, Miwa thought. *So be it.*

He raised his eyes to the screen once more, and scrutinised Magnusson. The older man was broad-shouldered, but not especially tall. Age had softened him somewhat — Miwa knew he was in his late sixties — but his jaw was still strong, and his features hinted at origins beyond Norway and Scandinavia. Magnusson's hair was silver-white and always immaculately combed, and he wore what Miwa had long ago come to think of as his uniform: an impeccably tailored suit in the darkest shade of charcoal, bordering upon black. His tie matched his eyes, in ice-chip blue, and his face bore the creases of a lifetime of both laughter and worry.

"I lodged the strongest possible protest, of course," Magnusson continued. His voice betrayed only frustration, not fear, though Miwa knew that the man carried the burden of an enormous emotional conflict. It was how he was kept under control, after all.

"But they insisted, nonetheless," Miwa said, and Magnusson's expression tightened.

"I hope you tidied up after yourself," the older man said, in a warning tone. *"If they find—"*

"There is nothing to be found on *Sverdfisk Gamma*," Miwa said softly, his eyes once again snapping up to meet Magnusson's. "It is exactly as it appears."

The other man's eyes narrowed. *"The platform is hardly the issue anymore. If they were to—"*

"Then they would be no further forward," Miwa interrupted again. "Intrigued, yes; but no more illuminated than today."

"The inspection itself shows that someone knows more than you expected," Magnusson replied. There was an open challenge on his face, and he leaned forward slightly, suddenly becoming the renowned businessman and industrialist that the world knew him as. *"There is a great deal to lose. Perhaps more for you than anyone else."*

There was a long moment of silence, as Miwa looked impassively at the older man's image. His own countenance was absolutely calm, and his brow uncreased. He knew that Magnusson would speak again, and he knew it would be only a matter of a few more seconds. Sure enough, he watched the tell-tale slight shift in the other man's position.

"I'm going out there myself, to make my protest in person, in the strongest possible terms. And our corporate counsel."

"That may be futile, Mr. Magnusson," Miwa replied. "And the ocean is a dangerous place. Your time would be better spent using whatever resources you have to settle this matter with the European government."

A hint of dark amusement crossed the other man's face. *"Dangerous? As I've told you before, you would be very unhappy if I met with an unfortunate end. I've made sure of it. And I've endured almost all the lies I can bear."*

Miwa nodded once more, the gesture somehow both

an acknowledgement and a gesture of reconciliation. "This is only a minor annoyance. They will find nothing, and your part in this is already over."

"My hands are red, but not as red as yours," Magnusson replied coldly, refusing to be pacified. *"Four people died on that damned ship. You had no right. There was no need!"*

"On that, we disagree," Miwa said, clasping his hands in front of him, "though I wonder if you realise that I regret the loss of life as much as you do. But it was part of the work."

"The work," Magnusson spat, his words heavy with disdain. *"I hired you for a single task, and it seems you have yet to complete it. Perhaps that ought to be your focus, before you bring disaster down upon us both."*

The older man's eyes blazed for a moment, and then the picture went blank as the connection was terminated remotely.

Miwa turned away from the screen and walked calmly over to his desk. *You hired me to clean it up, Magnusson,* he thought, pressing the single button set into a recess in the metal surface, *and that's exactly what I'll do.*

PART 2

Chapter 11

The rising sun was still low in the sky in Ålesund, but the heliport was already bustling with activity.

It was easy to spot the private air transport company's crown jewel: an Airbus H155 in silver-white, with a royal blue flash running across the tail. It was being fuelled via a dedicated line running from the edge of the pad it stood upon, and various ground staff busied themselves with myriad tasks.

No-one gave a second glance to the familiar AeroServ catering van as it was waved through the security checkpoint, and then drove along a connecting road leading past three other helipads and towards the fourth and most prominent one, looking dramatically out over the harbour. The man driving the vehicle stifled a yawn with one hand and simultaneously flexed his fingers, giving a casual wave to the guard, who returned the gesture disinterestedly and then resumed reading the newspaper in front of him. The identification badge clipped to the driver's uniform read *Tveit*, and it sat slightly crookedly.

Venter straightened his borrowed badge — not that its true owner would ever be reunited with it — before returning his hand to the wheel.

"That was easy," Reddy said from the passenger seat, his fingers drumming a staccato pattern on the door sill.

"It's early," Venter replied. "And the catering company changes staff constantly. Low pay."

Reddy smiled distractedly, his gaze already on the sleek aircraft up ahead. "They'll be changing staff again when these two don't show up for work tomorrow."

Venter didn't respond to his companion's remark, instead focusing his attention on parking the van in a bay below the oceanside heliport. He wasn't as enamoured with the more violent aspect of their work as Reddy was, but he accepted the necessity of it. Their employer was perhaps the most pragmatic man that Venter had ever met, which was a double-edged sword: he would tolerate no delays, and certainly not failure.

They misled us, Venter thought. He and Reddy had both been certain that they'd been unobserved at the warehouse in Bergen, but he was troubled by the contradiction between what they'd overheard and the sudden news yesterday afternoon of a surprise inspection at the drilling platform, to take place only a handful of hours from now. There were only two possibilities: either the people from Brussels had lied to Cross, or they'd known

— or at least suspected — that their conversation would be overheard. Either way, the situation had deteriorated more rapidly than anyone had expected, including Venter's employer.

"Let's get this done," he said, and Reddy nodded, his hand already on the door release. "No mistakes."

The other man paused to look over at him. He knew what Venter meant, and for once he didn't tell him to relax. Reddy knew just as well as anyone that a great deal hung in the balance. He also knew that their own disappearance would be arranged without the slightest hesitation if they became a liability.

"What do you suppose this thing costs?" Reddy asked, tilting his head in the direction of the gleaming helicopter on the raised pad ahead of and above them.

Venter shrugged. "The way they fit them out for executive transport, probably at least eight million Euros."

"*Fok*," Reddy spat, then his grin returned. "Then I'm really going to enjoy breaking it."

They got out of the van and went around to the rear doors, efficiently unloading a series of small cardboard boxes. They contained assorted airline-sized refreshments, utensils, napkins, and miscellaneous related items. Everything was designed to be placed into specific compartments in the helicopter's passenger cabin, in trays which mostly slid out at floor level, concealed behind padded leather panels. They had both familiarised themselves with the layout less than an hour before, courtesy of the van's two original occupants, who had been unfailingly helpful.

There was also an insulated pack with pre-crushed ice, stored in compartments separated by gel packs which kept the temperature down; Reddy slung this pack over his right shoulder via the attached strap, hefted all but three of the boxes into his arms, and went up the stairway to the helipad. A white-shirted employee of the aircraft rental company stood nearby, frowning at a clipboard, and he glanced up when he heard Reddy's boots clattering up the metal stairs. Reddy gave him a broad grin and a nod, but the other man just waved him towards the aircraft with only a cursory glance at his ID badge.

Venter followed, holding the remaining three boxes, with a PDA device on top. It displayed a full checklist of the cargo, and would accept a scribbled signature as acknowledgement of delivery via the stylus attached to a loop of flexible plastic. The checklist, however, was not exhaustive — there was one additional item packed in amongst the soft drinks consignment in the second-largest of the boxes that Reddy toted.

To an observer, it was simply another can of low-calorie cola, sitting amongst several others identical to it. Had the observer picked it up, however, they would have noticed that it was not only heavier than a normal drinks can — though not by much — but that its weight was markedly concentrated in the bottom.

The two men completed their task without a word,

packing the soft drinks in their normal position in the central aft lower storage drawer, which ran back into the body of the helicopter towards the rear of the aircraft. When closed, it was tucked beneath the luggage compartment, which was itself below the fuel tank.

Venter obtained a signature from the harried-looking employee who was by this point on his mobile phone, yelling something in Norwegian that Venter couldn't understand and didn't care to. He gave the man a nod, and then he and Reddy left with the now-empty cardboard boxes and cooler unit, dumped them into the rear of the van, and drove off into morning traffic under the rapidly dispersing clouds.

The morning was almost gone, and they had all been awake since long before dawn. The steady thud of the helicopter's blades might have lulled most travellers to sleep, but the spectacle beyond the aircraft's small windows was too compelling. Greenwood had been looking out at it for most of the trip so far.

The Norwegian Sea stretched to the horizon, dark blue and glittering in the midday sun. They seemed to hang in the sky, with only the occasional distant sea vessel to mark their progress. There was a striking sense of emptiness and isolation, and Greenwood could understand how the first sailors feared falling off the edge of the world. It was only from up above that the vastness and danger of the ocean was truly evident, vividly demonstrating how fragile humanity was, especially when the environment became inhospitable.

The cabin was spacious and comfortable, trimmed entirely in beige leather. The elite craft had been outfitted in VIP configuration, with club seats, power outlets, in-flight entertainment, air conditioning, and additional sound insulation. Greenwood had some idea of just how much money an aircraft like this cost to buy, and she doubted that a last-minute private rental of it — with a highly experienced pilot and full insurance — was cheap either. She again wondered what kind of strings Wuyts had pulled to arrange this kind of transport at the last minute, but she knew that she'd have to live with the mystery. She'd even been in this specific type of craft before, but that was prior to the maker's acquisition by Airbus. She was unsure of the current model number, but she recalled that it used to be the EC155 — and the manufacturer's previous name, appropriately, was Eurocopter.

Goose was sitting up front with the pilot, and the remaining four team members sat in the passenger area behind, leaving two vacant seats and plenty of space. They had taken off from Ålesund more than two hours earlier, and the view only became more and more foreboding as the journey continued.

Wuyts had made arrangements for the drilling platform to be temporarily and urgently remanned, diverting staff from both the mainland and a rig some eighty miles away with virtually no advance warning. Greenwood was still unsure exactly how the director had done that, either, but they'd received word as soon as they reached Oslo earlier that morning that their onward transportation would be standing by. Wuyts had also emphasised, in a rare overt show of diplomacy, the importance of treading carefully with the platform workers they would encounter. This entire operation was highly irregular, would doubtless be a source of rumour and gossip for years to come within the Norwegian energy community, and was undertaken despite the strongest possible protest from the rig's owning company.

Their pilot was pleasant enough, if tight-lipped, and he had no reason to be otherwise; a last-minute private charter for offshore flight and return would earn him a substantial extra chunk of income. Everyone else they'd see when they arrived was likely to be significantly less pleased to see them.

We have the authority, and the mandate, Greenwood thought. She didn't expect to find much evidence all the way out here in the middle of the ocean, but it was a place to start, and she wasn't going to let some surly and inquisitive engineers stand in her way.

She had her mission to carry out, and she had her team beside her. Dowling was snoring lightly in the seat to her right, and across from him Ramos was engrossed in her ebook reader device, which she guarded fiercely, refusing to be drawn on what sort of literature she enjoyed. Several weeks earlier, Goose had sworn he'd glimpsed the word "dragon" over her shoulder, but when asked, Ramos had remained as inscrutable and unflappable as always. She had reminded the Dutchman that the device was locked with a passcode, and that he really didn't want to get on her bad side.

Sitting directly opposite Greenwood, Aldridge had his arms folded, his head back against the well-padded seat, and his eyes were closed. At the heliport in Ålesund, the pilot had asked if they were all up to date with the mandatory training on what to do in the event of an unplanned water landing, and Greenwood had confirmed that they were, giving Aldridge a pointed look which he correctly interpreted as an order to remain quiet. In fact, while the rest of her team had not only received the military equivalent of that training but also all been involved in such landings previously, they hadn't yet had the chance to brief Aldridge — much less put him through the required drills and explanations. When the pilot wandered off to perform his final exterior preflight checks, Dowling quietly gave Aldridge the short version.

In most ways, it's just like a plane: there are life rafts deployed from the doors. Get onto one, and don't inflate your life jacket until you're outside. If things are more tricky and a craft goes under, they tend to roll, mate — and then water will start to come in. There's a few minutes of air in the canister on your jacket, and you need to stay inside until the rotors have stopped. Your instinct will be to remove your seatbelt, but keep it fastened; it's what gives you enough leverage to kick out the windows with your feet. Then unfasten the belt, swim out, and inflate your jacket. When you get to the surface, look for floatation devices first; if there's none, find someone else and link arms. Try to form a ring of people. If you're alone, cross your arms and legs and put your hands in your armpits to conserve heat. There's a locator beacon in your suit, and it triggers automatically in the water.

One corner of Greenwood's mouth curled into a grin as she recalled Aldridge asking how long they could survive in the water before fatal hypothermia set in. Dowling explained that, given the padded survival suits they were all wearing over their field uniforms and two additional thermal layers, they would probably be alright for up to a couple of hours, but beyond that the outlook was poor. Aldridge had frowned, and rechecked the securing straps of his lifejacket, but he'd also been first onto the helicopter, and now he'd apparently dozed off. He made quite the picture, sitting there in the bright yellow and black suit — sealed at the neck and wrists, with dressing instructions and warnings printed upside-down on the left thigh — and peacefully asleep.

The man continued to surprise and frustrate her in equal measure, but his expertise was her most valuable asset on this expedition, along with the case of equipment in the helicopter's small cargo hold. It was imperative that they find some clue about what Mark Cross and his crew encountered out here. Technically, the four people from the trawler were still classified as missing, but everyone seemed to have accepted the truth — even

Dr. Cross herself.

Whatever the light was, it killed them, she thought. *Wiped them out, leaving virtually nothing behind.*

She tried to imagine what must have been going through their minds; the confusion and the fear. When you got right down to it, everything was personal. No matter what was at stake, ultimately the cost would always be paid at the human level. It was something that Greenwood reminded herself of regularly, to ensure she never lost her perspective on the work they were asked to do. Decisions were often made at a political level, and it was all too easy to forget that the European Union — and the world — was composed of people, not nations.

When Greenwood's team got to the bottom of what had happened out here, whether they found a weapon, a new technology, some undiscovered kind of atmospheric phenomenon, or something else, the end result was still that Cross had lost her brother. The three other people on the *Hjørdis* presumably had families too, who would also never see them again. And if KESTREL failed to find and contain the source of the strange golden-orange energy field, the price would again doubtless be paid by ordinary people.

That's why failure is never an option, she thought.

"Ladies and gentlemen, we will arrive in approximately ten minutes," the pilot said over the intercom, and Greenwood saw Aldridge's eyes open and immediately focus on her.

"Can't believe I slept through the food service," he said, stretching his neck as he yawned.

Greenwood reached down to an underseat storage compartment, opened the front panel, and retrieved a single-serving packet of roasted peanuts, which she tossed at him. The foil container struck him in the chest and then fell into his waiting hand, and he grinned.

"Much obliged," he said. "Is this part of a Captain's standard duties, or am I special?"

"Oh you're special, alright," she replied, folding her arms and returning her attention to the seascape beyond the window and far below. She heard Aldridge tear open the packet and begin to eat the peanuts, and after half a minute or so, he leaned towards her.

"Everything alright?" he asked, his voice quieter than before, and when she looked at him she saw an expression she'd noticed several times in the past few weeks under various circumstances. It had elements of concern, understanding, and something else that she refused to put a label on.

"Did you know that more than ninety percent of helicopter emergency landings happen within sight of the planned destination?" she asked, her eyebrow raised in challenge. She made the statistic up on the spot, and she knew that he could tell.

Aldridge gave a small laugh and shook his head. "You learn something every day," he replied. "And fine, I won't ask. But did *you* know that if you ever want to talk…"

"Aldridge," she warned, her eyes flicking to the right towards Ramos and Dowling, both of whom seemed carefully oblivious to their conversation.

Aldridge raised his hand in capitulation, but he also gave her a meaningful look, before bringing his hand back down and picking out another peanut from the packet. A few moments of silence passed before he spoke again.

"So, are we talking *special* in terms of aptitude, or value to the team, or my long, long list of academic credentials, or—"

Greenwood rolled her eyes, then again looked over towards Ramos and Dowling. The other woman was reading intently, just as before. Dowling seemed to still be asleep, too, but Greenwood was almost certain he had the barest hint of a smirk on his face.

Less than ten seconds later, everything went to hell.

Chapter 12

The sound seemed to come from immediately behind Aldridge, and was so sudden and loud that he momentarily froze. It was a flat, metallic bang that reverberated through the entire airframe, and he felt it every bit as much as he heard it.

The helicopter lurched sickeningly in the air as if it had been struck, and Aldridge had a vivid mental image of some gigantic monster of the deep, reaching up with an impossibly long tentacle to swat at the bothersome artificial insect that flew far above the waves. An alarm blared from speakers in the ceiling, and the voice of the pilot filled the cabin.

"BRACE!"

Aldridge's chest tightened, and a moment later he could actually feel the blood leave his face as the craft tipped forwards, now dropping through the air as the ocean began to rise up like a vast wall. The main rotor was still spinning, but at nothing like its previous speed, and he was peripherally aware of a growing oscillation in the rhythm of the aerofoils. He locked eyes with Greenwood, who seemed to be falling away from him, backwards towards the sea, and then there was a shriek of metal as the craft gave a violent shudder. The port-side door adjacent to Aldridge's seat suddenly blew open and was immediately ripped off, flipping back on itself and smashing the window just inches from his head. Bitingly cold wind howled into the cabin, the sound of it almost drowning out the overhead alarm. He felt the sting of a shard of glass cutting the side of his face, and he instinctively shut his eyes.

"Were we hit?" Greenwood's shouted question came from somewhere in front of him, and Dowling's response was immediate.

"Explosion, chief. Something on board."

There were five rapid but smaller bangs, and Aldridge wondered for a moment if they were under fire, ducking his head further into his chest automatically before he opened his eyes again. The source of the new sounds was glaringly obvious: as well as the broken window and the gaping hole that had recently been the doorway, there was also a widening, jagged seam where several of the rivets in the superstructure had come apart under mechanical stress.

The helicopter went into a slow and nauseating spin, losing almost all of its remaining forward motion. Aldridge could see that Greenwood and Dowling were being held fast by their harnesses but still being pulled towards the rear of the craft, whereas he and Ramos were pinned back against their own seats. Suddenly, there was a cataclysmic rending sound, and the entire craft tumbled forward on itself. A moment too late, Aldridge realised that his own seat assembly was twisting to the right, on the verge of becoming unanchored from the floor.

His gaze went to Greenwood again, and his hammering pulse seemed to halt when he saw that her eyes were wide and her knuckles were white against her harness. He could suddenly smell smoke, and he thought he could feel heat coming from somewhere behind.

There was a final jolt from beneath him, and a brief sense of floating. The ocean vista loomed up to fill every window. He thought he heard his own name being called.

Then the remaining section of cabin wall beside him stripped away like tinfoil, and his seat plunged out into the freezing air.

Greenwood knew that the impact was only seconds away.

They were dropping like a stone. The helicopter had come out of its slow spin, but there was no control whatsoever. They were going to hit the ocean, and the front of the craft would take the worst of it. The one ray of hope was that the rotors had remained intact and continued turning after the explosion — whatever had caused it — and so they hadn't lost all lift immediately. The spin had also hopefully given the pilot a few crucial moments to signal for help. But the brief reprieve was now over.

She yanked downwards on the adjustment cords of her harness, pushing her boots against the vibrating floor of the cabin to press herself back against the seat, keeping her head in contact with the soft leather rest.

We're on fire, but the fuel tank hasn't breached yet, she thought. *If it goes up, we're all dead no matter what.*

Fighting her own instincts, she released her grip on the harness and instead clamped her hands around the front of the seat cushion. As the helicopter took another nauseating tumble in the air, she forced herself to close her mouth, bring her teeth together, and relax her jaw. She glanced at each of the other two members of her team who were still within the passenger cabin and in view. Dowling and Ramos were both braced, and she took a tiny amount of comfort from the other woman's expression: it was defiant to the last. She hoped desperately that Goose, sitting in the front beside the pilot, had found a way to bail out already — there was virtually no chance of surviving a crash like this from the cockpit.

Aldridge, she thought, her eyes automatically flicking to the jagged hole in the side wall, and then the exposed boltwork on the floor across from her where the seat assembly had been mounted. He'd gone out still strapped to his seat, which was light but reasonably tough, and padded. Still, it didn't give much cause for optimism.

The ocean filled her peripheral vision, and when she focused her gaze beyond the torn fuselage, she could see individual waves. There was no more time. As the helicopter made one last sideways twist in the air, she closed her eyes.

Aldridge felt the spray of the sea a moment before impact, and then all the breath was knocked from his lungs as the seat he was still strapped to hit the ocean surface with an enormous slapping sound, and a bone-jarring impact.

It had only been seconds since he fell from the helicopter, and already he was in the freezing water, tipping backwards as it lapped over his forehead and then his eyebrows. The weight of the seat assembly was pulling him underwater. He took one final gulp of air, and then his head and upper body were entirely submerged.

He barely had time to feel the panic rising in his chest before he heard a much larger impact somewhere nearby, but it was impossible to get any sense of direction. He was sinking, head first, and the icy Norwegian Sea felt like needles against the exposed skin of his face.

With an effort of will, he forced himself not to exhale, and instead blindly felt for the release mechanism on his harness. He grasped hold of it after several seconds that felt like an eternity, and he knew that if the harness failed to disengage, he was going to drown. He pulled the release handle, and immediately felt the vice-like grip around his body loosen. He wrenched the straps from his shoulders and opened his eyes, seeing daylight less than fifteen feet above him.

He had no other sense of which direction was up, and a detached part of his mind noted that if the crash had happened at night, he would be in even more trouble.

With his lungs burning, he kicked his legs and propelled himself upwards, and at long last his face broke clear of the surface, only to be drenched again immediately by a rolling wave. He gasped and took another lungful of air, and the pressure in his chest slackened.

Blinking seawater from his eyes, he looked around, treading water as best he could, and he was just about to inflate his lifejacket when he caught sight of an image that made his blood run even colder: one of the landing skids of the helicopter, and part of its undercarriage, just visible above the dark water a considerable distance away. There was ugly black smoke curling up from the rear, and the flicker of flames.

No, he thought, breaking into a front crawl that made his shoulders begin to burn within seconds, partially fighting a cross-current as he hauled himself through the waves, gaining on the crashed aircraft far too slowly. When he still wasn't even halfway there, he was startled by the sudden appearance of a bright orange object bursting from below the water, already immediately beginning to unfold and expand.

Life raft. Deployed automatically in water.

It didn't mean they'd survived, but nor did it mean they hadn't. He began to swim again, faster than before, his pulse thudding in his neck.

"Aldridge!"

The shout came as a surprise, and Aldridge spun around in the water. It was Goose's voice, and the man himself was swimming rapidly towards him, only about fifty feet away.

"The others?" Aldridge called to him as neared, but Goose just grimly nodded in the direction of the downed helicopter as he reached Aldridge, and they both continued towards it side by side.

"I jumped," Goose said between ragged breaths as they swam. "Saw you come out. I can't believe you survived."

"What about the pilot?"

The Dutchman shook his head. "Wouldn't come, but he ordered me to bail. He made the right call; it's his duty. He fought it down."

"Do you... do you think—" Aldridge started, but Goose cut him off.

"We're not writing anybody off yet."

Aldridge nodded, quickening his stroke once more.

They had almost reached the drifting life raft when three heads popped up from below the waves in rapid succession, and Aldridge felt a surge of relief. Greenwood, Dowling, and Ramos all slowly turned to look in their direction, and then Aldridge could see the relief on Greenwood's face too. As the two men swam the last few dozen feet, Ramos had already taken hold of one of the thin ropes strung along the base of the raft.

Aldridge and Goose reached the rest of the group, and Dowling nodded at each of them in a wordless gesture of welcome.

"Everybody in," Greenwood ordered between breaths, tilting her head towards the raft, and Aldridge frowned.

"The pilot?"

Dowling shook his head. "I already checked. He didn't survive the crash. Brave bastard still had his hand on the cyclic."

Aldridge finally started to shiver from the cold. "Damn it."

One by one, they swam over to the raft and hauled themselves inside with difficulty, alternating between the flexible ladders on opposing sides, fighting not just the waves but also the numbness of their hands from the shockingly cold water. It looked like a large, neon orange camping tent, floating on a black rubber base. The two doorways were on the longer sides, and were already drawn up and lashed at the top with attached reflective straps. The thick base afforded a measure of insulation from the chill of the ocean, but not much. Once all five of them were aboard, Dowling untied and zipped one of the doorways closed to shield them from the worst of the breeze.

"What's our communications status?" Greenwood asked, swiping her wet hair off her forehead.

"The pilot sent a mayday on the way down, and I heard the beginning of a reply," Goose said. "The copter had a GPS transponder. All of our suit beacons will have started broadcasting as soon as they were submerged."

"And we weren't far out from the platform," Ramos said. "In fact, I can see it." She pointed out the single open canvas doorway into the distance, and sure enough, they could see the silhouette of an oil rig in the middle distance, like the skeleton of a gigantic mechanical animal. As the raft rose and fell rhythmically with the waves, the platform seemed to swing vertically, disappearing first above the viewport and then below it.

"They'll send a launch," Dowling said. "Doubt they'll have a medic or a recovery crew if they were mustered to the rig just last night, but they'll definitely have some kind of boat." Goose nodded his agreement.

"So we wait," Greenwood said. "Any injuries?" She glanced at the cut on the side of Aldridge's face, but he waved her off.

They all shook their heads, and then Ramos patted an unzipped pocket in the body of her survival suit and pursed her lips in frustration.

"Your reading gadget?" Dowling ventured, and Ramos's brief glare was confirmation enough.

"The books will be backed up in the cloud, at least," Aldridge said apologetically, and Ramos shrugged.

"It's not the books," she replied. "It was a gift."

"Whoever just tried to kill us is going to buy you a

new one," Greenwood replied. "Goose, GPS will still work on our phones for location; mark the point the helicopter went down."

The Dutchman nodded, unzipping a watertight compartment in his survival suit and taking out his mobile. There was silence for a minute while he completed the task, and then Aldridge very pointedly stretched his back.

"They should pad those seats more," he said, wincing as he glanced over at Dowling. "And I'm questioning your advice about keeping my seatbelt on, Sergeant."

Dowling grinned at him, but it was subdued. They'd been damned lucky, and they all knew it. The situation had taken a very serious turn, and the priority was now to get out of the water, report their status to Wuyts, and find out who was behind the attempt on their lives. Aldridge loosened the neck of his suit, and it was obvious that his hands were shaking. Greenwood opened her mouth to say something, but he just gave her a warning look.

"Hell of a coincidence that we'd have engine failure on the way to the same rig where Cross's brother and his crew disappeared," he said, talking mostly to himself, and Greenwood nodded grimly at him before turning her head towards Dowling.

"So what do you think? Low yield explosive, but where? They'd have found anything external in pre-flight checks. It wasn't surface-to-air, and it was from the rear. Luggage?"

"There was nothing else in the hold when I loaded the field case," Aldridge said. "I looked. And I sealed it again myself."

Dowling shrugged. "Lots of little cubbyholes in the cabin, though. Pretty much everything opens. Easiest way is always consumables; comfort and catering. Could have been anything. Pack of napkins. Bottle of wine. Lots of options. Nearly half the panels go back into the rear airframe."

"So why aren't we all dead?"

Ramos's voice startled Aldridge, but the Spanish woman was still looking out of the open doorway towards the distant oil platform. She didn't turn her head as she spoke. "Rear airframe means the fuel tank, which is mid-height below the rotor assembly on an H155. Luggage hold is too conspicuous, so you use cabin storage. Direct the blast upwards, it ruptures the tank, then… *una bola de fuego*."

That's what we almost were, Aldridge thought. *A ball of fire.*

His stomach turned over at the thought of it. He pictured the structure of the helicopter, with the rearwards cabin storage compartments running back into the area immediately below the central axis of the craft. Stacked on top, the passenger luggage hold, then the fuel tanks, then the rotor assembly mounted vertically in the middle, extending upwards to join the aerofoils.

"My case of lab gear," he said.

"It's at the bottom of the ocean, mate," Dowling said.

"No use worrying about that now."

Aldridge blinked, and then quickly shook his head. "No, I mean the field case itself. It's not just some camera bag; it's military issue. Biometric locks, bulletproof, and *blast proof*."

Dowling understood immediately. "It'd have been a shaped charge, to make sure it travelled upwards to the fuel tank. But the case acted like shielding."

"Which is why we're alive," Aldridge said. "And I distinctly recall being mocked recently for bragging about my equipment."

"I'm sure the Director will give your box of toys a medal for bravery, if anyone ever sees it again," Greenwood said, but she wasn't smiling. It had been pure chance that they'd survived, and it was now very clear that someone didn't want anybody to investigate the platform. Aldridge knew that this turn of events would only strengthen Greenwood's resolve, and he also knew they had their work cut out for them.

"If they do take us to the rig, be alert," Greenwood said. "This is an uncertain and potentially hostile situation, and we've already had one casualty."

She looked at each of them in turn, letting her eyes rest upon Aldridge last. "Nobody wanders off anywhere alone," she added, and he gave a small nod.

As if on cue, they all suddenly heard the sound of an approaching motor.

Chapter 13

There were two men at the helm of the lifeboat, and neither was smiling. One of them, a squat man with a thick and wiry black moustache, threw a line which Ramos caught easily, drawing the raft in beside the hull.

"Injured?" the man asked, and Ramos shook her head, which caused the man to raise his eyebrows. He was about to say something when she pointed towards the waves below. "The pilot is dead."

The man paled, and to Ramos's considerable surprise, he crossed himself. After a moment's hesitation, he gestured to all of them to come aboard, not noticing that both Dowling and Goose sat directly opposite each other just inside the open doorway, ready to engage and overpower the two men at a moment's notice.

The boat's pilot joined his companion at the starboard side to help them all across, and then the raft was released for later recovery. The boat was small, but still more spacious than the raft, and they set off again immediately. Dowling sat immediately behind the helm compartment, facing inwards, and Ramos made a point of sitting opposite the other man from the platform, who earnestly enquired again about any injuries, finding it difficult to believe there were no broken bones, or worse.

There was no other conversation, and they made good time. *Sverdfisk Gamma* rose steadily higher above the churning waves, and it soon filled the sky above as they drew alongside. There were two more men waiting, both of them looking markedly uncomfortable.

Greenwood eyed them carefully, surprised that there weren't more people there — but they'd mustered only a bare minimum crew to accept their unwelcome visitors, presumably keeping the niceties to a minimum. That suited her just fine, because diplomacy was now the last thing on her mind.

She came forward as soon as they'd docked at the small floating jetty along the base of one gigantic leg of the platform, and she smoothly stepped up to stand toe-to-toe with the first of the two waiting men. He took a half-step back, with uncertainty written all over his face.

"I need to speak to the acting manager of this facility immediately," she said.

The man exchanged a nervous look with the boat's pilot, who remained silent.

"Of course," he said. "This way."

Dowling drew himself up to his full height, towering

over both the pilot and his colleague on the boat. "After you, gents," he said, pointing to the jetty. The pilot took a long look at the huge Welshman, and then at both Ramos and Goose, whose faces wore similar no-nonsense expressions, and then he simply nodded.

The party of nine ascended a zig-zagging set of metal stairways running up the interior of the platform leg, led by the two men who had been on the jetty when they arrived, then Greenwood and Aldridge, followed by the boat's pilot and his companion and finally Dowling, Ramos, and Goose. There were occasional short ladders, and it took several minutes before they finally reached the main deck. The breeze over the ocean was cold despite the sun having broken through the clouds.

Aldridge briefly paused at the top of the final stairway and looked out over the railing. The scene might as well have been from an alien world, or at the last frontier of human habitation on Earth. Every walkway and gantry was a steel grating, perforated with holes, making the ocean visible from virtually anywhere you stood. Adventurous gulls and other seabirds wheeled through the air above, and would occasionally perch on some remote point of the platform's superstructure. They never received anything in return for their curiosity, and soon moved on to another spot, or flew away. The waves were in ceaseless motion far below, and Aldridge found the effect of it all disorienting, despite the relative stability of the decking beneath his feet.

What did your brother find here, Dr. Cross? he

wondered, peering straight down towards the nearest two legs of the enormous rig, and remembering how one such pylon had been visible in the bizarre recording from the trawler. He could see a bright orange lifeboat covered with a red tarpaulin, attached to a pair of small cranes at the lower edge of the platform, and space for a second absent lifeboat next to it.

"Be careful," a voice said from behind him. "Long way down."

Aldridge turned, and saw one of the other platform workers standing close by, waiting for him to continue moving. This man had blonde hair instead of their guide's closely-cropped black.

"I'm a strong swimmer," Aldridge replied, not sensing any threat from the other man, but he laid his free hand loosely on the railing anyway. The worker just grunted. He seemed uneasy, and kept glancing away across the vast deck, as if he wanted to ensure they weren't being observed. He didn't say anything more, and after another moment Aldridge set off in the direction that Greenwood had gone.

They were led via a series of walkways towards a large building, several storeys high and lit from within. The exterior doors were heavy, and it looked like it took considerable effort for the still-unnamed man to wrench one of them open. The transition from the constant noise outside to the silence within was unnerving. To Aldridge's bemusement, one of the first objects they passed was a slot machine, plugged in but not switched on.

They ascended two further flights of stairs within the structure, some only dimly lit. Their increasingly nervous guide apologetically said that the platform was on minimal power, and there had been difficulties restoring various functions during the long night before. They stopped at a locker room, where they divested themselves of the survival suits, revealing their duty uniforms and field jackets. When the man saw their attire, he visibly tensed. Dowling and Goose hung the suits on a drying rack along the far wall of the locker room, and the Dutchman flicked a switch to turn on a heated air vent below, before turning to their escort again. The man nodded in acknowledgement, and led them onwards.

At last, they came to an ordinary door which opened to reveal a rudimentary meeting room, with four rectangular institutional tables all pushed together to form a larger surface. There were cheap plastic chairs stacked in the far corner of the room, and the tables themselves were battered and scarred. There were posters on three of the walls, including one that looked like it had been printed at least two decades earlier, giving instructions on resuscitation. The fourth wall had three large windows, looking dramatically out over the main deck of the platform. Clearly visible across from the building was the helipad they were meant to arrive on.

"Please wait here," their guide said. "Not long."

When Greenwood nodded, the man left the room

along with two of his three colleagues. The blonde-haired one remained behind, lifting chairs from the stack and placing them around the table. Once there were six, he crossed towards the door, and then stopped and looked back.

Aldridge made a subtle gesture with his hand at his side, knowing that the man wouldn't see it but his own people would. It meant *I'll handle this*.

"So what is it that you do here, exactly?" he asked, feigning polite interest.

The man looked at him for a long moment, and then shook his head. "Not here," he said. "Only today. Landing Officer." He jerked his head in the direction of the windows and the vivid green and yellow helipad that lay beyond. Aldridge could see it from where he stood. It had the phrase *SV. GAMMA* printed on it in large white letters. He nodded.

"And your friend that we're waiting for?"

The man's eyebrows knitted together for a moment, as if he didn't quite understand the words, but then he grimaced. "Platform Manager," he replied. "Not my friend."

Aldridge nodded once again, as if to say *Fair enough*. The man still looked uneasy, and Aldridge had a sudden vivid memory of one of his training sessions on informal interrogation. *Ask questions indirectly. Imply that you already know the answers. Leave gaps, and the subject will fill them.*

"I assume you know why we're here," he said, his

tone serious now, and with a definite air of authority. The other man did a double take, and then sighed deeply. When he spoke, he seemed to be struggling to translate his thoughts into English.

"I worked here. For eight years. I transfer, one year before now."

"So you know what was going on here," Aldridge said carefully, remembering his training. *After a leading question, deflect with a trivial remark. Let the subject bring the conversation back on topic.* "You must have wanted to transfer for a while."

The man shrugged, looking uneasily around for a few moments. "I see things. But always secret. They told the crew nothing."

Aldridge gave the man a rueful smile, as if he knew very well how it was. "They never do. But now *we're* here, and you know what we're going to do."

The room was silent. The man nodded, and Aldridge could see he bore the weight of a long-held burden; one he was relieved to finally share. He turned, and Aldridge thought for a moment that he was going to leave, but instead he walked over to the nearest window. After several seconds, he made a small gesture towards a building that stood at the far side of the rig's main level. It looked much like the accommodation and administration block they were in, but all of its windows bore steel shutters.

"You will find what they did there," the man said. "The others."

Aldridge told himself that it was just the unplanned swim he'd taken earlier, and the churning waves he knew were far below, but the temperature in the room seemed to drop. The man faced him once again, and scratched at the day's worth of stubble on his chin.

"I did have a friend. Dead now. They say accident; electricity. But it happened there. *He* did it. You will make him pay." He jerked his head in a gesture that clearly encompassed all of them, not just Aldridge.

Aldridge took a measured breath, and looked the man in the eye. "That's what we're going to do," he said. "All we need is a name."

The man turned to the window again and looked out to sea, and his gaze became unfocused for long moments. Just when Aldridge thought he'd miscalculated, the man gave a half-nod, and then grimaced again. He stepped away from the window and moved back to the door, resting his hand on the handle. When he spoke, his voice was quiet, as if he feared being overheard.

"*Miwa*," he said, and then he pulled the door open, and left.

The atmosphere in the meeting room crackled with tension. Greenwood took a step towards Aldridge and placed her hand on his shoulder for a moment, in wordless appreciation.

"Everyone take a seat," she said. "When the manager arrives, follow my lead."

There was barely time for the five of them to take

their chosen places around the table, Dowling and Ramos performing a quick visual survey of the room first, before the handle turned again.

A man entered, wearing a flannel shirt and dark jeans, with a high-visibility vest over the top. He carried a clipboard, and he wore a hard hat which he immediately removed and hung on a coat hook on the section of wall just inside the door. He made no move to take a seat at the table, instead standing and just looking at them. It was difficult for Greenwood to read his expression.

She stood up, and approached him. "I understand you're the platform manager."

"You are correct," the man said, his Norwegian accent lending a melodic quality to his vowels, but his expression was closed-off and he radiated animosity.

"I was hoping you'd say that," she replied. "I trust you've received instructions to accommodate us during our visit. We'll need full access to all areas of this platform."

The man folded his arms, and turned his attention to Dowling, who sat nearby. "This is no place for visitors. Dangerous. And private property."

Dowling kept eye contact, but he didn't respond, or even move. Eventually, the other man looked away. Greenwood stretched her neck as if to relieve a stiff muscle.

"I didn't catch your name, Mister...?"

"I did not give you it," the man replied gruffly.

Greenwood smiled.

"Then I'll call you John, I think," she said, and a look of surprise crossed the other man's face. "The thing is, John, we're not visitors, and I'm not asking for your cooperation — I'm telling you that you're going to give me full access to this installation, and you're also going to do anything else I ask of you. Because I've had a very difficult morning, as I think you've heard by now."

She took a step forward, and the man instinctively leaned back slightly. When she continued, her tone was softer; almost conspiratorial.

"And if you obstruct us in any way, I'll arrest you and tie you to one of these chairs myself, and when I'm ready to leave, I'll take you with me. You don't want that to happen, John; you can trust me on that."

The man's face flushed in anger and he looked quickly at Dowling and then at each of the others around the table, but he saw the same thing on every face: a hint of warning, and absolute loyalty to their leader.

So much for treading carefully, Greenwood thought, but she had neither the patience nor the time for this sort of needless obstacle.

The man licked his lips, at war with himself over whether to respond, but a moment later the choice was made for him. The door of the room flew open, and an imposing older man entered, flanked by two other figures. His suit was so dark as to be almost black, his ice-chip blue tie matched his eyes, and Greenwood recognised him immediately. The face of the platform manager went chalk white, but he might as well not have been in the room anymore, for all the attention anyone paid him now.

"This day just keeps getting more interesting," Greenwood said, sensing Dowling and Aldridge both appearing at her side. "It's a pleasure to finally meet you, Mr. Magnusson."

The mention of the older man's name seemed to shake the platform manager from his daze, and he was about to speak when Magnusson pointed directly at him without looking, and jerked his thumb over his shoulder towards the still-open door.

The platform manager flushed again, but he didn't say a word before he quickly gathered his hard hat and immediately left the room, quietly closing the door after himself. The two groups faced each other.

"Do any of you require medical attention?" Magnusson asked, ignoring Greenwood's previous remark but directing his question solely at her.

She was surprised, but didn't let it show on her face. She'd been expecting something more adversarial, given their intrusion on the rig and the inconvenience and cost to the company.

"No," she said. "But the helicopter pilot didn't survive. His body will have to be recovered."

Magnusson's head dropped and he closed his eyes as he exhaled heavily. Greenwood watched as one of the two people accompanying him, a woman in an expensive trouser-suit, stepped forward, but Magnusson waved her off without glancing in her direction. After a moment, he looked at Greenwood again.

"Perhaps we should sit down," he said, "and you can explain why you're here." He seemed absolutely stricken, and Greenwood wondered at the reason for it.

Guilt? Is he responsible for the bomb on the helicopter?

"Alright," she replied, and one by one they all took a seat around the makeshift table again. There were two more people than chairs, and Aldridge offered his to the woman accompanying Magnusson, but both she and the other man declined, preferring to stand at the edge of the room. Aldridge could see that Ramos was keeping a close eye on both of them, but the two people looked as unsettled as Magnusson himself.

Seeing their scrutiny, Magnusson gave a brief nod in the direction of the other two. "My personal assistant, and our corporate counsel," he said. "I fear their journey today has been wasted."

"And when exactly did the three of you arrive?" Greenwood asked. "There was no air traffic while we were in the lifeboat, so you must have been here for a while."

"Several hours," Magnusson replied, glancing at a wristwatch that Aldridge knew cost in excess of a quarter of a million Euros. "I came here to protest your visit personally."

"Someone already did that, in much stronger terms," Greenwood said cooly. "And I'd choose your return transport carefully. People have a habit of dying in the vicinity of this platform."

Magnusson paled slightly, but he simply nodded. "May I ask to whom I am speaking? You're not civilian investigators." His eyes flicked down to the insignia on the shoulder of Greenwood's field jacket, displaying the EU stars against a blue ground.

"I'm Captain Jessica Greenwood of the European Defence Agency. This is my squad, who someone tried to kill this morning. And I'm used to people being more surprised when I tell them who I am."

Magnusson indeed seemed to have been expecting them. "You were recently in Bergen," he said. The man at the door who had been introduced as CHX INFERIS's corporate counsel cleared his throat as if to speak, but Magnusson abruptly slammed his fist against the table top and then turned to pin him with a glare.

"Save your breath, Ivar," he said. "A man lies dead out there."

The lawyer simply nodded, his face betraying nothing, and after a moment Magnusson returned his attention to those sitting around the table.

"There is nothing for you to find here, but you may of course search wherever you wish," he said quietly, his face now grey. He looked years older than he had a minute earlier. Greenwood could see that he was conducting some sort of internal struggle with himself, but still trying to protect his company and its interests.

"There's always something to find, Mr. Magnusson,"

Aldridge said. "Like the objects from inside the bodies of Mark Cross and his comrades, found rattling around on the deck of the *Hjørdis*. All that was left of them."

"And then there's the matter of how they died," Greenwood added, before reaching inside her field jacket and producing a compact tablet device with a 7-inch display. She placed it on the table in front of her, then met Magnusson's eyes. "You'll want to clear the room now."

Magnusson held her gaze for at least ten seconds, and she knew he was deciding whether she was bluffing. At last, he sat back. "Leave us," he said, not breaking eye contact with Greenwood. The man and woman standing inside the doorway reluctantly left the room, and Magnusson clasped his hands on the tabletop.

Greenwood unlocked the tablet, tapped the screen a few times, and then turned it towards him. They could all hear that it was the video clip they'd managed to extract from the hidden recorder on the trawler, and as Magnusson watched it, he raised his clasped hands to cover his mouth. When the clip finished, he closed his eyes.

There wasn't a sound in the room, and Greenwood returned the tablet device to her jacket's inside pocket, content to give the man a few moments to come to terms with what he'd seen. The silence stretched beyond a minute before Magnusson opened his eyes again. He looked haunted, but there was also a quiet resolve about him.

"Now," Greenwood said, her voice even and controlled, "it's time you told me everything."

Magnusson blinked twice, and then he huffed with resignation. It was a tired sound, without humour. His lower eyelids had gained shadows beneath them, and the lines in his face looked more pronounced than they had been when he entered the room.

"I believe you are right," he said, and then he nodded as if confirming something to himself. "This day has finally come. So be it." He abruptly stood up, fastening the top button of his suit jacket, and squared his shoulders. "If you and your colleagues will follow me, Captain."

Magnusson dismissed his company's lawyer and his personal assistant, who were both waiting just along the corridor from the meeting room. The lawyer protested, but the old man was firm.

"The time for lies has passed," he said. Both of his employees left, and Magnusson led Greenwood and her team back down to the main deck level, and along a different set of corridors than those they'd previously entered through. He reached an exterior door and opened it easily, his strength belying his age. He walked with purpose, but he said nothing as they crossed the suddenly-loud open space, bird cries competing with the breeze from all around.

It was immediately obvious that they were being led to the same building the blonde-haired landing officer had alluded to earlier. Each of Greenwood's team was in a state of quiet alert, checking for any signs of danger within the structure they were fast approaching. Aldridge adjusted his field jacket, feeling the comforting weight of the pistol holstered within. Magnusson happened to glance backwards at the same moment, and without missing a beat he shook his head.

"You will find no need for weapons here," he said. "You have my word."

"And what *will* we find?" Greenwood asked immediately, unsettled at how perceptive Magnusson was. *I suppose it comes with being the CEO of a major energy company,* she thought.

Magnusson was facing forward again, still striding along, so he had to raise his voice against the wind in order to be heard. "Only the answers you seek."

"In the meeting room, you told us there was nothing to discover on this platform," Greenwood replied. Magnusson smiled ruefully.

"Indeed, there is not," he replied. "And I remind you that I am responsible for the welfare of a company that is the livelihood of thousands of people, so discretion is needed. But I can tell you a story, I think. One that is long overdue."

They reached the shuttered building, and he entered a passcode on a discreet keypad device hidden behind a waterproof panel. A green light flashed briefly, and then Magnusson opened the door. They all entered. Greenwood half expected them to be confronted by a squad of armed guards, but they just found themselves in a corridor much like the others they'd already seen, only with more exposed pipework. There was also electrical cabling strung from the ceiling, clearly not part of the original installation. Lights flicked on overhead automatically.

"This way," Magnusson said.

The air in the building was stale, and Greenwood felt on edge. There were no posters in this part of the platform, though there were indications that there once had been. Everything was stripped back, with cables going nowhere, mounting points for absent equipment, and patches of brighter paint along the corridor walls where furniture or machinery had once stood. There were many shadows cast by the harsh overhead lighting, and too many corners and alcoves.

"Do you know anything of the history of my people, Captain?" Magnusson asked suddenly, pulling Greenwood's attention away from her surroundings.

"I… well, every English schoolchild learns about the Vikings," she said, and Magnusson made a sound that might have been a laugh.

"And no doubt your teachers talk of them as raiders and looters, from Lindisfarne onwards," he replied.

"Not at all," she said, "but we all have violence in our history. Neither of our countries of birth can claim otherwise."

"Only in our history?" Magnusson asked, coming to a stop at an area where the corridor widened out into a broad hallway.

"The world has a great many problems, Mr. Magnusson, as you're certainly aware. But I like to think that some of us have advanced since the time of raiding parties attacking villages. More to the point, why are we talking about this?"

Magnusson's expression hardened, and he reflexively glanced over his shoulder, across the hallway towards a large set of double doors which were barely visible at the far side, their overhead lights not yet triggered by anyone's presence. Then he nodded to himself again.

"Advanced, yes. But some advancements only bring more horror."

Greenwood frowned. *What are you hinting at?* She was about to ask him directly when he started speaking again, the words flowing out of him quickly, as if a dam had burst.

"Tell me, Captain: as an Englishwoman, do you know of the term *tube alloys*?"

Greenwood sighed inwardly. "I'm a soldier," she replied. "Of course I do."

"And you," Magnusson said, turning to look at Aldridge. "Do you know what I would mean if I were to speak of *development of substitute materials*? And if I were to mention *Manhattan District*?"

Aldridge nodded. "Naturally. I have a Ph.D in particle physics. And the Scottish educational system is pretty good, even compared to Scandinavia."

Magnusson's eyebrows lifted, and his head moved in

what might have been a small nod of respect. He looked from Greenwood to Aldridge again, and Greenwood folded her arms.

"Very well, Magnusson," she said. "We'll play along, but I hope you'll come to your point soon. *Tube Alloys* was the codename for the secret British and Canadian nuclear weapons development project during World War II. It preceded and was later subsumed by the US project entitled *Development of Substitute Materials*, of which the portion conducted by the Army Corps of Engineers was called *Manhattan District*."

Magnusson shifted his gaze from Greenwood to Aldridge, who cleared his throat.

"But most people today would call it the Manhattan Project," he said.

Magnusson gave him a thoughtful look. "They would," he agreed.

"Are you implying that there's government involvement in all this?" Dowling asked, but Magnusson shook his head dismissively.

"Certainly not," he replied. "My point is that there are innovations not meant for the hands of mankind."

"Nuclear weapons put an end to a terrible war," Ramos said. Her tone was almost casual, and she constantly scanned their surroundings, not looking at Magnusson even when he replied.

"You are in favour of weapons of mass destruction?"

"I'm in favour of pragmatism," Ramos said.

"So the end justifies the means?"

"Life is rarely black and white."

"I know a man who believes it ought to be," Magnusson said, his eyes again becoming fixed on the shadowed doors that lay thirty or so feet away. "And perhaps we will all wish it were."

He set off again, directly across the wide hallway, lights flickering to life above him as he moved. They all followed, and it took only a few moments to reach the opposite side. Magnusson raised his hand towards the large sign on the wall to the right of the doors, but he pulled his arm away at the last moment, as if afraid to touch it. Greenwood frowned again, exchanging a look with Dowling.

The sign bore only two words: *WELL BAY*.

Magnusson spoke reverentially, like a man in church.

"There are dark places on this Earth, Captain. I expect you've seen some of them, and so have I." He let his hand fall back to his side.

"The sites not of atrocity, but of its origins. Where advancements are pursued and made, often in the name of *pragmatism*, but ending only in death."

The silence in the building was oppressive, and Aldridge felt a sudden deep sense of almost superstitious uneasiness that bordered on dread. Magnusson turned to look at them all.

"Beyond these doors, there is another such place."

Then he reached for the nearest handle, opened the door, and stepped through.

Chapter 14

Aldridge wasn't sure what he'd been expecting, but it wasn't this.

The well bay was wide and long, built on two storeys connected with metal interior stairways just like the ones they'd climbed to reach the main deck of the platform. Almost everything was painted yellow, and the walls held a profusion of pipes and ductwork in alternating yellow, blue, and silver. There were a handful of control panels on the edges of the room, but overall the sense was of almost everything having been removed. Stripped fittings and glaring spaces; too much room, and nothing to occupy it. The place echoed with their footsteps.

The dominant feature was a large area of floor with what looked like the capped ends of twenty large pipes which disappeared beneath, in a regular grid of four by five. There were markings painted around their edges, and a short structure had been built just above them, forming an elevated rectangular meshwork of narrow metal beams.

"That looks like where the cooling rods would be inserted into a fission reactor," Aldridge said. "But I'm guessing it's the wellheads from the drilling package that used to be here."

Magnusson nodded.

Aldridge walked over to one of the wellheads, and toed it with his boot. It sounded hollow, as expected. "What's under here now?"

"Only a long drop into the ocean," the older man replied. "Then darkness."

"And the subsea reserves of oil and gas," Greenwood said, trying to prompt him into continuing. "They've made you a wealthy and powerful man."

"These waters have given us much, it's true," Magnusson replied, with a sentimentality that Greenwood found puzzling, but then an expression of horror passed across his face. He took a monogrammed handkerchief from his jacket pocket and dabbed his hairline, returned the handkerchief to his pocket, and walked over so that he stood in front of the raised platform, which barely reached knee-level. Magnusson half-turned so that he was facing Greenwood and the four other members of her team.

"But the ocean also sent us something that should never have existed. It was almost four years ago, and it has invaded my dreams every night since."

He sat down heavily on the platform, tugging the knot of his tie loose and opening the top button of his shirt before resting his hands on his thighs. When he spoke, his eyes were unfocused, and directed at a point somewhere on the floor between himself and the others.

"*Klokken.*"

Goose's brow creased, and he exchanged a quick look with Greenwood, who gave the barest shrug. "The... clock?" he asked, and Magnusson looked at him in momentary confusion.

"Your accent; you are *Nederlandsk*? Dutch?"

Goose nodded. Magnusson gave a tired-looking smile which faded almost immediately.

"I suppose it would be, in your language," he said. "But no. *På Norsk* — in Norwegian — it means... *the Bell.*"

It was an innocuous term, but the context chilled Greenwood nonetheless. There was palpable fear in the old man's eyes, and he'd said it was a thing that should never have existed.

What has a bell got to do with all this?

"Four years ago," Aldridge said, taking a step forward. "That's when the accident happened at this platform. What *really* caused the oil spill here, Mr. Magnusson?"

The older man's face paled again, then he shook his head as if to clear it. Greenwood's team had slowly dispersed to ensure that the dimly-lit corners of the large room were indeed empty, but their attention was nonetheless focused on the conversation.

"A collision," Magnusson said at last. "The conductors were ruptured — all of them. Sheared in two. This facility was put into emergency shutdown, and a containment operation was launched immediately."

"A collision with what?" Dowling asked, and Magnusson looked over at him. There was a strange expression on his face; almost a kind of awe, or perverse amusement.

"An *Unterseeboot*," he said.

"By which you mean a submarine," Greenwood replied, puzzled at the sudden use of German instead of English or the man's native Norwegian.

"By which I mean an *Unterseeboot*, Captain," he said. He waited for his meaning to dawn on her. After a moment, it did.

"A German *military* submarine? They're not exactly known for crashing into things. I'd have heard about it."

Magnusson smiled. "Unlikely, since this vessel was launched by the *Kriegsmarine*."

The silence in the well bay was absolute. Aldridge slowly turned his head to exchange an incredulous look with Dowling, and could clearly read the disbelief on the Welshman's face.

"The *Kriegsmarine*," Greenwood repeated slowly, as if making sure she'd heard the word correctly. "The naval force of Nazi Germany, which hasn't existed since 1945, launched a submarine."

"In the closing years of the Second World War," Magnusson replied. "Lost to history, until three years and nine months ago, when for some reason — perhaps geological instability in the drilling region — its resting place was disturbed, bringing it into catastrophic contact with *Sverdfisk Gamma's* extraction apparatus."

Greenwood opened her mouth to say something and then closed it again, clearly at a loss for words. There were certainly several dozen U-boats still officially classified as missing; there were registries of such craft from wartime. But the vast majority would simply be undiscovered wreckage on the sea floor somewhere or other. The idea of a vessel from so long ago still being intact was very difficult to accept.

"What was its number?" Greenwood asked at last. She could at least check Magnusson's answer against known information from German naval history.

"U-7001K", Magnusson replied easily, and Greenwood immediately shook her head.

"The highest number was in the five-thousands for the *Kriegsmarine's* submarine fleet, and those ones were midget subs," Greenwood said. "I wrote a dissertation on the *Wehrmacht*."

"And yet, I have not lied to you, Captain," Magnusson said. "I have had cause to research the topic myself, as you can imagine, and this vessel seems to be unique. It was created for a single purpose: to smuggle its cargo from the ruins of the Third Reich, and take it beyond the reach of the Allied powers. The craft was designed for long-term submersion, and long-distance transport."

"A cargo submarine." Greenwood folded her arms. "And I suppose the ninety-year-old Nazis popped out after the collision to say hello, and sorry for the damage?"

Magnusson's expression darkened. "There was no more left of its crew than what Dr. Cross found on the trawler."

Seeing Greenwood's frustration, Aldridge raised his hand to forestall the retort he could sense was coming, addressing Magnusson again. "You're implying that the crew of the submarine suffered the same fate as Mark Cross and his colleagues, and that their cargo was responsible."

"That is the truth," Magnusson replied.

"And the cargo was some kind of… bell?" Ramos asked, her hands in her pockets and her face clearly showing skepticism. Magnusson sighed and shook his head.

"It is a machine," he said. "It resembles a bell in general outline only; the name is from the research documentation of its custodian on board the submarine — an *Obergruppenführer*."

Greenwood made a sound of surprise. "That's a pretty elite group of Nazis. During wartime, fewer than a hundred men were ever promoted to that rank."

Magnusson simply nodded, as if he were well aware of the fact. "But I cannot tell you which one. There were no identifying documents anywhere on board, for anyone."

Aldridge could see that the man was deadly serious. He felt profoundly uneasy, even though the story stretched credibility. But they had all seen the recording from the trawler.

"The light," he said, and Magnusson nodded once more.

"The Bell produces it," he replied. "It seems to be the device's sole function."

Goose's voice came from the far corner of the room. "And what does it actually do?"

Magnusson dropped his gaze to his own hands, which were still laid flat on his thighs. He swallowed thickly, and then took a ragged breath.

"That is a question I can answer with a direct quote from the materials written by the monsters who created it," he said. "*As best can be determined, the machine instantaneously disintegrates organic matter at the molecular level, creating a self-sustaining cascading effect in any suitable target which falls within range. Once initiated, unless shut down by its operator, the effect appears to spread indefinitely.*"

Greenwood didn't want to believe what she was being told — and on the face of it, the idea was ridiculous — but she felt the familiar creeping sense of dread and intuition that always arrived at some point during a mission. She stepped forward.

"You're telling me that Nazi Germany, more than

seventy years ago, created the holy grail of warfare: an infrastructure-safe, non-explosive, zero-fallout anti-personnel weapon. Then they put it on a submarine and secretly set off for god-knows-where, without ever using it in battle, but they ran into a snag en route and the whole thing has been lying at the bottom of the Norwegian Sea for twice as long as I've been alive."

"Again, that is the truth."

"What's the exact nature of the light field?" Aldridge asked, closing the distance between himself and Magnusson without even being aware of it. "Is it a radiation phenomenon? We didn't detect anything on the trawler. I can't even imagine what *physical mechanism* would cause molecular decoherence without—"

He was interrupted by Greenwood's hand on his upper arm, and he closed his mouth without continuing.

"Do you have proof of all this?" she asked, staring down Magnusson, and the older man sighed again.

"As you can see, neither the machine nor any of its documentation remains here," he said. "He took it all with him, just as I asked him to — and no, I do not know where it is now. He did not tell me everything — I didn't want him to. But if you will allow me to continue, I will share all that I know."

Miwa stood on the mountainside a few metres beyond a concealed cave mouth, looking down at the valley below.

An armed guard stood discreetly nearby, never looking directly at his employer, but he continually surveyed their immediate surroundings. The area of the mountain which held access points to the facility was entirely fenced off, and dotted with dire warning signs about unsafe conditions including rockslides. There was an electronic perimeter and extensive hidden surveillance, and any adventurous trespasser was soon met by armed men in Polish military uniforms, given a verbal dressing-down, and sent on their way with a stern rebuke and a warning to never return. The uniforms were genuine, but the men in question had no right to wear them.

The slopes were covered with spruce trees, and in the occasional clearing, the many multicoloured bands of the Precambrian gneiss rocks glittered in the sunlight.

Such beauty, Miwa thought. *But even this landscape is spoiled.*

There was the facility itself, concealed inside the jagged rock face rising up behind him. There was the fence, and the various supply lines for power, water, drainage, and so forth. There were the roads further down, and then a village, and not so far away, a city. And where there were settlements, there were human beings.

We have encroached everywhere. Even as far as the planet's poles.

It troubled him that he was so rarely able to enjoy the natural world anymore. Everything was tinged with sadness at the degree to which his own species had altered their environment, carelessly and destructively, and the consequences that were already all too visible. The future would be much worse. There were already more than 7.5 billion people on the Earth, and UN projections showed that the figure may grow by as much as a billion per decade through 2050. Mankind's demands and ceaseless consumption, coupled with a pathological inability to take a measured, long-term view instead of just living by convenience and exploitation, was sure to be its own downfall.

Too many, and too much, Miwa thought.

The sound of familiar footsteps roused him from his reverie, and a few seconds later he heard Tien clear his throat. Miwa turned to face him.

"The helicopter departed on schedule," Tien said, giving a slight bow. "There has been no further word, but we would not expect to know anything so soon. There were five passengers. Our colleagues obtained photographs from a distance."

"And the construction project?"

"On schedule, and virtually complete," Tien replied. "Another two weeks will be more than sufficient. It is most impressive."

Miwa nodded. "It has a long journey ahead. Along the way, it will bring great pain to the world."

Tien's face remained impassive. He knew that his master struggled with the ethics of their historic endeavour. A man burdened with the fate of so many lives could never truly rest.

"Its purpose is to herald rebirth," Tien said quietly. "And birth is always painful."

Miwa's lips moved, but it wasn't quite a smile. After a moment, he turned away to once again contemplate the natural beauty all around.

"Inform me when there is news from Norway," he said.

Tien gave an unseen bow, and left without another word.

Chapter 15

"You said that *he* took the device with him, and that you asked him to," Greenwood said. "I also know that this man was connected to at least one other death here, and I know that his name is Miwa. What I don't know is who he is, and how he's involved."

The shock on Magnusson's face was plain to see. "How do you know that name?"

"The worker who was supposedly electrocuted here had a friend. He was eager to see justice done."

Magnusson looked from Greenwood to Aldridge and back again, his mind putting the pieces together. "This friend is part of the temporary crew assigned here for your visit?"

"I want to make it very clear, Mr. Magnusson, that if anything should happen to *any* of the people now on this platform—"

"I am not a monster, Captain," Magnusson snapped,

and then his anger seemed to fade as quickly as it had risen up, being replaced immediately with a look of profound regret. "Though I may have helped unleash one upon the world."

"So you're not responsible for what happened to our transport?" Dowling asked from a short distance away, and Magnusson gave him a piercing look.

"I had nothing to do with it, I swear to you," he replied. "But Miwa… yes. I should have realised how he would handle this situation."

"I need you to start from the beginning," Greenwood said, and Magnusson nodded.

"Very well. The man we are talking about is Tsutomu Miwa. Does that name mean anything to any of you?"

Greenwood shook her head, though in truth the name did seem vaguely familiar. At her side, Aldridge shrugged.

"Doesn't ring a bell," he said. "No pun intended."

The remark seemed to go over Magnusson's head; either that, or he had judiciously ignored it.

"He is the founder and chief executive of MEC — Miwa Environmental Consulting Limited," the older man continued. "It's the leading services provider on all matters relating to energy and ecology, including sustainable sources. We have employed his company on a number of projects over the last seven years."

Goose frowned. "Sustainable energy consultancy, for an oil and gas company? I don't understand."

"CHX INFERIS is an *energy* company," Magnusson

corrected. "We look always for novel and responsible ways to satisfy our customers' needs."

"In other words, political pressure about pollution is starting to make you nervous." The comment had come from Ramos, and to his credit, Magnusson met her gaze without any apparent animosity, choosing to simply give a noncommittal shrug.

"In any case," he continued, "MEC already had a standing contract with us at the time of the spill caused by this platform's ruptured conductors. Decontamination is one of their primary specialities. Naturally, I asked Miwa to investigate immediately, under his existing contractual agreement. His access to expertise and equipment is unmatched in the industry."

Greenwood folded her arms. "So a World War II-era U-boat caused the spill. That's what Miwa found when his own people investigated. But not a word of the real cause ever leaked"— she glanced briefly at Aldridge, her look a clear warning that it wasn't the time for wit —" to the outside world."

"He is a businessman. Discretion is implicit," Magnusson replied. "Can you imagine how the public would have responded if they knew?"

Greenwood tilted her head in acknowledgement of the point. Oil being released into the ocean wasn't just an ecological disaster; it was also a public relations nightmare — and the spill had cost CHX INFERIS a great deal in both fines and stock value, at least temporarily. Adding a Nazi submarine into the mix would have ensured maximum exposure and outrage, even if it would probably deflect some of the blame due to its sheer unbelievability.

"This company has been my life's work, Captain," Magnusson said softly. "I will never allow it to become associated with the darkest period in modern European history."

"And Miwa's people found no-one on board the submarine," Aldridge said, to which Magnusson nodded.

"We attempted radio contact, and direct sound-conduction communication. There was no response. Given the obvious age of the vessel, we were not surprised. Miwa has subsea salvage and rescue personnel and craft, and they succeeded in docking over a hatch, equalising pressure, and opening it."

Dowling raised his eyebrows. "They can do that?"

Magnusson nodded once more. "They can. The equipment is exceptionally expensive, but it is available to us via MEC. We were not even charged. The situation caught Miwa's personal interest."

"I can certainly understand that," Aldridge said.

"The survey team initially thought they had found only discarded rank insignia and personal items, scattered throughout the vessel," Magnusson said, with a meaningful look at Aldridge.

"But it was actually the remains of the crew, strewn around by the collision," Aldridge finished on his behalf. "It must have been there for decades. So the device they were carrying was triggered somehow, while it was on board?"

"That was Miwa's eventual conclusion," Magnusson replied. "Once we saw what it could do."

"The supposedly electrocuted engineer," Greenwood said, and she felt a pang of sympathy at the sorrow which rose up on the older man's face.

"Yes," Magnusson replied. "One of my greatest regrets."

Haltingly, he told them how the survey team had found a lab on board the submarine, in a comparatively spacious rear section that had clearly been designed for this specific purpose. At its centre, the machine sat in a harness, attached to the U-boat's systems via an umbilical assembly that connected to the top of the device. There was extensive documentation in a row of filing cabinets, including a detailed hook-up and detachment procedure, and it was sheer luck that a member of the initial survey team was a native of Düsseldorf and thus could read the German manuals. Having satisfied themselves that the machine was not a bomb, and intrigued by references to its actual function, Miwa ordered its disconnection and removal from the submarine.

It was brought aboard *Sverdfisk Gamma*, and after a long period in temporary housing within a storage area while the platform's shutdown and decommissioning procedure slowly progressed, it was eventually moved to the cleared well bay. It was at this point that the first accident happened.

"Just a moment," Greenwood interrupted. "The documentation at least made it clear that this was a *weapon*, didn't it?"

"It was referred to always as an experiment," Magnusson replied. "but its builders had no idea what they would inadvertently discover."

"Then what were the goals of the experiment, as it was first conceived?" Aldridge asked, folding his arms. It wasn't unusual to find unexpected uses for an invention originally designed to do something else; it was particularly commonplace in chemistry and pharmacology, and history was replete with amusing anecdotes of accidental discoveries. "Everything we've seen so far implies that it's a field emitter of some kind. What did they originally hope it would do?"

Had he not seemed so profoundly saddened and exhausted, the expression on Magnusson's face might almost have been one of vague amusement.

"They had hoped to find a way to render their vehicles undetectable to radar, and eventually even to the naked eye."

Aldridge huffed in disdain. "A cloaking device, in the 1940s."

"A fanciful idea, I agree," the older man replied. "But it would have been a profound weapon. What they actually created was far worse."

Aldridge opened his mouth again, but Magnusson waved the expected question off.

"I do not know how it works. Miwa kept much of it

from me, and I had no desire to understand. I'm not certain that even *he* understands it fully. But he can control it, and much better than its builders ever could. They lacked our technology."

"He's computerised the control interface," Goose said, drawing a further nod from Magnusson.

"The engineer's death was truly an accident, and it happened early during Miwa's investigation. A foolish mistake."

"Maybe it was a mistake to bring the thing on board an oil platform," Dowling remarked, and Magnusson pinned him with another glare.

"You would rather it be left in proximity to a subsea oil field, in a potentially damaged submersible craft, for anyone to find?"

Dowling conceded the point with a lazy shrug.

"I agreed with bringing the device aboard," Magnusson continued. "My only desire, then and now, was to make it safe and then dispose of it. Miwa insisted that they must fully understand the device before deciding on its ultimate fate. It seemed reasonable. I often wonder just when he decided to mislead me."

There was silence for several moments while Magnusson was lost in thought. At length, he began speaking again.

"Initially, some of my own men were assigned to assist Miwa's people. It was a mistake, but it was necessary. They were sworn to secrecy. The engineer was called Falk, and he was passing in front of the Bell when it was inadvertently activated. The speed with which the field develops and propagates is as impressive as it is disturbing. Within moments, there was nothing left of him."

"You were there at the time?" Greenwood asked, but Magnusson shook his head.

"I tried very hard to be in this place as infrequently as possible, Captain, especially after the incident. I very nearly cancelled the entire endeavour then and there. I would have given the device to the Norwegian government. But Miwa convinced me it would be a foolish and dangerous act. On that, too, he was correct."

Greenwood could read his facial expression and body language with ease. "You feared that even your own country might use the device against someone."

"The Bell was *created* by a government that committed appalling crimes against humanity," Magnusson said. "And it has also already killed men and women in our own century; the crew of the trawler vessel, as well as the engineer I mentioned. My belief is simple: if a technology holds the potential for evil — as virtually all things do — then mankind cannot help but misuse it."

Aldridge lowered his eyes, considering the other man's words. Then he looked briefly at Greenwood before returning his gaze to Magnusson.

"You now believe that Miwa may do exactly that."

Magnusson nodded. "I do. It is the greatest fear of my life. And it is entirely upon my conscience, because it was I who gave him the means to carry out whatever plan he is now pursuing. I was too eager to believe him."

He told how he swore the few present members of his own crew to silence after the accident, paying them for their discretion as well as binding them to a nondisclosure agreement with the most dire penalties in the event of the information being released. The shame and frustration in his voice was evident. Miwa had insisted that the device be kept on the platform until it could be made truly safe for transport and disposal, and after the engineer's death, no-one argued with him. The slow and painstaking process of investigating its function and means of operation had been conveniently masked by the platform's multi-year shutdown process. Miwa had been in no rush to complete his work, and if anything, his zeal only increased as the weeks became months and the months became years.

"He saw some kind of potential in the machine," Ramos said. "Do you have any idea what he wants to do with it?"

"No," Magnusson replied, "but I fear the worst. Any government in the world would pay handsomely to acquire it for warfare, though they would claim to desire only knowledge, or to contain a threat. And if they could not buy it, they would take it nonetheless. Eventually, it would always be used."

"I tend to agree," Greenwood said, drawing a look of mild surprise from the older man. "But that brings us no closer to making sure it never happens. Did you close down this platform purely to provide an isolated environment for this… scientific investigation?"

Magnusson shook his head, just once, but forcefully. "Not at all. The field below had almost reached the end of its output, at least until newer technology becomes available. It was both practically and politically appropriate to decommission this facility. Our stakeholders would not accept a hastily-constructed excuse. The U-boat's collision was a curse, but it could not have struck a better location from the point of view of secrecy. It gave him years to study the machine. You may be surprised at how much is involved in ending a platform's active life."

"Warm shutdown, pipeline and topside cleaning, lighthouse mode, down-manning; I've read a bit about it recently," Aldridge interjected. "To say nothing of the planning phase beforehand, which is really the linchpin of the whole endeavour."

"Indeed," Magnusson replied, again with a flicker of respect visible for just a moment on his face.

"So it took a few years for this Tsutomu Miwa and his people to investigate the device's construction and operation, and during that time they added a computerised control system. To do what, precisely?"

"We always agreed that it was to make it harmless enough for transport on-shore, and its own decommissioning," Magnusson replied. "My instructions were that it never take another life."

"But Miwa lied to you," Greenwood said. It wasn't a

question.

"I would very much like to believe our goals were the same, at least initially. But he became seduced by something about the Bell. He saw the darkness in it, but also something else. He is a man who feels a great burden of duty to mankind, Captain. His work is sincere — otherwise, I would never have entrusted him with this task. But he also sees himself as possessed of a… how would you say, in English? A higher morality."

Greenwood nodded grimly, concealing the chill she suddenly felt. She had faced a great many dangers in her career, none of which the general public would ever know about. *The one thing they had in common was someone who thought they knew better than anyone else what was good for the world.*

"Something doesn't fit," she said, and Magnusson turned his palms towards her, inviting her to continue. "A strict code of ethics would preclude selling such an appalling weapon. Surely he'd want it to be destroyed just as much as you do."

"I would once have made the same judgement," Magnusson replied. "And yet, the incident with the *Hjørdis* shows otherwise. Miwa has clearly overcome the primary weakness of the device, and the reason it was never used in the closing years of the Second World War."

There was a pause, during which no-one in the room spoke, or even moved.

"He has done what the Nazis could not: learned to control the Bell's output with sufficient accuracy for targeting."

Venter put down his knife and fork and reached for his coffee, looking across at his colleague as he did so. Reddy was devouring a dripping hamburger with the zealousness that Venter had long ago become accustomed to; the other man's appetite was always at its most ravenous after killing someone.

"What?" Reddy asked, through a mouthful of ground beef, and Venter just shook his head.

His own meal had been much more Norwegian: a brunch dish with a hash of eggs, sausage, and potatoes, including a heavy dose of mustard. It was served in the metal pan it was cooked in, with strips of the ubiquitous dark rye bread alongside.

"Don't know how you can eat that crap," Reddy said, glancing distastefully at Venter's now-empty pan. Venter only shrugged, and was saved from replying by the vibration of his mobile phone — which he knew the Germans called a *Handy*, for some reason — in his pocket. He fished the device out and glanced around for a moment to ensure he was unobserved, then read the decrypted text message.

"Well?" Reddy asked, his mouth now empty, before reaching for the bottle of cola beside his plate.

"We're taking another trip," Venter replied, returning the phone to his pocket. He could read the other man's facial expression perfectly: *what a surprise.* "You'll be happy. Warmer weather."

"About bloody time," Reddy said. "Any shopping we need to pick up?"

The expression referred to acquiring specialist equipment, including weapons, for a mission. It always paid to be circumspect when discussing such matters, even privately — and certainly when sitting in a café.

"That depends," Venter said, motioning to a nearby waiter, who came over immediately. "*Regningen, takk,*" he said. *The bill, please.* He liked to learn useful phrases in the local language wherever he travelled. He considered it a perk of the job.

"Depends on fucking what?" Reddy asked, when the waiter had wandered away again. Venter grinned, enjoying his companion's irritation.

"Did you pack a bow tie?" he asked.

Magnusson waved away Greenwood's question about exactly who or what Miwa might target, and she didn't press the matter. Her intuition told her that the man was telling them the complete truth, and that he knew nothing more than he was letting on. She also sensed a great weariness and fear from him, and she understood it perfectly: it was the burden of responsibility, pre-emptive or otherwise.

"Then let me ask you two more things, Mr. Magnusson," she said. The man remained silent, which she took as an invitation to continue.

"When you first began to suspect something was wrong, why didn't you remove Miwa from the project?

You could have pursued the work yourself via other means, I'm sure."

"Perhaps," Magnusson replied, "but I realised too late that I had little choice in the matter. I knew that his team of engineers was our best hope of understanding the machine and containing its power. I also knew the consequences of failing to treat it with respect. I did voice concerns, but he was always quick to remind me of the dangers of such a thing falling into the wrong hands — he saw my own fears and used them to manipulate me. Finally, he threatened me with exposure. There was nothing I could do."

Greenwood could hear the rage that underlaid the man's voice. She could only imagine the burden he'd carried during the past several years, and how it could breed an impotent anger and hatred. For the moment, though, he mostly sounded defeated.

"Why not just dismantle it?" Goose asked, and Magnusson made a choked sound.

"It has been attempted," he replied. He took a breath.

"And?" Greenwood asked, but Magnusson shook his head.

"The documentation on the submarine warned against ever trying, but Miwa did. He had the sense to use a bomb-disposal robot, and some test subjects alongside."

Greenwood's expression darkened, and Magnusson raised his hand to deflect her protest. "Animals," he said. "Small primates. Reptiles. A dog. The robot removed the bolts without incident, but everything alive within the immediate area died when the casing cover was lifted away by five centimetres. They had a bad death."

"The Bell activated?" Aldridge asked, incredulously, but again Magnusson shook his head.

"No, not the energy field. A more conventional kind of radiation, I suppose; you would need to consult Miwa's findings. The creatures screamed, but only for moments. It looked like they had been burned."

"What the hell is inside the machine?" Greenwood asked, her posture aggressive now, but Magnusson only turned his hands over helplessly.

"I read a partial translation of some of the original notes. There is a liquid, like mercury, mounted inside a capsule in the upper central portion. It is essential to the device's function. There are coils of some kind, within cylinders; magnetic, thermal, I do not know. The external power source is electrical, of course. But none of it would work without the *xerum*, and once installed, it cannot be removed by any living being. For the same reason, the device cannot safely be destroyed in an explosion without risking contamination."

"Does this make any sense to you?" Greenwood asked, turning to Aldridge. He was rubbing his own jaw thoughtfully. He hadn't shaved that morning, probably in mild protest at the very early rise necessitated by the trip from Brussels to Ålesund, and the movement made a rasping sound that was amplified by the many metal surfaces in the room.

"Electromagnetic or thermal perturbation of materials can generate EM field effects, and even produce radiation, yes," he said, "but I've never seen anything like what we saw on the recording. The… reactant, or medium, or whatever it is, should also need to be replenished, but this one is still usable after seven decades, and the research documents said the effect would spread *indefinitely* while power was supplied. I don't know what to make of it, honestly. But I'll say this: I believe him, and it scares me."

"Then you are a wise man," Magnusson said. He looked at Greenwood again. "And your second question?"

"It sounds like you and Miwa aren't on the best of terms, despite being collaborators at the beginning of this enterprise," she said. "When did it all go wrong for you? It wasn't when your engineer died, at least."

"The trawler," Magnusson replied. "I had no idea — I only heard about it afterwards."

"It was another experiment," Aldridge said. "Like the animals you mentioned."

The older man nodded silently, his jaw working as if he was going to vomit. After a moment, though, he met Aldridge's gaze again and held it.

"I have thought about it many times. I believe that Miwa's connections in the environmentalist world must have allowed him to hear about the expedition in advance, so he was ready when they arrived here. He would have seen it as the perfect human test."

"And pretty easy to cover up, so far out at sea," Greenwood said. "People that nobody would miss for a while; activists and loners. The ocean is a dangerous place."

Magnusson looked away. "By the time I was informed, by Miwa himself, he had already departed from this platform. He took everything with him."

"Miwa told you because he knew that you'd be further implicated in the whole thing. There was no risk to him; it was just more leverage."

"That is correct, Captain," Magnusson said. "And it was I, in turn, who informed him of your unscheduled visit today — and you must believe me when I tell you I never thought he would attempt to murder an official delegation from the European Union. I can communicate with him in emergencies, but I have no idea of his location at the moment."

"All right," Greenwood replied. "We're going to look around a little, even though I'm fairly sure we won't find anything. Then we'll want to report in; do you have a communications link we can use?"

"You may use my own satellite phone," Magnusson replied. "My assistant will bring it to you when you're ready. And we can travel back together when my helicopter arrives. I have already instructed my people to perform an exhaustive check of the craft before it departs the mainland, but Miwa knows that I have my own contingency measures in place if anything were to happen to me. We will be safe."

"Bloody better be," Dowling rumbled. "One swim is enough for the day."

Magnusson didn't respond to the remark, but he stood up and turned to look at the neat grid of wellheads on the floor. His expression was thoughtful. Greenwood had turned away to allow him a moment to compose himself, but she looked around when he spoke once more.

"In German, the bell is *Die Glocke*," he said. "Language is fascinating. The similarities, and the differences. Wouldn't you agree, my Dutch friend?"

Goose exchanged a glance with Greenwood, and then he shrugged. "Yes, I suppose so."

"Because bells and clocks have always been closely related," Magnusson continued, as if he hadn't heard the other man at all. "In your language, *klokken* means *clocks*. In mine, it is *bell*. But there is always more to it than that. In Norway, a small bell is *bjelle*; a larger one, such as in a clocktower, is *klokke*. Sometimes one meaning, and sometimes the other."

"I'm not sure where you're going with this," Goose said evenly, and Magnusson tilted his head, without turning around.

"They had another name for the machine, you know; the Nazis. The project had a codename. It was *CHRONOS*. Do you know this word?"

Goose nodded. "I do. It's from Greek mythology. Chronos was the personification of linear time."

"It seems your team is well-educated, Captain," Magnusson said. "I admire that. Time is a subject I think about often. We have so little of it, even if we live to old age. And some of us have far less than others."

"Why did they give the project that particular name?" Aldridge asked. "Surely they didn't think there could be a temporal component to the device's function."

Magnusson made a dismissive gesture. "No man controls time," he said, almost angrily. "That is nonsense, for children and the weak-minded. What's done is done, and to change the past is impossible."

Greenwood's gaze flicked to Aldridge, and she saw a frown appear on his forehead for just a moment. She knew exactly what he was thinking about, and in her peripheral vision, she could see that he was momentarily the focus of the entire team's attention. An image flashed across her mind: a lightning storm above a gothic cathedral, but the colours were all wrong.

You'd be surprised what's possible, Magnusson, she thought.

She cleared her throat, looking towards the older man's back again. "You said some of us have less time than others. Are you concerned about your health?"

Magnusson turned to face Greenwood and he smiled, but there was a great sadness in it that confused her. "No," he replied. "I am as well as a man of my years could hope to be. I expect to be around for some time to come."

"But?" Greenwood replied, sensing that the man had

more to say.

"But those years will be haunted, as I am every day."

Once again there was a long moment of silence.

"We're going to do everything we can to—"

"You misunderstand me," Magnusson interrupted gently. "One is haunted by the past, not the future. Tell me this, Captain: when you prepared for this mission of yours, did you happen to discover my middle name?"

She shook her head.

"It is *Andrzej*. Not a common name in Norway."

"No," Greenwood replied, the curiosity evident in her voice. "But not uncommon in Poland."

Magnusson's eyes glinted, and he nodded. "It was my grandfather's name. He was Polish. The Nazis had a word for him also: *ein Jude*. Do you know this word too?"

"We all know that word," Greenwood replied, her voice softer now.

"My mother was eleven years old in 1939, when her own parents sent her away from Poland. They knew what was to come. She was adopted by a Norwegian family, and took their name. She met my father, they married, and I was born in 1950."

He looked again towards the wellheads, but his focus was the empty space above them, as if visualising the black machine that had sat there on a raised platform for several years, unsuspected by the outside world.

"She never saw her parents again, and I never met them. My grandparents, Andrzej and Solomea, were murdered in the camps. They wore the yellow star, and had numbers on their wrists."

He clenched his right fist, and raised it towards his face. Greenwood was surprised when he kissed the wrinkled skin on the back of his own hand.

"My given Norwegian name, Leif, means *descendant*, Captain," he said quietly. "I am defined by what my mother lost, and what I never had the chance to know. Can you imagine, then, my feelings when I saw this horror from the past reach out and claim more lives?"

"I don't think anyone here can fully know how you feel, but I believe I have some idea," Greenwood said. Magnusson nodded once more.

"I had Miwa remove Hitler's symbol from the machine's outer casing before I would permit it to be brought onboard this platform. They left it in the U-boat, with all the rest of the hateful insignia."

"Where's the submarine now?" Dowling asked. Magnusson gestured vaguely towards the wellheads protruding up through the floor, and the unseen icy waters far beneath their feet.

"It is still down below, even now," he said. "And may it rot there for all eternity."

Chapter 16

The last several hours of searching had been fruitless, and Greenwood was frustrated despite not being at all surprised. Miwa's team had been every bit as thorough as Magnusson promised.

There was nothing left to be found on the platform, whether in the well bay or elsewhere. She had used Magnusson's satellite phone to contact Wuyts, reporting the helicopter pilot's death and their own narrow escape. The rest had been communicated very briefly and vaguely, using arranged codewords. Their orders were to report to Brussels at the earliest opportunity, for a full debrief. Magnusson's own helicopter had already arrived and was being refuelled, under careful watch of Dowling and Ramos. Goose was performing a final check and restock of their survival suits, ready for their return flight.

Greenwood exited the main accommodation block,

shielding her eyes against the sun that had broken through the clouds. The ocean was a deep navy blue, but the waves now glittered in their ceaseless motion. She saw Aldridge about ten metres away, leaning on a railing at the platform's edge. He glanced around at her when he heard the sound of her boots against the metal surface as she approached.

"Let me guess," he said, "Wuyts is taking our travel insurance excess out of your allowance."

Greenwood pressed her lips together in a fine line as she came to stand beside him. She knew him a lot better now than she had a few months earlier, and she could tell that this particular flippant remark was a deflection. When something was bothering him, he tended to go on the offensive by pushing boundaries. He'd be expecting her to chastise him, or to just ignore him. She intended to do neither.

"What's bothering you?" she asked. Her tone was even, and she saw a flicker of something pass across his face even though his eyes were once again fixed on the ocean below. He shrugged.

"Magnusson took the engineer's death pretty hard," Aldridge said. "And the pilot's. I think he feels person-ally responsible."

Greenwood nodded, but it was in understanding as well as simple agreement.

"Don't do that," she said, and he looked around at her again with a frown.

"Do what?"

"You know damned well. You were right to bring Cross's dossier to my attention, and I was right to open an investigation. Everything that Magnusson said confirms that."

"If I hadn't pursued—"

"Then the engineer, and the crew of the trawler, and maybe a lot of other people in the future would all have died for nothing," she interrupted, "even if the pilot lived."

"Whereas now we have the chance to do something about it," he said, and she gave the barest nod.

"That's right."

"It seems like whenever I get pulled into things, innocent people end up dead."

"When *we* get pulled into things, we make sure the casualties are kept to a minimum," she corrected, turning to face him now. He still wasn't looking at her, but she continued anyway. "We keep people alive, Aldridge — and sometimes it means that somebody dies, so that a lot more don't have to. That's the job."

"The one I signed up for," he added, with a sigh.

"Getting cold feet?" she said, inclining her head towards the ocean below. She was rewarded with the hint of a lopsided grin.

"Figuratively? Nope," he replied. "It just… it bothers me. It's not OK."

"That's how you know *you're* still OK," she said. He only grunted in response, and then was silent for several moments, his eyes scanning the horizon. Finally he turned towards her, and she didn't step back even though they were separated by less than a metre.

"What about you?" he asked. "Big day so far, and more responsibility."

"That's the job," she said again, "It's what they pay me for. And I'm always OK."

Aldridge frowned in exaggerated annoyance, then tapped his fingers against the metal railing, listening to the sound reverberating. He broke eye contact, then moved his hand slightly closer to hers, stopping short of actually touching.

"You don't have to be, you know," he said.

This isn't the time, Aldridge, she thought, but then another part of her mind asked her when the time would be, exactly. She had no answer for that. She looked down at his hand on the railing, so very close to her own, then she pressed her lips together again. A moment later, she lifted her hand away.

"Yes, I do," she said, then she turned and began to walk back towards the accommodation block. She called over her shoulder as she went, without looking back. "You should get into your survival suit. We leave in twenty."

She thought she heard him say "Aye, Captain" but the wind carried most of the sound away. When she glanced back as she reached the nearest door, he was facing away from her, once again looking out to sea.

Magnusson's personal helicopter streaked above the

waves on its return journey from *Sverdfisk Gamma* to the Norwegian coast. The sun was getting low in the sky, and the clouds in the distance promised rain before long.

Unlike on its earlier outbound journey, the aircraft carried a full complement. Magnusson, his corporate counsel, his personal assistant, and all five of Greenwood's team were on board, and Aldridge had already remarked upon how the craft was the exact same model as the one they'd been in earlier. The comment earned him a rare sharp look from Ramos, and he'd been silent ever since, though Greenwood had noticed him fidgeting with his seat harness several times.

She looked around the cabin. Dowling and Ramos were both asleep, and Goose was calmly looking out the window, this time sitting in the rear passenger area with the rest of them. Aldridge seemed to have settled, but she still caught him looking over at her every few minutes. She'd raised an eyebrow in his direction, but he just mirrored the gesture then looked away.

The corporate lawyer had his eyes closed, but he swallowed periodically and shifted in his seat, betraying his discomfort. *Not a fan of helicopter rides*, Greenwood thought. It was understandable, especially today.

Magnusson himself was deep in thought, and his personal assistant sat beside him, working on a tablet computer. She paused suddenly, scrutinising something on the screen, and then she looked around at her employer. Magnusson became aware of the movement and glanced at her expectantly, and she turned the screen towards him. Greenwood watched as his eyes widened.

"Captain," he said, "would you perhaps like to ask my… colleague about his plans in person?"

The lawyer opened his eyes and looked at the older man, but he said nothing.

"I'd like that very much," Greenwood said carefully, "but you told me you didn't know his location."

Magnusson smiled, and for the first time there was a steely edge to it. "That was the truth, but it has been many years since I have needed to manage my own social engagements," he said, pointing to the tablet computer.

"Don't make me play twenty questions, Magnusson," Greenwood said, taking quiet satisfaction in the shocked expression that bloomed on the face of his personal assistant. Magnusson himself actually laughed.

"Very well," he replied. "A significant portion of Miwa's political access, and a not-inconsiderable revenue stream, comes from elite fundraising events. Invitation only, of course."

"Of course."

"And," he continued, "there is such an event taking place very soon. I regret that I will be unable to attend, but a man in my position could arrange for access to the guest list. There will be a number of charming and wealthy couples there, all with a keen interest in environmental causes. A late addition might be suspicious, but the risk is yours to take."

Aldridge folded his arms and looked at her expectantly. Greenwood ignored him.

"I think I'll take you up on that offer, if I can make arrangements in time," she said. "When and where? And don't tell me I'll need snow boots."

"Very much not," Magnusson replied. "I doubt you will even want a coat."

He leaned forward, the beige leather creaking as he moved.

"I would make your arrangements promptly. The event begins in forty-eight hours."

"There has been an unexpected development," Tien said, his head bowed and his entire demeanour projecting sorrow and regret.

"Specifically?"

Miwa was sitting at his desk once again, in his private office deep within the mountain. He had a great affection for the sterility and calmness of the bare rock walls, but he also felt horror at the origin of the place. Though he would never give voice to the thought, a part of him saw his presence here as a form of penance — albeit one that was being prepaid before the crime it would punish him for.

"The mission was unsuccessful," Tien replied. "The chartered helicopter crashed into the sea, but all onboard survived, except for the pilot."

Miwa closed his eyes for a moment, his face betraying no emotion whatsoever. "I understand. It has been confirmed?"

Tien nodded. "We intercepted a ship-to-shore communication to the Norwegian naval authorities, informing them of the accident."

"A communication made by the platform's temporary staff?"

Again, Tien nodded, understanding his master's unspoken second question. "There were no additional signals via the standard lines. But a satellite transmission would be beyond our reach."

And I have underestimated the resourcefulness of our European friends too often already, Miwa thought.

"I am concerned," he said, his gaze shifting towards the black rectangle of the video screen mounted on the side wall. It was currently switched off, and from this angle, he could see Tien reflected in it. The other man bobbed his head in a motion which somehow perfectly encapsulated both acknowledgement and apology.

Miwa allowed himself a minute of silent contemplation, and then he turned his attention to his trusted companion once more.

"An increase in security is prudent. Make the necessary arrangements."

"I anticipated your request. Our colleagues have already left Norway and are en route to your next engagement."

This time it was Miwa who nodded, but in satisfaction. Tien was fiercely loyal and unquestioning, but also ever-ready to show initiative.

"We will also bring our construction schedule ahead," Miwa continued. "Use whatever resources are required. I want to be ready in four days."

"It will be done," Tien replied immediately. "Are you certain you still wish to attend the fundraising event?"

"Completely," Miwa said. "The money is immaterial, but power is transferred in handshakes and polite greetings with those who already hold it. I believe this will be my last public appearance for some time."

He stood up, allowing his chair to slide backwards, then he walked over to the blank rock wall opposite the video screen. He laid his hands upon it, as he had countless times before, appreciating the cold, rough surface.

"What I am about to do has never been done, old friend," he said, "and it will never be forgotten — or perhaps forgiven. But is it right?"

Tien's gentle smile was almost paternal, and the question was a familiar one. "They may not think so in your lifetime," he replied quietly, "but history will speak your name with reverence. Empathy is too heavy a burden for the great figures of the ages."

"Empathy is our vaccine against the horrors we would otherwise bring upon ourselves," Miwa said, his tone thoughtful and his eyes unfocused. Then his brow furrowed for a brief moment before his face became expressionless again. "And empathy must often be purchased with pain."

Tien looked at his employer for several seconds, and then he silently stepped forward to the desk, placing a small rectangle of paper upon it. He bowed in Miwa's direction and then left the room.

Miwa wasted no time in moving across to his desk and picking up the piece of paper. It bore a word, in Tien's elegant handwriting: a surname, clearly Scandinavian. Miwa had seen several such notes before. One had said *Cross*, and another had been *Falk*.

The name on this one was not familiar to him, but he knew it belonged to the dead helicopter pilot. Tien was as well-prepared as ever. Miwa stared at it for long moments, burning it into his memory, before returning the paper to his desk.

Then he knelt down, the hard rock floor uncomfortable beneath him, and he prayed for the pilot's soul.

Chapter 17

The building rose up like something alien amidst the bustling city streets, immune to even the final blaze of the setting sun, as if a craft from another world had landed silently and inscrutably amongst a sea of up-turned faces.

It held hopes of one day being the tallest church in the world, but its construction process had already spanned thirteen decades, and was not yet complete. It was properly called the Basilica and Expiatory Church of the Holy Family, but to the inhabitants of its home city of Barcelona, as well as to the world in general, it had only one name.

Sagrada Família.

While its design was unconventional to the point of being shocking, and it divided public opinion even as the centenary of the architect's death approached, few would disagree that it was Antoni Gaudí's masterpiece.

Its three façades, of which two had been completed, stared out at the city, challenging onlookers not only to make sense of them, but to believe that they each belonged to the same building. The façade of Passion looked like a stark, angular portal being swallowed in the jaws of something from the black depths of the ocean, whereas the façade of Nativity rose like a baroque, nightmare sandcastle, its carvings and contours encrusting the myriad surfaces like barnacles. The building's sheer bulk, especially when topped with the ever-present cranes and scaffolding, served to keep its lowest reaches in shadow even at the height of the day, adding to the sense that it was a vast hallucination brooding on the Carrer de Mallorca.

By night, though, it glowed; lit from all around in a warm, golden haze that gave the impression that the sun had set within, to be released from the spires again the following morning. The church would normally have still been open at this hour, playing host to the final few clusters of its more than eight thousand daily visitors, but today it had closed early, hours before, in preparation for an exclusive and very private event. It was almost 8 PM in Barcelona, but the evening was just beginning.

Aldridge adjusted the sleeves of his suit jacket, but the action was entirely unnecessary; it had been tailored perfectly for him, and he already planned to ask if he could keep it after the mission was over. The cut on the side of his face from the helicopter's broken window had healed well during the past two days, and the mark was barely visible, but from time to time it itched a little.

Greenwood looped her hand through his elbow, and he was momentarily surprised until he realised that the gesture was for the benefit of any onlookers. He looked around at her, and with a wry smile on her face, she leaned towards him slightly.

"Stop fidgeting," she said. "Try to act like you belong here."

"I was refused entry to a nightclub in Edinburgh once for wearing my running shoes," he replied, and she laughed, but Aldridge wasn't sure whether it was genuine amusement or just more cover.

They had briefed Wuyts fully as soon as they arrived back onshore via Magnusson's personal helicopter. The director had readily confirmed the difficulty in finding Miwa; she was aware of his company, and knew that the man himself was an elusive figure. There was no current information on his whereabouts, so the donors' event in Barcelona seemed like the best available lead at the moment. The intervening day had been spent in hurried preparation, including the establishing of the identities they would be attending under, acquiring suitable clothing, and arranging transport. Wuyts had dispatched them to Spain with significant operational discretion, and had meanwhile continued her attempts to find out anything she could on the possible whereabouts of the device Magnusson had described.

The security line to enter the vast building via the

Nativity façade, at the top of a short flight of stairs, was short and efficient as befitted the wealth and power of those who were attending. Expensive vehicles approached the nearby kerb in a slow procession, delivering their occupants — and often one or more private staff — before smoothly pulling away to await the end of the evening and a summons to return. In some cases, luxury automobiles or even supercars were driven by their owners, and a valet parking service had been provided for the occasion. Aldridge winced at the idea of letting a stranger drive any of the gleaming machines he could see idling near the gated entrance to the grounds, but he supposed that if you were that rich, you could afford to repair any accidental scratches.

He and Greenwood had arrived in a sleek Bentley Continental Flying Spur W12 S, driven by Dowling, who wore a suit that would let him pass for either a driver or a guest if necessary. The car was a medium greyish-blue gunmetal shade to Aldridge's eye, and Greenwood had informed him that the colour was called Portofino. She had also actually turned her nose up at the vehicle when it was delivered to the hotel they were registered as guests at. Aldridge asked what was wrong with the car, and she'd waved the question away, merely remarking that she'd prefer something that looked a bit more sporty.

She stood by his side now, and he took another careful glance in her direction. She wore a sleeveless halter neck dress in ruby satin, ankle length, with a slit on the right side to mid-thigh. She had a diaphanous wrap sitting loosely on her shoulders, and a small purse in burgundy leather, on a fine chained strap. Her only jewellery was a pair of gold pendant teardrop earrings, and a bracelet which bore a delicate St. Christopher medallion, also in gold. Aldridge allowed himself a small smile.

Patron saint of travellers, he thought. *For protection when far from home.*

He allowed his eyes to drift from the bracelet to her slender but noticeably toned arms, the curve of her shoulders that he didn't think he'd ever seen before tonight, and the way the last rays of the Spanish sunset caught the auburn highlights in her hair. The overall effect was arresting, and served to distract him almost entirely from his discomfort about the evening that lay ahead of them, but he still didn't feel at ease.

It wasn't the stakes of their mission, because those were still somewhat unclear. It wasn't the impending confrontation with Tsutomu Miwa. It wasn't the formal occasion itself, either; although he'd never much enjoyed them, he could make polite conversation and he knew which spoon was for soup and which was for dessert. Nor was it even the fact of being amongst so many hugely wealthy people, because he was already an impostor in this place, so pretending to be rich seemed like just another small facet of the deception.

What's one more little lie between friends? Or colleagues, for that matter.

He looked at her face, unsurprised to see that she was casually scanning the people ahead of them in the line, the security staff at the entrance, and what she could see of the interior of the building. She wore an expression that would have looked to anyone else like simple, restrained anticipation for the soirée, but he knew that she was eager to get in there and challenge Miwa. She was planning and calculating, running scenarios and eventualities. The familiar fire was in her eyes, and in that moment he doubted that she was even aware of his presence beside her.

He'd felt powerfully drawn to Greenwood virtually since the day and hour they'd met, and he'd spent weeks afterwards telling himself that it was because of the events they'd experienced, and his gratitude that she'd saved his life more than once. As the weeks became months, however, the explanation had felt more and more flimsy. She intrigued him, and he knew that truthfully he was a little in awe of her. Her strength and intelligence were clear for anyone to see, but he'd also learned of her overriding drive to protect, and to sacrifice, and to tirelessly shoulder the responsibilities that came with this strange life they led. She was a warrior, and she was fiercely private — he often wondered if she realised how lonely she seemed to be, carrying whatever burdens he could sometimes see chasing across her eyes before being hurriedly pushed away again.

She was also a very beautiful woman.

In this situation, with her appearance softened by the

dress, and the heels, and the hint of makeup, and the light upon her hair, it was difficult for him to think of much else.

Greenwood looked around at him suddenly, and after a moment he saw her eyes widen, before she quickly faced forward again. When she spoke, her voice was quiet, and lacked the humour it had held a minute earlier.

"You can stop that too," she said.

"Seek and leverage all available sources of verisimilitude," he replied, and he could have sworn that she gave the barest shake of her head. They both knew it was a direct quotation from the basic field training course on covert infiltration operations; the idea was to use anything you could find to help you blend in and seem authentic while undercover.

"So you *can* read," Greenwood said, and he felt a mock-congratulatory tap from the fingers of the hand she still had curled at his elbow.

The line moved forward, and Aldridge once again mentally recited the details of their cover identities. *I'm Alisdair Lewis, representing a private investment group in Aberdeen with various interests in the petrochemical industry; we're looking to make our portfolio more environmentally friendly, and improve our political influence accordingly. She's Claire Morton-Fellowes, an advisory member of our group who's based in London, interested in philanthropic causes, and independently wealthy via her family's textiles import business.*

Keeping his voice low, he half-turned his head towards her to speak without being overheard.

"Why do you get to be the rich and charitable one?"

"Because a bash like this will be overflowing with bored wealthy people with a lot more money than sense, looking to write a cheque and rent a sense of purpose," she replied in an equally quiet voice. "They won't even give my identity a second glance. It's useful. And that's why you're—"

"Whoever you need me to be," he interjected. She gave him a warning look, but he met her gaze without blinking, and just shrugged. "That's the job, remember?"

Greenwood swept a strand of her hair back into place with her free hand, and they both lapsed into silence for a few moments. Aldridge heard her take a measured breath, and then she was speaking again.

"Just don't spill any drinks on my dress."

He grinned without looking around. "Wouldn't dream of it. Spilling a drink, I mean. I might dream about the dress, though. Is it yours?"

She tilted her head to one side. "It is now," she replied, and Aldridge's grin widened.

"Any plans to wear it outside of work?"

This time she did glance at him. "Still inquiring about things that are none of your business, *Alisdair*. Let's just try to concentrate on the job at hand, shall we?"

"Fair enough," he replied, just as the queue moved forward once more. They were now second in line. "For what it's worth, though, *Claire*... you look beautiful tonight."

She was silent for long enough that he thought she wasn't going to acknowledge his words, but then she gave him another quick look.

"You look alright too, I suppose," she said.

Aldridge had the good grace to simply smile, then he quickly directed his attention to the security checkpoint ahead. Greenwood had already assured him that it would be a cursory examination. *The guests are too wealthy to pat down, and some of them will absolutely be armed anyway, including their own security. The venue's staff will have a quick look at coats and bags, and that'll be it.*

It made sense, but he was still uncomfortably aware of the ceramic-bodied pistol in an underarm holster hidden beneath his shirt. He also wondered whether there'd be an electronic wand that might detect the tiny earpiece transceivers they both wore, but he couldn't see any sign of such a thing up ahead.

"The last thing you want to do is look nervous," Greenwood said, apparently having read his body language. "Just don't tell them that my lipstick is actually a hand grenade."

He was about to respond when they were called forward by an Asian woman in a strapless blue sequinned dress, holding a small tablet computer. Aldridge took their invitations from his jacket's inside pocket. They were printed on heavy-gauge paper, exquisitely inlaid with bands of subtle colour around the edges. Each bore their names, with holographic elements overlaid, presumably to prevent duplication. There were barcodes in the lower left corner, and also the flag of the country of origin of each guest. Beside the flag, there was a number in boldface; the accompanying footnote indicated that it was the country's annual carbon dioxide emissions in kilotonnes.

He handed the invitations to the woman, who quickly scanned them using the tablet's camera and confirmed their identities. She looked up at them with one eyebrow raised, and Aldridge felt his heart stutter in his chest, but then the woman smiled. Her accent, to his surprise, was slightly but unmistakably French.

"England and Scotland," she said, referring to the flags on their respective invitations. "I thought you didn't get along."

Greenwood gave her widest smile as they both stepped forward to enter the vast building.

"What makes you think we do?" she replied.

The balcony doors of the suite were fully open, allowing the Mediterranean breeze to sweep through the room. The sound of the city all around was constant, and Miwa stood motionless just inside the threshold, with his eyes closed.

He knew that the event would be just beginning, and the impressive venue was only a few minutes away by car, but it would still be a little while before he'd go downstairs to make the brief trip to the church, and then his grand entrance in front of his many guests. He knew his speech by heart, for he had already delivered it on a number of occasions before this one. It was updated periodically according to which way the political winds were blowing, the sensibilities and idiosyncrasies of whichever country he was in, and the most recent environmental outrage that would be most likely to draw fervour, sympathy, and financial commitment. But ultimately, each of these occasions was just another instance of the same evening. He held at least one per year, and the attendees were always generous and enthusiastic.

How would they respond if they knew what their donations had funded in recent years?

The truth was that some of them might approve, at least in principle. The wealthy saw themselves as set apart from the general public in more aspects than living arrangements and attainable luxuries. They often supposed themselves to be among the great figures of history. But Miwa knew that true visionaries must ultimately always take action.

Tien was elsewhere in the luxurious but very temporary residence, making the various small preparations for the evening, and monitoring their larger projects far beyond this particular city. They had arrived only a handful of hours ago, and Miwa would not even spend a single night here. There was a knock at the outer door beyond his private hallway, and he heard the soft footfalls of his faithful friend and servant moving in that direction.

Miwa remained motionless and still looking out at the urban vista as Tien escorted Venter and Reddy into the lavishly appointed living area, before discreetly disappearing again. The two men stood in silence, waiting for their employer to address them. Miwa allowed ten seconds to pass, enough to emphasise the power relationship in the room, but not enough to be egregiously impolite, then he turned to face them.

"Gentlemen," he said, and they both nodded, having learned long ago not to attempt a bow.

Venter was the more self-assured of the two, his posture relatively relaxed, simply awaiting instructions. His slightly younger counterpart was as restless as ever, and clearly uncomfortable in his evening attire. Miwa could tell that Reddy itched to tear the tie from around his own neck, but the man nonetheless kept his hands by his sides, his expression a vague grimace.

"After the events in Norway, we must be prepared," Miwa said, clasping his hands behind his back and regarding each of them in turn. "Mr. Magnusson's internal conflict has been evident for some time. We may have uninvited guests this evening. You know who you must look for."

Venter nodded again. "And if we find them?"

Miwa fixed him with a look that was both calm but also somehow ominous. "Then we will take them elsewhere, to speak privately. We must find out what they know, and avoid the further spreading of any such knowledge."

Neither of the two killers in front of him knew very much about the Bell itself, or the precise details of Miwa's plans for it. In his view, they were blunt instruments, no matter how ingenious they could be when required. He saw them as a necessary evil, and one to be purged if their existence became a liability.

"What if they don't want to come?"

It was Reddy who had spoken, and Miwa watched as Venter threw a cautionary glance in the other man's direction. But it was a reasonable question.

"Discretion is required," Miwa replied. "I would prefer to avoid upsetting our other guests, because then I too would become upset." For him, it was a simple statement of fact, but he knew that it would be interpreted as a threat. Such inferences were helpful, and he knew that his message had been received.

"Understood," Venter said immediately. "We'll be downstairs whenever you're ready, sir."

Miwa turned away again without responding, and the other two men wasted no time in leaving the suite. Virtually as soon as the outer door had clicked shut behind them, Tien re-entered the living room, coming to stand at a respectful distance from his master. The older man also waited in silence, as usual.

"Almost five million people," Miwa said. It was the population of the urban area of Barcelona. He knew that Tien would understand without further clarification, and the other man indeed remained silent. "And the haze of their energy demands rises above it all." He gestured vaguely towards the skyline before continuing.

"The sixth most populous urban area in the European Union. Within Spain, it is second only to Madrid. But globally, it does not appear in the first *ninety*."

Tien nodded patiently, having heard such numbers before. "The spread of humanity, and its impact," he offered.

"Too far and too much," Miwa replied. "And too many. It must change."

"Everything is proceeding as you instructed," Tien said. "We will be ready. If I may suggest, we should move the device soon."

Miwa nodded distractedly. His excellent memory tormented him, relentlessly supplying facts and figures that would be useful in his impending speech, but which also horrified him. As necessary as events like tonight's reception were, they were also frustrating. He had to walk a fine line regarding his tone when speaking to the attendees; they had to be energised and even frightened, but they also had to believe that their contributions could be of real benefit — they had to think that there was still a chance. And there was, even though several points of no return had already been passed. So his words could be passionate, but not unvarnished. He had to keep the doomsaying at least partially hypothetical, and thus he could never convey the truest extent of his own fears.

Even the idle rich must sleep soundly, he thought. *And so they will… for a little while longer.* The world would be a very different place by the time the next new year dawned.

Miwa turned to face Tien, and he could see from the other man's face that his next words would come as no surprise.

"I believe it's time to get ready," he said.

Chapter 18

Aldridge felt Greenwood subtly elbow him in the ribs for the third time in as many minutes. He knew she was telling him to stop staring at their surroundings, but that was impossible. He'd never seen anything remotely like it.

They stood within a forest of light, amidst pale grey columns stretching far above, giving an ethereal air of sanctity to the cavernous space. Sagrada Família was lit from the outside with spotlights, to ensure the huge array of stained glass windows looked their very best. It was simultaneously reminiscent of a grand temple from high fantasy, and also the skeletal rib cage of some prehistoric monster, vast beyond all imagining. Geometric patterns were everywhere, mostly inspired by marine forms, and the interior walls were carved to look curiously like the closely-packed façades of other buildings. In combination with the radiant light overhead, the effect was to create a vague sense of confusion as to whether they were indoors or not.

The enormous tree-like columns split outwards after three-quarters of their height, extending organic-looking stone branches to support the roof. Bulbous golden discs marked the points of divergence, and archways and supports led the eye off into the distance, emphasising the sheer scale of the construction.

"If Poseidon existed, this would be his summer home," Aldridge said, drawing a glance from Greenwood. "It's like something out of Greek mythology. Or Tolkien."

"First time here?" she asked, and he nodded without taking his eyes from a grand balcony several storeys above them, and at least forty feet away across the floor.

"And you?"

"I've been once before," she replied. "Sightseeing."

Aldridge's eyebrows lifted in curiosity that he made no attempt to conceal. "With a friend?"

She ignored the question. "I just wish you'd stop looking like such a tourist. We're amongst the rich and vaguely famous; these people don't gawk. They… appreciate. In a bored sort of way."

He turned to look at her. "You don't like rich people," he said, his tone implying that it was an insightful deduction. She wrinkled her nose in the way she did when she profoundly disagreed with something.

"I don't like *pretentious* people," she replied dryly. "Whether they're wealthy is neither here nor there."

"Well I can't imagine what it costs to rent this place for the night," he said. "Look at all this stuff."

Aldridge assumed that there would normally be pews somewhere, or at least seating, but it had all been cleared away to make room for the evening's event. There were a number of large, free-standing display screens which must each have been at least a hundred inches diagonally, mounted on sleek aluminium legs. They ran a looping presentation, silent but subtitled, showing statistics on environmental damage, human impact on the climate, the planet's dwindling natural resources, and the work of Miwa Environmental Consulting. There were free bars at several strategic points, and in the area that would usually serve as the nave, there was a raised stage area, currently cordoned off. Soft music played from hidden speakers all around, infusing the space with inoffensive orchestral covers of the popular songs of previous decades.

Greenwood's eye drifted to the various staff who milled around, wearing permanent smiles. She noted an array of hostesses soliciting donations with electronic card-reader machines, at least thirty waiters carrying trays of either drinks or hors d'oeuvres, and a discreet but visible security presence.

Aldridge followed her gaze, and wondered whether the security personnel were employed by the church, the city, or Miwa's organisation. He could also see various people who stood near to several of the guests, not participating in conversations but instead keeping a watchful eye on their surroundings, and he knew that they must be private bodyguards.

"See anybody whose autograph I should get?" he asked, and Greenwood gave a slight shrug.

"I think I saw the new chief executive of Anfruns Industrial Technologies a minute ago," she said. "But you'd probably be more interested in that musician who wears the red tinted glasses all the time. He's at most of these things."

"I'm starting to feel a bit underpaid," Aldridge said. "That's not an official complaint, by the way. How much money do you need to have to get these invitations?"

Greenwood leaned in towards him, lowering her voice. "The entry fee for tonight was a registered donation to a specified environmental cause; a minimum of 250,000 Euros. Per person."

His head whipped around to look at her, but thankfully no-one else noticed. "Bloody hell. Do we have that kind of money in the budget? I had to fill in a form to get *pens*."

Her eyes sparkled even as her jaw visibly tensed, and in a flash of insight Aldridge knew that she was biting back a laugh.

Interesting, he thought, and he wondered if her amusement at his remark when they'd been waiting in the entrance line earlier might have been genuine after all.

"Come on," she said, tilting her head in the direction

of a busier part of the enormous floor area, where a dozen or so couples were actually dancing languidly. "We shouldn't stand out in the open."

"Half a million Euros for us to be here," he muttered to himself, deliberately just loud enough for her to hear, as they began to move. "The sausage rolls had better be incredible."

They'd walked only ten metres or so when Greenwood spoke again, in a conversational tone that belied the seriousness of her subject. "We've got to assume that whoever was behind the helicopter crash also got a good look at us on the pad. They might not expect us to be here, but I think that Miwa probably errs on the side of caution. We should avoid any close scrutiny from security."

"Especially since we were last-minute additions to the guest list," Aldridge replied, but Greenwood shook her head.

"We weren't; like Magnusson said, it'd be too suspicious. Alisdair Lewis and Claire Morton-Fellowes have been on the list for months. We're just taking their places."

"We're *real* people?" he asked, his voice dropping to a whisper but losing none of its incredulity. Greenwood simply nodded.

"And that's an advantage. If they do think we'll gate-crash, they'll be looking primarily at the serving staff, and even the security personnel. Anyone who could easily be added or substituted at the last minute."

"And how did we manage it, exactly? Where are our namesakes right now?"

Greenwood gave a one-shouldered shrug, which drew Aldridge's eye for a moment. "The director is an extremely resourceful woman. I don't make a habit of looking a gift horse in the mouth. Or questioning her."

Aldridge nodded, conceding the point. "I do have one other question, though. Is your lipstick really a hand grenade? Because I never know when you're joking. About anything."

Her lips curled into a wry grin, and she was about to respond when Aldridge caught sight of a security guard exiting a side door and beginning to stride purposefully in their direction. He felt himself tense up as he met Greenwood's gaze again, and he could see from her expression that she'd noticed the change in his posture. He acted immediately.

Her eyebrows shot up as he took hold of her right hand with his left, and with a smile and a quick mock bow, he pulled her along with him into the vicinity of the dancing couples. His right hand found her waist, and he felt her fingers settle upon his shoulder as he casually glanced in the direction the guard had been coming from.

The squat, frowning man was stuffed into a suit that was clearly a size too small for him, and his gleamingly bald head reflected the light from the stained glass windows like an emergency beacon. He marched past without sparing them a single look.

As they moved slowly to the music, Greenwood gave an appreciative nod. "That was a bold move. And quick thinking."

"Make sure you write that on my report card," he replied.

"Hmm, we'll see. And what was the plan if the guard had come over and tapped you on the shoulder?"

"I just assumed you'd incapacitate him," Aldridge shrugged. "And I could create a diversion. Though that's more difficult when I'm not wearing my kilt."

Greenwood rolled her eyes. "Probably for the best, since we're trying to keep a low profile."

She checked to see that the guard had continued on his course, and to her relief the man was now nowhere to be seen. Aldridge saw her shoulders relax slightly.

"Maybe," he said, drawing her attention once more. "But it's still thirty degrees Celsius outside. Honestly, I could do with the breeze."

Dowling had parked the Bentley a block and a half to the south of the plaza which housed the magnificent church, in a side street not far from a mobile phone store. He stood beside the vehicle, casually leaning against the closed driver's-side door, with the window open. His arms were folded, and he looked every inch the chauffeur-bodyguard combination that he was playing tonight.

In the rear of the Bentley sat Goose and Ramos. The Dutchman was dressed to blend in with the other guests at Miwa's event, even though he had no invitation, and a plan had been made to get him inside with local police credentials as a supposed security precaution if it turned out to be necessary. Ramos was in casual, nondescript clothes, and also carried Barcelona police ID. Greenwood wasn't generally in favour of assuming the authority of civilian law enforcement, but it did conveniently open a lot of doors — and her team was usually long gone by the time any questions could be asked by the public.

Goose held a tablet computer, and both he and Ramos periodically glanced at it. The screen displayed a live video feed from a camera-equipped micro drone that Ramos had flown onto the roof of a tapas bar which straddled the corner of Carrer de la Marina, diagonally opposite the Nativity façade where Miwa would no doubt enter Sagrada Família at some point after all the other guests had arrived. They were positioned to keep Aldridge and Greenwood informed about any significant developments outside the building, and to take any action which might later become necessary.

All three of the other KESTREL team members wore the more conventional external earpiece communications devices, more noticeable but also more comfortable than the in-ear and nigh-invisible models that the two inside the church were using. The external versions had two other major advantages: much longer battery life, and the benefit of a small mute switch to deaden the built-in microphone, allowing them to speak amongst themselves without being heard remotely. The mute switches were currently all engaged.

"Aldridge is a brave man," Goose said. Ramos looked at him but didn't respond. Standing outside the car, Dowling grinned.

"That's one word for it," he replied. "Persistent little bugger."

"Do you think he's just kidding around?" Goose asked, and Dowling flexed his shoulders.

"Nope. I think it's just his style; humour, you know. She says it's his *defence mechanism*." His Welsh accent punctuated each lilting syllable in an uneven tempo.

"And she lets him get away with it," Goose added. "I've seen her give a dressing down to men your size, Larry, for just a misplaced look. Or punch them."

Dowling chuckled, nodding his head at the truth of it. "It's different with him, apparently. I've known her a long time. Longer than either of you two have."

Ramos chose that moment to speak up. "I don't think the Captain would appreciate you two gossiping about her," she said. "Though it's much more interesting than your usual conversation."

Goose huffed in amusement as he looked across at her. "You're in an unusually good mood."

The Spanish woman shrugged, then gestured vaguely to what lay beyond the car's heavily tinted rear windows. "I'm home," she said.

He nodded in understanding, then glanced at the tablet device again. "And you're right. None of our business. No sign of the man himself yet."

"When he shows up, you should get nearer the place, Alicia," Dowling said. "You're first in, if need be. We'll be right behind you. But I'm hoping it won't be necessary."

"You don't think he'll risk drawing attention with so many high-profile guests around," she replied, and she could see the big man nodding from outside the vehicle.

"I think he'll want to hush it up. Take them somewhere else. Or just deny everything and try to scarper. Then we can nab him."

His voice was calm, but he didn't sound entirely convinced, and nor was Ramos.

"Let's hope it works out that way," she said.

"Normally, you should actually *ask* a lady if she wants to dance first," Greenwood said. Her tone was relaxed, but she was still subtly observing the vast area around them, and the other attendees and various staff.

"So that's what I've been doing wrong all these years," Aldridge replied.

No-one seemed to be paying them much attention, which was just as Greenwood had expected. All the same, it made sense to go with the crowd, move around as much as possible, and deter any casual conversational approaches from other guests.

"When do you think he'll show up?" Aldridge asked, his focus on a passing waiter who held a tray of canapés.

"In a little while," she replied. "Magnusson said that Miwa always arrives after the start, but not by too much. It's to encourage punctuality in his guests."

Aldridge nodded. "Fair enough."

"But he'll still allow enough time for everybody to get suitably…"

She tailed off, then nodded towards the nearest of several freestanding bar areas, where a small group of their fellow attendees were ordering drinks. From the look of it, most of them wanted elaborate cocktails.

"Lubricated," Aldridge supplied. "That's what we say in Scotland."

"You say a lot of things in Scotland," she replied archly, and he grinned.

"That we do."

"Talking of which, maybe we should head over towards the bar there. Everyone else has a drink. And before you ask: nothing alcoholic. We're here to work."

Aldridge sighed, but he placed his hand on the small of her back and guided her in the direction she'd indicated. They both walked over towards the counter, weaving through the other dancing couples. They were served almost immediately, asking for two lime and sodas. The request drew no surprise at all, and indeed Greenwood heard another woman asking for something non-alcoholic too. She briefly wondered if it was because they were in a church, but she realised it was probably more about the calories.

Their drinks in hand, they drifted away from the bar

again, this time in the opposite direction, and within a minute they'd found a good vantage point just past one of the large pillars that lined the nave. They could observe most of the main area, but weren't particularly noticeable. They would also see anyone coming in via either of the two primary entrances.

They stood in silence for several minutes, both appreciating the cold drinks after the heat of the evening, though the interior of the basilica stayed remarkably cool and pleasant. At one point they both tensed as one of the doors of the Nativity façade swung open, but it was just another guest arriving.

Greenwood was just about to ask Aldridge what time it was when he spoke first.

"Will her majesty give you back the rest of your holidays once this is all over?"

She shrugged. "I suppose so. Don't see why not." She knew he was referring to Director Wuyts, and chose not to warn him — yet again — about the disrespectful appellation.

"That's good," he said. She could hear the note of apology in his voice, and she turned her head slightly to look at him. Aldridge was leaning against the base of the pillar, staring off into the distance.

"Besides," she added, after taking a small sip of her drink, "I can go away anytime. I just pick a place, and book a flight. To explore, and to recharge. It's pretty easy when you don't need to coordinate with anyone else."

He met her gaze, and in his eyes she could see his acknowledgement of what she'd admitted to him. He tilted his head to one side. "You know, travelling is a lot more fun when you're with someone. It's a widely-accepted fact."

Greenwood used her drink to gesture at their impressive surroundings. "Like this, you mean?" she asked, but Aldridge shook his head.

"Nope. Like you said, this is work. Not the same thing at all."

He took a gulp of the cold liquid in his own glass, chancing a quick glance at her over the rim.

"You trying to ask me something, Aldridge?" she said, her tone somewhere between teasing and warning, and she was surprised when his expression suddenly lost all its humour.

"Maybe later," he replied, his voice quieter now. "Right now, I think we should direct our questions towards *him*."

Greenwood was careful not to follow the direction of Aldridge's gaze too quickly. The doors of the Nativity façade were both open now, and then a noticeable hush descended. When she finally allowed her focus to come to rest on the entranceway, she saw a group of four men coming in.

The two who flanked the others were clearly quite capable of defending themselves, and looked positively uncomfortable in their suits. There was also an older man, moving economically but fluidly, and holding a compact leather binder.

The final member of the group, encircled by the rest but at a distance which afforded him full view of his surroundings, stood out. His mandarin-collared pale grey suit sat immaculately upon a slender frame, and his jet black hair and unlined skin gave him an ethereal, ageless appearance that was at once commanding and vaguely unsettling. He came to a halt a few metres inside the doorway. He did not look around, but every eye in the vast space was upon him.

Tsutomu Miwa had arrived.

Chapter 19

The scene before Miwa was just as it always was.

Faces that were all turned towards him, and the expected range of expressions. There was admiration, but not to excess — this particular demographic tended to control the display of such emotion. More visibly, the predatory hint of what they hoped to gain from the evening. And then there was the third and most common emotion: a tempered sort of optimism, combined with concern, and flimsily masked with cultured indifference.

No matter the venue, or the country, they always sought the same things.

Direction. Advantage. Hope.

He would give them all three, as he always did, and he would begin by giving them what they *least* wanted, and the thing which underpinned all their other needs: fear.

The building was beautiful, but it had not been chosen idly. No part of his substantial business enterprise was accidental, and he prided himself on making his influence felt in even the smallest part of it. He delegated a great deal, as all leaders must, but only to those who had earned the required trust. He saw all of his employees as projections of himself, and their rewards — and punishments — were of corresponding magnitude.

It took an average of five seconds after he entered a room like this for the murmur of muted conversation to begin, even as all of the assembled audience's eyes remained fixed upon him. It was why he always paused after coming in; to allow them to look. Be seen, but stand apart. Be real, but separate. It was one of the many secrets of influencing both hearts and minds.

He knew that the whispered words were a form of both excitement and tension, and he knew just how to release it. He smiled, and bowed. The room erupted into applause, which the basilica's hard surfaces and soaring ceiling amplified into the adulation of thousands.

Miwa moved forward with his entourage, the crowd parting to allow him passage. He wasn't an imposing man physically and nor was Tien, which was why he had the two other men flanking him, their own body language making it very clear that Miwa shouldn't be approached at this point of the evening. They made their way steadily towards the stage area, and at the foot of the short, three-step stairway which led up onto the raised platform, Venter and Reddy stopped and turned around, forming a barrier to anyone who might think of joining their host on the stage. The very visible presence of personal security was mostly for show; there had never been any trouble.

Tien proceeded to the lectern and set the leather folder upon it. He opened it out flat, revealing a tablet computer, and connected a cable to it which ran from the top edge of the lectern. He then walked to the front of the stage and raised his hands, palms outwards, at shoulder height. Once again, silence descended upon the vast space immediately. Tien turned to his master, attached a lapel microphone to Miwa's suit jacket, bowed, and then left the stage to stand with Venter and Reddy.

Miwa himself remained at the rear of the stage, his eyes downcast towards the floor. He raised his hands and steepled his fingers together, then allowed his eyelids to slide shut. He knew that scores of people were watching him, but he pushed that thought away, and sought his point of balance. He envisioned it as a pearl, suspended between the protective temple of his palms, perfectly in focus despite his closed eyes.

Within, he saw a miniature ocean, roiling and turbulent, washing ceaselessly all around the interior of the cloudy sphere. He could almost hear it. Chaotic, yet contained. Ever-changing, with its own wild beauty. And all of it overlaid with the shadows cast by his slender fingers. He felt his shoulders fully relax, and he inhaled deeply through his nose. With the oxygen flowing into his lungs, the pearl seemed brighter, and less opaque; the ocean within was more visible now. He opened his eyes.

"Welcome, my friends," he said.

Another round of applause, more brief this time. *As expected*, he thought.

"The building in which we now stand is very special to me, because it embodies two principles which have guided my work and my life. First of all, that the forms and creations of the natural world should be a guide to humanity. And furthermore, that the proper attitude of our species towards nature should be one of reverence."

More applause. *And now, to humility.*

"It is not only our duty, but also our unique privilege as the self-appointed stewards of the Earth, to protect this world that has sheltered and nurtured us. It warms my heart to know that you, my honoured guests, feel the same way — and it is my own privilege to be amongst you tonight."

A sea of smiles. *Like domesticated beasts, conditioned to respond.*

"I trust that the symbolism of this jewel of Barcelona was not too heavy-handed. Obtaining its use for this evening was certainly not cheap."

A smile of his own, and a chorus of polite laughter from the crowd.

Then flattery.

"You are not here because of your wealth, my friends.

What this world requires of you is what has really brought you here tonight: your vision. Your principles, your determination, and your desire to effect positive change for your fellow human beings. Even for those who would look upon your status with envy or ill will, for they require your help most of all. It is here, amongst your peers who have reached the pinnacle of what our civilisation has made possible, that we can take a moment to consider a word that many of you will not often see: debt."

Heads nodding. A few shifts in posture. Some fading smiles. *Let them anticipate the key-change before they hear it, to heighten its impact when it comes.*

"You have found great success and privilege. You have earned it. You have been rewarded. Your fellow men and women look up to you, no matter what they might sometimes say. You have nothing more to prove."

He took a measured breath, as if to steady himself from a swell of emotion which, while genuine, had long ago become so familiar as to fade into the background.

"But now, all that you have worked for is in grave danger."

The images flashing past on the screen mounted behind the stage were like an assault. One after another, relentless and horrifying. Miwa's voice, with its even tone and quiet conviction, counterpointed the disturbing visuals.

"Chernobyl. Bhopal. The Kuwaiti oil fires."

The screen showed the 2,600 square kilometre exclusion zone in Ukraine, and the abandoned city of Pripyat. The face of a young victim of the methyl isocyanate gas release in India. Oil fields and entire lakes burning at the tip of the Persian Gulf.

"The Aral Sea of a thousand islands, which is now a desert."

Ships, rusted and faded by the merciless sun, standing aground in yellowed scrub, like something from post-apocalyptic science fiction.

"The *Exxon Valdez*, and of course *Deepwater Horizon*."

Half a million barrels of crude oil spilled into the Gulf of Alaska. Almost five million barrels spewed into the Gulf of Mexico, and a fireball visible from forty miles away.

"And my own country's Minamata, and Tokaimura, and Fukushima Daiichi."

Methylmercury poisoning from an industrial plant. Improperly mixed uranium solution and the effects of the resulting radiation release. And three nuclear meltdowns after a tsunami disabled the emergency generators which powered reactor-cooling pumps.

There were burned faces, twisted forms, and bodies covered in sheets. Unseeing eyes, including those that had witnessed only a handful of years since birth. Poisoned marine life and seabirds. A carnival of horrors that had many of the wealthy and powerful people in the basilica lowering their drinks away from noticeably paler faces.

"Polar ice is melting at an unprecedented rate," Miwa

continued. "Ocean levels are rising. Extreme weather phenomena are on the increase, and spreading. Respiratory disease is endemic in entire cities where pollution levels exceed our capacity for measurement."

He paused for a moment as he surveyed his audience.

"Forest and brush fires burn out of control. Temperatures soar, annually setting new records within recorded human history. Droughts ravage agricultural land, bringing food insecurity, population migration, political instability, disease, and starvation. For humankind, the future looks dark. Indeed, to prevent climate change, it is already too late."

Another pause. *Having broken them down with fear, now they will eagerly accept any morsel of hope.*

"But the story of our species is one of survival," he said. "It is a story of enlightenment conquering irrationality, however slow the process may be. The human intellect, properly applied, creates wonders almost daily. We have improved our own lives immeasurably, even in the last handful of decades. Our knowledge stretches further with every passing year. We know now, more than ever, how special — how rare — our world is. And we know that it must be protected, not just for our own survival, but for that of millions of other species with whom we share our home."

The mood of the audience began to shift, as it always did at this point in the presentation, and the images on the screen changed correspondingly. There were seabirds in flight now; the majestic animals of the

Serengeti; exotic deep-ocean life; primates in a rain forest; a little girl running across a field of green grass with her Labrador puppy close at her heels; a spider's web glistening with dew; a sunrise reflected a thousand times in the glass sides of closely-packed skyscrapers.

"The task ahead is difficult, and extensive, but it is not impossible. We must moderate our energy usage, reduce greenhouse-gas emissions, adopt environmentally safe and sustainable energy sources, pioneer new recycling methods and technologies, and radically alter our global food provision, transport, manufacturing, and settlement habits. Education, investment, and action. Political lobbying and leverage. A holistic and active approach to heeding the message that Earth is unequivocally sending us. The apathy must end now. This planet is not going anywhere, but humanity may, unless we find a new respect for our cradle of life."

The crowd broke into applause. Miwa allowed it to continue for a few seconds before raising a hand to once again request silence.

"The real question for tonight is that of responsibility. It is one of the fundamental truths of existence that those with vision must often bear the burdens of being saviours to those without. A few great men and women who can see further, and who understand the larger context of our lives, and our ecosystem. Allies of both this world and its inhabitants, who are willing to *act* in order that we can all be saved."

Miwa stepped forward now, bypassing the lectern to

stand at the front edge of the stage, mere metres from the nearest of his assembled guests. He spread his hands, palms upwards and tilted slightly towards the rapt audience.

"My friends, I believe that those people of vision are in this room tonight. Thank you."

This time, the applause was thunderous.

Another evening, and another city, but always the same, Miwa thought, bowing humbly before the crowd. After a few seconds, he straightened up again, surveying the throng before him.

All I ask for is your money, he thought, before beginning to move down the steps to join them. *The responsibility will be mine alone.*

Chapter 20

"As you probably heard, Larry, his speech is over now," Greenwood said. "Stay alert. We'll make the approach when possible." She heard a soft click in her earpiece as Dowling disabled the mute function of his own headset's microphone.

"*Acknowledged, chief,*" came his voice over the communications channel. "*We're ready if you need us.*"

Miwa was surrounded by admirers after his presentation, and Greenwood knew it would take a little while for the crowd to disperse. At the foot of the stairs he'd made an impassioned plea for generosity, pointing out the various staff members placed throughout the basilica with handheld terminals for transacting donations. Anonymity or publicity were available at the donor's discretion, and tax relief was assured. From Greenwood's vantage point, every person who had encountered one of the relevant staff had eagerly produced a bank card.

"I could probably chip in fifty Euros, if it's going to save the world like he said," Aldridge remarked, and Greenwood threw a quick glance in his direction.

"I've been authorised to make a donation, if it proves tactically advantageous," she said. "You can hang onto your wallet."

"I'm not even going to ask how much walking-around money you've got to play with," he replied, and she nodded as if to confirm the wisdom of his decision.

"I'm hoping it won't be necessary. We'll hang back for a few minutes, then start to make our way over there. When there's an opportunity to speak to him, we'll very politely introduce ourselves."

"And bring up some uncomfortable topics?"

"Exactly," she replied. "Then we get him somewhere quiet, and make it clear he's coming with us."

"He might not be happy about that," Aldridge said casually, with a vague smirk on his face.

"Nobody ever is," Greenwood replied. "He'll just have to live with it."

Her eyes followed the two bodyguards or mercenaries who had accompanied Miwa into Sagrada Família. They remained near the stage, but always within ten feet of their employer. Greenwood understood the positioning; they could obtain a higher vantage point at a moment's notice, while still being only two quick strides from the man himself. She had no doubt that they'd been ordered not to stay glued to his sides, for the sake of the comfort of his many patrons.

Miwa handled them with the practised manner of someone long accustomed to working a room. Graciousness and poise, gratitude and humility, and what looked like a brief and customised exhortation to aid the cause, before giving a firm handshake and then moving onwards. Everyone got their moment with him, and the next person they each encountered was one of his mobile cashiers, followed by a waiter bearing sustenance. It was all very elegantly done.

Greenwood and Aldridge watched the proceedings for almost ten minutes, occasionally moving closer to their quarry. When the crowd around Miwa eventually began to thin, the older gentleman who had arrived with him used the opening to approach his employer, and leaned in to discreetly say a few brief words. Miwa nodded.

"That's our cue," Greenwood said, tapping Aldridge on the elbow for good measure. "Stay beside me."

"Just try and stop me," he replied, already moving to take her drink and deposit both glasses on a narrow table nearby apparently set up for that purpose. They moved easily through the dispersing crowd, their approach covered by the buzz of animated conversation and laughter from all around.

Relieving stress after being confronted with difficult information, she thought. It was a normal human response. The whole structure of the event was designed to manipulate that reaction to maximise the amount of money taken. She had no particular problem with it as long as the funds did indeed go towards good causes — but she suspected that most of the people here might be surprised and dismayed to learn about some of their host's other special interests.

"Making approach now," Greenwood said under her breath, and she immediately heard a confirmation from Dowling in her earpiece.

"*Understood.*"

She and Aldridge were within a few metres now. Greenwood took a breath, and smiled widely.

"Mr. Miwa! What a wonderful speech."

The man of the hour turned towards her, already wearing the same gracious smile she'd witnessed a dozen times in as many minutes.

"I am grateful for your kind words, madam," he replied smoothly, extending a hand. "Tsutomu Miwa."

"Claire Morton-Fellowes," she said, shaking his hand enthusiastically. "And allow me to introduce my colleague, Alisdair Lewis."

"Pleasure to meet you," Aldridge said, shaking Miwa's hand in turn.

"The pleasure is assuredly mine," Miwa replied. "Thank you both for being here tonight. It is one of the great privileges of my life to meet like-minded people."

"We feel the same way," Greenwood replied. "And we're eager to support your work in any way we can. In fact, I think we may already be involved in similar areas."

"Is that so?" Miwa asked politely, folding his hands in front of him.

"Indeed. I believe we've even met with some of your own colleagues regarding ventures in Scandinavia. I wonder if you might recall."

Miwa bowed his head apologetically. "I am fortunate that my business interests have become quite widespread in recent years. Could you be more specific?"

Greenwood smiled again, noticing that the older man who had been standing a short distance away now closed the distance to stand beside Miwa. She felt more than saw Aldridge's posture shift beside her, and she gave the older man a quick glance. His face was stern, and she knew immediately that he'd recognised her, even if Miwa himself hadn't yet.

"Oh, of course; naturally," she said, focusing her attention on Miwa once more. "I'm sorry. You're a very busy man. We were in Bergen on business just recently, and I understand that some of your men used the same car rental agency. And then I think we might all have been at the same heliport in Ålesund the following day. A remarkable coincidence, don't you think?"

She saw the exact moment that Miwa understood. His facial expression didn't change at all, but his eyes did. Beside him, the older man gave a single glance to the other two at the stage front, and they were at Miwa's side in a few seconds.

"Remarkable indeed, madam," Miwa said. "I do hope that your business was concluded to your satisfaction."

"It was a productive trip," Aldridge said, drawing the attention of all four men standing opposite him. "We even had time for a swim. Tell me, Mr. Miwa, do you happen to have any current operations in the Norwegian Sea?"

"Not at the moment, Mr. Lewis," Miwa replied, his sharp eyes contrasting with the continued mellowness of his voice. "Now, if you will excuse me, I have a number of people to see, and limited time."

He fixed his eyes upon Greenwood for a moment, and then began to turn to leave. He stopped in place when she spoke in a hushed voice.

"I know what it's like to be on a tight schedule, Mr. Miwa. And I also know about *CHRONOS*."

Miwa's face flickered with momentary surprise and alarm, then he schooled his expression once more. He looked from Greenwood to Aldridge and back again. After several seconds, he spoke. "May I ask who I'm actually speaking to?"

"We represent the European Defence Agency," Greenwood replied. "This is an official matter, you're within our jurisdiction, and I'm feeling courteous enough to be interested in your side of the story."

The two bodyguards didn't move so much as a muscle, and nor did the older man Miwa had arrived with.

Miwa nodded. "Perhaps we could discuss this matter privately," he said, glancing briefly at his elderly companion.

"My thoughts exactly," Greenwood replied.

The older man immediately gestured towards a grey set of double doors on the far wall, set below an elaborate balcony that looked like the front of a building. The two mercenaries stepped slightly closer to Greenwood and Aldridge, making it clear that they should move in that direction.

"Shall we?" Aldridge asked, but his gaze was fixed on the nearer of the two serious-looking men. His own expression was one of quiet confidence, underlaid with threat.

Greenwood nodded, adjusting her purse on her shoulder, then they began walking. Miwa and the older man were slightly ahead, and the two other men flanked the group, directing other guests out of the way. At one point, a woman approached with a smile on her face, clearly intent on talking to Miwa, but the older man informed her that he had an important matter to attend to, and would return shortly to speak with her.

"I appreciate your willingness to avoid creating a scene," Miwa said to Greenwood, after the female guest had moved away. "I will of course wish to have my legal counsel present for our discussion."

Greenwood's instincts raised a note of warning at his remark. *You have no intention of talking to us. You're stalling until we're out of sight of your crowd of benefactors.*

As if to confirm the thought, she caught a brief movement from the corner of her eye: the shorter of the two bodyguards flicked open the button of his suit jacket. She glanced in the opposite direction, making eye contact with Aldridge. He blinked at her, and she knew he'd seen it too.

The older man quickened his pace and reached the doors ahead, opening the righthand one. There was a small atrium beyond, with a spiral staircase curving upwards on the right. There was also a conventional set of steps leading down below ground level.

When they were almost at the threshold, one of Greenwood's heels seemed to skid a few inches on the smooth surface, causing her to lose her balance just enough for her purse strap to slip from her shoulder, depositing the small bag on the floor beside her. She steadied herself with a sigh of irritation.

Both of Miwa's bodyguards twitched in momentary alarm, but the movement had looked completely natural and accidental. Greenwood simply raised an eyebrow at them, causing the shorter of the two to give a sneering grin.

Because of the distraction, no-one noticed the quick and fluid motion of Aldridge's right hand as he reached inside his own suit jacket, made an adjustment, and then resumed his prior posture, all in the space of a couple of seconds.

Greenwood extended her arm down towards the dropped purse, bending slightly at the knees.

"I should have worn different shoes," she said.

Outside the basilica and diagonally across the Carrer de la Marina, a raven-haired woman sprang from a plastic chair on the pavement outside a tapas bar and ran towards the Nativity façade, weaving through the slow traffic effortlessly.

Not far to the south, a greyish-blue Bentley Continental Flying Spur hurtled from the mouth of a side street, its twelve-cylinder engine growling.

Greenwood's hand was only a few centimetres from her purse when it abruptly changed course, reached into the split that ran up the skirt of her dress on the right side, and expertly withdrew a compact pistol from the holster on her inner left thigh. She straightened up and spun around in an instant, in time to see Miwa's taller bodyguard's eyes widen.

She was peripherally aware of three things. Aldridge had drawn his pistol in the same instant. The taller bodyguard, instead of going for his own weapon as his colleague now was, dived towards Miwa. And the older man, somehow much nearer than he'd been a moment ago, was holding a cruel-looking knife.

In the stone-lined entryway to the atrium, below the overhanging balcony and opening out into the vast pillared space of the Sagrada Família itself, the first gunshot sounded like cannonfire.

Venter reacted without thinking, knocking Miwa to the ground with his own body and pinning him there for a moment, one hand pressing into his employer's chest to keep him down, and the other reaching for his own pistol. There was barely time to disable the safety before he heard the flat, echoing report of a shot being fired.

The sound was deafening.

There was a moment of perfect stillness, and then everything happened at once.

Screams, from back over towards the nave. Shouts, and running footsteps. Then a second gunshot, and this one came from a short distance away. He heard Reddy curse in Afrikaans, and he risked a half-turn to assess the situation.

The man and woman they'd been escorting out of the event were no longer visible. Reddy had taken a firing position behind the limited cover provided by a short pillar supporting one of the arches of the balcony's underside. His suit had a gash ripped through it along his right bicep, and blood was visible. His grip on his weapon looked normal, though there was perspiration on his brow. It looked like he'd been either quick or lucky, and suffered only a flesh wound.

The first gunshot was Reddy's, Venter thought. *The woman has six bullets left, or five if she was the one who returned fire.*

He could see Tien standing implacably in the middle of the entranceway, right out in the open. He had some kind of knife balanced in his fingers, and was looking off towards the nearest major column of the nave proper. Venter would bet a month's pay that it was where the man and woman had taken cover. Most people would think the old man was crazy, but Venter knew single-minded loyalty when he saw it. He doubted that the man or woman would fire on someone who didn't have a gun, so right now Tien was a voluntary human shield for Miwa.

Good enough, Venter thought. And if Tien was wrong and the others were willing to shoot through him, Venter really didn't care very much at all.

Without wasting another moment, he rocked back from his knees and into a crouch, then grabbed fistfuls of the front of Miwa's suit, hauling him up and then spinning him around.

"Move," Venter said, pushing his boss hard towards the atrium. Miwa stumbled for a moment and then found his footing, propelling himself rapidly forward. "Then left," Venter called after him, seeing Miwa swerve immediately and disappear from view.

Venter spun around, exchanging a look with Reddy. He was angry now, and his meaning was clear.

Let's flush them out.

"You never answered me about whether your lipstick is a hand grenade," Aldridge said, his back pressed to the broad column, with Greenwood at his side.

"Afraid not," she replied. "And this is hardly the place for explosives."

"We've got a lot of company coming," Aldridge said, seeing several security personnel cautiously making their way from the nave towards them. Some were from the venue, but there were also a few he recognised as the private staff of some of the other guests. The situation could get very messy, very quickly.

"Got to contain this," Greenwood said. "And we need to catch up with Miwa. There might be another exit from where he ran off to."

Suddenly, one of Miwa's own two bodyguards came into view, running at forty-five degrees from his previous position to get a better vantage point on their hiding place, and Greenwood barely had time to duck before a puff of dust blew out of the column just a few inches from her head. She twisted into a half-crouch and snapped off a return shot, aiming low, but her attacker had already moved out of her sight line. It was the sneering man.

At almost the same moment, an over-zealous member of someone's personal security staff ran towards the fray, obviously intent on direct intervention to keep his employer safe. Miwa's other bodyguard, still guarding the atrium, gave a look of disgust before putting a bullet in the man's forehead from fifty metres away. Now the screams of the guests resumed in earnest.

Aldridge could see that both primary sets of doors to the basilica had been pushed partially open, and people were streaming out into the night, practically climbing over each other to escape.

Good, he thought.

A moment later, he heard a shout from down towards the opposite end of the nave, in a voice he recognised well.

"*¡Policía!*"

It was Ramos, her weapon already drawn and her

Barcelona police credentials clipped to her belt, shouldering her way through the tide of guests.

"Larry, where are you?" Greenwood said, and as usual the response came immediately.

"Just arrived outside now. Bit of a circus here."

"Stay there. Miwa might use a different exit. Help where you can. Alicia has the Nativity entrance covered."

"Got it, chief. We'll keep an eye out for him."

"The real police will be here in the next few minutes," Aldridge said, with tension evident in his voice. "We don't have a lot of time."

Greenwood bit her lower lip, assessing the situation. "Alright. We need a clear approach. Circle round and get the drop on the guy trying to flank us. I'll cover you."

"Can do," Aldridge said, feeling the not unpleasant buzz of adrenalin through his system. They weren't wearing bulletproof vests because of their attire, and their weapons were small calibre to ease concealment. "I almost forgot: I brought you a gift."

At her confused and irritated glance, he reached into his inside jacket pocket and retrieved one of the two spare ammunition magazines he was carrying, dropping it into her palm.

"Just what I wanted," she replied. "No bloody pockets on this dress."

"Don't I know it," he replied, then he dashed off towards the cover of an adjacent freestanding bar area without giving her the chance to reply. He heard Greenwood fire a covering shot almost as soon as he was in motion.

It was answered by another shot barely two seconds later, allowing both of them to pinpoint the bodyguard's location. He was only about eight metres from Aldridge's position, behind a metal-sided concierge station where guests could make donations privately via electronic funds transfer if they so desired.

"Sorry about the bumpy ride the other day, sweetheart," the sneering man called out. "Helicopters can be temperamental things."

Aldridge could readily imagine how Greenwood's eyes must have narrowed at the remark. *So it's the same two from Ålesund,* he thought. *And probably from Bergen.*

The man popped his head out to take another shot in Greenwood's direction, and Aldridge could hear the impact of the bullet against stone.

"I hope your friend is a little more effective than you are," Greenwood called back, snapping off three more shots at one-second intervals. Each struck metal sheeting.

Thank you, Captain, Aldridge thought, in motion before the sound of the first shot had dissipated. He reached the concierge station in silence, crouching on the opposite side, less than half a metre from the other man. He could hear his breathing, and knew he'd rise to aim again momentarily. Aldridge took a measured breath through his nose, and as soon as he heard the squeak of leather shoes, he forced down his own instincts and lunged upwards.

The man barely had time to bring his pistol to bear on Greenwood's hiding place before Aldridge's face appeared above him, and he didn't even see the blur of his arm before everything went dark.

"He'll feel that in the morning," Aldridge said, quickly disarming the unconscious man. The angry red imprint from the butt of Aldridge's pistol stood out vividly across his left cheek and the side of his forehead.

Greenwood quickly joined him, evading a bullet from the other of Miwa's men. Reaching cover, she quickly looked out and saw the second bodyguard exchange a look with the older man and then turn and run through the doorway into the atrium, going in the same direction Miwa had. Ramos was now closing in on the older man, who still stood out in the open, barring her way.

"Got to be a side entrance," Aldridge said, as Greenwood reloaded her weapon. "Larry, Goose: Miwa and one armed guard, possible exit on south-west corner. The same guy from Norway. Six feet, well built, black dinner jacket and bowtie, brown hair."

"*On our way,*" came Goose's voice over the intercom, his breathing indicating that he was running.

"We'll follow them out," Greenwood said. "Be careful in case they're still inside. Let Ramos deal with the old man."

Aldridge nodded. "I've got a cable tie for this one," he said, tilting his head towards the downed man in front of them, but Greenwood shook her head.

He watched as Greenwood reached up to grasp her right earring and twisted the gold teardrop portion. It came off in her hand, leaving the upper part of the earring untouched. She bent down and slid her hand into the man's jacket, pushing the tiny object deep into the inside breast pocket.

"Right," she said. "Alicia, bring the old man in. Let this one go. Aldridge, let's move."

They both ran diagonally across the open area leading to the doorway beneath the balcony, and disappeared inside without looking back.

Once Greenwood and Aldridge had vanished into the atrium beyond, Ramos slowly advanced on the older man.

"I could choose any one of about ten things to arrest you for," she said. "Don't make this difficult."

The man's heavily lined eyes didn't blink, but there was the faintest trace of a smile on his lips. He had the knife balanced in his right hand, and his arm was completely steady.

"You already know that I will tell you nothing," he said. His voice was warm, and almost jovial, as if they were two long-lost friends meeting by chance. Ramos gave a one-shouldered shrug.

"We'll see," she replied. "Put down the knife. I'd prefer to do this peacefully."

"I regretfully cannot comply," he replied, subtly adjusting his footing. His tricep now bore most of the weight of the knife, and was extended to about two-thirds of its range of movement. He could snap his arm forwards and send the knife hurtling through the air in an instant.

Ramos's heart rate increased by a notch, and she consciously controlled her breathing. She knew that she could readily incapacitate or kill him without trouble, but she didn't want to.

"Your stance is good," she said. "You've been practising for years. The knife is beautiful. If I'm not mistaken, it's older than you are."

The man gave a small nod of both confirmation and respect. "It has served others before me. I desire this no more than you do."

"I believe you," Ramos replied. "But that doesn't help us unless you drop the weapon."

The man only scrutinised her silently.

You're devoted to your master, she thought. It was a noble thing, but there was limited time, and she didn't have the luxury of trying to reason with him at length.

Slowly, she lowered her pistol, and then holstered it inside her jacket.

"A gesture of good faith," she said, and the man once again nodded. Ramos kept her muscles loose, and lowered her gaze just a couple of inches, from his eyes to his mouth. It would scarcely be noticeable to her opponent at the distance they were from each other, but it provided a small but crucial improvement in her focus on his stance.

Several seconds passed, and then the man spoke again.

"You are a woman of honour," he said. "And so I must apologise."

His arm whipped forward and the knife whispered through the air in the blink of an eye, but Ramos was ready. She let her left knee buckle while pushing from the ball of her right foot, twisting through the air as she pivoted one leg behind her and ended up in a crouch, several feet to the left of where the knife had passed straight through the empty air where her chest had been. She immediately exploded from the ground and ran at the older man.

His expression still didn't change, even as he rebalanced his weight in a classic loose martial arts pose, his front shoulder low and his gaze locked on her as she approached. A lifetime of training showed in every inch of his stance and attitude, but that lifetime had been a few years too long. The confrontation was over in moments.

The old man moved with surprising speed and grace, his fist looming in Ramos's peripheral vision, but she was too fast for him. She spun easily out of reach, continuing around to catch his upper arm and use it as leverage to pull him forwards and off-balance, allowing her to drive a knee into his solar plexus. To his credit, he barely made a sound, and immediately lashed out with the heel of his hand. She anticipated the move and stepped just out of range. A sharp downwards blow with her elbow to the base of his skull ended the fight.

Ramos caught his collar as he fell forward, pulling him back up and then laying him down gently. She checked his pulse and respiration, then rolled him onto his front, pulled a plastic tie from her jacket pocket and cinched his hands behind his back, then turned him onto his side.

"My target is down and cuffed," she said, aware of increasing clamour at the far end of the nave. "I could use some help transporting him."

"*Roger that,*" came Dowling's voice in her ear. "*But can it wait a minute? We're a little busy.*"

Ramos reached down to grab the older man and at least drag him out of sight. She was about to ask Dowling if perhaps he was the one who needed help, but she froze when she heard the unmistakeable sound of another gunshot over the intercom.

Venter put a bullet through the exterior door's lock mechanism, then kicked the handle assembly hard enough to make it fall to the floor, the door bouncing back from its stops in the frame and opening inwards. He stuck his head out and looked left and right, and then nodded to his employer.

Miwa's thoughts were a blur.

The European Defence Agency knows about the Bell.

The only logical conclusion was that Magnusson's discontent had finally evolved into treachery, due to both his burden of guilt and the new outrage of the helicopter pilot's death.

Understandable, he thought. *I sympathise.*

He followed Venter's directions and jogged easily along the side of the enormous building. The perimeter fence which bordered the Carrer de Sardenya was high and not suitable for climbing, but there was a gate near-by. Ordinarily there would have been a security guard posted at it, but with the commotion, the outpouring of guests, and the approaching police sirens, it was deserted.

Beyond, cars were lined up all along the road, most of them presumably belonging to Miwa's guests for the evening. He saw three uniformed valets standing nervously together, and with Venter at his side, he ran directly towards him.

One of the young men turned at the sound of their approach, and his face immediately paled when he saw Venter's handgun.

"Necesitamos un auto," Miwa said, pointing towards the nearest vehicle, a beautiful Maserati Quattroporte GTS GranLusso in alpine white.

The young man hesitated for only a moment before simply nodding, and with an unsteady hand he reached into the nearby portable lockbox and took out a set of keys, which he carefully gave to Miwa before retreating with his hands raised.

Miwa rounded the vehicle, going for the driver's door, and he waved Venter towards the passenger side.

"In case of pursuit," he said.

They both got in, and a moment later the big V8 engine snarled to life, and the car leapt away from the kerb.

Chapter 21

Greenwood and Aldridge burst from the side door of Sagrada Família just in time to see the Maserati leaving.

"Damn it," Greenwood snapped, breaking into a run immediately. Aldridge was close behind, and they reached the cluster of valets in moments. One of the three young men still had his hands raised in surrender, drawing a questioning look from Aldridge.

"Relax," he said. "You're safe now." He holstered his pistol to emphasise the point, but the valets were still silent, apparently frozen in shock.

"*Estás a salvo*," Greenwood said, repeating Aldridge's assertion in Spanish. She kept her own pistol at her side as she glanced quickly around in frustration, then she fixed her gaze on the valets again. She snapped her fingers in the air a few inches from the nose of the nearest young man, and he flinched. When she spoke, her voice was louder and more commanding than before.

"¡Escúchame! ¿Cuál es el coche más rápido aquí?"

The man blinked, looking lost for a moment, then he shrugged and pointed down the row of vehicles towards a sleek black machine that glistened in the night-time lights of the city. Greenwood turned her head to look, and then her eyes lit up.

"Now that'll do nicely," she said, before turning to the valet once more. *"Las llaves. Ahora."*

She had barely finished speaking when a set of keys was pressed into her hand. She nodded in thanks, and she and Aldridge both broke into a run, reaching the car in seconds. Aldridge's eyebrows shot up as he recognised the distinctive winged badge on the front lip of the bodywork, and the two words contained within.

"This evening keeps getting more and more James Bond," he said.

"Get in," Greenwood replied, but Aldridge grabbed her forearm before she could move.

"You know how this is going to go," he said. "I'm certified for urban pursuit, but we both know you're the better marksman. Or woman. Now do you want to drive, or do you want to shoot?"

She gritted her teeth for a moment, then grudgingly pushed the keys into his hand. "Fine," she said. "But if you scratch the bodywork, it's coming out of your lab budget."

Aldridge grinned, running around to the drivers side, and they both got in. He slid the keys into his trouser pocket, knowing the keyless entry and start system would do its job, and pressed the starter button beside the steering wheel. The engine gave a throaty growl and the dashboard illuminated automatically.

"Try not to put us into the side of a bus," Greenwood said, fastening her seatbelt as Aldridge did the same.

"Oh ye of little faith," Aldridge said, then he put the car in gear, depressed the accelerator, and they hurtled away from the line of parked cars.

"They took a right up ahead," Greenwood said, and he nodded, making the turn with ease before he poured on more speed. The vehicle handled like a dream.

"Is this a bad time to tell you I've got three penalty points on my UK driving license for—"

"Failing to obey a traffic signal, yes; I know about that," Greenwood replied as she kicked off her heels into the footwell and reloaded her gun. "I had the endorsement cancelled when you joined up. Your record is spotless. But the night is young."

Aldridge huffed out a laugh, twitching the car into the oncoming lane to overtake a delivery van before pulling back in and immediately blowing straight through an amber light.

"Pretend you didn't see that," he said, pouring on more speed as he heard a chorus of honks from the traffic behind him. "You think they can outrun us?"

"In an ideal flat race, not a chance. They're in some kind of fancy Maserati. This is an Aston Martin DBS Superleggera. I didn't think this model was even out yet."

"Rich people," Aldridge said, grimacing as he threaded the car through a narrow gap between an off-duty ambulance and a tiny sub-compact electric vehicle, to the significant alarm of both vehicles' drivers.

"But it's *not* a flat race, and we're in a major city," Greenwood said, her eyes constantly scanning the road ahead. "Larry, are you still with me?"

"Right here, chief. I take it Miwa got away, then?"

"We're in pursuit. Take Goose and get inside via the side door. Help Alicia get the old man out and away from the scene. I want some answers from him. And pick up my purse."

Aldridge heard the Welshman chuckle.

"Roger that."

"There they are," Aldridge said. Greenwood spotted the white vehicle immediately, seeing that it had been caught at a major junction while several buses were crossing the perpendicular street. The traffic was clearing now, and sure enough the Maserati roared out onto the crosshatching while the light was still at red.

Aldridge urged the Aston Martin forward even faster, his hands tightening on the wheel as he hoped there would be another gap in the flow of vehicles ahead. They weren't far behind now, and as they sailed across the junction without incident, he could see the moment when their quarry became aware of their pursuit.

The Maserati was approaching an area of construction at the side of the street, with a coned-off area containing several men in high-visibility jackets, one with a pneumatic drill. The lanes had been narrowed to accommo-date the work, and the opposite side of the street was occupied by yet another city bus. As Aldridge watched, Miwa's vehicle mounted the pavement to shoot past the construction area on the pedestrian side, prompting immediate shouts of alarm from the workers. Thankful-ly there were no pedestrians there, and Aldridge twisted the wheel to follow them.

Reaching the road surface again, the Maserati made a hard, screeching turn onto a wider avenue that cut diagonally through the city going north-east, with the Aston Martin right on its tail. Terraced houses and the occasional semi-hidden square blurred past, dozens of heads turning to mark the passage of the two powerful vehicles.

"They're going to kill someone if they keep going," Greenwood said, unfastening her seatbelt as the dash-board chimed in protest, and she pressed the control to wind down the passenger-side window. She sat forward and refastened the belt behind her, across the seat back, then half-turned to wind her left arm through it and grip the cross-strap. She curled her legs up under her to crouch sideways facing the driver's side, then leaned backwards and extended her arm, head, and shoulders out of the window.

Her first shot shattered the Maserati's nearside rear light assembly, and the car swerved to the left before its driver regained control. Almost immediately, she saw the barrel of a pistol appear out of its own passenger-side window, and she pulled her head down as a bullet ripped through the air just above her.

Aldridge swerved the Aston Martin to the left, straddling lanes, in an attempt to move Greenwood out of sight of the gunman in front of them, but the Maserati matched the move a moment later.

Then let's try something else, he thought, accelerating harder. The car ate up the road, easily gaining on the Maserati, and then he quickly pulled to the right, giving Greenwood a clear view of their target's rear left tyre. She took the shot, but Miwa had the presence of mind to swerve in the opposite direction, and the bullet ricocheted uselessly off the tarmac a third of a metre to the side of the wheel.

"Well played," Aldridge muttered to himself.

The Maserati whipped across another junction, this time narrowly avoiding an open-topped truck and several mopeds. Aldridge glanced in his rear-view mirror and saw blue lights several blocks behind, but he couldn't hear the sirens yet. He hoped the Barcelona police were setting up a roadblock somewhere ahead, but he had his doubts; the situation had developed too quickly, and they would have lost precious time in assessing what happened back at the basilica.

His brow creased into a frown as he read the road ahead. Signs indicated that they would soon reach an on-ramp for the primary route north into the region of wildlife parks that led to Andorra, the Pyrenees, and France. According to Greenwood, there was no way the

Maserati could outrun them, so it was likely that Miwa would bypass that road and instead loop east, which meant staying in the metropolitan area with all its corresponding dangers during a high-speed pursuit.

The Maserati juked to the left, running an oncoming postal van off the road, and Miwa's bodyguard fired at Greenwood again. Aldridge steered in the opposite direction, and through the open window he could hear the sound of something at the side of the street being blown apart.

Got to end this, he thought. *Ideally before somebody dies.*

The buildings were a blur on either side. Aldridge pressed the accelerator harder, feeling the finely tuned vehicle respond immediately. The growl of the engine filled the interior.

"Greenwood?" he said, raising his voice so she could hear him with her upper body leaning out the passenger-side window. He was trying for nonchalance, but the note of tension in his voice was unmistakeable. The Maserati loomed ahead of them, despite its best efforts to get away.

"What?" Greenwood shouted back. "And that's Captain to you!" Another bullet zipped over the roof, missing the bodywork by what seemed like barely an inch, and Greenwood ducked down. They were less than three car-lengths behind now. The rear-view mirror was filled with pursuing blue lights.

"I just want you to know that I've had a lovely evening—" Aldridge twisted the wheel abruptly to the left, narrowly avoiding a slow-moving minivan as it changed lane "—and I hope we can do this again sometime."

He risked a quick glance in her direction, and was gratified to see the grin on her face as she carefully took aim at the rear right tyre of the car ahead, her hair whipping backwards in the breeze, and pulled the trigger.

The bullet narrowly missed the edge of the tyre and instead found the hub of the alloy wheel, splitting one of the caps into several jagged pieces. They skittered across the road as the Maserati made a screeching left turn in front of two fire trucks en route to a call, adding the blast of horns to their emergency sirens.

There was nowhere for the Aston to go. The roadway to the left was blocked by the fire trucks, and there was no room to go around. Aldridge regretfully stood on the brakes, and the car bit down onto the tarmac and came to a smooth halt without a hint of lateral movement. He slammed his hand onto the dashboard fairing as Greenwood drew back inside the window.

"They were lucky, that's all," she said. "Nothing else we could have done. We'll be seeing Miwa again soon."

"I'm going to ask him for a refund of our entry donation for the evening," Aldridge replied. "And maybe punch him in the face."

It was only a few seconds later that the two leading police cars skidded to a halt, their occupants immediately leaping out and drawing their weapons.

"I love dealing with local police," Greenwood sighed,

dropping the pistol to the floor and putting her hands flat on the dashboard, as Aldridge first rolled his window down, then switched the engine off and moved his fingers to the top of the steering wheel.

A very angry-looking police woman approached the driver's side door with her service pistol pointing squarely at Aldridge's chest. He smiled apologetically at her.

"I've just realised the speed limit is in *kilometres* here," he said.

Chapter 22

Miwa and Venter arrived at the small airfield on the edge of the Barcelona-El Prat complex within twenty minutes of outrunning their pursuers, keeping to a less conspicuous speed and driving style. Miwa assumed that most of the city's police would already have converged on Sagrada Família anyway, but it always paid to take precautions.

His aircraft and its pilot were waiting, and they were joined only minutes later by Reddy, with an angry-looking mark on the side of his face, and an even angrier expression on the rest of it.

"They took the old man," Reddy said. "I saw them carry him out. Unconscious, not dead."

Miwa paused. *Tien has been captured. But he will tell them nothing.*

He felt a pang of guilt for the plight of his oldest friend, but he knew there was no real danger. Tien would be interrogated according to the law, but nothing would be learned, and the authorities would charge him and process him appropriately. Miwa had significant legal and political resources, and this situation would easily be resolved in due course.

By then, they will have a great deal more to worry about.

"That bastard cold-cocked me," Reddy said through gritted teeth. "Next time I see him and that fucking woman—"

"Silence," Miwa interrupted. The look of rebellion on Reddy's face was momentary, before quickly being quashed by a sharp look from Venter.

"We will depart immediately," Miwa continued. "Make the necessary arrangements, and bring me a secure phone."

Venter nodded, giving Reddy a glance that clearly indicated he shouldn't say any more, and then all three men boarded the jet. Within minutes they began to taxi, and they were airborne before a further quarter of an hour had elapsed.

A satellite phone lay face-up on the mahogany trimmed table beside Miwa's reclining leather seat. He picked it up and held the 3 key for a moment, hearing a long string of tones being dialled. There was silence for five seconds, then a series of brief clicks, and a single ring before the call connected.

"Our timetable has altered," he said immediately, without waiting for the other party to speak. "Begin evacuating the facility immediately. Move the machine first. I want it in transit within the hour."

A pause, as he listened for a few moments.

"I am going on ahead. Bring it to me for final installation."

He pressed a button to terminate the call, and set the phone back down before glancing out of the window. They were passing through the cloud layer, but the lights of the city were still visible below. Miwa could hear some sounds from the jet's galley area, where he presumed that Reddy was applying ice to his injury, but he paid them no heed.

He was relieved.

After years of preparation and hard work, his plan was now in its final stages before execution. The presence of the European Defence Agency was, in a way, a welcome development. The situation was now simple, and the path ahead was clear. There need be no further contemplation, nor any delay. It was time to act, and that's exactly what he would do.

He had a single remaining responsibility before taking the Bell to its target. *The mountain base must be stripped of as much information and equipment as possible.*

Miwa now proceeded on the assumption that the base would be located and captured within the next twenty-four hours. It was the tactically sound assumption to make. The device would already be long gone, but there was a great deal of computer equipment, stored data, machinery, and printed matter pertaining to the project, to say nothing of the biological test subjects and the scientific staff. Transport of the removed items would also be awkward, having to be either via helicopter or down mountainside paths. Pre-emptively collapsing the structure via explosives wasn't an attractive course of action, as it would bring immediate scrutiny down upon them, and Miwa was keen to salvage as much of the research material as possible — but when the time came, he would not hesitate.

He knew that any information they might glean would be of limited use given the short time frame before he commenced his operation, but his adversaries had proven both resourceful and fortunate thus far. Once again, the next move was obvious, and he wouldn't allow the cry of his conscience to stand in the way; there was far too much at stake.

We will remove as much as we can, and then allow them to capture the deserted base, he thought. *And then, when they are secure in their victory, we will destroy our own former stronghold with them inside.*

It took a little too long to deal with the Barcelona police, but Greenwood and Aldridge were finally on their way back to Sagrada Família. Goose had made the wise decision to involve Wuyts as soon as he'd heard them being ordered out of the Aston Martin over the communications channel, and orders had quickly come down from above to allow them to leave. The police officers hadn't been happy about it, and Greenwood understood their frustration.

"For whatever it's worth, I'm sorry," Aldridge said, an expression of frustrated disappointment on his face as he navigated the late evening traffic, now only minutes away from the basilica which was certain to be swarming with police and journalists. Greenwood glanced around at him in confusion.

"About?"

"They got away," he replied. "Now we're losing time."

Greenwood returned her attention to the cityscape beyond the Aston's windows. "Not your fault, Aldridge, and we're hardly back to square one. We've got the old man, for a start—"

"Who isn't going to tell us anything, as you well know," Aldridge interjected, drawing another quick glance from her.

"—and Wuyts also said she's found something she'd like us to see."

Aldridge just grunted, clearly still mulling over the evening's events. Greenwood knew what he was thinking: that he'd failed in his duty, or had let people down, or that whatever would come to pass would now be his own fault. None of it was true, but she could clearly remember the voice in her own mind that said those things regularly about herself. Responsibility was a double-edged sword. The best way to handle the misplaced guilt was to push forward even harder.

"Listen," she said, "we've got about four hours to return this car, get to the airport, be briefed by Wuyts, and do whatever else we can think of to prepare for our next move."

"And then your earring wakes up," he replied, and she nodded.

"I know exactly how you're feeling right now; I really do," Greenwood continued. "But you did everything right, and we're further ahead than we were this morning. We're going to find out exactly what Miwa plans to do with that machine, and we're going to take it away from him before he can."

Now it was Aldridge's turn to nod. "Fair enough," he said.

"Besides," she added, "that was some pretty fancy driving. You're not up to Alicia's or Goose's level just yet, but you've come a hell of a long way in a few months. I'll be noting in my report that I was impressed."

Aldridge gave a tight-lipped grin as he manoeuvred the car through the final junction and turned away from the throng of gathered gawkers, photographers, news media, and emergency services at both of Sagrada Família's entrance façades. The police cordon predictably skirted the valet parking area, allowing the rich and powerful to leave quietly after their ordeal.

He found a space approximately where the car had originally been parked, and slid the Aston into it, then put the vehicle into reverse to bring it in more neatly. One tyre lightly bumped the kerb, and he sighed.

"But on second thought..." Greenwood said with

amusement in her voice and a glint in her eye, and Aldridge switched off the engine before twisting in his seat to face her.

"I'll have you know, Captain, that it's been a very stressful evening."

A little over thirty minutes later, they were seated on their own jet, hidden by the doors of a small hangar at Barcelona-El Prat. The aircraft was fully fuelled, and only needed a flight plan. Dowling, Ramos, and Goose were already there when Greenwood and Aldridge arrived, and the older man they'd arrested — whose name was apparently Tien — was already en route to Brussels under military guard. Everyone had already changed back into ordinary civilian clothing, though Greenwood hadn't yet removed her makeup. Wuyts's face appeared on the mid-sized flat panel display mounted above a shallow metal work-surface in the cabin.

"We have limited time," she said. *"I have troops from the Battlegroups standing by for immediate covert deployment, but I'd like to have an idea of what they'll be up against. You still have no information on whether the weapon can be defended against or neutralised?"*

Greenwood shook her head. "No, sir," she replied. "We're not even sure how he plans to use it, or where. It seems to kill people and leave almost nothing behind, without damaging structures or machinery. He could sell it for almost any price to virtually all the governments of the world."

"The spread of this technology must be prevented at any cost," Wuyts said. *"But whatever else he is, Miwa is a principled man. I doubt he'd just hand it off to some warlord, no matter how much money was involved."*

"What are you thinking, sir?" Greenwood shifted in her seat, gratefully accepting a paper cup of coffee that Dowling handed to her.

Wuyts paused for a moment, then cleared her throat. *"I have some disturbing news,"* she said. *"I assume you're all familiar with the annual Bilderberg meeting?"*

"It's a conference in a hotel in Oosterbeek," Goose replied. "Politicians, industry leaders, bankers. They're global capitalists and power-brokers."

"And according to some people on the internet, they want a unified world government," Aldridge added. Wuyts gave him a brief look, and tilted her head to the side ever so slightly in a gesture that Greenwood couldn't quite decipher.

"There are similar meetings everywhere, of course," Wuyts continued, *"but substantially more secret. I have attended a number of them. But I was unaware of a particular group which Miwa met with late last year. I was able to obtain footage secretly recorded at that meeting, and it raises a troubling possibility."*

"He mentioned the Bell?" Ramos asked, and Wuyts shook her head.

"No. I wouldn't expect him to. I've prepared a brief extract."

The image of Wuyts moved into a small inset rectangle in the lower right corner of the display, with the main portion being taken over by a low-resolution video that looked like it had been recorded from chest height. The rightmost quarter of the recording device's field of view was obscured by something, but it was easy to see that there was a large conference table, oval in shape and made of dark wood, with people around it. Whoever had made the recording was one of the attendees, and the narrow viewing angle meant that only one person was fully visible.

"That's Miwa," Dowling said.

The man looked the same as he had earlier today, albeit in a darker suit. There were some figures in the background, at the edges of the room, but they were indistinct. One of them might have been Tien, but Greenwood couldn't be entirely sure. In the recording, Miwa nodded, then he began to speak.

"I agree in principle, but I'm afraid that your perspective is limited by political concerns. The problem exists on three fronts, not two — and only one of which is currently intractable. You are deliberately overlooking an additional avenue of intervention because you find it unpalatable."

There was a moment of silence, and then a male voice spoke off-camera.

"And what is this third axis of our shared problem?"

Miwa steepled his fingers on the wooden surface in front of him. *"We have discussed climate change, which cannot be reversed by any known technological means or otherwise, though further damage could of course be avoided.*

There are some promising theories and experiments, but we are all aware that the next century will bring marked changes to our way of life. We have also spoken of impending resource shortages, which can potentially be mitigated somewhat by a number of means, though neither quickly nor completely."

He sat back again, allowing his hands to lift from the table, still together.

"A consumption problem requires three factors in a state of imbalance: the environment of consumption, the rate of consumption, ... and the number of consumers. The time has come to consider all these factors, and how they are interrelated."

The hidden male speaker began to voice an objection, but Miwa spoke over him.

"The duty of any single government is to ensure the survival, safety, and prosperity of its people. The duty of a civilisation, however, is to ensure its own continuity. Everyone in this room has seen our studies. These two goals have lamentably become incompatible. Only a fool would argue otherwise."

"We all know that, Miwa," the male voice said, *"but what would you have us do? No government would survive a deliberate policy of..."*

"The word itself is not painful to speak, Prime Minister," Miwa replied. *"Depopulation is the most profound sacrifice, but there are scenarios in which it is necessary. Our planet now finds itself facing such a scenario."*

Then a female voice spoke up from off-camera, with an accent that might have been Russian. *"The forecasts make it clear that resource shortages and the proliferation of extreme weather events will combine to do that work on our behalf."*

"*But too slowly, Madame President,*" Miwa said, turning his head to look at a different point across the table, still out of view of the recording. "*The gradualness of the process will guarantee the breakdown of social order at the national level, and of international cooperation, posing an existential threat to human civilisation.*"

"*So we should exterminate a percentage of our populace? Those dark days are lost to history.*" The male voice, angry now.

"*I abhor killing in all its forms,*" Miwa replied. "*As you said, no government would survive such a policy, making it non-viable for any nation. I believe in natural selection and the survival of the fittest, not mass murder — but I also believe that pragmatism must be the ultimate determinant.*"

"*Then we are back where we started,*" the female voice said. "*Even if this horror could be contemplated, there is no practical way to accomplish it while preserving some measure of public order, at least in the interim.*"

Miwa lowered his hands to the table once more, and he was silent for several long seconds. Then he looked in the direction of the female voice.

"*But what if there were?*"

Wuyts's face filled the screen again. The recording had cut off after Miwa's last question, leaving a gulf of silence and a chill in the air.

"My god," Greenwood said.

Wuyts pursed her lips as if in distaste, but she said nothing.

"To be clear," Aldridge said, "what we're talking about here is… a planned genocide. You think he's going to use the Bell to achieve a partial human depopulation — which it seems to be readily capable of — in the name of ecological conservation."

"At this point, I believe it has to become our working assumption, yes," Wuyts replied.

"And we don't know when or where he'll activate it," Goose said.

"To make a meaningful difference to human consumption and environmental impact, you'd have to get rid of a *lot* of people," Aldridge mused aloud. "If you want to hit more than ten percent of the human race, even choosing the most populous countries — China, or India — the area of effect would have to be enormous. Several million square kilometres. Even supposing the field that the Bell generates can be sustained over such an unimaginable distance, which I don't for a moment believe that it can, the propagation delay would be significant. In the video from the trawler, it looked like it moved at a handful of metres per second at most."

Aldridge thought for a few moments, then nodded. "Even if Miwa situated the Bell centrally in China and activated it, and supposing the field propagated at five metres per second — which is faster than we saw in the video — it would take over a *week* to reach the country's eastern and western borders. India would be faster, but it would still take days to reach the north and south. And both countries have a nuclear arsenal, which would presumably be no more affected by the Bell's energy field than the trawler itself was. Miwa would never have the chance to make much of a dent on population size before the target country's military attacked the epicentre and destroyed the machine."

"And you said he's a principled man, sir," Greenwood said, looking at Wuyts's face on the screen, and the other woman nodded. "So I doubt he'd eliminate an entire nationality. He'd want to… distribute the losses, somehow."

"I also expect he'd have particular reservations about targeting Asia, given his own heritage," Wuyts said.

"And there's the problem of collateral damage," Aldridge said. "Animals and plants within the effect radius would be eliminated along with human beings. That hardly seems like something Miwa would want. It'd be completely counterproductive. The whole biosphere would suffer catastrophic damage."

"So what the hell is he going to do with it?" Dowling asked. "Make more of them, and spread them out? Set them all off at once, in major cities?"

Aldridge was already shaking his head. "Magnusson said they couldn't even disassemble the device, much less build more of them. And he'd need a supply of the liquid in the capsule within it. What did he call it? The *xerum*. He didn't say anything about there being any more of it on the U-boat."

"So we have some advantages, at least," Greenwood said. "Even if depopulation is his goal, the practicalities make it enormously difficult, and he probably only has one machine. If there was any sudden light-show like we saw on the trawler's recording, especially in a densely-populated area, we'd hear about it almost immediately."

"Which means that we still don't know what his real plan is," Ramos said quietly, drawing the attention of everyone else. "He's anything but a fool, and I heard him over the comms channel when he was trying to lead you away from his other guests tonight. He sounded confident. Like he had the upper hand. And it's been months since he abandoned the oil platform."

"What are you saying, Corporal?" Wuyts asked. Ramos looked up at the display screen thoughtfully for a moment before replying.

"I think he's already entering his endgame," she said.

There was silence in the cabin. At last, Wuyts spoke.

"I'm inclined to agree. Your captive will be arriving here in Brussels before midnight, but we're not going to get anything from him, leaving us with limited options."

Ramos nodded.

"What about other outgoing flights?" Goose asked. "Miwa will have wanted to leave the country immediately."

Wuyts sighed in frustration. *"You can imagine the number of executive charters and privately-owned jets leaving the metropolitan area tonight, under a variety of colourful identities, none of whom we particularly want to detain without good cause. Especially after the exciting evening they've had."*

Greenwood nodded wearily. The exodus of politicians, industry magnates, celebrities, and the idle rich created the perfect cover for Miwa's escape. Most of those people routinely travelled under assumed names for reasons of privacy and safety.

"So what's our next move?" Aldridge asked.

"We get ready," Greenwood said. "We need to be prepared for a direct engagement on a larger scale. Miwa knows about us now, and his priority will be keeping the device out of our reach and moving ahead with his plan. He moved it from the oil platform, and I'm betting he's got plenty of security wherever it is. We're going to find it, and we're going to take it — by any means necessary."

"Our assembled unit from the EU Battlegroups is equipped and prepared for transport," Wuyts said. *"They'll muster centrally in Belgium within the next two hours, and deploy as soon as we have a location. I'll be placing them under your command, Captain."*

Greenwood nodded. "I'll contact you as soon as we know where we're going, sir. I'll need our specialists too, from the base. In the meantime, we're going to try to get some rest. I expect we've got a long night ahead."

"Very well," Wuyts replied, *"and I'm looking into Miwa's business dealings during the past several years, but I'm not optimistic about finding anything useful. I hope you'll*

have more luck. Keep me informed." Then the display went blank.

"Alright," Greenwood said, turning to face the rest of her team. "One-hour shifts monitoring comms and keeping watch. Wake me if there's anything either way. Larry, you're first up. Everyone else, get some sleep."

Dowling gave a makeshift salute, and moved to a small station further forward in the cabin, hooking a headset over one ear and settling into the adjacent chair. He logged into the computer terminal secured to the shallow metal work surface, and his fingers began to glide over the keys.

Ramos and Goose went immediately to a pair of reclining seats towards the rear, sat down, and closed their eyes. As soldiers, they'd long ago fallen into the habit of sleeping whenever and wherever they got the chance.

Aldridge stood up, but didn't immediately head towards a more comfortable chair, instead choosing to watch Greenwood as she distractedly ran a hand through her hair. When he spoke, it was in a subdued tone that didn't carry very far.

"There's something wrong with all this," he said. When she quirked an eyebrow at him, he gestured vaguely. "I mean, besides… everything we just heard. It doesn't add up; the numbers don't work."

"I know," she said. "And that only makes me more nervous, not less." Aldridge nodded in agreement.

"We'll work it out," he replied. "Try to rest for a

while. Speaking as a doctor, that's the best thing you can do right now."

The barest flicker of a grin appeared on Greenwood's face. "You're not that kind of doctor."

Aldridge smiled at her, and then leaned in as if to impart a secret. "Doesn't mean I'm wrong, though," he replied.

Chapter 23

Greenwood's wristwatch indicated it was only a few minutes past one in the morning when there was a crisp and prolonged beep in unison from two of the nearby tablet computer devices.

"About time," she said. In a chair nearby, Dowling and Goose opened their eyes immediately. Ramos was working at the comms station, and she swivelled her chair around. Aldridge was already hovering nearby.

"Why does the earring wait four hours before sending its location, again?" Aldridge asked, and Greenwood tilted her head slightly in his direction without looking away from the tablet device she'd picked up.

"We've had situations where periodic-transmission bugs have been detected early, due to the RF output," she replied. "No-one can decrypt the actual data, but the signal itself can easily be detected. The thinking is that a four-hour delay lets the target escape and reach their destination, then pass through any security apparatus while the transmitter remains dormant. Then it sends a high-intensity pulse, and shuts down for another four hours."

"And why is it inside an earring?" Aldridge asked, placing one hand on the back of her chair as he peered over Greenwood's shoulder at the tablet's screen.

Greenwood shrugged. "They put them inside all kinds of things. Anything small enough to conceal within the target's clothing. Now if this thing would just… ah, we've got a location."

A map appeared on the tablet's screen, with a blinking marker in the middle of a contoured green area.

"Owl Mountains, Poland," she said. "It's about eighty kilometres southwest of Wrocław."

Dowling immediately stood up and went to the front of the plane to inform the pilot of their destination. Greenwood was already entering commands on the tablet device.

"Our own forces will rendezvous with us at a staging point in the local area. I want to depart immediately."

Dowling had just come back from the cockpit, and he nodded. "Flight time is about two hours and thirty minutes to Wrocław, chief; it's our nearest viable muster point. Tower has given us a slot in ten minutes, so we're going to start taxiing any moment now."

"Alicia, coordinate with our troops. I want a briefing as soon as we land," Greenwood said. "Make sure onward transport is waiting — land, not air, or they'll know we're coming."

Ramos was already consulting her computer at the comms station. "We'll need to allow ninety minutes for the drive. In the best case, we'll be on site some time after 06:00 local."

"Fine," Greenwood replied. "And line up a helicopter to hold in the city — I want to bring our specialists in rapidly once we secure the location. Inform Wuyts. Everybody belt up." She turned to look at Goose. "You know the drill."

The Dutchman nodded. "Terrain, transport access points, and live satellite. I'll have it up once we're in the air. Looks like it's some kind of national park, which should mean at least a basic road system for maintenance. They also had to bring the Bell in, plus a lot of equipment and personnel. Could have been by air, but that's risky."

Greenwood nodded. "Let's hope nobody's out for an early hike."

"And there's something else, Captain," Goose said, looking over her shoulder at the tablet device. He pointed to a cluster of figures. "Judging by the geography, these coordinates are centred on one of the peaks, but look at the transponder's altitude reading compared to the terrain profile."

"That explains how you hide a testing facility in a nature reserve," Greenwood replied. "Alicia, make sure we have blasting equipment and standard rock climbing and traversal gear. Lights for everyone."

Ramos nodded without looking around, her typing not faltering for a moment.

"Lights?" Aldridge asked, settling into a chair and fastening his seatbelt. "It'll be almost dawn when we get there."

Greenwood looked around at him. "It will be," she replied. "But according to this information, they're inside the mountain."

Aldridge hadn't expected to sleep on the brief flight to Poland, but he managed to get an extra hour of rest nonetheless. The last ninety minutes in the air were spent speculating on the physics behind the Bell's operation, but there was just too much they still didn't understand.

He knew there was a very real prospect that the device would be waiting for them, and could be used offensively. Despite his best efforts, he could do no more than guess at possible defences against it. There had been no radiation signature on the trawler or in the objects left behind when Mark Cross's crew were killed, so there was no reason to suppose that any form of radiation shielding would be effective. Likewise, physical barriers were no guarantee of safety either, especially given the energy field's disturbing movement in the recording from the *Hjørdis*, flowing in three dimensions, appearing to act as something between a liquid and a gas.

His advice to Greenwood was to equip as for any

tactical incursion, proceed cautiously into larger chambers, and maintain a constant path of rapid retreat — but that was all common sense. He'd also requested a cache of directed and projectile EMP weapons, as well as conventional ranged explosives as emergency countermeasures.

They landed at a military airfield just south of Wrocław, and were met by an EU transport plane and a Polish air force helicopter. The plane held twenty-five soldiers already in forest combat camouflage, and fully equipped. A variety of flags were visible on their left shoulders, with their right bearing the circular blue insignia of the European Union. Also on board were several scientists and engineers from KESTREL's own base in central Brussels. Aldridge warmly but briefly greeted Dr. al-Ahmed, clapping him on the shoulder. He was told to be careful in return, and he had waved off the request with a confidence he didn't feel.

It was now 06:28, and they were en route towards the mountains in a convoy of four covered trucks. The terrain had already been tending upwards for a while when Aldridge checked his rifle one final time. Greenwood was sitting across from him, quietly conferring with Dowling and Goose. Ramos sat beside Aldridge, taciturn as always.

"You know, there really are owls in the Owl Mountains," he said, and Ramos glanced at him. "The Eurasian eagle-owl has distinctive ear tufts and orange eyes."

"Are they likely to be a problem?" she replied, and Aldridge gave her a confused look for a moment before shaking his head.

"Oh, not at all, no. They're mostly nocturnal. And they eat… the usual owl stuff. Field rodents, small birds, fish and insects; that kind of thing. I was just making conversation."

"Hmm," she said. "I seem to recall you had an interest in birdwatching."

"I read about them on Wikipedia while we were in the air. I like to be prepared."

"You like to annoy the Captain with irrelevant information," Ramos replied, with a glint in her eye, and Aldridge smothered a laugh.

"Why, Corporal, I'm flattered that you're paying so much attention," he said.

"And," Ramos continued as if he hadn't spoken, "I think you're worried about the mission, and you cover it with jokes. Which she also knows." She nodded slightly towards Greenwood, and Aldridge's eyes flicked in that direction for a moment.

"I don't suppose there's much point trying to deny it," he replied in a quieter voice, "and you're right; I am. There are a lot of unknowns, and we're asking these people to risk their lives without the benefit of a proper understanding of what we're up against."

"That's the job," Ramos said, and Aldridge gave a faint grin. When Ramos raised one eyebrow in a silent question, this time it was Aldridge who nodded towards Greenwood.

"That's exactly what she'd say."

"And she would be right," Ramos replied.

Aldridge exchanged another glance with her, then he once again focused his attention on the conversation Greenwood was having on the bench across from him.

"No mains supply?" Greenwood asked, and Dowling shrugged.

"Nothing we can find. If he's using the grid locally, it's minimal, chief — nothing to raise any suspicions. He's got to have generators, or be pulling power in from somewhere else. God knows how, though."

"Which means we can't cut power on the way in," Greenwood replied. "Then we play it by ear. Handle any resistance we encounter, and take the facility. Then we conduct a survey, and go from there. If we find the device, we let the clever people decide whether we can safely move it."

"I'm going to assume the *clever people* includes me," Aldridge interjected, "and I can tell you with certainty that we can indeed move it — because Miwa moved it from the U-boat onto the oil platform, and then from that platform to somewhere else, maybe here in Poland. Evidently it's possible to make it safe for transport."

Greenwood gave him a withering look, but she also nodded. "And it'll be your job — and that of your colleagues — to make it happen. We need to get that machine into responsible hands."

"By which you mean the military," Aldridge quipped,

and Greenwood pressed her lips together for a moment.

"By which I mean the European Defence Agency, your employer," she replied. Aldridge raised his hands in surrender, and Greenwood turned her attention to Goose and the portable, toughened tablet computer he was working with.

"We've got a live satellite feed," Goose said, touching the display and pinching his fingers apart to zoom in. "There's an old road here, and we're on it right now. Probably a logging route in the past, but this is a protected area now. It's the one vehicle path that goes high enough to intersect the transponder signal's altitude."

"Then this is our way in," Greenwood replied. "We'll go as far as we can, and then proceed on foot. Three groups of ten, with a thirty-second gap between the first two. The third group will hold position at a perimeter we establish, until ordered otherwise."

She flicked a switch on the side of her earpiece, now speaking to everyone in all four of the trucks. "Alright, you've all been briefed. We don't know what we'll be up against, but our objective is to secure a concealed facility suspected to house an experimental energy weapon. The weapon is a black metallic cylinder, two metres in approximate height, vertically mounted, with cabling running from the top. It produces a visible and rapidly spreading illuminating field which is one hundred percent lethal upon contact. It's electrically powered, and the field itself is non-irradiating, but the internal mechanism is highly radioactive if exposed. We have no knowledge of any defence against the weapon's effects."

Some of the EU Battlegroups soldiers exchanged looks, but none of them said anything.

Aldridge also flicked his headset's broadcast switch. "When it's in operation, the machine produces a characteristic signature: a high amplitude, low frequency hum. Auditory and vibrational. As the Captain said, it's absolutely *vital* that the casing's physical integrity be preserved. Do not direct any fire or explosive force in its direction. It's also unknown what the result would be of severing its umbilical power connection, but that would be a preferable option — though only as a last resort."

Greenwood nodded, having watched him as he spoke. "If you encounter the energy field, or suspect that you're hearing or feeling the hum, retreat immediately. Again: do not engage the device while it's operational, under any circumstances. If you have an opportunity to disable the facility's electrical power in that context, do so without hesitation."

She looked at each of her teammates in turn, then she continued speaking. "We also don't know what kind of resistance we'll face. Use discretion, and minimise casualties whenever possible — but our priority is to secure the weapon. Lethal force is authorised. Stay alert, and good luck."

Greenwood disabled the broadcast function and sat back, resting her hands on the rifle in her lap. Less than a minute later, they all felt the truck braking, then it came to a stop.

"Fencing ahead, one hundred metres," the driver called back. "Gates are open."

"How welcoming," Aldridge remarked, just as Greenwood got to her feet, crouching slightly under the low tarpaulin ceiling. She nodded towards the rear of the truck.

"Let's get it done," she said.

There were six men in total, including Venter and Reddy. Venter was in command, and he knew how crucial his team's mission was. He adjusted his position, getting comfortable for the period of inactivity ahead of them.

The chamber was very small indeed — only about five square metres, with bare rock walls — but it was well ventilated and tolerably warm. It had probably been a storage area or an incomplete utility space back in the early 1940s, when this was a different land, and when this facility had been built by the back-breaking labour of slaves. Today, it was simply a waiting room.

The bomb was surprisingly portable, given its destructive power. Modern technology had fashioned it in two parts which connected together to automatically prime it, with the detonation countdown already preprogrammed. Each of the two pieces fit easily into a slim backpack, one worn by Venter himself and the other carried by an Albanian who Venter knew only by the nickname Priest.

Venter had been surprised at Miwa's plan, but he

would carry it out exactly as ordered. Miwa had informants at every airfield in the region as a precaution, and his influence extended even to the military. The scientific personnel at the Owl Mountains facility had been evacuated alongside the Bell, but there was still a considerable amount of equipment and related materials to be removed. Time had run out, though, when they heard of an EU military transport plane making a short-notice landing outside Wrocław.

Miwa's instructions were clear: allow the base to be captured, unopposed. It would be quickly occupied by both military and scientific personnel, and searched thoroughly. They would begin to inspect the remaining equipment for whatever secrets they could find. Their guard would be down. Then, when the opportunity presented itself, Venter's team would detonate a bomb in the Bell's harness chamber on the lowest level, destroying the facility and its remaining contents, and hopefully killing as many of the intruders from the European Defence Agency as possible.

It was a bold move, which was to be expected, but it was also uncharacteristically bloody for Miwa. Venter had learned never to question his employer, though, and he had to admit that there was a sound tactical motive behind it: cripple as much of the enemy's forces as possible in a single location, to allow time for the final phase of the plan to be carried out.

By Venter's estimate, assuming that the EU troops would travel by road to avoid drawing unnecessary attention, they would arrive very soon indeed. It wouldn't take long for them to find their way through the base after that. He and his team would be waiting for an hour or two at most. Their hiding place was adjacent to the harness chamber, accessible through a narrow bored channel which was obscured with a shelving unit. The channel continued for a short distance before opening into the chamber they waited in now, and there was a further extension of the passage behind that chamber, ending in a long vertical shaft which opened onto the mountainside near the peak.

They would wait in silence for a short while, then seize an opportunity to set the explosive device in the harness cavern before escaping via the exit shaft, to be picked up by a helicopter which stood ready several kilometres to the north. Venter glanced around at his five companions. All were lying on the rock floor, face up, and four had their eyes closed. Reddy, though, was awake.

Silently, he repeatedly threw a combat knife into the air, watching it arc end over end above his head, reaching its peak and then slicing back down towards him. Each time, he caught it effortlessly.

Chapter 24

"Vehicles arrived and departed here recently, sir," said the young French soldier as he inspected the ground around the perimeter fencing. He kept his rifle at the ready, but his eyes were focused on the earth at his feet. "Heavy loads. Several."

Greenwood nodded. It fit the profile of a hurried evacuation, which was the logical move for Miwa. Nevertheless, that didn't mean there wouldn't be any nasty surprises waiting inside. Sentries left behind, traps, even the Bell itself, rigged to activate when someone entered.

"Move in," she said. "Let's be careful. And someone look into tracking where the vehicles went."

They had split into three groups as ordered, with Greenwood, Dowling, and Aldridge heading up Alpha team, Ramos and Goose leading Bravo team, and Charlie team holding the perimeter at the fence. The trucks had been turned around and positioned in staggered formation at a wide separation, for rapid escape if necessary.

Greenwood's team went forward in two rows of five. She and Dowling were at the front with three of the Battlegroups troops, and Aldridge joined the remaining four bringing up the rear. They moved quickly and quietly, staying several metres from each other. The fence extended out of sight in either direction, and the dirt track which ran through the open gates continued for thirty metres before ending at the rockface. Once they reached that point, they saw that an area of trees off to one side, not visible from the fence, had been cleared away long ago.

There was a prominent warning sign about unsafe conditions, including rock slides and unstable mine shafts beneath the surface. There was also a one-man outpost hut, emblazoned with faded Polish military insignia, but it was empty. A few metres beyond, recessed into the rock wall, was a corrugated metal shutter door large enough to drive two of their trucks through side by side. It was open.

Greenwood gave a hand signal, and one of the soldiers crept forward to take up a position to the left of the opening. After a moment, he quickly peered around the edge into the passageway beyond, then withdrew his head once more. He gave a different hand signal in return, and Greenwood nodded.

Clear, she thought. *But that's no guarantee.*

They proceeded cautiously, followed shortly afterwards by the second team of ten. The entrance passage was surprisingly long, and virtually straight. It bored directly into the rock face for a distance of forty metres, going through another shutter door which also lay open. There were tyre marks on the ground, and some scattered small items off to one side. Aldridge crouched down to inspect them, but they were just discarded chocolate wrappers, crumpled cigarette packets, and an empty water bottle.

Lights were mounted regularly along metal rails which ran across the ceiling, and the facility's power was clearly still on, because they were all illuminated. Greenwood felt deeply uneasy about it, since anyone further in would be able to see them all with perfect clarity, lit from above and silhouetted against the rectangle of daylight from outside. So far, though, there was no sign that anyone else was present.

A large cavern opened out in front of them, with further passageways leading to the left and right, and a small set of double doors in front. The doors were closed, but the branching passageways were empty, and they sloped markedly downwards, presumably following the terrain beyond. The rightmost had some kind of conduit constructed at its base, along the left wall, protected by railings. It was metal-sided, and ran the full length of the passageway, vanishing off around a curve in the distance. It was marked with the lightning bolt symbol readily understood almost anywhere to mean electricity.

"So they *are* bringing in power from elsewhere," Goose said, walking over to the conduit. "But where?"

"I might have an idea about that," Aldridge said, looking all around with considerable interest. Overhead, as well as the lighting rails, there was routing for cabling, and colour-coded pipework. Alongside these newer installations there were also much older, and clearly now unused, pipes and what looked like mountings for electrical wiring. The facility had been there for a long time.

He turned around to look in the direction they'd come, and sure enough there were also older, bare mountings just inside the boundaries of the open shutter doors. Even the doors themselves had been replaced.

"Captain," Aldridge said, in an awed tone, "I think this is Project *Riese*. Or at least an undiscovered part of it."

Of course, Greenwood thought, with a flash of recognition. *That's exactly what it is.*

Riese, or *Giant*, was a vast Nazi construction project during the closing two years of the Second World War. A series of underground structures, some linked together, spread throughout Lower Silesia, and created for an unknown purpose. Built by forced labourers, prisoners of war, and concentration camp inmates — many of whom died in the process.

Aldridge's brow furrowed, and he walked over to a nearby portion of the electrical conduit. It was mounted at knee-height, and below, back towards the tunnel wall, was the yellowed and faded edge of a piece of paper. He pulled it out, accompanied by a cloud of dust that made him cough briefly, then he unfolded it. He stared at it for several seconds, then held it up. The contents were brief and in German typescript, detailing a shipment of miscellaneous provisions and construction materials. The date was 12th March 1944. There was a scrawled signature at the bottom, and the top-left corner of the paper bore the German eagle standing atop a swastika within a wreath of oak leaves. The eagle was looking towards its left shoulder, not its right, making it the *Parteiadler* of the Nazi Party: the Iron Eagle.

"When this place was built, it was in Germany," Greenwood said. "And that explains how they're routing electrical power here without it showing up on the local grid. These tunnels could go anywhere else in the region. If this facility was never found, it stands to reason that there could be more like it too."

"Explains another thing too, chief," Dowling said, his rifle held at the ready as he surveyed their surroundings. His expression was uncharacteristically dark. "Too much of a coincidence otherwise. The only way Miwa could know about this place is if there was a record of it in the submarine."

The air seemed to grow colder. Greenwood looked from Dowling to Aldridge and back again. She knew that his conclusion was logical, and almost certainly correct. It was Ramos who spoke the words that were at the front of everyone's mind.

"He brought the Bell home," she said.

There was silence, but it only lasted a few moments before Greenwood spoke again. "Then let's do the job we came here to do. Get that door open, Larry. Post a guard here too, and send some men to reconnoitre the first hundred metres of each of these side tunnels."

Dowling nodded, and went over to the set of double doors which lay just ahead. He checked around the edges for anything that indicated a trap, then he took a deep breath. With a quick backwards glance to make sure no-one else was standing close by, he twisted the handle and pulled. The door swung open effortlessly, revealing another large chamber beyond. He stepped through with his rifle trained on the space ahead, and after a couple of seconds he called back through. "Clear."

They filed in one by one. There was a sunken floor area with rows of metal-framed desks, all of them empty. Office chairs sat at various angles, as if abandoned in a hurry. Small sets of three steps carved into the rock led from the lowered section to the primary floor. There was another door towards the rear, and a corridor leading to a well-lit area that looked like an internal lobby of some kind.

They moved forward again, with soldiers checking the underside of every desk in the open-plan working space. Aldridge ordered two of the EU troops to check the corridor and report back, while he and Greenwood approached the single door on the far side.

"Twenty Euros says this isn't a janitor's cupboard," he said, and Greenwood threw him a glance.

"No bet," she replied, twisting the handle then kicking the door open. They found themselves looking into a spartan room whose walls and floor were mostly bare. There was a sizable metal desk in the rear half of the room, also empty, with an expensive-looking chair behind it. The wall to the left of the desk had an open doorway to a bathroom, and a large monitor mounted on the blank rock surface.

"Miwa's office?" Dowling asked, and Greenwood nodded.

"Looks that way. But no sign of the man himself."

One of the soldiers Aldridge had sent to check the corridor outside returned, and now stood in the doorway.

"There's an elevator just down the hall, Captain," he said. "A stairwell too. Looks like two more floors below."

"I don't know about the rest of you, but personally I'd *love* to go deeper into the creepy Nazi lair hidden inside the mountain," Aldridge said.

"Then it's your lucky day," Greenwood replied, without any humour. She motioned to the door, and they set off along the corridor towards the elevator lobby.

It took fifteen minutes to explore the second floor. There was yet another lateral tunnel leading gradually downwards, and Goose judged that it probably intersected with those from the upper floor, as a means of moving large items around the complex. There were several small laboratories, some dormitories with lockers, a kitchen and canteen-style dining room with a huge larder, toilet and shower facilities, and a surprisingly extensive leisure area — including a projection TV, pool tables, a small library, armchairs and sofas, and in a further room, a well-equipped gym.

There was also a small chamber with prefabricated walls and soundproofing installed, split into two booths. Each one had a chair, and a narrow table with a kind of small stand upon it. A surveillance camera was mounted in one corner of the ceiling in each booth. Goose was puzzling over their function until Ramos pointed out that they were probably just a modern sort of phone box, but for audio or video chat using mobile phones or tablet computers that the occupant would bring with them.

"For the staff to keep in touch with family members, I suppose," Dowling said, and Ramos nodded.

The third and lowest floor had no such human touches. There was a further access ramp, ending in a large machine room with huge generators and various working areas, showing signs of recent and hurried abandonment. More disturbingly, there was a morgue facility, complete with autopsy room and refrigerated storage — entirely empty — and an incinerator. There was only one other chamber leading off the hallway.

Fifty metres beyond the elevator lobby on the lowest floor, there was a set of large blast doors. An access portal was set into the rightmost door, with a black biometric panel set into the adjacent surface. The portal lay partially open, but the chamber beyond was obscured by the angle of the door. The air was noticeably cooler here, and Greenwood could even see water vapour escaping from the area ahead.

Last stop on the tour, she thought.

"Alright," she said to her assembled team. All four other members of KESTREL stood with her, plus eight additional soldiers. All had their weapons at the ready. There was a noticeable tension in the air.

"If Miwa's machine is still here, it's in that room up ahead," she said. "And that's the better of the two scenarios. Let's move."

Dowling was the first through, rifle aimed into the vast chamber ahead, and a directed EMP handgun in an additional sidearm holster on his belt. There was no sign of anyone else beyond the blast doors, but he still came to a halt at the sight before him.

The cavern was sixty metres wide, and the main feature was a pool in the centre, taking up more than ten percent of the total floor area. An elaborate mechanised gantry overhung the pool, and there was a structure that looked like a control booth set back near one of the walls, with cabling running along a channel in the floor between it and the gantry.

The Bell was nowhere to be seen, but it was obvious that it had been previously mounted directly above the pool.

"Damn it," Greenwood muttered. "Alright, search the rest of the level again, and assuming we're alone, I want the specialists here in twenty minutes."

Towards the rear of the room, there was a doorway leading to a series of holding cells, both animal-sized and human. Most of the cells were empty, but there were still a few small mammals and reptiles in cages, and even a heavily sedated chimpanzee in what looked like a mobile containment trolley mounted on small rubber wheels.

"Take the animals topside," Greenwood ordered three of the Battlegroups soldiers. "Put them in one of the trucks for now, and make ready to evacuate them when we bring the specialists up."

There was a large glass-fronted set of cabinets under temperature control, holding a variety of organic samples, and Aldridge exchanged a pointed look with Dowling. It was clear that this was a testing facility for the effects of the Bell device.

When they went back out into the main cavern, Aldridge noticed a perimeter of small containers around the edges of the pool, and he approached one of them cautiously. "I think these are biological samples," he said. "They've been experimenting here. That's what the animals were for. And whatever poor bastards they kept in the holding cells."

The ceiling of the vast space was still slightly misty, though they could all hear the faint rumble of air conditioning units. Other than the ambient sound, and their own footfalls, the entire facility was shrouded in silence.

"I'm going to head back up to the second level and see if there's any useful data in the labs. There were a few computers still in there," Aldridge said, and Greenwood nodded her approval. "I'd also like al-Ahmed to take a look at the containers around the pool when he gets here. Can we have him escorted down here as a priority?"

"I'll handle that," Ramos said, receiving a nod and smile of thanks from Aldridge.

"Do you think they built it in this room? In the 1940s, I mean," Goose asked, and Dowling shrugged.

"Stands to reason, I suppose," the big man replied. "But the real question is where the bloody thing is now."

Forty minutes later, Aldridge was working in one of the labs on the second level of the complex. There was some promising data on a laptop there, and he was making a copy of it on a flash drive he'd found in a desk drawer. When the copy was complete, he pocketed the drive and then began to open files on the laptop at random.

He'd barely begun to read when he heard Greenwood's voice over his shoulder.

"You'd better not be playing Solitaire," she said, and he grinned without looking around.

"I was actually thinking of downloading Minecraft," he replied, "but my boss wouldn't approve."

"No, I wouldn't," Greenwood said. "What have we

got so far?"

"I've only just started to look, but I've taken a copy of it all already. I can upload it once we get back to civilisation. This machine's networking is completely locked down."

"Think you've got anything that'll be useful to us?"

Aldridge tilted his head to one side. "Hard to say. So far, it looks like a lot of chemistry. I'm also pretty sure there's an unlicensed copy of Photoshop, in case you want to add to Miwa's list of serious crimes."

"I'll inform the European Commission immediately," she replied dryly, and Aldridge looked around at her, but Greenwood's focus was on the laptop's screen. "I'm sure they'll ask for a very detailed report of his business software and its provenance."

"Half a billion people in twenty-eight countries, and our most fearsome weapon is bureaucracy," Aldridge replied, with a small shake of his head.

"Down to twenty-seven soon," she replied, and he gave her another look, this time a wince. The UK was scheduled to leave the European Union in a matter of months, after a highly divisive referendum characterised by murky politics and appeals to bigotry and xenophobia.

"Not our finest hour," he replied. "And my lot voted against the damned thing. Everyone down south will live to regret it just like us."

"Yes, they will," Greenwood said with a sigh. "But I wonder how *well* they'll live, at least in the short term.

I'm just glad my other passport says I'm a Belgian citizen."

"I'm covered too. The Chancellor was very grateful for what we did in Hamburg. I'm a proud dual citizen of *Deutschland* now."

"I'm well aware of that," she replied.

Aldridge opened another file, and besides a mass of text there was a small diagram which was unmistakably a cross-section of the Bell. He felt Greenwood's hand grip his shoulder, and he nodded quickly.

"I see it," he said distractedly, scrolling the document. "I think this might be—"

The screen suddenly flashed, then a single word appeared in the upper-left corner: *ERASING.*

"What's happening?" Greenwood asked, but Aldridge didn't have a chance to respond. Barely a second later, all of the lights in the facility suddenly went off, plunging them into darkness.

Chapter 25

Venter tightened his grip on his assault rifle. It wouldn't be long now.

They'd just sent the erase signal to all devices on the facility's internal network, and then triggered the remote shutdown of main power. The backup generators had been decoupled from the electrical systems too, so there would be no emergency lighting anytime soon either. The inevitable ensuing confusion would be the perfect cover for their task.

Reddy and the four other men were crouched nearby in readiness, and Venter could feel the solid but surprisingly light casing of his half of the modular bomb. He pressed a small button on the side of his wristwatch to illuminate the dial, then used the momentary dim light to wave his hand in the air and draw everyone's attention. He gestured towards the narrower of the two openings in the chamber's walls, which was currently blocked by the rear of a shelving unit. From the front, it looked solid, but there were castors mounted on the underside and concealed by a panel. It could be moved virtually soundlessly, if they pushed it slowly enough. Priest and one of the others took hold of the unit's frame and very gently moved it outwards and then to the side, revealing a short passageway leading to the testing pool cavern.

They could hear confused voices up ahead, and there were scattered flashes of illumination from handheld torches, but Venter knew they were certain to have the element of surprise. Reddy had switched off the sole light in their hiding place five minutes earlier, to ensure their eyes had all adjusted to the darkness in advance. Their combat gear was black from head to toe, and they were mere shadows in the small space. Now, it was time to carry out their plan.

Without a word, the six men advanced one after the other, vanishing into the greater darkness ahead.

"Larry, report," Greenwood said, already unslinging her rifle and making it ready. A light clicked on just a few feet away from her as Aldridge found his flashlight, keeping it initially pointed at the floor to avoid dazzling either of them.

"We've lost power everywhere, chief," Dowling replied on the communications channel. *"Seems like the emergency generators aren't connected to the system either. Got a bad feeling about this."*

"Me too," Greenwood replied. "All team leaders, we have possible enemy action. I'm going down to level three. I want everyone on alert. Start escorting the specialists back outside immediately. If there's any sign of —"

Her words were cut off as her earpiece relayed the unmistakable sound of a gunshot echoing against rock walls, and a man's scream.

There was another single shot almost immediately afterwards, and then a burst of semi-automatic fire, then Greenwood heard an ominous thud followed by a muted curse in a distinctively Welsh accent.

"*Hostiles are on site. Repeat: hostile forces, level three,*" Dowling said. They heard the flat report of his own weapon being fired twice, and then the answering sound of a ricochet that was far too close for comfort. "*At least two men down. Get those bloody generators on!*"

"Aldridge, get the data out of here; that's our priority," Greenwood ordered, and Aldridge immediately opened his mouth in protest. She pinned him with a glare. "I don't have time to argue. There's a lot more at stake here, and you know it. Get it out of here, and take our civilian staff with you. Do what you can on the way."

Aldridge hesitated for only a moment, then he nodded, readying his own rifle. "Just... be careful," he said. "I'll see you topside when it's over."

Greenwood crossed to the door first, took a single glance back at him, then pulled the door handle and moved fluidly out into the corridor. They could both still hear sporadic gunfire over their earpieces, but there seemed to be no incursion on the second level. There was an equipment pack sitting against the wall nearby, left there by one of the Battlegroups troopers. She quickly retrieved two narrow, thirty-centimetre long plastic tubes from it, and attached the objects to one of the lashing points on the right thigh of her field uniform.

"Charlie team, secure the base exterior and our transport. Make ready to evacuate civilian staff. Team leaders, I need a report," Greenwood said, keeping her voice low as she methodically swept the corridor with the flashlight mounted along her rifle. She reached the open door of the stairwell without encountering any opposition, where she paused briefly to listen to the voices coming over the communications channel, then she switched off the flashlight and aimed her rifle's barrel into the stairwell itself. She could hear muted sounds from below, but nothing nearby — though that didn't mean there wasn't a nasty surprise waiting below.

Voices in her ear told her that there was no external sign of hostile forces at the main entrance, nor any reports of engagement on the upper or middle levels.

So either there's an additional entrance that goes straight to the lower level, or they were waiting here for us all along, she thought. *Or both.*

Greenwood quickly reached the midpoint of her descent to level three. She expected to be on the receiving end of gunfire at any moment, but she made it to the lower door and into the wide corridor without encountering anyone. The sounds of battle were louder now, and she could hear that they were coming from the testing cavern up ahead. She stuck to the left wall, flashlight still off, navigating by the periodic flashes that showed through the access portal set into one of the blast doors.

A shape suddenly surged out of the darkness ahead, and Greenwood had her rifle trained on it in an instant, but at the last moment she recognised the face of one of the biologists from her own base. The young woman looked terrified, and was clutching her left forearm. There was a dark patch against the fabric there, and Greenwood guessed that she'd caught a flesh wound from a bullet.

Greenwood grabbed the woman's other arm, pulling her away from the opening, and she gasped but didn't cry out.

"It's Captain Greenwood. You're safe. You're alright," she said, and the young woman's shoulders sagged in partial relief.

"They're shooting at us," she whispered, eyes wide enough to be faintly visible in the darkness. "They killed some of the soldiers."

Greenwood felt her gut clench, but she kept her tone steady. "Can you tell me anything about the size of the enemy force, where they came from, or their current location?"

The other woman shook her head. "I don't… I just, I saw one man go down. Someone shot him, in the head. He fell and he didn't move. They were shooting from the back of the cavern at first. I could hear their boots on the floor."

Greenwood nodded. "OK. That's helpful. You've done well. Now listen to me carefully, alright?" She didn't wait for a response before grasping the woman's hand from her uninjured arm and placing it flat against the nearby wall. "You're going to stay quiet, and follow this wall. Keep your hand on it. Don't go too fast. You'll get to the door of the stairwell. Go up two levels. Some-one will meet you and get you out. You'll do fine. Go now."

The woman's was breathing raggedly, but she nod-ded and immediately hurried off into the darkness, her palm making a faint scraping sound as she led herself along the wall and away.

"I have one of our science personnel on the way up the stairwell from three," Greenwood said after flicking the broadcast switch on her headset. "Female, unarmed. Minor injury, left forearm. Evac and medic."

"*Acknowledged, Captain,*" came the voice of the same French soldier who had read the tyre tracks on the ground outside earlier. It seemed like it was about a week ago but had really only been a couple of hours.

"Larry, I'm outside the blast doors and coming in. How does it look?"

"*Small hostile force, chief. Five or so; one down. They were on top of us right away. Probably hiding here since before we arrived. We've got casualties too. I think we lost someone from Bravo."*

Greenwood nodded to herself, forcing down the grief and frustration of losing someone under her command; there would be time to deal with that later. The main problem right now was that there was something very wrong with the scenario.

"Five isn't many. What's their objective? They can't effectively engage our forces above, and they can't get out this way either."

Dowling didn't immediately reply, and Greenwood crouched and stuck her head briefly around the edge of the portal in the blast door, but the cavern beyond was a void, occasionally lit by a spark of gunfire. Dowling and whoever else was with him in there had clearly switched off their flashlights, otherwise they'd have been sitting ducks.

"We've taken cover behind the control booth," Dowling responded at last. *"That's on the left as you come in, on your side of the room. They're not trying to get to the doors. They're up to something in here. I think I saw a pack on one of them."*

They must have another exit back the way they came, Greenwood realised, and the next thought was automatic. *They're a demolition crew, and they want to catch as many of us as they can in the blast.*

"All teams, this is Greenwood," she said. "Evacuate the facility immediately via the main entrance. I repeat:

evacuate, and get clear. Larry, I think they want to bring the place down around our ears."

"That was my thought too, chief," Dowling said, snapping off another shot. *"And one more thing: we've still got al-Ahmed in here with us."*

Shit, Greenwood thought. They'd have to extract the man as a priority, but the elevators went offline with the mains power, and the ramps were a much longer way around. There was no guarantee that whatever secret access route the hostile forces had used would be accessible to a wheelchair, or would allow carrying a man out. The situation was deteriorating, and it was time to go on the offensive.

"Who else have you got in there?" she asked, pulling the plastic tubes from their place in the lashing point on her right thigh.

"Two from Alpha, al-Ahmed, and me. Not nearly enough."

"Then let's even the odds," Greenwood replied. "Chem lights in five."

"Roger that," Dowling replied, and Greenwood could hear the neat metallic click of a fresh rifle magazine being clipped into place over the intercom.

She quickly bent both of the tubes, feeling the inner containers break immediately, then she shook them violently. Both objects instantly gave off a strong glow, one green and one blue, and Greenwood mentally counted down from three before hurling first one tube and then the other in different directions through the portal and into the gloom of the cavern ahead.

A burst of covering gunfire immediately erupted from somewhere in the near-left corner, and Greenwood used the opportunity to advance through the doorway, sending a stream of fire towards the cluster of shapes she could faintly see at the other side of the central area. The enemy forces had taken cover behind one of the primary securing points of the gantry that overhung the pool.

The chemical lights gave out a harsh glow that didn't reach the furthest walls of the vast space, but it was more than enough to allow an effective counterattack. The blue light had landed a few metres in front of the control booth, but the green light had overshot the ring of small sample containers around the poolside and actually fallen into the water, which now shone with an eerie luminescence that rippled on the rocky ceiling above.

Greenwood only had a moment to assess the scene before she simultaneously heard and felt a bullet slice through the air just to the right of her head, and she dived in the opposite direction as she returned fire. She could hear what was almost certainly Dowling giving her more covering fire as she sprinted in the direction of the control booth. Even as she reached it, she could see movement in her peripheral vision, and knew that their enemies were advancing.

"Better late than never," Dowling said with a strained smile, and Greenwood threw an acknowledging glance in his direction.

"They're making a push forward," she said. "They can't have set the device yet. We've got to get control." She turned her attention to al-Ahmed, who was backed up against the rear wall of the booth. The man looked tense but not at all panicked, his hands sitting loosely open on the armrests of his wheelchair. "How are you holding up, Qadir?"

"I'm grateful to see some excitement, Captain," he replied. "It reminds me of the old days."

Greenwood nodded slowly, and then her eyes widened as a thought occurred to her. *He lost his legs in a bomb disposal accident.*

"You were in the military. That's where you were injured."

Al-Ahmed nodded. "I was, and I'm still rated for firearms. If I can help, I'm ready and willing."

"I had something else in mind," Greenwood replied, putting a hand on the man's shoulder. Before she could continue, he was already nodding, with a knowing look in his brown eyes.

"You'd like me to try to disarm whatever explosive device they've brought with them."

"Yes, I would," she replied. "I don't want to order you, and you're free to say no. But you understand that I have to ask. You're a potential resource, and I'm responsible for all of your lives."

Al-Ahmed smiled, and there was an element of sadness to it. "You need not explain, Captain. I'll do whatever I can."

"Thank you," she replied, just as there was a fresh and sustained volley of weapons fire from further into the cavern. She thought it sounded closer than before.

"Sorry to interrupt, chief, but we've got a new problem," Dowling said from his position at the far left side of the rear wall of the control booth. "One of them just took something from his pack. They're placing it behind one of the support legs on the opposite side of the pool. And there's another guy with a pack working his way forward."

"What do you make of that?" Greenwood replied, but she was talking to al-Ahmed instead. The man frowned, one fist now clenching the rim of the large wheel on the right side of his chair.

"It sounds like a modular device," he replied. "They're relatively new. Stackable, to manage the magnitude of the explosion. The components are usually safe to transport in isolation — unless pierced or detonated, of course — but when attached to each other they're automatically primed. They allow for custom payloads: conventional explosives, binary agents, chemical, biological. All they need to do is choose the placement, and clip the modules together."

Greenwood and Dowling exchanged a look. They might have only moments to intervene. "Alpha team, cover us and escort Dr. al-Ahmed to the device when possible. Larry, you and I are going to stop them assembling it."

Dowling nodded, checked his weapon, and with a

final nod from Greenwood they both sent a stream of bullets from the left and right edges of the booth, resulting in a momentary interruption to the incoming fire. They seized the opportunity and moved out into the open, firing at the enemy position as they went, and the two EU Battlegroups troops immediately took up their previous positions, providing covering fire.

Two of the black-clad intruders had moved to the other leg of the gantry on the far side of the pool, in an attempt to cut off any access to the area where the first module of the bomb had been placed. Dowling's next shot hit one of the men in the left arm, spinning his rifle around to his back on its shoulder strap. Greenwood put a bullet in his chest, and he went down like a felled tree.

"Four left," she called out. Now the enemy force was outnumbered, but she wouldn't be celebrating victory anytime soon. The other man at the nearest leg of the gantry was firing indiscriminately, and then his rifle abruptly clicked. Dowling and Greenwood surged forward as one, Dowling stopping halfway to take a firing position, but Greenwood continued running, reaching the man just as he raised his weapon again. She spun as she moved, using her own momentum to twist past the barrel of the rifle and bring her elbow crashing into his face, breaking his nose instantly. He fell backwards, bouncing off one of the support pylons of the enormous metal leg of the gantry, then tipped forward, arms flailing as his own blood sprayed the stone floor. Greenwood brought the butt of her rifle down on the topmost vertebra at the back of his neck with a crunch that made Dowling wince, before finally diving alongside the base of the gantry's leg just in time to avoid a volley of bullets that bit holes in the floor and kicked up puffs of dust.

"Three," she said, already analysing how to reach her next target. A moment later, the decision was taken from her, as one of the remaining men who were clustered around the device on the floor twenty-five metres away suddenly lunged in their direction, snapping off sloppy shots that went slightly wide, one even hitting the metal leg they sheltered behind. A burst of fire from the two Battlegroups troopers at the control booth made him reverse course immediately.

Greenwood watched as the three men ahead broke for the only door they had a hope of reaching: the entrance to the side chamber which housed the cells for biological specimens. There was no way out of there as far as she knew, but it was also a very defensible position.

And I'm betting they won't consider surrender, she thought. As the intruders reached the relative safety of the holding chamber, Greenwood waved Dowling onwards, and they both cautiously advanced towards the modular bomb component that sat on the bare stone. Their weapons were trained on the holding chamber's doorway, which was little more than a black rectangle in the dim light.

In her peripheral vision, Greenwood saw the two Alpha team soldiers escorting al-Ahmed from behind the control booth, bringing him around the south side of the pool, to head directly underneath the test gantry and ultimately to where the slim, grey device lay awaiting its sister component. Dowling was first to approach, but he ignored the bomb, his eyes ceaselessly probing the darkness ahead. Al-Ahmed was only fifteen metres or so away now, flanked by his two guards, and Greenwood just had time to wonder if they might manage to remove the already-placed module and retreat back through the blast doors to rendezvous with a larger force.

Then everything seemed to happen at once.

PART 3

Chapter 26

All three of the mercenaries burst from the doorway ahead in quick succession, and one of them — an Eastern European with black hair and a face entirely devoid of any emotion whatsoever — immediately turned his weapon upon the soldiers escorting al-Ahmed. They returned fire immediately, and theirs was the better aim: a dark hole appeared on the mercenary's forehead, and he crumpled to the ground dead. Less than two seconds later, the Alpha team soldier who had fired the shot suddenly pirouetted awkwardly to his left, several shots going wild as he spun, a spray of scarlet jetting from his neck.

"Bastard," Greenwood said, taking five rapid shots at the man who had killed her soldier, but her target had already dived behind another support pylon. There were now only two enemy combatants, the taller one wearing a compact backpack, and the shorter one who had killed the Battlegroups trooper. There was no fear on either of their faces, but the shorter man had a disturbing grin on his face, which was turned into something wicked by the green fluorescent light glowing from the water nearby. Two seconds later, he dashed from cover, heading straight towards al-Ahmed and the remaining member of Alpha team.

"Larry!" Greenwood called out, but it was unnecessary: Dowling was already taking aim, but in the confusion of shadows and the glare of the chemical light beacon, his shot was wide. The mercenary was more accurate, and two bullets punched through the chest of the Battlegroups trooper.

Al-Ahmed is alone out there, Greenwood barely had time to think, then the mercenary trained his rifle on the wheelchair-bound biologist and squeezed the trigger. It clicked, and the man spat, reaching for his sidearm automatically — but a final shot from the dying trooper startled him and the pistol clattered to the floor and skidded across the surface. It seemed to move in slow motion, and then it slid over the edge of the pool and sank out of sight.

Bullets from Greenwood and Dowling sliced through the air and rang out against the iron gantry, carefully away from al-Ahmed, and the shorter mercenary snarled and was forced to double back to where his companion crouched reloading his own rifle, barely three metres from the bomb module on the floor.

Greenwood dropped to one knee, finding a more

stable firing position, but her eyes widened in disbelief as she saw al-Ahmed twist his chair around and rapidly pump his arms to move to the edge of the pool. He flicked the brake lever, and then used his thick arms to launch himself from the seat. All four pairs of eyes looked around at the huge splash as he entered the water, immediately dropping out of sight.

What the hell? Greenwood thought, but she had to immediately roll to one side as a bullet slashed through the air only centimetres from her neck. The taller of the two mercenaries was firing recklessly, and she could see the other man behind him, removing a disturbingly familiar device from his tactical backpack.

"Running out of time, chief," Dowling said from several metres to her left, just as another roar of gunfire cut through the air between them. Greenwood barely registered another much smaller splash from the direction of the pool, and then the impossible happened. She heard the sound of a single gunshot, then the taller mercenary jerked to one side, falling away from his cover and sprawling across the floor. He twitched once and then lay still, a puddle of dark liquid spreading around his head. The other mercenary shouted something like *Venter!* and the word echoed around the rock walls.

Greenwood's head snapped towards the pool. Al-Ahmed's forehead was visible over its edge, still in the water. One arm rested along the tiled perimeter, supporting his weight. The other held the pistol that had fallen in. He nodded to her, and after a moment, she nodded back.

The distraction had taken a moment too long. There was a muted beep, and then a new light appeared just ahead. The shorter mercenary was running again, but this time it was towards the back of the cavern, furthest from the blast doors, into an area still shrouded in darkness. Where he'd been standing, the two modules had been clipped together and a red digital countdown had appeared in a panel on top.

01:58

01:57

01:56

No, Greenwood thought, then she reacted immediately. She pointed to the pool, but Dowling was already almost there.

"No time to go back out," he shouted, and she nodded in agreement.

"Can you lift him?"

"Already have," Dowling grunted, standing fully upright with the biologist pulled across his massive shoulders. Al-Ahmed held Dowling's own rifle now, his soaking clothes dripping water on the floor.

"Stay behind me," Greenwood said. "They must have a way out back there, and we're going along for the ride." She flicked the broadcast switch on her earpiece. "All teams, detonation in one minute forty five seconds — *evacuate and get clear.*"

With a final glance at the bomb, she confirmed that

Dowling was still with her and then raised her rifle and ran in the direction the last remaining mercenary had gone.

It took only moments to cross the rest of the cavern, and their enemy's exit was immediately apparent: a passage concealed behind a movable shelving unit, twisting out of sight. She flicked on her rifle-mounted flashlight and moved forward, counting down in her head. The passage wound to the right and then left, going through a wider area that had doubtless been the staging point for the incursion. Then it continued a short way towards a dead end, with an iron ladder bolted to the wall, rising at an angle within a diagonal shaft cut through the mountain. The faint clang of boots from above was an unneeded confirmation that their quarry was only moments ahead, but suddenly an entirely new sound, low and rhythmic, filled the air.

Greenwood felt her chest tighten as she remembered the video recording from the trawler and the low hum of the Bell, but half a second later the noise resolved into the heavy beat of helicopter rotors, amplified by the narrow channel of rock.

"Can you get Qadir up this thing?" she called back to Dowling, and the Welshman gritted his teeth.

"Whether I can or I can't, I'm bloody well going to," he replied, adjusting al-Ahmed's weight on his shoulders. Greenwood looked back at them and gestured towards the ladder.

"Up you go, then," she said, indicating that the two

men should go first. Dowling looked at her for an instant, but the expression on his face was easily readable: he knew she'd tolerate no argument. He nodded and approached the ladder's lowest rungs, and to his surprise al-Ahmed dropped the rifle, reached up, and pulled himself off Dowling's shoulders vertically, easily ascending several rungs using his arms alone, then stopped to briefly rest before continuing onwards.

"That was easier than I thought," Dowling muttered as he picked up his rifle and slung it over his shoulder, then he jumped up to grab a rung above his head and quickly pulled himself up too, his boots clanking on the narrow iron bars. Greenwood followed after them, and they had ascended the entire stretch in less than half a minute, reaching a passageway barely two metres long which ended in an open doorway. Light filtered in from beyond, through foliage that whipped back and forth in a powerful breeze. The sound of thudding helicopter rotors was deafening.

Greenwood readied her weapon and sprang out into the cold daylight, leaving Dowling to follow more cautiously behind with al-Ahmed once again slung over his shoulders. The sleek black helicopter had already picked up its passenger, and Greenwood could see the face of the one remaining mercenary through the craft's rear windows. His previously sneering expression was now a snarl, and there was murder in his eyes.

She briefly considered shooting at the aircraft's fuel tank, but immediately decided against it — there was no way to tell who else was onboard, and the wreckage was likely to make a bad situation much worse.

"He's gone," she shouted over the receding rotor noise, "we need to move." Greenwood glanced rapidly around, finally settling on a small copse of pine trees slightly downhill and about forty metres away. "Get behind those trees!"

Dowling grunted and broke into a strained run, sweat beading his forehead, with Greenwood bringing up the rear. As they went, she counted down in her head.

Not going to make it, she thought. There were only seconds left.

A sudden breeze cooled her brow for a moment, and she had a vivid mental image of her final evening run during her holiday in Italy, five days ago — but it felt like five years. Then Aldridge had called, and set them on the path towards this moment which might be her last.

As if on cue, her headset crackled, and she heard Aldridge's voice in her ear.

"Greenwood! Did you get clear?"

Before she could summon the breath to reply, the entire mountainside exploded.

Aldridge heard the explosion over the communications channel first, and an instant later he was thrown from his feet. He had already hit the ground by the time he heard the actual sound through the air. It was like a thunderstorm within the earth.

He rolled onto his stomach then got to his knees before standing up warily, reaching out to help one of the civilian scientists nearby. They had evacuated everyone several minutes earlier, and at Greenwood's command had fallen back to a safe distance down the mountain path. Even so, the trucks were now rocking on their suspension, and the air above was filled with flapping wings as hundreds of birds took flight and left the area. A vast cloud of dust billowed from where the exterior gate to the facility had been, and rocky debris rained down on much of the forest that immediately surrounded it. A few smaller stones had even managed to reach their position, breaking one of the trucks' headlamps and striking a Portuguese soldier in the chest. The dust thinned by the time it reached them, but several people still coughed as it drifted by on the wind.

Aldridge knew it would be madness, and entirely pointless, to rush headlong into the dust cloud and the unstable terrain ahead and above. His earpiece was silent, and there was a band of tension across his chest. His stomach felt like it was filled with ice. He toggled the broadcast switch on his headset again.

"Greenwood, this is Aldridge," he said, his finger pressing the device tighter into his aural canal to pick up the faintest sound. "Repeat: this is Aldridge. Please come in."

He looked around, and saw Ramos and Goose standing nearby, their field uniforms streaked with dirt after they'd been thrown into the undergrowth by the shockwave. They were both looking back at him silently.

He'd seen a helicopter, just briefly, over the peak of the mountain a minute or two earlier. It had descended rapidly out of sight, but it could only have touched down for a moment before lifting off again, then it banked and accelerated away and out of sight towards the north-west.

Maybe they all got on board, he thought, but he knew it was unlikely. There hadn't been much time, and it was obviously escape transport for whoever had planted the device that destroyed the facility.

"Greenwood, it's bloody impolite not to answer," he said, his voice wavering on the last word. There was silence for a long moment, before everyone's headsets abruptly made a clicking sound.

"Why do you always call me when I'm running?" Greenwood replied, and Aldridge let out a choked laugh. There were sounds of relief all around, and a couple of the scientists blinked back a sudden bright sheen in their eyes. Ramos and Goose exchanged a grin, and the Dutchman clapped his colleague on her shoulder.

"I'm fine too, mate, and thanks for asking," came Dowling's voice over the channel, breathing heavily.

"Sorry, who's this again?" Aldridge replied, and he could have sworn he heard Dowling mutter *cheeky little bastard*.

"If you're both quite finished, we've still got a job to do," Greenwood said, but there was no rebuke in her tone. She sounded a little out of breath, and wired in the way

that a near-death experience tends to cause. *"We're on the opposite side of the peak, probably at a lower altitude than you. There are trees, just beyond some landslide defences that saved our arses. I can see the access road about a hundred metres farther down. We're going to work our way to it, so meet us there with the vehicles."*

"Understood, Captain," Ramos replied, immediately gesturing to the Battlegroups troopers to get everyone into the trucks.

"We saw a helicopter," Aldridge said, and he heard Greenwood huff in frustration.

"One of them escaped. I think we saw him in Barcelona too. And I'd like to see him again. Goose, do we have any way to give chase?"

"I'm afraid not," the Dutchman replied apologetically. "The helicopter we borrowed from the Polish air force only managed to touch down for long enough to deliver the civilian staff, then we had to send it back — there isn't exactly a suitable pad anywhere around here. It'll take twenty minutes to bring it back up here, and honestly I'd advise against a landing near this point until the geological situation after the explosion is more clear."

"Alright," Greenwood replied, with the frustration very clear in her voice. *"You made the right decision. Contact the Polish Ministry of National Defence immediately; I want to know where that aircraft was headed. And get in touch with base — use satellites, flight plans, airfield surveillance... whatever you need."*

"Right away, Captain," Goose said, turning and striding away as he took a phone from one of the pouches on his uniform.

Aldridge became aware of the distant sound of a siren, and he knew that every emergency services vehicle within ten miles was probably en route to their location already.

And the army, I bet, he thought.

Looking around, he saw that almost everyone had boarded the trucks, and he made his way towards the nearest one. "We're leaving now, Greenwood," he said. "Rendezvous within five minutes, give or take."

"*Copy that*," she replied. Aldridge could hear that she was moving at a brisk pace. "*We've got al-Ahmed here, but he had to leave his chair behind.*"

"We passed a hospital on the road from the staging point in Wrocław. I'll send someone in to borrow one on the way back. See you in a bit."

He heard a click in his earpiece, then he took a last look around. The scenery was just as beautiful as earlier, but the air was misty with the last of the dust thrown up by the detonation and shockwave. There were no bird sounds whatsoever; only the breeze rustling the leaves of hundreds of trees. The facility which had lain undiscovered for seven decades was now only rubble somewhere further up the slope, burying the birthplace of the Bell permanently. The sound of approaching sirens grew louder.

Aldridge sighed, then crossed quickly to the tailgate

of the nearby truck and hopped up into the covered rear area. Goose sat close to the back, talking intently into his phone. Ramos looked up at Aldridge from her own position on the other one of the long and uncomfortable benches along either side of the space. He sat down beside her, then slapped the metal panelling of the truck that held the simple backrest of the bench. The trooper in the driver's seat glanced around through the open partition.

"Let's go," Aldridge said.

The coffee was every bit as acrid as the last cup, but Aldridge thought he might be getting used to it. At least the aroma partially masked the ambient reek of diesel.

The military airfield's hangar was too brightly lit and too cold, and he hoped they weren't going to be stuck in the vast space for much longer. It was a little after 1 PM, and they'd been there for the last two hours, in a growing state of tension. They'd been held up for half an hour on their return journey by the regional police and the Polish armed forces, who had now been given the unenviable task of dealing with the destroyed mountaintop. Local and national news were already running stories on a loud noise heard in the vicinity of the *Park Krajobrazowy Gór Sowich*, and a minor ground tremor. The government had made a statement confirming a landslide in the area, which was now under control, but thankfully with no injuries or fatalities due to the early hour.

They'd had an uncomfortable and frustrating briefing with Wuyts, where the Director confirmed that Tien had revealed nothing, just as expected. The man was loyal to Miwa beyond all question, and he had now been transferred to a secure holding facility pending the outcome of the mission. During the video call, Goose received word from the Polish Air Force that the helicopter which briefly touched down on the northern slope of the mountain had gone to a small airfield towards the north, and shortly later an executive jet took off for an unknown destination. The filed flight plan had indicated a landing in Brussels, which Greenwood knew was just Miwa's way of sending a message of defiance. The ground crew at the airfield also told of how a large cargo plane had departed only a handful of hours before the jet, having been loaded from a small convoy of trucks that had arrived from the direction of the Owl Mountains.

Greenwood had been pacing the hangar, giving orders and wrestling with the problem of what Miwa's next move might be, as the rest of the team tried to find any possible lead or clue. They were in crisis, and running on caffeine and nervous energy, with no real progress made since they arrived. Goose was gathering satellite and air-traffic data across a wide radius, Ramos was focusing on national intelligence agencies and surveillance, Dowling was continuing to pursue the business interests of Miwa's company, and halfway across the huge space, at a makeshift desk that was actually a tool bench for aircraft repairs, Qadir was focusing on the biological testing reports, using a wheelchair they'd temporarily borrowed from the nearest hospital in Wrocław.

Aldridge had begun inspecting the data he'd copied from the computer at the facility's lab as soon as they reached the hangar, and upon confirming that a substantial portion of it was indeed chemistry, he'd transmitted it to KESTREL's headquarters with instructions that Lily Cross should look over it. It had taken an hour for her to prepare a summary for him and send it back, which he'd been reading alongside the rest of the original data ever since. He glanced up from the screen when he heard familiar footsteps approaching.

"We need a break, and soon," Greenwood said, dropping into the empty swivel chair next to him. The chairs had been taken from an office furniture warehouse two blocks from the military base, commandeered by Polish soldiers amidst the strenuous but useless protestations of the warehouse's manager.

"Lunch break, tea break, or sudden insight into a certain environmentalist's plans?" Aldridge asked, and he knew how stressed Greenwood must be when she didn't even look around at him for the remark. She was sitting in her chair backwards, her arms folded across the top of the backrest, staring at the laptop's screen in a way that he knew meant she wasn't really reading any of it.

"All of the above," she replied wearily, "but I'd prefer

the insight first."

He looked at her for a moment, noticing the slightly pursed lips, the lines of tension at the side of her mouth, and how noticeable her cheekbones were under the harsh lighting.

"Have you eaten anything since we got back here?" he asked, and this time she did look at him, raising an eyebrow.

"What are you, Aldridge; my mother?"

"Do I need to be?"

She held his gaze for a second or two before her eyes flicked back to the screen. "I've been a little busy, in case you haven't noticed," she replied. There was no real annoyance in her voice, though, and he smiled even though she wasn't looking at him. He reached into one of the pockets of his field jacket which was draped around the back of his own chair and pulled out a protein bar, then he reached over and poked her arm with it.

She looked around again, and she was just opening her mouth to refuse the offering when he pushed the bar into her hand instead.

"Look, I'll tell you what I've found out so far," Aldridge said placatingly, nodding towards the laptop, "but you might as well eat while I'm talking. I was a university lecturer, remember, and I only take questions at the end."

This time she did give him a withering look, but she also took the protein bar and tore open one end of the foil before taking a large bite. She made a sound of appreciation that had Aldridge momentarily forgetting what he'd been going to say.

"Uh, well," he began, clearing his throat, "we've been able to determine a few interesting things, mostly about the control interface for the Bell, and what it's capable of."

Greenwood nodded, reaching for Aldridge's coffee and taking a gulp of it before wincing and looking at him in disbelief. He just shrugged apologetically before continuing.

"It's two things, really. First, the device can be *tuned*. It changes the nature of the field it generates, somehow. There are controls that manage a complex set of factors like the electrical energy input and distribution, the spin rate of the central mechanism, the aperture dilation for the chamber that contains the xerum capsule, and the operation of something that might be a kind of con-denser. We're not sure how it works, but when it was built, these were all discrete systems. Miwa's people have unified and computerised the interface to control it all. It's one of the two primary modifications that can be made to the Bell's operation. Miwa's scientists called it the *organic tuning interval*."

Greenwood frowned. "Interval? What does that mean?"

Aldridge tapped a few keys, bringing up a diagram. It showed a horizontal axis with a series of value labels that were indecipherable to her. They looked like something between mathematics and chemistry, and there were two boundary markers plotted on the scale as bracketed lines, connected by a thicker horizontal line. Each end of the indicated area was labelled with a Greek letter.

"This is the interval, conceptually," Aldridge continued, pointing to the area between the boundary markers. "The endpoints are movable, via the control interface."

"And what's the scale?" she asked, crumpling the empty wrapper for the protein bar and putting it down on the desk.

"Essentially, it's molecular complexity," he replied. "There are some nuances to it that I don't have a firm grasp of yet, but basically this is a means of targeting organic forms of a given chemical sophistication. And *that,* " he said, pointing at the screen in emphasis, "is why the decking of the *Hjørdis* was stripped clean, but the fixtures and fittings themselves were still there, including the deck plating. The Bell was configured to target — or rather, to contaminate — the kind of chemical complexity you find in a human being."

"So we were right," Greenwood said, in a quieter voice. "He's going for depopulation."

Aldridge just shrugged one shoulder. "All I can tell you is that the Bell's operational mode when the trawler encountered it would seem to match this detailed example in the control interface documentation. In this mode, any living thing which the field came into contact with would suffer catastrophic and virtually immediate decoherence of its molecular structure."

There was silence for a few seconds, then Greenwood looked at him again. "Alright. In a way, we already knew all this, except for the details. You said the *interval* was one of two modifications that can be made to how the thing works. What's the other one?"

"Field geometry," he replied, tapping more keys on the laptop's keyboard. A schematic replaced the chart, showing a cross-section of the Bell itself, with a series of internal panels highlighted. They formed two parallel open rings around the upper and lower thirds of the device, within the main casing. "These are control surfaces."

"In the aerodynamic sense?" Greenwood asked, and Aldridge tilted his right hand back and forth in a gesture that clearly meant *kind of.*

"They change the field emission parameters to control how it flows from the machine, so it's a valid analogy," he said. "It can radiate uniformly, be directed upwards or downwards in a conical pattern of varying projected circumference, and so on. It looks like it uses magnetic deflection at the point of origin, within its shell. The surfaces can apparently be repositioned either via the remote interface, or at a small override terminal on the Bell itself, at the point where the umbilical connection is attached. So it's eminently possible to operate it in a controlled way, minimising any risk to the operator — not that I'd want to be anywhere near the thing when it's active."

"How comforting," Greenwood replied. "Last question: you used the word *contaminate*. How?"

"It's another analogy, and it's the scary part," he replied, automatically lowering his voice. "Whatever reaction the Bell sets in motion — whatever physical mechanism causes the molecular disintegration effect — it doesn't require complete immersion in the field. That's why the woman with the pistol in the trawler recording vanished so quickly. The reaction *chains* through interval-targeted substances."

Greenwood's face paled. "So if the light touches your little finger and then shuts off—"

"You're still gone. Yes. That's exactly it."

"And we're no closer to finding the damned thing than we were yesterday," she said. There was a long silence before Aldridge spoke again.

"We're going to find it, you know. We'll figure out what Miwa plans to do, and we'll stop him, somehow." He kept his voice low, but his tone was steady and certain.

"What makes you so confident?" Greenwood asked, and he shrugged.

"Millennia of the patriarchy, mostly. Makes you believe you can do anything."

She gave a tired laugh.

"See, that proves it," he continued, tilting his head towards her. "Two impossible things accomplished in five minutes: you ate something while you're working, and you laughed at one of my jokes."

"You're keeping track of my eating habits, Aldridge? I'm not sure how to feel about that."

"I'm just… paying attention," he replied. "Dowling tells me it's the mark of a good soldier."

She turned in the chair, and her face was earnest again. When she spoke, he had to lean forward slightly to hear her. "And what do you see, exactly, when you're paying attention?"

Aldridge inhaled deeply, then folded his arms, contemplating her. After a moment, he spoke. "I see the most dedicated and driven person I've ever met. A fighter. One of the good guys. Somebody you definitely want to have on your side."

He warmed to his subject, adjusting his position in the chair.

"I see my leader, who's saved my life more than once, and who's got a stubborn streak a mile wide. I see someone who knows the difference between right and wrong, and also knows you have to keep checking where the line between them is. I see someone who puts other people first, maybe more than she should. And who looks amazing in a red dress."

She dropped her gaze, but he kept talking.

"And I see someone who probably knows there's something missing in her life. I think I see someone who's lonely, and doesn't need to be."

"Well, *I* see you're still learning about the chain of command," she deflected. "The way it works is that the buck stops here." She tapped the rank insignia on her field uniform. "That means this whole thing, like every mission, is my responsibility alone, and—"

"You don't have to do anything alone, actually," he interrupted, keeping his voice low. "Not this, and not anything else. We're not meant to. But I see *you're* still learning that."

She looked at him in surprise, and he held her gaze for a moment with the barest hint of a smile, before suddenly waggling his eyebrows.

She huffed and tucked a strand of hair behind her ear before reaching for his coffee cup again and taking another sip. "Stop being so bloody charming. It's incredibly irritating."

"That usually means it's working."

There was a lull in the conversation, and Aldridge began scrolling through the documents on the laptop, skimming them, hoping that something might jump out at him.

"Are we going to talk about the elephant in the room?" he asked at last, risking a quick sideways glance at her, and Greenwood sighed.

"Which one? I thought we just did that."

"The one related to this mission."

"It doesn't matter," she said, shaking her head briefly. "We've got our job to do. Miwa doesn't get to make that kind of decision on behalf of everyone else."

"But—" Aldridge began, and she interrupted him before he could finish the thought.

"But he's basically right; I know. Climate change of the catastrophic kind is probably inevitable at this point. Our lives are going to radically change during the next few decades. And we're still moving in the wrong direction. The USA withdrew from the Paris Agreement. Someone is producing CFCs again in east Asia. We're seeing temperature records broken on an annual basis. People are still burning coal, for god's sakes. The list goes on."

"I think…" Aldridge began, scratching at his chin, "Well, you heard him in Wuyts's covert recording of the conference. He thinks he's doing the right thing in less than ideal circumstances. He might not even be wrong about that. You said that he doesn't get to make the decision for everyone, but… do we?"

She sat up straighter in her chair. "We're on the side of hope, though. That's the difference."

"Even if it's foolish?"

She looked at him again, taking a moment to let her eyes roam over his face. "Even if it's foolish," she said, and after a moment, he nodded.

Greenwood put her hands behind her head and stretched, arching her back. "I'd be more hopeful if I knew what his goal was," she muttered, looking idly around the hangar. Aldridge followed her gaze.

I feel like I've spent most of the last week in planes and helicopters, he thought. *Not very eco-friendly, considering the context.*

The smell of diesel intensified, and he looked around

to see a Polish soldier filling a portable fuel canister attached to the back of a military jeep.

"For an environmentalist, he's quite the frequent flier," Aldridge said. "He's had us chasing him across half of Europe. I wonder how much carbon offsetting he has to do for his own jet just so he can sleep at night."

Greenwood gave the barest lopsided grin, without much feeling behind it. "He probably sees it as a necessary evil," she said distractedly, now looking over to where Goose and Ramos were working.

An image flickered across Aldridge's mind, just for an instant, and he frowned.

Greenwood sighed in frustration. "I should have been able to stop him by now. *We* should have. What the hell are we missing?" Her right hand curled into a fist, and she brought it down on the work surface hard enough to make the coffee cup shift a few millimetres, but the sound was lost in the ambient noise of the hangar. Then she felt Aldridge's hand on her arm. She looked up at him, expecting him to offer some words of consolation.

"Cross," he said.

She rolled her eyes. "I'm not cross; I'm bloody furious. With myself. We don't have time to be sitting around here and—"

She stopped abruptly when he shook his head, his eyes wider now. "No, I mean *Cross*," he said. "Dr. Cross. When we spoke on the phone earlier, after she sent her analysis of the data from the lab."

"What about her?" Greenwood asked. Aldridge released her arm, his mind whirling with images now.

Frequent flier.

"She said… she said that the organic tuning interval allows the Bell to target anything from higher life forms down to the very simplest chemical compounds."

Greenwood nodded slowly. "You already explained that. So?"

Aldridge glanced around again. The soldier had finished filling the canister on the jeep, and was screwing the cap back on. There was another whiff of diesel.

He felt his forearms prickle with gooseflesh. "Do you know the common definition of an organic compound?"

Greenwood thought for a moment, letting her mind drift back to high school chemistry. "Something that contains carbon."

Aldridge nodded.

A necessary evil.

He sprang out of his chair, breaking into a jog towards where Dowling was researching all of Miwa Environmental Consulting's business interests around the world. The big Welshman glanced up as he approached, and Greenwood caught up to them after a couple of seconds.

"What have you got, Aldridge?" she asked insistently, and her tone drew the attention of Goose and Ramos too.

"Larry, does Miwa's company have any oceanographic holdings of its own?" Aldridge asked, raising his palm towards Greenwood to request that she wait for a moment.

Dowling nodded. "Absolutely; I've seen a few in the records. The company has a huge research wing. They do all kinds of impact assessment, and that sort of stuff. Got a small survey fleet, spread around the world."

"Can you give me a list of places?" Aldridge asked, and Dowling nodded again, tapping keys rapidly. The names of various world cities appeared, with many in Europe — but not all of them.

Aberdeen. Alexandria. Bilbao. Christchurch. Marseilles. Oslo. Palermo. Sitra. Tromsø.

"Sitra," Aldridge said, with something like awe in his voice.

"Aldridge, *tell me* what you're thinking," Greenwood said.

"It's in Bahrain," he replied. "That's where he's going. That's where he's taken it."

"Why there?" Greenwood asked. Ramos and Goose had now joined the other three in a small circle, and all eyes were on Aldridge.

"It's in the Persian Gulf," he said, as if it explained everything.

"We know where Bahrain is, mate," Dowling said, and Aldridge blinked at him for a moment before speaking again.

"That's the missing piece," he said. "We've been assuming he'd use the Bell for direct depopulation — targeting a high molecular complexity interval like human beings. But he can get what he wants another way, and much more easily. Hitting just a few different targets would cause global chaos."

He looked from Greenwood to Dowling and back again.

"Some of the most rudimentary organic compounds are *hydrocarbons*. He's going after the *oil fields*! Think about it: if you eliminate a big chunk of the world's petrochemical reserves, overnight, then—"

"Civilisation falls apart," Goose said. "You get hyper-inflation of oil prices, resource wars, an end to international transport and trade, food shortages, disease, riots…"

Aldridge was nodding intently. "And inevitable de-population, but as a side effect. You get rid of a major cause of atmospheric pollution that also happens to be the world's energy source, and then let scarcity and panic do the rest of the work for you."

"And the Persian Gulf…" Greenwood began, her face noticeably paler than before, but she tailed off. Aldridge supplied the rest of the thought.

"Is home to the largest offshore oil field in the world: *Safaniya*."

Greenwood's heart pounded in her chest. She ran the scenario through her mind again and again, trying to find a flaw, but everything fit too perfectly.

An organic target, but of the most rudimentary kind. A huge environmental threat in itself, and highly symbolic. A guaranteed means to worldwide upheaval, with a virtually immediate and drastic change in human civilisation. And a readily achievable plan.

He'll use the Bell to destroy Safaniya, then in the confusion and alarm he'll move to the next target, and so on. Anywhere with direct access to a well or subsea field would work. And it doesn't matter how large the reservoir of hydrocarbons is.

"But how can he do that?" Dowling asked. "We're talking about the ocean floor. Is he going to lower it down there? What about the pressure?"

"There's pressure-stress data in the files I took from the lab," Aldridge replied, "but it doesn't need to go down very far. The energy field can be shaped to flow downwards, and it propagates at a few metres per second; Miwa could just mount it on the underside of a vessel, or lower it just far enough beneath the surface to ensure his own safety. The Persian Gulf is less than a hundred metres deep, at most. And even if he targeted the bottom of the Mariana Trench — the deepest point on Earth — the Bell's field could reach it in a little over an hour."

"Even so, surely he'll need time for the light to spread through an entire oil field?" Ramos asked, and both Aldridge and Greenwood simultaneously shook their heads.

"That's what Aldridge was just explaining to me," Greenwood said gravely. "The light creates a chain reaction in the substances it targets. Miwa only needs to hit a single point in a reservoir, for just a moment, to set it off."

"Jesus," Dowling said. "It'll all go to hell."

Goose nodded. "I'd predict total geopolitical destabilisation within a year at the most. Can you imagine how the United States would respond? And the Russians? I'm not even sure anyone would live long enough to experience the humanitarian disaster."

"Maybe," Aldridge said, thoughtfully. "But maybe not. I don't get the feeling Miwa wants the human race to be all but eradicated. Maybe he's…"

"He's what?" Greenwood asked when he tailed off, and Aldridge locked his eyes on hers.

"On the side of hope," he said. "Perhaps he thinks it'll push us to innovate and adapt. We just need the incentive of dire necessity."

"That's a hell of a bet to make with billions of lives, and frankly I don't feel optimistic about the odds," she replied. Aldridge tilted his head to one side in a non-committal gesture.

"It's surprising how much people can change, when they have to," he said, his voice quieter now. "I know a bit about that."

She held his gaze for a moment, biting her lower lip. "Well I'm not ready to find out just yet," she replied at last, before turning to Goose. "Get me the Director."

This time, the video conference took less than ten minutes. Wuyts unilaterally authorised an immediate covert incursion into an extra-jurisdictional nation, arranging for onwards transport to be waiting for them at their destination, which was to be Kuwait City. By

Dowling's estimate, if Miwa was going to sail northbound from Sitra towards the Safaniya oil field, they could intercept him just before he reached his target by approaching from the opposite direction.

Aldridge asked Greenwood what means of travel they'd use, but she refused to be drawn on the subject, merely indicating the proximity of the ordinary Polish army troopers at the other end of the hangar, none of whom had security clearance for any of this. He had heard her request that something called *Guideline* be immediately flown to Kuwait in preparation for their arrival, and Wuyts assured her it would be in the air within the next fifteen minutes.

Ramos and Goose quickly obtained aircraft arrival records for all runways and landing strips in or near Sitra, and sure enough, they found mentions of both a large cargo plane and an executive jet arriving in the early hours of that morning. Dowling had found an online magazine piece about the pride of Miwa's research fleet, still under construction and as yet unnamed at the time of the article, but due for launch within the coming months. An elaborate survey and scientific vessel with a stated mission of investigating the long-term effects of sustained oil and gas extraction on local marine life, it was capable of deploying manned and robotic submersibles to great depths, and was outfitted with an exotic array of sensors and analysis equipment. They knew immediately that it would make the perfect delivery platform for the Bell, and it came as no surprise that its registered home port was Miwa's facility in Bahrain.

They were all keenly aware that Miwa already had a substantial head start, and it would take another four hours to reach the Gulf by air. Having arranged for return transport to Brussels for her civilian staff, Greenwood bid a brief farewell to the Polish base commander, then she and the four members of her team stepped once again out into the grey afternoon light to board their own jet.

Her wristwatch read exactly 2 PM when she was pressed back into her seat as the aircraft accelerated down the runway and then lifted off from Wrocław, en route to Kuwait.

There's a very real chance that we'll be too late to stop this.

She glanced around at the others, seeing four grim faces each lost in their own thoughts. Greenwood had a feeling that the same scenario was playing out in their minds too.

But we'll give it everything we've got, she thought. *Including our lives, if necessary.*

Chapter 27

The ship was called *Hyperion*, and it was a stunning sight.

A hundred and ten metres long, with a 20,000 kilometre range and capable of up to three months of autonomy, it was painted in Miwa Environmental Consulting's fleet livery of light blue paired with vivid yellow. Its intended complement included a crew of twenty, plus forty researchers, each of them comfortably accommodated for both work and leisure. Twin spherical antennae clusters sat atop the bridge on its uppermost structure, two large crane assemblies sprouted from the fore and aft of the ship, and the lowered rear deck bore the mounting berth for a submersible.

The berth was already occupied, but its tarpaulin-covered load was no submarine.

Named for the Greek Titan characterised as the god of watchfulness and wisdom, the vessel's name was a message regarding its owner's vigilance on matters of sea pollution, marine habitat encroachment and damage, and shifting ocean pH, amongst many other things.

But *Hyperion* was also the god of light, and this namesake of the ancient deity would indeed deliver a unique type of illumination — to destroy the poison that humanity had been enslaved by for so long.

We have come this far, and now the time has come to finish the task, Miwa thought.

It was almost 6 PM in Sitra, and he'd been there since the early hours of the morning when he'd arrived from Barcelona. He felt completely alive, his body coursing with both eagerness and dread. It was a similar sensation to how he'd once felt when giving speeches before large crowds, but it had been many years since those situations had last provoked any lingering reaction in him.

Now, though, he felt reborn.

There was a note of sadness, too, that Tien would not be present to witness the culmination of their work in person, but he would learn of it soon enough via the international media, along with the rest of the world.

The *Hyperion* was at the quayside of Miwa's own facility on the east of the island, and if he looked northwards he could easily see the massive Gulf refineries stretching into the distance. The various governments of the region had initially resisted his company's presence there, but arrangements had readily been made, as always. Receiving his reports up to a year in advance, the authorities had quickly realised that it was in their best interests to have responses and promised actions already in place by the time the wider environmental community obtained any data about marine contamination. Miwa had accepted the ethical compromise in the name of access both to the region and its various rulers, and for several years now his research facility had been merely paying lip service to its stated role, whilst focusing on the development of a suitable mobile delivery platform for the Bell.

The Safaniya oil field was fifty kilometres long, and capable of producing 1.2 million barrels of crude oil per day. It was an appropriate first target. The remainder of the itinerary would be adapted to the developing circumstances, but the second strike point would ideally be Abu Dhabi's Upper and Lower Zakum fields, followed by Saudi Arabia's Manifa. All were in the Persian Gulf, and readily reachable during a single voyage.

With luck, we will have depleted all three reservoirs before their owners and operators have realised what has happened. And with this act, mankind's long journey back to symbiosis with the world will truly begin.

Miwa walked along the quay until he entered the shadow of the ship, and then he turned alongside it, moving from the stern towards the bow.

"Balance in all things," he whispered to himself, the words disappearing amidst the sound of the waves and the breeze almost as soon as he'd spoken them.

He often pondered the question of what his grandfather would say if the old man were alive today and had learned of how his grandson was going to change the human world so profoundly during the hours that lay ahead. Miwa would like to believe there might be some understanding, at least, but it was a question that would never be answered.

The sun would set in less than thirty minutes, bringing a long night that he had been imagining and planning for since he'd first realised the potential of the machine dredged up from the bottom of the Norwegian Sea. The Nazis who created it would doubtless have used it to perpetrate more horrors upon their fellow men and women, but even they would never have dreamed of doing this most radical and unthinkable of things.

When the sun rises over these waters in eleven hours, it will shine down upon a world that has changed utterly — though its inhabitants may not yet know it.

As usual, he felt the weight of pre-emptive guilt and shame settling in the centre of his chest. Miwa knew very well how events were likely to unfold once the major oil-producing and exporting countries realised that their most valuable resource, and the key to their security, prosperity and power, had abruptly vanished. The truth would be concealed for as long as possible, but realistically the gravity of the situation would be known by most foreign governments within a matter of days at most. Fuel rationing and stockpiling would begin immediately, with a rapid curtailing of movement for most populations. Fuel prices would skyrocket, closely followed by the cost of almost everything else. The richest countries would be the most paralysed with anxiety, and international tensions would spread and escalate too quickly for diplomacy to soothe.

Civilisation is a luxury, purchased with freedom from need, Miwa thought. *Our most noble values will always be the first, and furthest, to fall.*

Resource wars on an intercontinental scale were inevitable, but in this modern age they were likely to be settled rapidly by long-range and devastating attacks, up to and including the use of nuclear weapons. Internal law and civic order would fall apart regardless of international events, as enforced isolation, and food and water insecurity, quickly turned once-proud and rational people into the two oldest factions in existence: the hunters, and the hunted.

The lower edge of the Sun's disc had slipped beneath the horizon now, seeming to set the waters ablaze, painting the waves and sky in orange and gold.

Thus death will claim more souls than in any conflict, plague, or disaster in the entire history of our species, each of them upon my conscience alone.

Miwa glanced up at the primary deck of his ship, seeing two of the dozen or so black-clad soldiers of his security detail, painstakingly vetted and hired for the upcoming voyage. There would be only a skeleton crew of scientists and engineers on board, watched over carefully by these mercenaries, to ensure there were no unpleasant surprises.

Reddy appeared in the doorway of the quayside facility, and walked briskly towards his employer. The man had arrived two hours earlier, and presented a terse report of what had taken place in the Owl Mountains. Since then, he had been pacing ceaselessly, and had begun to draw irritated looks from the other security personnel. Miwa turned to face him as he approached.

"I am saddened by the death of your colleague," Miwa said. "Mr. Venter completed his mission bravely, and at the ultimate cost."

Reddy's eyes were disturbingly blank as he nodded slowly. "Your man in there said we can launch in two hours," he replied.

"We have all made sacrifices," Miwa continued, "But by tomorrow morning we will have achieved the first and most important part of our goal."

"And I'll be a million Euros richer," the other man said, to which Miwa simply nodded.

"Inform the administrative staff that they may finish for the day and take a long weekend, with pay," Miwa said, and Reddy raised an eyebrow.

"Why not just kill them?"

A shadow fell over Miwa's face, and the air seemed to become very still. He looked at Reddy for several moments, unblinking and unmoving. When he finally spoke, his tone was icy.

"They know nothing of our cargo or route. Send them home, as I instructed."

For almost ten seconds, Miwa didn't know whether Reddy would obey or not, but finally the man shrugged and took a leisurely step backwards towards the quayside facility before adding a final remark.

"What if one of them talks to someone?"

Miwa turned away, once again looking up at the metal hull of his ship. His gaze tracked along the primary deck, then moved to the tarpaulin at the rear which hid the Bell and its umbilical control connection.

"By morning," he replied, "it won't matter."

Reddy's footsteps slowly receded, and Miwa took a breath to centre himself once more, before resuming his walk along the quayside in the shade of the ship's towering hull.

Either our whole world survives, or nothing does. It was the point that so many otherwise rational and sensible people failed to grasp, or insisted on denying. The Earth was a delicate symphony of interconnected ecosystems, each dependent on the others in a multitude of ways. Tiny fluctuations in climate could readily eradicate entire species, causing a knock-on effect that would all too quickly result in famine, pestilence, and the rendering inhospitable of previously thriving habitats — for insects, animals, and humans alike.

Yes, there was proven adaptability; it was the nature of things. Evolution used the mechanism of random mutation, tested in an uncaring environment, to self-select for advantageous qualities. But evolution had taken place mostly in the context of slow changes, over hundreds or thousands of millennia. Anthropogenic industrial pollution had created a radical change in the biosphere in a mere century. Adaption had limits, and the truth was that no-one really knew how resilient the ecosystem as a whole actually was. That the planet itself would still exist was certain. But its inhabitants, and the balance between them, were more fragile than most people liked to believe.

Bees. Coral reefs. The rainforest. Our multitude of critically endangered species. All irreplaceable. Yet we choose to bury our heads in the sand where seas once were.

If humanity could adapt to a future without fossil fuels, that would be one modest part of restoring its own viability. But if it couldn't, then who was to say that the hand of evolution wasn't also at work? A species that destroys its own habitat, food sources, and its very air to breathe, surely could be judged as self-selecting for extinction.

But we will not go quietly, Miwa thought. *Clean energy is almost within reach. Renewable fuel technologies advance yearly. Developed cultures are awakening to the need to dramatically alter food selection and consumption patterns. And selective carbon reclamation is plainly possible, because in a manner of speaking, that is exactly what the Bell does.*

He reached the bow and continued onwards, his pupils contracting at the sudden glare of the setting sun that was no longer obscured by the vessel. The fiery disc had almost completely sunk beneath the horizon now, seeming to take its fire down below the waves.

There will be another fire in the depths of these waters tonight, he thought, feeling a chill that was partly horror and partly anticipation. It would not be long now. At this part of the quay there was no-one else around, and he tried to enjoy the precious moments of solitude, even if there was no longer any peace of mind to accompany it.

Accelerated evolution requires an intolerable threat, but no creature on Earth can rival us. Thus, we must become the agents of our own peril.

Miwa had told Reddy that they had all made sacrifices, but he knew that the greatest sacrifice was destined to be his alone. He also knew that, consciously or otherwise, he had been preparing for this task for virtually his entire life.

The breeze from the gulf was picking up now, and he felt its chill through his light suit, relishing the sensation. He imagined it seeping through his skin and settling in his bones, hardening him to what needed to be done. As if in final acceptance of his duty, his next thought was spoken aloud, into the strengthening wind.

"So be it," he said. "Tonight, I will be the nemesis that humanity so desperately needs."

Chapter 28

At 20:04 local time, KESTREL's jet touched down in Kuwait City, on a private strip a few kilometres to the east of the primary airport. As soon as Dowling opened the cabin door, Greenwood could see a black helicopter sitting on a pad a hundred metres away, with the Persian Gulf stretching out beyond it. They transferred to it immediately, and were airborne again in less than five minutes.

At 20:17, Goose loaded an updated satellite image on the mini-tablet device he carried, and his mouth tightened into a narrow line. He turned the device so that Greenwood could see it. Like the previous series of images they'd been monitoring during the flight from Poland, it showed Miwa's oceanographic research facility at the harbour in Sitra. Unlike the previous images, however, there was no vessel docked at the quayside. Instead, at the edge of the image's frame, the rear of the ship was just visible, heading out into the Gulf.

Miwa has embarked, she thought, feeling dread settle into the pit of her stomach. She flicked the intercom switch on the bulky corded headsets they all wore, connected to the aircraft's internal communications system.

"Target is en route," she said, and four pairs of eyes locked onto her simultaneously. "Looks like departure was within the last ten minutes. We're a little over twenty minutes out from our connecting transport. Goose, make sure they're on course and up to speed. We're not going to have much time when we land if we're going to keep to our intercept schedule."

The Dutchman nodded, tapping a message out on the tablet device while Greenwood continued.

"Everything should be waiting, but if anything's missing, we proceed anyway. I want to minimise our sailing time as much as possible. The moment we're within viable launch range, we go straight to *Guideline*."

"Understood, Captain," Ramos said. "I've been looking forward to getting acquainted with it."

Aldridge glanced from one woman to the other. "And you're still not going to tell me what that is, exactly?"

"You'll see soon enough," Greenwood replied, with a quick bob of her head towards the pilot of the helicopter. The soldier was in plain clothes but was vaguely recognisable as an EU Battlegroups trooper whose identification Greenwood had reviewed en route to Kuwait. There were limits to the man's clearance, hence the circumspect wording.

At 20:39, a light became visible on the water's surface below. There had been nothing there before, and the illumination had only just been activated, revealing a makeshift helipad towards the rear of a nondescript cargo ship. Several people were barely visible outside the ring of lights. The pilot brought the helicopter down smoothly, landing with ease despite the moderate swell of the waves, and the rotors had barely begun to slow when Dowling hauled the side door open and five sets of boots hit the metal deck plating. Ramos slid the door closed again behind them, and the moment they were clear of the pad, the rotors increased speed once again and the helicopter lifted up into the black vault of the sky. The noise receded quickly, and Aldridge blinked in an attempt to adjust his vision to the sudden darkness after all the lights around the helipad blinked out.

"Captain," a man said, stepping forward. His accent was unplaceable, and Greenwood recognised him as their covert deployment contact in this region, an Egyptian by birth whose cover name was Sameh. She nodded a greeting.

"I want to make best possible speed," she said. "Is everything here?"

Sameh gave a tight smile. "All is ready. Go below and see. You will have ninety minutes before we must begin the preparation sequence and checks."

"Alright," Greenwood replied. "Radio silence, and stay alert. I want this entire operation to pass right under the noses of Saudi Aramco and the Kingdom."

"Of course," Sameh replied, bowing his head briefly before walking off into the darkness of the foredeck. Greenwood motioned to the rest of her team, and all five entered a nearby doorway.

The interior was as dilapidated as above deck, and Aldridge had the sense that it was kept that way on purpose, to avoid the attention that a newer or better-maintained ship might attract. They descended two flights of metal stairs within, finding themselves at the meeting point of two corridors. One led aft, with a variety of doors along each side. The other stretched towards the bow of the ship, ending in an unassuming hatchway. It was this that Greenwood headed for, and upon reaching it she set her hand on the latch.

"Alright, Aldridge," she said, "since you waited so patiently."

He stepped forward, noticing the twinkle in Dowling's eye as he stepped past the big man. "If this is a surprise birthday party, I really think it's an inappropriate time," Aldridge replied. "I mean that literally. My birthday is months away."

Greenwood twisted the hatch handle, and began to swing the door inwards. "No cake and candles tonight," she replied. Lights blinked on within the chamber ahead automatically. Aldridge stepped up to the threshold and peered in, just as the room became fully illuminated.

"This," Greenwood said, "is *Guideline*."

Aldridge stared for several seconds, then looked

around at her with a grin forming on his face.

"We get the *coolest* toys," he replied.

Reddy glanced around at the multitude of control panels and instruments on the bridge of the elaborate science vessel, before once again turning his attention to the wraparound windows which formed the entire front of the bridge. The waves of the Persian Gulf flowed rapidly by on each side, and a crescent moon hung balefully in the night sky.

He knew that it wouldn't be long now. They were making good time northwards, and they'd reach the optimal point within the oil field's vicinity by midnight. If necessary, they could even deploy the Bell slightly earlier, according to Miwa.

He didn't care about his employer's goal, or his motives. The important thing was that Miwa had both money and power, which were the two most useful things in the world when the situation entailed risk. Money was the reward for it, and power was insurance against it.

A million Euros for each successful voyage, he thought. *And he's got plenty of them planned.*

Miwa said that not all of his targets were accessible from the oceans, and that there would be overland and subterranean strikes in future. Reddy didn't care about that either. He'd do what was needed, as long as he was paid. The truth was that he enjoyed it, and he'd probably do it anyway, but his philosophy was that if you were going to have fun, you might as well make some money at the same time.

Besides, he had a score to settle. Miwa had made it clear that, sooner or later, he was expecting more trouble from the English bitch and her squad. The Arab in the wheelchair had put a bullet in Venter's head, and the other guy had damn near broken Reddy's cheekbone with the side of his pistol.

Venter had been uptight and prickly about protocol, but they'd worked together for years, long before this latest venture. Neither of them considered the other to be a friend, but they were close comrades in arms, and while he was never going to shed a tear, Reddy was going to make sure that Venter's death was avenged — brutally.

Miwa wasn't convinced that the others could catch up to the ship so soon, but Reddy knew better. He'd learned that the only thing you needed to prepare for in life was the worst — and once you did that, you were prepared for everything. So for him, it was only a matter of time until the bitch turned up. And that was just fine.

Actually, he was looking forward to it.

"On a scale of one to Bad, how bad would it be to ask the Saudi authorities for their help with this?" Aldridge asked. "It's their oil field. They'd send the whole three-ring circus out to stop Miwa's ship."

Greenwood was standing a short distance away at a desk in the large bay on the cargo vessel's lowest deck, poring over a tablet device showing a satellite map overlaid with two moving markers. She barely turned her head when she replied.

"Bad," she said. "And you know it."

"Because…?"

Greenwood sighed, stretching her neck and rolling her shoulders. "Because we're outside our jurisdiction, so it wouldn't be *help* as much as taking over. There's no way we can allow the Bell to fall into the hands of a foreign government. And definitely not the Saudis, who would probably use it in the same damned way that Miwa's going to, but to secure their own monopoly in the global oil and gas industry. Or as a weapon of war, for that matter."

She turned around now, folding her arms and leaning back against the edge of the desk. "This kind of job is the reason we exist. It's our purpose. The small print is that sometimes we're beyond the EU or its aligned nations, and it comes down to just the five of us."

"Five of us and that thing," Aldridge said, nodding towards the hulking shape held by clamps, suspended above a purpose-built channel in the floor. It was about the length of a minibus but only three metres wide, and it looked like an enormous bullet. There were no markings of any kind on its smooth, dark surface.

Guideline was the project codename for a state of the art stealth mini submarine, capable of carrying up to six people for five hundred miles beneath the waves, at depths up to 45 metres. It was an autonomous submersible vehicle, and its design minimised weight and complexity by operating under a wet configuration — occupants were in full diving gear, and the interior was flooded at all times. It had one intended function above all others: to covertly deliver a fully-equipped strike force directly to difficult-to-reach targets.

"So you like the sub?" Greenwood asked, already knowing the answer. She wondered how he'd feel when they actually deployed. The plan was to drop-launch at sea, straight from the cargo ship, and intercept Miwa's vessel before he could use the Bell. Diving gear made some people claustrophobic, though Aldridge hadn't shown any sign of it during his training, and the close confines of a flooded environment were a further psychological challenge for anyone.

"It'll do," he replied, "but for the record, subs are meant to keep you dry when you're underwater."

Greenwood was inspecting the satellite map again, and Aldridge stepped over towards the desk to stand beside her. He saw the marker that represented Miwa's vessel, and the one that showed their own position. There was also an irregular shape overlaid on a portion of the Persian Gulf between the two, showing the extent of the Safaniya oil field. Finally, their own ship's marker had a faint line attached to it, linking it to Miwa's position. A number bisected the line, and it was counting down rapidly. Aldridge estimated there was less than half an hour before it reached zero.

"It's our distance from minimum deployment range.

The sub is slower than this old crate," Greenwood said, noticing the focus of Aldridge's attention. She gestured at the walls of the cargo ship around them. "When that number reaches zero, we can launch *Guideline* and manage to intercept Miwa ahead of his probable strike point. If we launch earlier, we might not get there in time. So it's a balance. We don't want them to see us coming, but we want to hitch a ride for as long as possible before we deploy."

Aldridge nodded. "Fair enough. And how are you feeling?"

"I'm relieved, honestly," she replied. "No more chasing around. We stop him tonight, one way or another, and then it's over. Now why don't you ask what you really want to ask?"

Aldridge slid his hands into his pockets and sighed. "Alright" he said, "I agree that the Bell can't stay in the hands of a private individual, and especially not an activist. It's too precarious. I get that. But..."

She straightened up again, turning to face him again. "But?"

"You know that phrase about being on the wrong side of history?"

Greenwood lowered her eyes for a moment. "History will never know about any of this."

"Not really my point," Aldridge said, and there was a note of sadness in his voice. "They'll put it in a warehouse somewhere, under guard. They'll study it. Maybe some good will even come from it all, but there's a part of me that wants Miwa to do what he set out to do. Not to the extent he's probably planning; it'd be tantamount to genocide. But as a… I don't know. A shock to the system, for all of us."

She looked at him for several long moments. "Is that your way of saying you're going to disobey my orders, Aldridge?"

He huffed. "I'm not going to dignify that scurrilous accusation with a response. You know bloody well that I'll follow wherever you lead. And *I* know that you agree with me."

She tilted her head to one side. "I have my orders too. Some decisions are above my pay grade."

Aldridge leaned towards her slightly, giving her a piercing look. "You don't believe that for a second," he replied quietly. "And if you did, you wouldn't be half the leader that you are."

"If it turns out to be the wrong choice, then I'll just have to live with the consequences," she said.

"And you're still not alone in all this," he replied, then he shrugged in acceptance. When he spoke again, a familiar note of teasing had returned to his voice. "I bet you had real problems with sharing when you were little."

"I was an only child," she replied, turning her attention back to the satellite map. "I didn't have to share."

"That explains so much."

The door behind them opened and Dowling walked in, followed by Goose and Ramos. Greenwood glanced up briefly, then checked the satellite map again.

"That dip in the Norwegian Sea the other day has put me in the mood for a swim, chief," the big Welshman said.

"Not that there's much else to do here anyway," Goose added, drawing a nod from the other man.

Greenwood looked around at each of the other four members of her team. Her colleagues, her friends, and her family. There had been other moments like this one; a brief period of quiet contemplation before waging a small and secret war. In the most optimistic scenario, they would survive to see more situations like this, again and again, for however long they were needed and capable. But that was the job, and the life they'd all chosen. It was who they were.

And only fools deny their own nature.

She nodded decisively.

"Let's suit up."

Chapter 29

Miwa wore a black wetsuit with silver reflective stripes running down the sides, and a simple utility belt fastened around his waist. There was a small zipped pouch clipped to the left side.

A holster was attached to the belt and strapped around his right thigh, bearing a 9mm pistol. His boots were low-profile waterproof tactical grips, and there was a combat utility knife lashed to his left calf. His diving watch's lume glowed green on his wrist.

The waves all around looked like oil in the moonlight. A vast, restless ocean of black, opaque and toxic, ready to burst into flames at the merest stray spark and reduce the world to ashes.

And we light the fire willingly.

He stood out on the narrow observation deck in front of the bridge windows at the port side, a slender figure whose short hair was barely troubled by the ceaseless breeze. *Hyperion* cut easily through the dark waters, speeding onwards to her destiny but unaware of her pivotal role in human history.

Like Enola Gay before her, Miwa thought, turning to look back along the side of the ship towards the lowered rear deck. The tarpaulin covering the ship's unique cargo was just visible from his position. *And the machine existed even before that infamous day.*

The Bell had probably already long since been taken from Germany on the day that Hiroshima was all but destroyed, and seventy-three winters had come and gone since. It had lain buried and forgotten below waters just like these, its stewards having fallen to the ill fortune that seemed to seep from its black skin even when the fire within was dormant. But it had found him nonetheless.

And tonight, he thought, *even CHRONOS will find redemption, in exchange for one final atrocity.*

Aldridge knew he was less than twenty metres below the surface, but it felt like he was entombed at the bottom of the ocean.

He kept his breathing even and steady as he'd been trained to do, occasionally glancing at the four other partially-obscured faces around him. Their diving masks had faint illumination around the visor, allowing for useful eye contact, which could be disabled with a gentle touch on a control on the right side. Their intercoms were of the earbud variety, separate from the mask, and rated for immersion up to forty metres — which was substantially deeper than they'd be going — but they couldn't use them with the diving regulators in their mouths. As a backup communications mechanism, they each had a flexible touchscreen cuff strapped to their left forearm, as a text messaging system.

Remember, even at twenty metres we need to decompress on the way back up, Ramos had reminded him when they launched from the cargo ship. He'd acknowledged the statement despite his focus mostly being on the submarine being lowered slowly into the waves through a hatch in the base of the ship, then held there until the craft filled entirely with water.

The sub would handle decompression stops for them, automatically altering its depth as they neared their target, to finally deploy them when they were less than three metres from the surface. Their approach was from the north, and they would split into two boarding teams: Greenwood, Dowling, and Ramos for the starboard side towards the fore, and Aldridge and Goose for the port side aft. Miwa's ship had two crane assemblies which would prove useful as latching points to grapple if necessary, and there were also inset ladders in the vessel's exterior hull.

The mission was very clearly defined: prevent Miwa from using the Bell, via any means necessary. Preemptive deadly force was authorised. There would be no support, and no second chances. If the Bell couldn't be secured, then sinking or otherwise destroying the ship was an approved fallback option. They each had both compact rifles and pistols, spare ammunition, and a small selection of ranged and placed explosives.

Aldridge was startled by a crisp female voice in his ear.

Five minutes to deployment point. Five minutes.

There had been no other audible range updates, but he supposed that they were unnecessary. He locked eyes with Ramos, who was sitting directly opposite. She pointed towards the front of the black cylinder they were sealed into, where there was a single illuminated display just above a small H-shaped metal wheel fastened to the interior front wall. Her meaning was clear: *That was the computer talking.*

He gave a small nod, then turned his head slightly to look towards Greenwood, who was sitting two places to Ramos's left, opposite no-one. He could barely even see her eyes within the diving mask, and her face was almost entirely in shadow, with the small visible portion of her jaw looking unnaturally pale. She sat perfectly still, her soaked hair held tight against her head by the straps of the mask, and he had a sudden disquieting mental image that seemed almost like a premonition.

This is how she'd look if she died out here tonight.

He immediately pushed the morbid thought away, chastising himself for giving any voice to it, and then she suddenly looked around at him. He couldn't read her expression, but he saw her blink before turning away again.

Aldridge glanced at his wristwatch, then adjusted the position of the rifle strapped to his chest. Four minutes to go.

If anyone asked, he'd say he didn't believe in luck — good or bad — but many of the other beliefs he'd held as inviolable during his life had been shattered since he first met the people who now sat with him in the watery darkness.

His left hand rested on his thigh, invisible in the black glove that sat against the same colour of wetsuit. Slowly, and as inconspicuously as he could, he crossed his fingers.

Ramos was the first to board the *Hyperion*, moving silently up the ladder on the starboard side, at a point equidistant between the bow and the bridge tower. Greenwood followed her, and then Dowling. When Ramos reached the top, she looked carefully over the edge of the main deck, immediately spotting a black-clad soldier with an M4A1 carbine assault rifle.

She made a series of hand-gestures visible to Greenwood beneath her on the ladder, quickly surveyed the rest of the nearby area, then went back down a single rung and out of sight. She pressed one hand flat against the hull, feeling the unhurried approach of a pair of heavy combat boots whose sound was virtually drowned out by the wind, waves, and the engines of the ship. She stepped back up one rung, crouching on the ladder, and when a shadow fell across the edge of the deck she used her legs to propel herself upwards rapidly, grabbing the leg that came into view and pulling it directly outwards. There was a thump and a crack as the man fell backwards onto the metal deck, his head hitting the unyielding surface with sickening force. Ramos reached up and over the edge to grab his belt, then pulled him out through the gap in the guardrail and just over the top of the ladder. She quickly snatched the radio from the front of his combat vest, flicking the earpiece connector away with her thumb, then she grasped his belt again and drove her elbow backwards, hauling him over the edge. Greenwood and Dowling had already moved to the right side of the rungs they stood on, and the man's body fell silently past them to finally hit the waves below. The splash it made was completely unnoticeable above the surrounding noise.

They waited in silence for a count of twenty, then one after another they climbed smoothly up and onto the main deck, vanishing into the shadows within seconds.

Aldridge and Goose crouched beside the base of the aft crane, hidden behind the bulk of the tarpaulin-covered Bell. Despite the imminent threat of the two patrolling soldiers they were tracking, Aldridge felt a sense of awe at being so close to the object of their mission.

A machine built secretly in the closing years of the Second World War, resurrected from the depths of the Norwegian Sea, and now turned to an entirely unpredicted purpose. It was a weapon of death the likes of which the world had never seen, but it could also be the means to a new beginning for humanity. He could readily understand why Miwa had become seduced by the device, and its dark potential.

Goose tensed at his side, and Aldridge responded in kind. No communication was necessary. They both knew exactly where the two nearby soldiers were, and that they were fast approaching their hiding place. Four seconds later, the first of them came around the left side of the Bell, nearest Goose. The Dutchman silently delivered a vicious chop under the shelf of the man's jaw on the left side, bringing him immediately to his knees, already unconscious before he could fall forwards to the deck. Goose caught him and gently rolled him under the edge of the tarpaulin, the whole operation unnoticed by his counterpart, whose eyes were trained on the railing running along the port edge of the rear deck.

The second man stepped closer to the railing, looking over and downwards to check the ladder approach. The next thing he knew was darkness, as Aldridge drove the underside of his elbow into the base of his neck. The man's unconscious form joined his companion, and both had their wrists and ankles zip-tied together behind them then lashed to the base of the crane assembly. Aldridge exchanged a nod with Goose, and they began to move forward towards the bridge tower that rose up before them.

Everything's going too well, Greenwood thought.

There was no question of walking into an ambush —
they could clearly see the patrol patterns of another
three of Miwa's security personnel up ahead — but she
always felt deeply uneasy when a mission was proceeding uncharacteristically smoothly. Usually, it meant that
something was about to go badly wrong.

Dowling appeared from the shadows to one side of
her, moving to flank the trooper who was smoking a
cigarette twenty feet away, off to one side of a doorway
and beneath the shelter of the overhanging walkway
above.

Probably hiding from his boss, Greenwood thought. *Well
he's got more to fear tonight than a reprimand.*

A little over ten seconds later, the man suddenly
jerked and then fell to one side, partially behind an
exterior storage compartment that was bolted to the
deck and painted in high-visibility orange. His boots
were visible for a moment, then they were dragged out
of sight.

Greenwood was just on the verge of thinking they'd
achieved another undetected neutralisation when a
bullet suddenly thudded into the storage compartment,
coming from a high trajectory.

"Bugger," she muttered, readying her rifle and taking
aim at the soldier who was now visible two levels
above, on a balcony set back from the deck below, training his own weapon on Dowling's hiding place. Greenwood steadied herself against the mild roll of the waves,
aimed, and squeezed the trigger. The man crashed back

against the wall behind him, his left arm becoming entangled in a ring buoy, and the force of the impact propelled him forwards again and over the guard rail. He crashed down onto the main deck with a thump that Greenwood and Ramos could both feel regardless of the distance, and the ring buoy followed him, reaching the end of its retaining cord barely a metre above the deck plating. It hung there, snapping and twisting above the man's lifeless body like a grotesque neon vulture.

Two seconds later, an alarm klaxon began to blare.

The primary deck was flooded with the white glare from a bank of floodlights mounted below the bridge windows on the fifth level, and more soldiers immediately poured from doors on three of the raised walkways.

Greenwood quickly counted them before taking cover, knowing that there could be more elsewhere. *Six up there at least, and they have the high ground.* Ramos was right beside her, and she could just see the large shape of Dowling, who had retreated ten feet to get behind taller cover.

"We're eight metres from the port aft exterior stairway to level 2," came Aldridge's voice over their headsets. *"Next stairs are another six metres forward."*

"Three hostiles on 3, and three more on 4," Ramos replied. "Even spread. Dowling is pinned down."

"I'm going for level 3, port side," Aldridge replied, and he immediately made a break from cover and quickly closed the distance to the foot of the metal staircase that

clung to the side of the enormous tower, tucked beneath the wings of the broad bridge structure that overhung the four levels below it on each side. Bullets punched into the deck plating just behind him, but he reached the cover of the first level's walkway without being hit.

"Two more, level 4 aft," Goose said. *"I'll handle them."*

"Stay on the main deck, Goose," Greenwood said. "When possible, try to get below and find the engine room. I want this ship dead in the water."

"Understood," Goose replied, then Greenwood heard the sound of a rifle being discharged in three-shot burst mode, with the answering ring of a hard metal surface.

"We need to move," she said, and Ramos nodded. Both women emerged at the same moment, concentrating their fire on the left side of each of the two forward walkways above, to draw the fire of all six of Miwa's soldiers. They both felt a salvo of returned fire chewing up the deck plating as they ran, shooting half-blind. Ramos took a position beside a service hatch with cover from a ventilation riser, and Greenwood went straight to the place where the guard had been smoking earlier, his cigarette still faintly glowing on the hard surface of the deck until it was crushed by her boot. There was an abrupt cry from above, and she knew that Ramos had further narrowed their enemy's numerical advantage.

"Level 4 forward, one down," Ramos said over the communications channel, and Greenwood updated her mental tally.

Seven left outside, to our five. Miwa inside, plus an un-

known number of further hostiles and probably some civilian staff and crew.

Bullets struck the doorframe just centimetres from her head, and she ducked, preparing to return fire. Before she could, another single gunshot from above her position was accompanied by a clang, and then an assault rifle fell through the air, skipped off a hand railing, and slid over the edge to fall into the sea.

"Level 4 aft, one down," came Aldridge's voice.

Almost immediately, Dowling popped up from his position and sent two rounds at a high angle towards the fourth-level balcony, just below the floodlights. Both hit their targets: one of the enormous lights shattered, and the soldier who had been using the glare as cover was launched from his feet as the bullet punched upwards through his throat.

"I make that even numbers now, chief," Dowling said, and Greenwood was just about to order him to rendezvous with her when they heard a series of three-round bursts from above that also echoed in their earpieces.

"Getting a little close for comfort up h—" Aldridge said, then they heard him grunt at the same moment that the unseen enemy fired again, followed by a thud.

"Aldridge, respond," Greenwood said insistently, gesturing to Dowling and Ramos to take the stairways on opposite sides of the tower. She readied her own weapon, rolled from cover, and in a single motion she put a bullet through the chest of one of the soldiers on the third level above. The man collapsed to his knees, his head lodging in the narrow gap below the handrail, and never moved again.

"Talk to me, Aldridge," Greenwood said, already on the starboard side stairs going upwards, her rifle sweeping the whole walkway above. She knew that Aldridge was on the opposite side of the structure and he would have been on level three at most, and she hoped she could make it back around somehow. She reached the first walkway, sprinted the handful of metres to reach the second set of stairs, and then ascended even more quickly. It was only her heightened senses from the adrenalin coursing through her veins that made her notice a slightly deeper area of shadow eight metres away on the balcony area overlooking the forward deck area below. She snapped off a round into the centre of it as she dived for the shelter of a supporting pillar, and another soldier slumped to the ground in the moonlight.

There was intermittent fire from all around, and two of the remaining black-clad troopers retreated upwards to the level below the bridge, going through a doorway and pulling the hatch shut behind them.

Leaves one outside, two inside plus unknowns, and Miwa.

"Anybody got eyes on Aldridge?" she asked, and she felt her chest loosen in relief when his own voice answered her in her earpiece.

"I'm fine," he groaned. *"One of these bastards—"*

His words were cut off by the roar of a gunshot, so loud in her ear that Greenwood flinched and felt her pulse kick up another few notches. A moment later, Aldridge continued.

"*—put a bloody hole through my belt pack, left side. Didn't actually hit me, but it knocked me back down a flight of stairs. I just missed him too. He's gone around towards you.*"

"*I can see him from here, mate,*" Dowling said. "*He just went into the port door, level 4.*"

"Then they're all inside now," Greenwood replied. "Two went in on this side. There's a door here on level 3, starboard; Alicia, you and I are going in here. Larry, join Aldridge and take port. We're going to meet on the bridge. Goose, now's the time to go for the engine room."

"*Already going below, Captain,*" the Dutchman replied.

Ramos joined Greenwood within moments, and they took positions on either side of the unsecured door hatch. Greenwood exchanged a look with the other woman, spun the handle, and pulled the heavy door open.

They counted to three, then went inside.

"We must hold them off at any cost," Miwa said, and Reddy nodded grimly.

They were both on the bridge, behind the panoramic glass panels which were bulletproof and embedded ten centimetres into their steel surrounds. A large angled display panel set into a console surface showed a hydrographic map of the surrounding portion of the Persian Gulf, with sea-floor contours and hazards. *Hyperion's* navigational computer piloted the vessel automatically, and a countdown was prominently displayed in the upper right section of the screen.

MINIMUM VIABLE RANGE: 05:03

Miwa tapped a panel on an ancillary display and was immediately connected with the ship's chief engineer. "Lock all access immediately," he said. "Engine room and umbilical connect bay." A nervous-sounding voice acknowledged the order, and began to ask what was going on, but Miwa terminated the voice link without responding. All of the civilian crew and scientific staff — a handful of people — had been secured below decks as soon as the alarm was triggered.

"Seal the observation deck door," Miwa said.

Reddy's only response was to slam a fresh magazine into his assault rifle. He was using armour-piercing rounds which would rip through the ship's walls as if they were made of tinfoil, and the weapon was enhanced with a Heckler & Koch M320 grenade launcher module with electronic targeting system, chambered with a single 40mm projectile. He walked over to the only exterior access door from the bridge itself — a portside hatch that led to a narrow deck in front of the bridge windows, looping around to connect with a stairway down to the outer level below — and he pressed a small lever that locked the door.

The rear of the bridge was another reinforced glass wall, with a large door set into it, bearing its own viewing panel. It led to a further chamber, with separate rear-facing balcony access overlooking the deployment crane which held its tarpaulin-covered load, five levels below on the lowered aft deck. There was no other entrance to this room, and it held a single console: the remote control interface for the Bell.

Miwa walked to the door, pressed his thumb to a panel, and it slid open. He stepped inside, and motioned for Reddy to follow him. When both men were inside, the door slid smoothly closed in front of them, separating them from the bridge with five centimetres of reinforced glass.

"If there are any remaining security personnel below, tell them to use the scientific staff and crew as hostages if it becomes necessary," Miwa said.

At the same moment, they heard the sound of gunfire from the interior stairwells on both sides.

Greenwood and Ramos drove the two soldiers upwards as aggressively as they could in the narrow confines of the bridge tower's interior, both women intensely aware that there was very little time left.

One of the men made the mistake of lifting his rifle over the upper railing to fire blindly down into the stairway void. Ramos put two rounds straight through the five-centimetre gap in front of his feet from three metres below, one punching through his left kidney and the other lodging in his right lung.

The other man disappeared through the door at the top of the stairs, the harsh illumination from within spilling out and painting his shadow on the walls of the stairwell. Greenwood knew they'd reached the bridge, and she ran straight for the opening, then crouched when she was still ten steps from the top, using the bottom edge of the doorway as a rest for her weapon. The soldier was attempting to take cover behind the decorative unit that held the ship's ornate brass wheel, at the very front of the large space. He sent at least ten shots in her direction, several of them ricocheting off the door frame. Greenwood put a single bullet dead centre in his forehead, and then there was an eerily sudden silence.

As Ramos joined her near the top of the stairway, Greenwood could hear another exchange of gunfire in her earpiece, followed by the ever-calm tones of Dowling.

"One hostile down, port level 4 inside stairs."

"Two down here. That's all of them from before. Entering bridge now," she replied, and she nodded to Ramos. They went in one after another, and both immediately trained their rifles on the familiar mercenary who stood behind the glass just metres away, holding his weapon casually. To his side, at a solitary console, stood Miwa.

"Good evening, madam," Miwa said, glancing briefly over at her before once again focusing on the console. "Though we met only yesterday, I don't believe you've properly introduced yourself."

Greenwood assessed the situation. The glass was

clearly bulletproof, but that wouldn't be a problem for the thuggish-looking man she recognised from the Owl Mountains and elsewhere; the hardware he was carrying could cut through the barrier easily with the right ammunition, and she was willing to bet that he had plenty of it. She looked over towards what was probably the navigational control console, and saw a red electronic banner across it that said *LOCKED*.

"Captain Jessica Greenwood," she replied. "We didn't get a chance to finish our last conversation."

Miwa's lips curled into a faint grin, but only momentarily. "Indeed. And I regret we will not do so here either. As I'm sure you are aware, I have a task to perform. As does my associate Mr. Reddy, whom you've also met."

In her peripheral vision, Greenwood saw Dowling and Aldridge running across the short deck that extended in front of the bridge. They stopped outside the glass, looking in, and the man named Reddy clearly saw them too. Miwa and Reddy were in the rear chamber facing all four of them, with Ramos and Greenwood inside the bridge, and Dowling and Aldridge behind the two women and outside of it.

"It doesn't have to be like this," Greenwood said, and now Miwa looked up at her again for a moment, before walking the few paces from the console to stand in front of the thick glass. The state of the art intercom made it sound like they were all in the same chamber.

"True," he replied, and Greenwood quirked an eyebrow in surprise before he continued. "But the alternative is the death of all humanity, and many other species besides."

"There are other ways it could go," she replied. "You know that. Necessity is the mother of invention. Human ingenuity—"

"—is not in question, Captain," Miwa interrupted. His voice was gentle, as if correcting a beloved child. "The problem is of integrity, and altruism. Individuals may truly desire change for the greater good, but our social *structures* will always reveal man's true heart: avarice and solipsism."

"We have our problems, yes, but this isn't the answer. The technology in that machine itself could—"

"—never be entrusted to any government or private enterprise on the planet," Miwa said. "Mr. Magnusson was entirely correct in his fears. Corruption and horror would be the inevitable results."

"What gives you the right to decide?" Ramos asked, drawing a sneer from Reddy but a contemplative look from Miwa.

"I have no right," Miwa replied quietly. "Such a right does not exist; *cannot* exist. And yet, I have taken action because I am able to. Power is responsibility, but not in the way most people think. If a moral being is capable of acting, then he or she is ethically compelled to do so."

"So your own morality is superior to that of several billion other people?" Greenwood said, the disdain in her voice coming through clearly. "You're not saving your species, Miwa; you've already given up on all of us."

"I freely admit I've always been deeply troubled at what I must do, and I remain so. But surely a woman in your position understands the concept of sacrifice. You have killed a number of my men on this very ship tonight."

"I regret each and every one of those lost lives," she replied with a steely look in her eyes, "and I hold you responsible for creating the situation where our actions were tactically necessary. How can *you* be sure that the atrocity you're about to commit is really the only way? I have plenty of blood on my hands, Miwa, but if you do this, you'll kill more people than anyone else in history. You said it yourself: no-one can ever have the right to make that choice."

"But your government has nevertheless granted you the authority to make life-and-death decisions as a matter of course," Miwa said quietly. "I admire your idealism, Captain. I share it, in a way. Where we differ is that I no longer have hope that humanity will find its own solution."

Ramos took a small step forward. "It sounds like you think of humanity as separate from you," she said. "We've met men like you before. Are you not human too, *Señor* Miwa?"

" *No estoy seguro, señora,*" Miwa replied easily. "Can a man who willingly throws the world into chaos really claim to be?"

We're losing control of the negotiation, Greenwood thought. When Ramos asked if he was a human being like the rest of them, Miwa had replied *I'm not sure*, and that was always a cause for concern. He was beginning to psychologically distance himself, having already settled into the role of some perverse kind of martyr for mankind. Ramos was right when she said that they'd met others like him, though none had been so principled.

"I understand what you're trying to do," Greenwood said, drawing Miwa's attention again. "We all do. And I even sympathise. I've been struggling with all of this since Norway. I know that our species is on a collision course with self-destruction, but I haven't given up on us yet. There has to be another way. We can find it together. We have to, no matter how long it takes. You don't need to do any of this."

"Unfortunately, Captain," Miwa replied in a tone of profound sadness that chilled her to the core, "we don't have the luxury of unlimited time."

Greenwood's eyes flicked automatically to the console near Miwa, and then she looked around at the main navigational controls in the bridge area where she stood. She lifted her gaze to see Aldridge standing outside, beyond the large panels of glass. His rifle was held loosely at his side, and he was looking only at her.

A loud chime sounded overhead. The accompanying synthesised voice message was perfectly clear.

"Viable target zone reached."

A bank of monitors mounted at roof level and angled downwards from the front of the bridge all flicked on at the same moment. One showed a high angle of the aft crane on the lowered rear deck. The second showed only a close-up of corrugated metal. The third seemed to be a direct feed from beneath the ship, showing the depths of the Persian Gulf falling away into blackness. On the first monitor, a ring of small tethering loops popped open in unison, freeing the tarpaulin to immediately be lifted by the breeze. It whipped and cartwheeled away towards the stern, and dropped into the water beyond. Its movement revealed the two still-unconscious men tied to the base of the crane assembly, a few metres away from the object that was now completely visible.

The Bell was blacker than the night that surrounded it, its thick umbilical cabling snaking down the side of the *Hyperion* to presumably disappear into a secured control bay. From this elevated viewing angle, Greenwood could see faint bolt-marks on the machine's upper surface where a metal plate had once been attached, and she knew that if she had seen it seventy years earlier, it would have borne a swastika.

"I love humanity, and all that we have built, but we have become a cancer upon the Earth," Miwa said. "Our unhindered encroachment and accelerating overpopulation have already brought us to a precarious age of dwindling resources and growing tension."

Miwa's gaze moved between Greenwood, Ramos,

Aldridge, and Dowling as he spoke. "When lower animals endanger an ecosystem, we perform a cull. I choose to follow that age-old wisdom." Slowly, he turned and walked back to the lone console.

Greenwood lunged forwards, and Reddy lifted his weapon, but she only stood with the toes of her boots pressing against the glass barrier, her eyes fixed on the display that Miwa now stood in front of again.

"That machine has poisoned you, Miwa," she said. "You've become just like the monsters who created it. Think about what you're going to do. Think about the pain and suffering you're going to cause, for so many people. Think about *them*."

"I think about them every moment of every day," Miwa replied, and Greenwood could see the latent anguish on his face. She could also see that he wasn't going to be swayed by any argument.

"So let them live!" she called out. "At least give them the chance to find a better way."

Miwa lowered his head. "They can't all live, Captain, but our species can survive. *CHRONOS* was conceived in hatred, by murderers and bigots... but perhaps their greatest crime was that their vision was too limited."

His hands hovered above the touchscreen.

"They are long dead already, but the Bell's makers will have their second genocide after all."

Ramos suddenly fired three shots from her rifle, but each of them merely made a pucker mark in the surface of the glass. Reddy sneered again, but Miwa didn't even glance around. Instead, he touched a control that Greenwood recognised from the diagram Aldridge had shown her in the military hangar in Poland: it was the upper boundary marker of the Bell's organic tuning interval.

He slid the marker to the right, expanding the interval to encompass what she knew was not only rudimentary hydrocarbon molecules, but complex organic patterns including human beings. When triggered, the field wouldn't just eradicate Safaniya's oil; it would also be instantly lethal to any living thing it came into contact with.

Miwa tapped another control and then pressed his thumb to a panel alongside. The synthesised voice spoke again.

"Deployment commencing."

The mechanical sound was faint but immediate, and Greenwood knew that the crane's hydraulics were powering up for a pre-programmed lowering of its load over the side of *Hyperion's* hull.

Miwa stepped back from the console, then drew his pistol and put four bullets into the touchscreen. It shattered, spewing electronic debris on the floor around its pedestal, its innards sparking briefly before becoming inert. He holstered his pistol again, and nodded to himself.

Greenwood turned away from the scene, and took two steps forward into the centre of the bridge. She glanced up at the overhead monitors and saw that the crane had slowly begun to lift the Bell clear of the rear deck. She carefully set her rifle down on the floor, and when she stood back up, she was met with the stricken faces of Aldridge and Dowling beyond the bridge windows.

"Aldridge," she whispered, far too quietly for the bridge intercom to pick up but easily registered by her earpiece microphone, and he gave a tight nod.

"Right here," he replied, moving so that Greenwood was directly between himself and Miwa, obscuring the other man's view of his lips. "And feeling bloody useless. I'm so sorry."

"You said there's an override. On the machine's body, at the upper connect point." Her tone was intense, but her words were barely audible.

Aldridge's eyes flashed. "Yes. Yes! But… well, if it's set for a simple molecular structure, then theoretically it'd be safe to—"

"It's not," she replied. "He widened the interval before he destroyed the controls. But I'm going anyway. *This is the job.* The rest of you stay here and commandeer the ship. That's an order." She saw the panic flare across Aldridge's face, and when he spoke his tone was full of warning.

"Listen to me. One point of contact is all it takes," he said, pressing his fist against the glass, and she could see the deep frown on Dowling's face too. "One molecule. You'll be two metres from the field *at most*. It'll bloody kill you!"

"It'll be angled downwards," she said, glancing again

at the monitors above her head. The Bell was now swinging out over the edge of the deck. She reached into a compartment on her belt and pulled out a small foldable breathing unit, concealing it in her palm and along the inside of her wrist. It would give her around five minutes of air.

"For god's sake, Jessica!" Aldridge shouted, but she just gave him a sad smile. After another moment, she briefly shook her head.

"That's Captain to you," she replied.

Then she abruptly ran to the port side of the bridge, flipped the lever to unlock the door, and in a single fluid motion she hauled it open, dashed outside, and sprinted along the outer gangway to the furthest guard railing. The drop was straight down to the black surface of the ocean. There were a thousand stars visible in the sky above, and she could see that the lowest part of the Bell had now entered the water.

Greenwood stepped over the railing, clipped the respirator into her mouth, and then she dived into the darkness.

Chapter 30

Miwa immediately understood what Greenwood planned to do. He turned to Reddy, and pointed towards the bridge area in front of them.

"Finish this," he said, and the other man grinned, but Miwa was already moving. He crossed to the only other door from the rear chamber, opening onto his private aft balcony. He didn't even notice the change in temperature as he stepped out into the night, breaking into a run as he went in the same direction that Greenwood had gone moments before. He was an accomplished free diver of remarkable endurance. Further equipment would be unnecessary, and would cause an unaffordable delay.

He didn't hesitate for even a moment when he reached the railing, vaulting directly over it and transitioning into a dive that looked like he'd practised it a thousand times. The fall took less than two seconds, and then he vanished beneath the waves.

Ramos sprinted for the doorway that led back to the stairwell as Reddy raised his rifle, and she barely cleared the threshold when she heard the sharp crack of tungsten carbide rounds punching clear through the bulletproof glass that separated the rear control room from the main bridge.

Aldridge and Dowling hit the deck as several of the rounds lodged in the front panoramic windows of the bridge, making the glass bubble at the impact point.

"Another couple of shots and he'll have it all down," Dowling said, looking around for any surface or object that might provide protection, but finding none. "And he's got a bloody grenade launcher on that thing."

"*Not likely to use it at close range,*" Ramos replied in his ear, sounding out of breath. They could hear her boots clanking on metal, and knew she must have descended to level four below.

"I'm assuming our vests won't help here," Aldridge said, rolling inwards toward the exterior base of the bridge windows where the metal surround was thicker.

"Not a bloody bit. Those rounds would go clean out the other side, and the shock will be what kills you, whether he hits your chest or your ankle."

Another volley of shots battered into the front windows, and two of them sliced out into the night. Aldridge risked a glance over the rim of the lower surround, and saw Reddy kicking aside the ruined glass between the bridge and the control room. It fell in strangely-shaped pieces like chunks of ice, and when it hit the ground it sounded more like heavy plastic.

"He's through to the bridge," Aldridge said, slamming a fresh magazine into his rifle. "He'll be out here in ten seconds, if that."

Dowling reached into a pouch on his belt as more rounds slammed into the barrier above them, and he was about to pull out a compact grenade when the sound of gunfire suddenly stopped. Aldridge took another quick look over the rim. His next words weren't any comfort.

"He's going after Ramos," he said.

The water was cold, though not unbearably so, but Greenwood was long past noticing it.

The pressure in her ears rose until she swallowed and felt them pop painfully. The Bell was clearly visible below her, its supporting chains still paying out, but she knew that it must already be almost at its activation point. She couldn't make out anything on the top portion where the umbilical line connected to the primary casing, but she knew the override had to be there somewhere. She fought to keep her breathing steady as she forced her muscles to work harder, dragging herself further below the waves.

Suddenly, she heard a muted clunk as the mechanism stopped spooling out, and the Bell hung almost motionless in the water.

Not yet, she thought, feeling the panic rising in her chest. *Just give me another few —*

The sound seemed to come from every direction at once. A gentle and almost sonorous hum, rhythmic and pulsing every two or three seconds. Its pitch was low, and it didn't seem to be loud, but it nevertheless effortlessly drowned out everything else around her. She felt the hairs on the back of her neck stand up, and a moment later she flinched, instinctively stopping her own descent.

A rich, golden-orange light burst from the lower two-thirds of the machine's surface, moving through the water like ink. It curled and ran, billowing downwards at a sharp angle, propagating with shocking speed.

Greenwood kicked her legs and twisted to the side to regain her downwards motion, and it was only by sheer luck that the movement pulled her from the path of the lethal-looking diving knife that suddenly loomed in her peripheral vision.

Aldridge was up and kicking at the damaged bridge windows within a second. After three heavy blows from his heel, a large chunk of glass fell inwards, and he and Dowling ducked through the space and into the bridge. They immediately ran for the stairwell that Ramos and Reddy had gone down.

They paused at the top, listening for a moment, and immediately pulled back when a volley of rounds punched ragged holes through the ceiling immediately above the door frame.

"Bastard," Dowling muttered. "Alicia, we're on our way."

"*No hurry*," she replied, her voice barely above a whisper.

Aldridge quickly looked back at the overhead monitor that showed an underwater view, and he felt his heart stutter in his chest. The Bell was active, flooding the water with its eerie liquid fire down below, the luminescence framing not just the black outline of the machine itself but also a man and a woman locked in combat.

Come on, Greenwood, he thought, then he heard Goose's voice in his earpiece.

"*The engine room has been locked from the inside. It'll take a while for me to get in. Should I come back up?*"

"Negative," Dowling said, his voice raised as he fired down into the stairwell. "Follow your orders. We need to take control."

"*Acknowledged. Good luck.*"

Dowling fired again, and this time he was rewarded with a roar of pain as one of his shots caught Reddy in the upper arm. No more than five seconds passed before they heard the clank of boots on metal, and a hail of gunfire sprayed the whole ceiling of the enclosed area, ripping open holes large enough to see starlight through.

"Jesus," Dowling said, ducking and rolling back through the doorway and onto the bridge, closely followed by Aldridge. "He's coming back up."

"Fall back to the observation deck?" Aldridge asked, but Dowling shook his head.

"We need to end this. Alicia, we're making a stand here. Might want to stay down there."

"*And let you have all the fun?*" the Spanish woman replied, her voice louder now, and Dowling's lips twisted in a smile that looked more like a grimace.

Dowling hurried to the port side of the bridge, and Aldridge followed him halfway and then stopped, looking towards the navigation console which now stood framed by a large empty window, with pieces of glass strewn across the floor.

"The controls are locked, mate," Dowling said, getting into a firing position on one knee, slightly out of the direct line of the doorway from which they could hear Reddy approaching even faster now.

"Not what I had in mind," Aldridge replied, dashing to the console and then going behind it, to the side that looked out towards the front of the ship. He grasped something and pulled, and a panel swung open. Then he locked eyes with Dowling.

"I might have an idea," he said.

Greenwood swam desperately down into a vortex of boiling fire.

She had managed to deflect Miwa's attacks, but only narrowly. The man was in superb physical condition, and had no breathing apparatus. His moves were swift and calculated, using his own body weight and hers, and at least twice he'd come very close to plunging his utility knife into her body. She'd deliberately discharged air bubbles from her compact regulator unit to momentarily blind him, then driven her heel into his solar plexus and used the recoil to surge backwards and down. It had been like kicking a plank of wood, and she knew he would be scant metres behind her.

She neared the Bell, slowing slightly as she saw the undulating field of energy pouring from its surface below, almost close enough to touch. The hum from the machine seemed to be inside her head, vibrating through her bones, and she could swear that even the portions of its casing that weren't emitting the field were still nevertheless slightly luminescent.

She clamped one hand onto the thick umbilical cable's shielding, and then she saw it. Mounted just under the joining point, there was a rectangular control unit about the size of a television remote control, but twice as wide. The majority of its front face was taken up by a toughened display that she assumed was touch-sensitive. She sent up a small prayer to whomever might be listening that it was the type of touchscreen that worked when wet.

Greenwood reached out and gripped its top edge, finding a release lever, and she pulled it. The handset immediately popped entirely free of the machine, and surged up towards her. She grabbed at it instinctively, and then she understood: it felt too light for its size.

There's an air-filled chamber inside it. It's designed to float.

Her grip seemed to automatically waken the display, and she saw that it was divided into three sections, marked *Interval*, *Geometry*, and *Power*. She stabbed her finger at the master power control, but then noticed that it was bordered in red and greyed out, just like the Interval controls. The message on the screen momentarily stopped the breath in her throat.

INSERT MASTER KEY.

Sure enough, there was a silver key slot on the right side of the unit to accept a conventional key — a key she didn't have.

Damn it, no, she thought. *Not when we're so bloody close.*

It was more intuition than anything she saw or heard, but she instinctively spun to her left, narrowly avoiding a sharp right cross from Miwa, who had caught up with her again. His momentum meant he had to grab the umbilical cable to avoid overshooting and coming into contact with the energy field, and Greenwood used the brief reprieve to frantically look at the override unit again.

The only section of controls that were enabled were those for the field geometry. The interval couldn't be modified without the key, so the light was lethal. It was directed downwards, and would very soon intersect with Safaniya's subsea oil reserves.

At her heart, she was a soldier, and she made the only decision that provided at least a chance of success.

The interface was intuitive to the point of extreme

simplicity, and it took barely a second to switch the Bell to radiate upwards instead of down. The pitch of the hum changed subtly, and it was immediately apparent that the topmost extent of the energy field had started to rise.

It'll kill everyone on the ship above if it gets that far, but it's my only move.

Miwa had already noticed what was going on, and she saw his eyes widen. He propelled himself explosively upwards by pushing off from the topmost portion of the Bell's casing, avoiding the energy field by mere centimetres.

Greenwood lifted her arm above her head, then released the override unit. It bobbed for a moment and then began to move upwards of its own accord. She kicked her legs, filled her lungs from the regulator, and rapidly typed four letters on her wrist-mounted communicator.

Then she fixed her gaze on the tiny, receding form of the override unit, and she swam for her life.

The entire ceiling of the bridge was puckered with jagged holes, and Reddy had almost reached the top of the stairs.

"If this doesn't work, I'm using a grenade," Dowling said, and Aldridge only nodded. Two more rounds tore through the floor near the doorway to the stairs, and he knew it meant that the mercenary would reappear at any moment. Sure enough, less than two seconds later,

Reddy's face appeared in the doorway.

Aldridge swung the butt of his rifle viciously downwards, breaking off the nozzle of the fire extinguisher he'd taken from behind the navigation console. The plastic headpiece skittered away, and the pressurised carbon dioxide caused the lightweight gas bottle to shoot across the floor directly towards the doorway. It struck Reddy in the upper chest, shattering both of his collarbones instantly, and sending him cartwheeling back down a single flight of stairs to crash down in a crumpled heap on the narrow landing.

Dowling and Aldridge immediately ran back across the bridge, but they came to a halt at the sound of a single gunshot from below. They heard slow footsteps coming up the metal stairs, and Aldridge raised his rifle, but then he lowered it again a moment later as Ramos came into view.

"It's finished," she said.

Dowling reached out and clasped her shoulder for a moment, then turned to look up the overhead monitors.

"Mother of Christ," he said. Aldridge and Ramos followed his gaze, and Aldridge felt the blood rush from his cheeks. The entire field of view of the underwater camera showed only the blossoming liquid fire of the Bell's energy field, now obscuring the machine itself, and expanding *upwards* towards them. Barely visible against the ever-shifting glare were two human shapes, swimming desperately for the surface.

"Larry, you need to go down to the engine room and

help Goose get in there," Aldridge said, surprised at the calm in his voice. Dowling glanced briefly at him in surprise, then he nodded.

"On my way," he said, and then he ran off. A moment later, Aldridge and Ramos both looked at their wrist communicators as the devices simultaneously buzzed. There were only four letters on each screen: *EVAC*.

"We should launch the lifeboat," Ramos said. "At least for the ones who are still alive. Maybe there's time to—"

"There isn't, and we both know it," Aldridge said quietly. "But... maybe if I went down there to help her, I could..." He tailed off, and then he sighed. He knew there was nothing he could do except the most difficult thing: watch what was going to happen.

Ramos stepped forward to stand beside him, her eyes fixed on the monitor too.

"It's up to her now," she said.

Miwa's hand fastened around Greenwood's ankle like a vice, and she immediately twisted and kicked downwards with her other foot.

He was anticipating the move, though, so he easily dodged to one side and caught the other foot too, pulling her closer to him before suddenly releasing her and sending a vicious uppercut towards her chin.

Greenwood saw it coming. She jerked backwards, but not far enough, and Miwa's punch knocked her respirator out of her mouth, breaking the mouthpiece in two.

She had a lungful of air, but nothing more after that.

Miwa smiled, seeing victory within reach, and Greenwood brought her arms up in a defensive posture as he prepared to strike again. Everything was perfectly illuminated by the surging light from below, and in a chance movement of Miwa's arm that made its shadow shift against his body, she saw a small pouch attached to the left side of his belt.

If that's just his wallet, I'm going to be really upset, she thought.

Miwa lunged, and she pivoted to take the blow on her shoulder, rolling to dissipate the force. She reached out and grabbed the pouch, planting both her feet on his abdomen, then she crashed her other fist into the bridge of his nose before kicking her legs out as hard as she could, ripping the pouch from his belt and simultaneously propelling herself upwards as she pushed him down. She didn't look back.

He tried to recover, but the blood from his nose and the pain were both disorienting. He was aware of light and warmth, and he whipped his arms out, still tumbling head over feet, to try to right himself. The last thing he ever felt was a sensation vaguely like static electricity, just brushing against the back of his left hand — and then every molecule in his body blew apart like dust.

Greenwood could see the override unit only a handful of metres above. Her lungs were bursting, and the light all around her was growing in intensity.

Not like this.

All she could think of were the people on the ship above her. Her comrades. Her friends. Her family. She sensed her vision beginning to darken around the edges.

As she brought her hands together, she ripped the pouch open and felt around inside, and her fingers found a small metal key. She willed her legs to move faster, and she could practically feel the last of the oxygen in her bloodstream being absorbed into her muscles. She reached out, and her hand closed around the solid metal shape of the override unit.

Abandoning her attempt to reach the surface, she flipped the unit over, blinking to try and find the slot, and finally she did. She tried to insert the key, but it wouldn't go in, and panic threatened to completely overwhelm her.

She willed herself to focus, and she rotated the key a hundred and eighty degrees. It went into the slot easily this time, and the screen lit up again when she turned it. The power control was now bordered in green.

She felt warmth blooming up out of the coldness of the water, right at her back. The light was everywhere. There was no more air, and no more time.

She pressed the control, and she closed her eyes.

EPILOGUE

The ocean looked like it was on fire.

Aldridge stood motionless, unable to tear his eyes away from the spectacle before him. The breeze blowing in over the waves filled his nose with the sharp smell of the sea.

"Quite a view."

He glanced around at the sound of Greenwood's voice, and saw her walking over to where he stood at the edge of the airfield, looking out at the dramatic sunrise over the Persian Gulf.

The waves were lit in every shade of gold and orange and red, the shimmering disc of the sun only halfway above the horizon. It was 05:32 in Kuwait City, and it was the end of a very long night.

"It really is," Aldridge replied. "You could take the rest of your holiday here. Just pick up where you left off."

"Mm, I could," Greenwood said. "Though I heard that travelling is more fun when you're with someone." There was a pronounced note of teasing in her voice.

"Whoever told you that needs to get some new chat-up lines," he replied, and she grinned and nodded.

I can't believe we're all still here, she thought.

The Bell's energy field had dissipated immediately after Greenwood triggered the override unit's power shutdown. There had been no sign of Tsutomu Miwa's body afterwards, but Wuyts was already arranging a story for the world media about a tragic diving accident while taking his newest research vessel out for its maiden voyage. The chief executive of CHX INFERIS Group had promised a statement of sadness and condolence, praising an environmentalist who had bridged the gap between principle and pragmatism, leaving behind a legacy of profound ecological awareness and progressive action.

Hyperion was docked less than half a mile from the airfield, and its scientific staff and crew were already in custody aboard the Boeing C-17 Globemaster III transport plane parked a hundred metres from where Aldridge and Greenwood stood. The vessel had been escorted there by their own cargo ship, to which *Guideline* had automatically returned after deploying them.

Aldridge turned to look at the hulking aircraft, and saw the tail end of a familiar tarpaulin-covered object being loaded aboard.

"What exactly is the European Defence Agency going

to do with the Bell?" he asked, leaning back against the railing. Greenwood shrugged one shoulder.

"Study it, I suppose," she replied. "And then hopefully lock it away for another seventy years."

"I was going to ask if we could put it on top of that really big Christmas tree they bring out in Brussels around early November."

"You're a ridiculous human being, Aldridge," Greenwood said, folding her arms as she turned back around to look at the sunrise.

"That's not a *no*, though."

"Oh it's a *no*, alright."

They stood in silence for several minutes, just enjoying the morning air and the growing warmth of the sun. It was a relief to be out of the wetsuits. They each wore civilian clothing now, and would be departing shortly on their own jet, flying directly to Brussels for a full debriefing with Wuyts.

A ship's horn sounded somewhere out on the horizon.

"I saw you were on the phone earlier," Greenwood said, and Aldridge glanced over at her.

"Cross," he replied.

"Should I be?"

He laughed, then it faded to a faint smile. "I just wanted to let her know that it was over. That the people responsible for her brother's death had been brought to justice, and the weapon wouldn't be a threat to anyone else."

Greenwood nodded, considering his words for a moment. "I wonder if that's what happened," she said. "Was it justice? Because I'm really not sure."

"That's above my pay grade, boss," he quipped, but then he noticed the slight crease on her brow, and his expression sobered.

"His death was a tragedy," Greenwood said, her voice quieter now. "And everyone will say so, but they won't really know just how true it is. He was a great man. I can't even imagine the kind of conviction needed to do what he tried to do. And yes, his methods were horrific… but what no-one's going to admit is that he cared more about our fate than just about anyone I've ever met."

"I think that you and he have some things in common," Aldridge said, and she looked quickly around at him, but he raised a hand to forestall any objection. "I mean that you both have responsibility in your blood. You were born to sacrifice yourselves. Maybe you're both a little too eager to do it, too."

She looked back out at the waves, and it was almost half a minute before she spoke again.

"Maybe. But we'd be lucky to have more people with his bravery."

"No argument there. But here's hoping they're optimists," Aldridge replied.

The scent of jet fuel drifted by, and he frowned. It had troubling connotations for him now, and he was willing to bet that she felt the same way.

"I have to believe that there's another way forward," Greenwood said. "That's what I told Miwa, and I want it to be true. I just don't know what it might be. The signs aren't exactly encouraging."

Aldridge nodded. "Seems like a whole lot of little efforts that don't really add up to much, and the big stuff gets pushed back by governments who only care about the next election. Plus a lot of countries just can't afford to go renewable on the scale that's needed. Try getting China or India to switch to green energy. And the Americans are going backwards."

"The diplomacy doesn't work, so we're praying for a technological miracle," she said, then she tilted her head in the direction of the transport plane. "And there's one sitting right there. Maybe they can use it somehow. Or learn from it."

"Fingers crossed," Aldridge replied. "And in the meantime?"

"We keep fighting. It's all we can do."

Aldridge nodded again, and was silent for a few seconds. "What happens if time runs out?" he asked.

The sun was higher now, its disc almost completely above the waves, and its light flooded the entire vista before them. Its warmth felt like rebirth, but eventually it would set once more. It was always in motion, never stationary.

"Well, then we..." Greenwood began, but she tailed off and just shook her head, unfolding her arms and letting her hand fall to the railing.

"Just enjoy the view?"

She glanced around at him with the beginnings of her customary expression of exasperation, but he wasn't looking out at the spectacular sunrise as she expected. He was looking straight at her. She held his gaze for several moments before looking off towards the horizon again.

"I'm really glad you're alive," he said quietly.

"I feel the same way," she replied, and she didn't have to look around to know that he'd grinned.

"Now we're getting a little ahead of ourselves."

"Well we certainly wouldn't want to rush," she said.

Aldridge didn't respond to that, and there was a short silence that was neither awkward nor entirely comfortable. Then she saw him step closer in her peripheral vision, and she assumed he was going to head over to the jet. When she looked up, though, he was standing right beside her.

The look in his eyes was one she recognised, and she felt her pulse quicken. The question or quip or rebuke, or whatever she'd been thinking, vanished from her mind.

"He was right about another thing," Aldridge said. "Miwa, I mean. When you were on the bridge, and I was outside. I could hear him over the comm channel."

"Oh?" she replied, and she was surprised at how steady her voice was.

Aldridge nodded slowly, his gaze flicking from her eyes to her hair, and finally to her lips.

"We don't have the luxury of unlimited time," he said.

He leaned in slowly, giving her every chance to step back — or sweep his legs out from under him, or knock him unconscious — but she didn't. She froze for only a moment when he pressed his lips to hers, then her eyes closed.

The kiss was gentle, both a statement and also a question. Her palm came up against his chest and he thought she would push him away, but she didn't move for several seconds. Finally, he felt a soft pressure, and he withdrew, but only by half a step.

There was a slight flush to her cheeks, and Aldridge thought she'd never been more beautiful. Greenwood cleared her throat, and her tongue unconsciously flicked out to smooth over her bottom lip.

"I thought we talked about doing things without properly assessing the consequences," she said. Her voice was a little breathy, and Aldridge was sure that she must have been able to hear his own heart thudding in his chest.

"We did," he agreed. "But I decided it was worth the risk."

She dropped her gaze to his chest. "That's the kind of thinking that could end badly for you," she said, her voice quiet again. Aldridge reached out instinctively, taking hold of the fingers of her left hand, just for a moment. He waited until she looked up at him again.

"I'm on the side of hope," he replied.

* * *

"I could sleep for a week," Goose said as he helped Ramos stow the last of their gear in the tall lockers within the jet. He was looking forward to getting airborne, so he could write up a preliminary field report and then get at least a couple of hours of rest before the debriefing at headquarters.

"I'll settle for a full night, at home in my own bed," Ramos replied. "I think they'll give us some leave in a day or two."

"Next week, more likely," Goose lamented. "Plenty of loose ends to tie up first. Dr. Cross, the Bell, Miwa's assistant, the scientists from the ship… I think there's a lot of paperwork ahead."

Ramos pursed her lips in mild irritation, but it was mostly for show. She didn't mind work, and she preferred to finish a job herself rather than hand off the responsibility. Her wife understood the demands of her job.

"What do you think, Larry?" Goose asked, calling to the big Welshman who was standing at the front of the jet's cabin, just inside the open doorway. "Should we ask them to pay us overtime?"

Dowling's arms were folded across his chest and he had a faint grin on his face as he looked over towards the railing that bordered the airfield, watching the two silhouetted figures there.

"You know me, mate," he replied, stepping away from the door and moving into the cabin wearing his usual easy smile. "I think we should just do what we're bloody told."

Greenwood and Aldridge walked slowly back across the tarmac towards the waiting jet, keeping a discreet distance apart. Neither of them spoke.

They stopped to watch the huge Globemaster accelerate down the runway, lifting into the air slowly but steadily, and then begin a long curving climb out over the Gulf. When the noise of its engines had mostly receded, they crossed the short remaining distance to the foot of the folded down steps of their own aircraft.

Greenwood seemed like she was about to say something, but then she apparently decided against it. She took one last glance around the airfield and then over to where they'd previously been standing, before turning to Aldridge. She looked every inch the military captain, shoulders square and radiating confidence. She checked her wristwatch, then nodded towards the plane.

"Well, it's getting late," she said.

"Or early," Aldridge replied. She gave the barest shrug of her shoulders, as if to say *same difference*.

He gestured towards the steps with just the slightest movement of his arm, indicating that she should precede him, but she shook her head.

"After you."

Aldridge opened his mouth to protest, but Greenwood silenced him by raising one elegant eyebrow.

The sun was well above the waves now, on its long

climb back up into the sky, bathing everything in golden light. It shone on her hair like fire, and its embers sparkled in her eyes. One corner of her mouth curled into the hint of a grin.

"That's an order," she said.

Afterword

Dear Reader,

I'm Matt Gemmell, the author of this book. This letter is for you. Thank you for reading *TOLL*!

If you'd like an exclusive **bonus chapter**, plus previews of new novels and more, I'd love to send you my readers' newsletter:

mattgemmell.com/news-toll

I hope you've enjoyed reading this instalment in the KESTREL series. I deeply appreciate the investment of time and trust you've made. Writing a novel is a tough job, and what makes it worthwhile is the idea that someone, somewhere, is reading your words.

Today, right now, that someone is you. From one human being to another, thank you. You're the reason I'm doing this.

If you enjoyed the book, I'd be very grateful if you left

a review on the online store of your choice. Authors live and die by those reviews. A minute of your time would mean a great deal to me.

I'd also love to hear from you, and keep you informed about new books, behind-the-scenes articles on writing, bonus and deleted chapters, and more. Here's how we can stay in touch:

My newsletter: mattgemmell.com/news-toll
On Twitter: @mattgemmell
On Facebook: facebook.com/MattGemmellAuthor
My web site: mattgemmell.com

Thank you for reading.

Matt Gemmell
Edinburgh, Scotland
26th October, 2018

KESTREL will return.

Acknowledgements

The first book is the hardest, so they say. Then the second book is the hardest, and so on. That's how it works. So far, they're right.

I'd like to thank my wife, Lauren Gemmell, for her support during the writing of *TOLL*. It was a long haul — longer than it needed to be — and she walked the line that loving partners do, giving encouragement at various levels of severity. The book is better because of her input, and my life is better because she's in it.

My profound gratitude goes to Lisa and Chris Tayler, my petrochemical industry consultants, who went above and beyond to answer all my questions — in person over Christmas dinner, at the Oil & Gas Museum in Aberdeen, and remotely via WhatsApp from an oil rig in the North Sea. Any errors, exaggerations, or wholesale fabrications are mine alone; sometimes dramatic license can look a lot like incompetence, and vice versa. (But the slot machine on the drilling platform is completely authentic. I've seen proof.)

Writing can be a lonely endeavour, but Whisky our labradoodle made sure I had company every step of the way, including as I write these words now. Thanks, big pal.

I'm grateful to Stuart Bache at Books Covered for continuing his excellent work on *CHANGER* by creating the cover for *TOLL* too. Seeing the results of his talent is what makes each book feel real to me. Here's to the next one.

To my family and friends, who have learned when to ask and when not to, thank you. I'll keep you posted.

This book wouldn't exist without the kind, generous, and remarkably optimistic people who are patrons of my writing via my site's membership programme. To those noble few: this book is yours, and we're just getting started. Adam and Grace Jaworski, your names will always be synonymous with the KESTREL series — and I'm pretty sure that Adam is my uncle at this point. And to dear Lloyd: I think Greenwood et al were probably just as happy to see you again.

The story you've hopefully just read would be substantially poorer if not for the sharp eyes and careful critique of those who braved less-than-finished versions. It's not an easy thing to wait two years and then have to blast through it all in a few days. Anders Kierulf (lightning fast, two out of two), Mark Aufflick (even when ill), Rys Sommefeldt, Daryl Baxter, Regine Horteur (Greenwood's biggest fan), and of course Lloyd Nebres: you must be crazy, but you're truly appreciated. Any flaws that remain are wholly my fault.

Most of all, dear reader, my thanks go to you. Let's do this again sometime soon.

A few notes on places and things. Sant'Agnello, where Greenwood's holiday is so rudely interrupted, is real, and I've stood on the terrace where she takes her phone call. KESTREL's headquarters in Brussels is something I can neither confirm nor deny, but you can visit the grand library above it yourself. Sagrada Família in Barcelona is incredibly beautiful, and utterly worthy of your time and attention — I'm very sorry for the bullet holes. All the locations in the magical country of Norway are real too. I'd go there in winter, if I were you.

The series of underground installations created by Nazi Germany and collectively called project *Reise* do exist, and you can explore them — including in the Owl Mountains — but Miwa's base is the product of my imagination.

The various vehicles all exist too, or have been only lightly modified. The luxury cars and assorted helicopters are entirely of our world. Miwa's *Hyperion* is based on Australia's magnificent RV *Investigator*, and KESTREL's own *Guideline* is a marginally improved version of Huntington Ingalls Underwater Solutions Group's *PROTEUS* minisub.

As for the Bell... well, who knows? You'll find a wealth of conspiracy theories related to it online and in various books, both fiction and non; try searching for *Die Glocke*. There are also a number of *Kriegsmarine* U-boats which remain unaccounted for, to this day. *CHRONOS* has been a dark fascination of mine for years, and I felt the time was right to try telling a tale about it from a contemporary angle.

Everything in this book about climate change, population growth, environmental disasters, rising temperatures, fluctuating weather patterns, nuclear accidents, oil spills, decimated coral reefs, and so on is one hundred percent factual, I'm sorry to say.

The world is changing, and we're the ones who are responsible. I'm a little more afraid each day. I don't know what the future holds for us.

But I'm on the side of hope.